SPY ONE

To: Jim
My first novel - I'm still writing

Kenneth C Kent

Sept 9, 2021

SPY ONE

KENNETH C. KENT

COPYRIGHT © 2012 BY KENNETH C. KENT.

LIBRARY OF CONGRESS CONTROL NUMBER:		2012918958
ISBN:	HARDCOVER	978-1-4797-3145-9
	SOFTCOVER	978-1-4797-3144-2
	EBOOK	978-1-4797-3146-6

All rights reserved. No part of this book may be reproduced or transmitted in any form or by any means, electronic or mechanical, including photocopying, recording, or by any information storage and retrieval system, without permission in writing from the copyright owner.

This is a work of fiction. Names, characters, places and incidents either are the product of the author's imagination or are used fictitiously, and any resemblance to any actual persons, living or dead, events, or locales is entirely coincidental.

This book was printed in the United States of America.

To order additional copies of this book, contact:
Xlibris Corporation
1-888-795-4274
www.Xlibris.com
Orders@Xlibris.com
120928

Dedication

This story is dedicated to my loving wife Lucy Lee, my daughter Laura, my son-in-law Michael and my grandchildren Kaitlyn and Tyler for giving me the time to pursue my desire to write.

I wish to thank a special group of people for their help in reading the proof copies to catch any spelling errors or incomplete thoughts and for their feedback regarding the story. Their comments are listed on the back cover. Their help has been invaluable since I read and reread and still found mistakes. I also wish to thank numerous friends and family members for encouraging me to continue on this incredible journey with my writing.

All characters and events in this book are fictional any similarity is purely coincidental. I did use locations and dates liberally to give a time line and a local feel to the story.

Kenneth C. Kent Author

Chapter 1

The school bus stopped at the corner; the tall long-haired blonde girl with designer cut jeans got on board and waved at the other students on the bus and said hello to the driver. Today, I noticed it was not the same driver that drove the bus for the past three weeks. It was a young woman that appeared to be in her middle thirties, with dark brown hair cropped short in a bob; she was not wearing a wedding band but she had a Bluetooth or something stuck in her left ear so she could communicate with whomever she was talking to. She acknowledged the blonde girl, looked at her student ID, and checked her log sheet to make sure she was supposed to be on this bus. Then the bus proceeded down the street until it got to the next corner, where it stopped to pick up other students.

As for me I could continue my surveillance. The blonde girl named Elisia is the daughter of the man I am following. He is believed to be a spy from an eastern European country that was once part of the Soviet Union. Since the breakup of the Soviet Union, most of the satellite countries have their own networks. Why he is under surveillance is not my concern; my boss Rodger Allen McCray, Field Supervisor, Chicago office of International Intelligence (IIA) issued the order. Keep an eye on Karl Buranski, record his every move, and keep an eye on his family to see whom they are in contact with. I am just following orders. Take photos of everybody he talks to and get license plate numbers of the cars, log everything, and research his contacts. Seven-forty-five, I see Karl back his car, a three-year-old BMW silver-gray sedan out of the garage; so I wait and follow him once he turns at the traffic light. He turns left toward the office where he works. He does not notice my car today. I switched cars from the previous week as a precaution in case he noticed somebody following him; it pays to not be too obvious when you are in this business. In my job, we need to blend in with all the other people out there and look like we live in the neighborhood and belong where we are. For me, this was an easy task since I have a teenage daughter of my own and know the concerns most parents have for their own children.

From the information I have on Karl Buranski, his occupation is listed as superintendent for KBW Construction LLC that does home remodeling in the suburban Chicago area. He moved here in 2007 from Bulgaria with his family to start a new life. From the information supplied to me, he is originally from Germany or even Poland since he does not have a typical Bulgarian name. His wife's name is Ana and looks a lot like the daughter, both tall and blonde. The office is in Orland Park, right next door a used-car dealership that specializes in European imports. For the past three weeks, he takes basically the same route to work and home. The only variations to his schedule are when he goes to jobsites to check the status on the jobs or stops at the market on the way home. He doesn't seem to run around very much; one day a week he makes the rounds of the jobs and works most days until around seven o'clock and then heads home. It normally takes about forty minutes from the office to his house. Once he gets home, he stays home during the week. On Saturdays, he meets some of his friends for an early breakfast and then goes to the office for a couple of hours to catch up on his reports. If the weather is nice, he will meet a couple of friends and they play a small golf course by his office before heading home. In a few weeks that will change since all the courses will be closed for the winter.

For the life of me, I fail to see why my boss is determined I need to keep a close eye on him. He seems like the sort of hard worker and family man everybody wants for their friend. Never out carousing or trying to be a big shot, hard working, keeping his nose clean, and not getting into arguments with the workers and then be able to move up in the company. He seems to know his stuff and all of the projects his crews are working on are on time and in budget. Most of the remodeling they are doing is second stories on older bungalows and ranches in close in suburbs of Chicago that are seeing a change in the nationalities of people moving in. A lot of them are from Eastern Europe and such so it is a good fit for them. Perhaps that is the link

McCray is looking for but I haven't seen him talk to any of the people they are doing the work for. His boss handles lining up the jobs; he gives Karl the drawings and the list of materials they need for each project, tells him when the completion date is, and how much they have to spend so they can make twenty percent after the job is finished. It is Karl's responsibility to make that happen. No sloppy work if they want to keep getting the jobs.

McCray just called; he got word there is a meeting that is supposed to take place this afternoon and wants me to be sure that I am in position to listen and note who is coming to the meeting. This must be why he has been so antsy, wanting me to stick to Karl like glue. McCray doesn't miss a thing. I know he was in Marine Corps for six years and then moved to the bureau for five years; then IIA got interested in him and offered him a promotion; plus he likes doing this sort of thing, and he has a unique sense of when something is going to happen. He has been my boss for the past three years, and he has been right every time. Damned, if I know how he does it, but he does. Right now, I have about two hours to kill before the meeting takes place. It would be nice if there was a coffee shop in the neighborhood; that way I could get a fresh cup of coffee; right now the one I am drinking is ice cold, but I better stay put. I have my laptop, so I can work on my research while I wait. I have a good vantage point, where I can see everybody that comes to his office and still not be seen by any prying eyes.

It is four-forty-five as I look at my digital clock on the dash. I thought they were supposed to start the meeting now, but I haven't seen anybody even slow down in front of his office. Maybe the meeting was postponed; but then if it was, McCray would have called me; I guess I am the one getting antsy now. Years ago I would be chain-smoking cigarettes at this point but since I gave those up a long time ago, I fiddle with the knobs on the dash board or drum my fingers on the dash board until the tension slacks off. I checked all my equipment; I will be able to hear everything that goes on in Karl's office. It is a good thing McCray has some inside help that made getting the bug in place real easy; I doubt they even suspect that we did that. If they haven't found it by now, they never will. Looks like we may be getting company; two black Escalades just pulled up in front of the office. Four men getting out, two from each car; the drivers and the sidekicks stay put. Damn the way they are walking, I can't get decent photos of any of them—heads tilted down and hats on their heads. I never saw any of these guys around here before, so this must be what McCray was hoping for. These guys don't look like they are looking to get any remodeling done. They look like mob types—black suits and shoes—and could be packing. I did get the plates; nothing special about them, loaded the photos and the plate info in the computer, and forwarded it to McCray.

The meeting is starting, I didn't see Karl's boss come in although he is inside with them. Perhaps he was here all morning working on a proposal for another project and just now went into Karl's office. I didn't think he would be around for this meeting from what McCray said; this was a hush-hush meeting between Buranski and some person of interest to McCray. Those four guys looked serious, like they had something definite in mind when they walked in. They are talking about a special project that needs to be done. No details are being talked about, like Karl and his boss know what they mean. They did say this project needs to be finished before the holidays since they have something real important to take care of; if it can't be done by then, they will go elsewhere. That doesn't sound like they are real confident that Karl and his boss can handle the project. Perhaps they just want to stir things up a bit. Karl is telling them that this project will be done even before then if they come up with enough money, and he will make sure it is done sooner. His boss is just letting Karl do all the talking. He doesn't like strong-arm types telling him he can't do something on time. After all he has been in business for sixteen years and always completes his jobs on time. These guys wave him off and say this is not your run-of-the-mill second story job; this is much bigger than that, if you know what I mean. Karl once again tells them everything will be fine, just leave it to me and bring the money tomorrow. The older guy tells his associate, "You see I told you, this guy Karl can fix anything. Bring him the money tomorrow so we can get the wheels in motion."

The older guy tells them, "An associate will be here tomorrow with the money so you can get started with the project." I am wondering what project, since nothing was discussed. Karl seemed to know more about what was expected than his boss, which was real strange since his boss Grozdan runs the construction company. Perhaps McCray knows more than he is letting on, like who tipped him off about the meeting and why Grozdan was not surprised when the four guys wanted to talk only to Karl. He must have been there more as an adviser, if Karl needed somebody to back him up. Four on one isn't good odds, but still that surprises me since he is more of a control person than a consultant type. After the four guys leave, Buranski says, "Thanks for being here; I was told there would only be two of them. Why they both needed bodyguards to talk to us was not part of the deal. Tonight I will go talk to Radko since we might need some muscle." His boss says, "I told you when you came to work for me, don't get me involved with anything other than the construction business. I don't want or need any trouble. I worked too hard to build this business for you to mess it up." To which Karl replied, "Yes I know what you told me and trust me you will not be involved. I am doing this for Nikoli Filchev. You know him, right?" To which Grozdan says, "It's your neck." Then he left the office, got in his car that was parked out back, and drove away.

    Karl stayed in the office and it sounded like he was opening and closing file drawers looking for something. This went on for some time, and then I heard a phone ring. It must have been his cell phone, since it wasn't the company phone. He walked out of his office with his cell phone up to his ear and mumbled something that I took to mean "hold on," and then I could not hear anything at all. He walked out the back door and talked in a muffled voice like he didn't want to be heard. A few minutes later he walked back into his office, shut the door, and went back to the file cabinets. This time he found what he was looking for since I heard him say, "Ja so that's where it was." At six-thirty he called his wife Ana and said, "I will be home later after nine. I have a meeting tonight. Save me a plate of cabbage rolls, I'll eat when I get home. Yes, I'll be fine; I ate my lunch late today. See you after the meeting, tell Elisia good luck tonight."

    He went out back and got in his car; he was carrying an attaché case and a small duffle bag, which seemed odd if he was going to a meeting. I waited until he pulled out and called McCray and said it looked like it would be a late night. I said he told his wife he had a meeting and would be home after nine. I told McCray I would keep him posted and that I was following him at a safe distance. Buranski went east on 159th Street to Harlem Avenue and turned left and pulled in the lot next to Gold's Gym, which surprised me. He got out of his car, grabbed the duffle bag, and went inside. I waited outside for about five minutes and then went in to see what was going on. I was stopped by an attendant, and he asked if he could help me. I said, "I wanted to check the place out and find out what you have to offer. I have been meaning to get back on to a fitness routine, but with my job I never know when I can work out." He had me follow him to a desk, and I saw Buranski; he had changed from his work clothes to sweat pants, a mesh shirt, and athletic shoes. He looked pretty fit, like he worked out a lot. I figure he must have a gym at home or something. I talked to the manager at the desk; he offered to show me the facility and told me that as a member I could come and work out pretty much at any time I want. So he gave me a tour of the place.

Buranski was talking to another guy; this guy looked like a wrestler if I ever saw one. I thought Radko. I asked the manager about any special programs they have. He told me they offer a full range of fitness programs; they even have some special instructors that can teach some of the basic fighting techniques like wrestling, self-defense like judo and karate, and even kick boxing for those that think the other stuff is too tame. I pointed at the wrestler; he says, "Radko, he has been here about ten years and has helped a lot of members hone up their wrestling ability." We were not real close to them but I could hear Buranski. He said, "Radko you know me, I wouldn't come here if I didn't need your help." Radko goes, "So what do you need?" Buranski says, "We need to talk someplace private." Radko says, "Tree place, three o'clock tomorrow." Buranski says good-bye and walks over to the weight rack and does about thirty minutes of lifting weights; then he spends time on a stationary bike and then heads to the locker room. I thanked the manager for showing me around, and I told him I would be back after I made my decision. The price for unlimited use was two hundred dollars a month. I wrote that on the business card he gave me. I told him my name was Jim Huggins. I wanted to get out of there before Buranski came out of the shower.

    I went outside and called McCray to tell him what I found out inside but it went right to voice mail. About ten minutes later, Buranski gets in his car. He puts the cell phone up to his ear and starts talking. He pulls out of the parking lot and heads north on Harlem Avenue. I follow to see if he is going to make any other stops. Forty minutes later, he is on his street; he clicks the garage door opener and pulls in. I look at the clock, nine-o-five, not too bad. I call McCray but get his voice mail again, so I leave a message for him to call me. I am heading home after I grab something to eat.

    I stop at a little place in the area called Maple Street Café; it is a neighborhood place that serves home-cooked meals and great coffee. The waitress is one of those that like to make you laugh; she likes to harass the regular customers, but it is all in fun. She works her tail off most nights since the place is usually pretty busy. The owner of the place, Tony was Chicago Police Department before he was injured on the job and he bought this place. Val has been here, I think, from day one. Most of his regular customers are CPD guys that stop here all the time. Val tells me, "Hey, Jimbo you look beat." I said, "Long day plus I haven't eaten since breakfast." She says, "Today is Yankee pot roast." I said, "Sounds good to me." She already was pouring my coffee and then yells, "Tony we need a pot roast for Jimbo." He dishes it up and brings it out and sits down next to me; he grabs his coffee cup and we talk for a few minutes. They usually stay open until ten, and then they start putting the chairs up on the tables so the cleaning guys can mop the place. Val is busy filling the sugar jars, putting the creamer away, and making sure all the condiments are put away. The food is always good; the place is always spick-and-span and the food is reasonably priced. That is a hard combination to find in a lot of restaurants. I finish my dinner and tell Tony and Val goodnight and head home. Today was a long day indeed, 6:30 a.m. until 10:30 p.m.,—sixteen hours keeping an eye on Buranski. It's time to take a shower and try to get some sleep.

Chapter 2

Six a.m., I am up and ready to head out the door to get a cup of coffee and a cinnamon roll and the cell phone rings. It is McCray; he apologizes for not calling last night but he was tied up with his boss, the Director of the Chicago office, Patrick M. Schaunessy, no less. He told me they were going through files trying to put names with the four guys' photos that were at Buranski's office. They are sure about two of the guys; they are enforcer types for Alfonso Mariano family. The other two they couldn't get any information at all. They ran the photos through all the normal channels and still nothing. McCray said they were in touch with Scotland Yard and Interpol and hoped to get a lead on them today sometime. Radko, they found, was a wrestler on the Bulgarian Olympic team in the mid-nineties, and he is part owner of the Gold's Gym and works with aspiring wrestlers that need help to make an Olympic team. He has been here for ten years and never had any problem or ties to anybody that would cause him to draw IIA attention.

McCray says, "Stick with Buranski today, find out who comes to the office with the money and follow him to his rendezvous with Radko, but stay out of sight, he may be getting cautious. Use the telephoto camera and send me the photos as soon as you get them. We need to find out what this project is, so we don't get caught napping." I said, "I read you load and clear. Do you want me to follow him from home or just get to his office after ten to see if the money guy shows up?" McCray says, "That sounds fine since he doesn't vary his mornings. Ten sounds good since nobody gets moving before then, they don't want to sit in traffic. Keep me posted."

This gives me a couple of hours so I can work on some of my research. Now, at least I know a little bit more about the people that were at Buranski's office yesterday. I am still puzzled about the other two that they can't find any information about in any of the databases. I'll run the photos on my computer and see if I can notice anything different; then I'll head over to Orland Park, but first I need to get my coffee and some breakfast. Talk about coming up empty almost two hours and nothing. It is getting close to nine; I better get moving if I am going to be there on time. I pack the telephoto equipment and head to Buranski's office. Nine forty-five, I am in position and can get the photos I need if they show up. To test the camera, I zoom in on the used-car lot just to set the focus and make sure I can get good shots. Ten-thirty and Dragan from the used-car lot walks over to Buranski's office. That is not unusual; for the past three weeks, he goes to Buranski's office at the same time. They sit and talk for about twenty minutes, and Dragan heads back to the used-car lot. I ran Dragan through the database; nothing extraordinary. Runs the used-car business, been here about ten years, click, coincidence. Dragan and Radko both have been living in this area for ten years. Make a note to look for a connection. He doesn't look like the wrestler type or weight lifter. Lighter weight on his feet a lot and active, maybe track team sprinter or something along those lines. When I get home tonight, I will check the Olympic Teams from that era.

It is almost lunch time and nobody has shown up at Buranski's office. His phone rings; he picks it up and says, "KBW Construction, Karl speaking. A change in plans, when? Yes, I will be able to meet you here later. What time? 7 p.m. Okay no problem, I'll clear my schedule for tonight. See you then." After he gets off the phone, he goes out the back door with his cell phone up to his ear. Once he goes outside I can't hear a thing; our plant is only good in his office. He goes back inside and looks at the list of projects they currently have going. He has a schedule board on the back wall; I can see it through the telephoto lens. He makes a couple of notes on the board and tells Grozdan, "I better go check this project; the guys are falling behind and they want more material. When I saw the plans, we ordered everything you had on the list that we were going to supply, something is wrong someplace." Grozdan says, "Good thinking, I know you and if you think there is a problem you can usually spot it right away. Are you coming back this afternoon?" Karl says, "I have to see Radko at three, but after that I will be back, the other guy is coming tonight at seven about that special project. Are you going to be around?" Grozdan says, "Only if you need me to watch your back." Karl says, "Maybe to be safe, I'll be back by five."

He calls his wife and says, "Ana, change in plans for tonight; I know I told you I would be home but something came up; I'll call you later when I know what time. Tell Elisia tomorrow night I will be there for her game at school. I saw the schedule on the note board. I promise I will not miss this game; that school is tough but she should do well." He waved to his boss, took his attaché case, and went out the back door. He got in his car and was just about to pull away, and he remembered he didn't have something. So he got out and went back into the office to get what he was missing. He came out carrying a tube with the plans for this project. I waited until he pulled out and I followed him. To my surprise, he drove about three blocks and pulled into a restaurant that serves Gyro's. I thought he must need some lunch; I do too. After he went in, I waited a few minutes and went in to pick up a sandwich for me. They also had Italian Beef and Sausage combo, which was what I ordered. The Gyro's are good but I would have to sit in there and eat it and didn't think that was too wise; Buranski might recognize me from the gym. I ate my sandwich in my car and played with my laptop. I waited for Buranski to leave and followed.

He headed right to the jobsite, which was in Palos Heights. They were putting a second story on an older ranch home; the people wanted to stay in the area since the children were growing and they needed more room. They tried selling the house so they could move to a larger home, but the market is terrible so they couldn't sell their place. From the looks of the neighborhood, a lot of people have done the same thing. I parked far enough away, but close enough such that I can use the telephoto lens to get some photos. I figure I might as well take a couple of photos to look at later. I zoomed in on his crew that is working on this job; they look like the typical construction crew, wearing the Carhartt jackets and hard hats. Buranski is talking to the job foreman, trying to figure out why they are short on material and running behind. He is looking at the plans again and seemed to get real agitated. The foreman shook his head, and Buranski got in his face and poked him in the chest with his finger like he was trying to make a point. The foreman nodded like he got the message. Buranski turned around and headed back to his car, and one of the workers followed him and walked over to his car and said something. Buranski got out of his car and headed back over to the foreman. He looks like he is going to read him the riot act or something. He walks up to the foreman and tells him something; the foreman looks around and sees the guy that Buranski asked about, and he motioned for him to come over where they were. He walked over and the foreman took the guys hard hat off and threw it on the ground and spit on it and gave the guy a motion like "get out of my sight, you're off the job." The guy reached down, picked up his hard hat, wiped it on his pants, and turned and walked away. I could tell Buranski was not pleased; he said something to the foreman, and he called the rest of the crew over. Once they were there, he talked to them as a group; when he finished, they all gave him a thumbs up. Finally, satisfied, he walked back to his car and drove away. Boy, I wish I had a microphone on one of the crew so I knew what they were talking about. I have never seen him upset with his guys before. He plays hardball from the looks of it and doesn't take any crap from any of the men.

It is two-fifteen when he leaves the jobsite. He heads right toward 294; I follow him and try to keep him in sight. I know where he is going but not sure which route he will take or where exactly at the arboretum he is supposed to meet Radko. He gets on 294 northbound; that is a good sign he will take it to 88 and go west to the exit at Lisle. The traffic isn't too heavy yet, but give it a couple of hours and it will slow down for sure. We are clipping along at about 60; other cars are driving past like we are in the slow lane. Some, I swear, were going 80; no troopers around; they show up after 3:30 to get ready for rush hour and figure where they want to sit. I see Buranski signal to exit for I-88, so I follow suit. No backups anywhere; before I know it, he is getting over to get off at the Lisle exit. I back off a little; he goes through the toll booth, and I follow three cars behind. He drives to the main entrance, pays his fee, and drives to the main parking area. He grabs his small duffle bag from the trunk and goes into the visitor center. A few minutes later, he comes out wearing a track suit and starts doing some stretching exercises. He is doing those; and I spot Radko walking over to him. Radko is dressed the same way. Damn, it looks like they are going to run one of the trails. I didn't think of that. McCray thought somebody else would show up but to me it doesn't look like that is going to happen. Radko nods to Buranski and starts off toward Meadow Lake. Buranski says, "Two laps, then we walk." Radko asks, "How about five?" Buranski says, "Not today." Off they go. I watch they are running at a moderate pace, neither one trying to outdo the other. They are running side by side and talking all the while. After two laps, they start to walk and take a path away from the lake and head toward the 4 Columns. Once they start walking that way, I follow them; I have walking shoes, jeans, a sweatshirt, and a Denver Broncos hat on. I pretend to look at the trees and stuff around me while keeping an eye on them. They get to the 4 Columns area, and there is an older gentleman there. Buranski and Radko see him, and I go, "Is this who they are meeting here?" I have a small camera with me, not the telephoto job. Hopefully, this will get a good enough photo of him. I can enlarge it on the computer.

I stay a few yards behind them; the older guy starts talking right away. I can't understand what he is saying, plus I am not close enough since I don't want to be spotted. They continue walking, and the older guy seems to be the one doing most of the talking. Buranski and Radko don't say very much. They get to a fork in the trail; the older guy says something to them and goes off to the right, and they take the left fork. My problem now is do I follow the old guy or tail them. I decide I'll follow the old guy. He walks to an area where it looks like a maze and walks through it. I follow at a safe distance. On the other side of the maze is the visitor center. I follow him; he goes in and finds the restroom; I wait until he comes out and then finds a concession stand to get a coffee. I get a fruit juice and drink that. He walks out to the front, and there is a car waiting. He gets in, and they drive away. I copy down the plate info; I don't figure it will help much since it was a livery service. I walk back to the main parking where I am parked and here come Buranski and Radko at the same time. They exchange good-byes and Buranski says, "Call me later, after you get off work, on my cell phone. We'll talk more after tonight's meeting." Radko asks, "After ten OK?" Buranski says, "Ja." I look at my watch; it is four-fifteen. Buranski told his boss he would be back by five. Good timing on his part. Unless we run into heavy traffic, we will be in Orland Park right at five.

We get to Orland Park at five minutes after five. Not too bad considering that the traffic was a lot heavier coming back. He parks in back and goes into the office. His boss is still there. I turn on my receiver to listen to what they have to say. Grozdan asks "Did you find out what the problem was with the project in Palos?" Karl says, "Yes, I think a member of the crew was swiping stuff from the job to use on a side job he was doing for a friend. The foreman made a big stink; so I talked to the whole crew and told them we can't afford any more of that. They all agreed, so I think we will be good. The foreman said the guy was going to replace the stuff he borrowed in hopes that he could get his job back. I told the foreman to do what he needed to do. If he takes him back, I don't want to see any shortages again. He told me there won't be." Grozdan asked about Radko, "Is he going to help you if you need him?" Karl says, "Yes, he will call me after he gets off tonight after ten to discuss it more. Right now, I can't tell him anything since the meeting is at seven tonight. I just want him to be available in case I need his muscle." Grozdan says, "I am going out for dinner, you want something?" Karl asks, "What are you getting?" He says, "Lamb Kabob's." Karl says, "Sounds good, I had a Gyro for lunch and after my run and the walk I need something. Thanks." The boss goes out the back door and drives away. Buranski is putting his plans and stuff away and making some notes on the schedule board. I load the photos into the laptop and send them to McCray. I looked at them before I sent them. This guy looks familiar in a way; I don't know from where right off, but I have seen him before someplace. I wish I had stopped someplace on the way back here to get a fresh coffee. This stuff in my travel mug is ice cold.

It is six o'clock when Grozdan gets back with dinner. Karl says, "That smells really good, what do I owe you?" His boss says, "It's on the house tonight." They are sitting in his office eating and the phone rings. Karl answers, "Yes, are you on your way? OK twenty-five minutes, that will be fine. You coming alone? Good. Ring the bell, since the door is locked. I'll come to let you in." Grozdan asks, "You believe him?" Karl says, "No, but I wanted to hear what he said. Those guys never come alone." Grozdan says, "I need to take care of a couple of things in my office tonight anyway, so I will stick around just in case." Karl says, "Is Dragan still at the lot?" His boss says, "Yes, I saw him when I came back, why do you ask?" Karl says, "He told me if I needed help tonight, he might be here. I told him, I thought we would be OK; he asked me to give him a signal if I need help. I asked what kind of signal? He told me to flip the lights on and off four times. So I said, I can remember that." He said, "I'll be watching you can't trust those guys. They come to my place all the time trying to see if they can make a deal, but they only want the deal on their terms. Nothing down, take forever to pay if you are lucky. Otherwise you get the car back; it is trash. So I tell them, I don't work that way. They are always looking for a free ride; they make a lot of money but they don't want to pay for anything." Grozdan says, "He's smarter than he lets on. I see him studying a lot. He always has a book in his office, trying to improve his mind. He told me 'When I came here, I had nothing; I was an athlete, but no brains. I figured if I learned something, I would be better off. So, I'm trying.' Now if he could find a good wife, he would be much happier." Grozdan says, "I'll be back in a few minutes." And he heads to his office. Karl is straightening up his desk and fiddling with something; then I see it, a luger he took out of the desk drawer. I guess he wants to be prepared. Some meeting, if he needs to be armed. I wonder if he has a permit for that thing. McCray could run a check through his network. Maybe it's just for show. Time will tell. Now, who is getting antsy? Boy, I can't believe this. I need to focus right now. I take the camera out with the telephoto lens and get ready. We don't even know who is coming to the meeting tonight. Need to put names with faces. Then maybe we can figure out what this special project is.

Ten minutes to seven, a black Escalade pulls up in front. There are two guys in front, and one guy in back. The man on the right gets out and opens the door for the one in back; he is carrying a small briefcase. He motions for him to get back in the car. He walks to the office door and pushes the bell. Pretty smart of him to have the other two wait in the car. Maybe Buranski won't need his equalizer. Karl comes down and unlocks the door, and the guy goes in. From what I remember, the other day this guy wasn't one of the four that were here yesterday. Maybe he is just the money guy delivering the money. They walk into Karl's office, and Karl asks, "Is it all there?" The guy says, "See for yourself, as he opens the case." Karl examines the contents, takes a stack of bills out, and flips through it to make sure it isn't just phony money. He counts the stacks and does a quick tally on his adding machine. He said, "100 down, the balance when the job is finished right?" The guy says, "That was what I was told. When do you start?" Karl says, "Right now. After you leave, I will start the wheels in motion. I may need your guys to clear a couple of things for me since I don't have any contacts in Permit Department." The guy says, "I should be able to clear that for you. Let me know when you need the permit and what you say you are going to be doing, so we can put a dollar value on the project. They charge the fee based upon how much the final bill is going to be." Karl says, "I should have the numbers tomorrow, but I need to go see the building, just so I get seen there, so it will not be a surprise when I show up to start getting the place ready and my crew shows up." The guy says, "Al said, you would be thorough. I can see what he is talking about. You don't want to leave anything to chance." Karl asks, "Whom can I call tomorrow to get me inside the house?" The guy says, "Call me, I will arrange it." He hands Karl a card with his phone number. No name, just a number. Karl asks, "How will I know it's you?" The guy goes, "How will I know it's you?" The games begin. Karl walks him to the door, unlocks it, and lets him out.

Grozdan comes out of his office and walks into Karl's and says, "That went pretty smooth. I guess we won't need Dragan tonight." Karl says, "I had the jitters earlier, wondering if he was going to show. I need to put this money in the bank tomorrow. I'll take it home with me and stop there in the morning. I don't want it around here." His boss says, "I don't blame you. I don't think I have ever seen that much cash at one time." Karl says, "This is peanuts; if we pull this job off, the next job will be bigger." His boss says, "This job you are doing, what is it?" Karl says, "We need to remodel a couple of rooms and add a high-class electronics system with state-of-the-art listening devices, some small disks like Dish Network. The neighbors will think they are switching from cable to Dish. We can't get within five hundred feet, but with these we should be able to hear what we want. Nikoli said his customers think that our subject will be talking to some really high-level people and what he has to say would have a huge impact on what happens in the area over the next few months. That is all I know right now; that is why I need to see the place." His boss says, "I didn't know you were an electronics specialist?" Karl says, "That was my main field; the construction was cover, and it has helped me with special projects." His boss asked, "Where is this job?" Karl says, "I can't tell you right now. I need to check it out; it might not even get the results they want. After I check it out, I'll know more." His boss says, "If you are going to do this under the company name, I will need that information." Karl says, "You will have it. After the bank tomorrow, I will call about what time I can see the building; then I have to go to the electronics place to make sure I can get all the stuff I need and the list of materials for the remodeling. I will call you if I run into any snags. I should be here after four tomorrow." Grozdan says, "Good luck." Ten minutes later they both leave.

I called McCray and told him everything I just heard. He said, "The guy at the arboretum was from Bulgaria's crime syndicate. He is one of the lieutenants that were sent over here after the breakup of the Soviet empire. He is friends with a bigwig in the Bulgarian government. This sounds like it is a political favor. Why he is involved in an operation like this seems strange. To me it sounds like somebody is trying to expand their territory by promising to get top-level information. We just have to thwart their plans." I said, "I knew the guy looked familiar, but I couldn't place him; he doesn't get around much, not like the guy at the Consulate." McCray says,

"Anything on the guy at the meeting tonight?" I said, "It was too dark to get a good photo even with the telephoto lens. I will send it to you, but it is not good. The guy must have some contacts, since Buranski said he might need some help getting the permit cleared and he said he could take care of that. So I am thinking he must have friends in that department, plus he used Alfonso's name right off the bat. You know more about Chicago politics than I do." McCray says, "That does sound like there is some shady dealing going on. If we knew where they were looking to do the work, it would help; we could check our sources." I said, "After Buranski goes to the bank, he is supposed to call his contact about seeing the house and set the time and then he has to see an electronics guy. Once he does those things, it should give us more insight." McCray says, "You following him now?" I said, "Yes, he just left the office with the money and is heading home." McCray says, "Good work, have dinner and we'll talk in the morning. I will try to figure out who this guy is. It might save us some time."

After Buranski got home, I decided I would go see Val again. At least today I had some food, not like yesterday. I walk in and Val says, "Jimbo, two nights in a row. Don't you ever eat at a normal time?" I said, "Sometimes. Tomorrow I should get to eat at a regular time, if everything pans out the way it is supposed to." I asked, "What's today's special?" She said, "Today is liver and onions." I said, "I'll pass, have Tony cook me a steak medium rare, almost mooing, sautéed mushrooms, fresh not canned, baked potato, extra butter, and vegetable, as long as it isn't broccoli." Val goes, "You must be hungry," as she pours my coffee. I said, "Busy day, but I did get lunch today. But now I'm starved." Tony brings my dinner out and sits down across from me and says, "I hope you like it. I don't usually use fresh mushrooms; but you, I know, don't like canned. Are you always so fussy?" I said, "For the most part I like everything fresh. I don't even buy canned at home, not that I cook a lot but I just like fresh." I cut the steak and said, "Looks great!" Tony asks, "So what job are you working right now on?" I look at him and shake my head. He says, "Jim, you know me, I wouldn't tell anybody." I said, "I know, but I can't tell you; after this one is done, I will tell you about it."

Tony says, "I'll hold you to that, just be careful. I know what you do for a living." I said, "I try."

Val comes over and asks, "What was that about?" I said, "Tony was snooping again; you know me, I can't tell him anything." She said, "I know; he talks to the boys in blue all the time too, and they tell him the same thing. He really misses being in the action. He likes running this place, but it's not the same if you know what I mean." I said, "That I do. I don't know what I would do if I couldn't do my job. Most of the time, it is just tailing people and keeping an eye on what they do; sometimes it can get exciting but I still love what I do." Val says, "So is that why you aren't married?" I said, "I tried that, but it didn't work out. My wife could never understand the demands of my job. I never could keep a regular schedule; even now my schedule is whatever the job demands." She says, "You should try it again before you get too old." I said, "I might, when I want to take life a little easier. Right now, I don't know when that might be." She says, "Jimbo, you are a good-looking guy; I bet you would have the ladies falling all over you if you gave them a chance." I said, "Why, thank you Val, and why aren't you married?" She says, "The right guy hasn't asked me yet." I finish my dinner and tell Val and Tony good night and head home.

I get home, flip on the computer, and load the new pictures into my computer. I look at the clock and think, Wow! It's not even ten o'clock and I'm home and have some time to do some research before grabbing a shower and getting a decent night's sleep. I enlarge the photo of the guy at the meeting tonight, trying to put a name with that face. I run it through my normal channels and draw a blank; then I think maybe I should be looking for somebody that works for the city. Chances are if he is friends with Alfonso, he might be working in one of the departments, maybe as a supervisor. He didn't look like a street worker. He said he could get the permit pushed through and cut a lot of red tape. After about an hour of jumping around from department to department, I am getting really frustrated. None of the pictures they have are doing me any good; they only show department superintendents, and a lot of the pictures are outdated, I'm sure. I know some of the people they showed, and they are probably five or ten years older now but the photo hasn't been updated. A lot of these are fifteen—and twenty-year employees in the same position. They get a lot of time off and extra pay for working the taste of Chicago. Not a bad gig I guess, if you don't mind not being able to advance. Somebody above you has to retire, die, or get arrested for taking bribes or something. Not my kind of job, that's for sure. I wish I had a name; he gave Buranski a card with a phone number on it, but no name. I look through the photos; the number is almost legible when I blow the image up but it is distorted, so I play with it a little—708 . . . It's of no use; even if I got the number, that wouldn't help a lot, I figure it is a cell phone that won't be used again. I look at the clock, it is eleven-thirty. I log off the computer, take a shower, and hit the sack.

Chapter 3

Five-thirty, I am up. Why? I don't know. I guess I have too many things on my mind. I toss on a jacket and drive over to the donut shop to pick up a coffee and a cinnamon roll. I look at the thermos they have there and think why not, I'll need more than my travel mug today, plus it will keep it hotter. Twelve bucks, I think that is worth it; they even filled for me free. That's what I call a bargain. I don't splurge too often but every now and then I get the urge. I drive back to my place and log on to the computer. I figure I have an hour or so until I need to leave, so I'll look again in a different department. I am taking my time so I don't miss anything. My cell phone rings, it is McCray. He asks, "Did I wake you?" I said, "No I have been out and picked up coffee and breakfast." He asks, "Cinnamon roll right?" I said, "Yes, you know I never get tired of them." He says, "You really should try something healthier like hot oatmeal; it sticks with you longer and gives you more energy." I ask, "Did you find out anything on the guy from last night?" He says, "Not really, I ran it through every department I could think of and he doesn't come up." I said, "I tried going into the city database looking for pictures but I couldn't find him there either." McCray says, "Maybe we are looking in the wrong place, maybe he is with county sheriff department or water reclamation. If I know Mariano, he has guys in there too. While you follow Buranski, I'll do some checking; I have a friend at the sheriff's office, he'll know if he is in that department." I said, "I'll keep you posted."

I head to Buranski's house since I don't know what time he is going to head to the bank. I get to his house right after seven-thirty. There is his daughter waiting for the bus; he backs the car out and stops by his daughter to say something to her. I think he wants to assure her he will be home to go to the game as promised. That's a good father. He pulls away; I wait a couple of minutes before I follow him. The bank they use for the business is in Countryside. I guess it is convenient for them or something, First National Bank of Countryside. Maybe the boss knows somebody at the bank from a business deal. I know for Buranski it is a little out of the way since he could just get on 294 and zip right to Orland Park. There are a bunch of banks in Orland Park, who knows why they chose this bank. He parks and waits until they open, gets out of his car, and goes inside. I figure he is going to the safe deposit box; they aren't going to report 100G's as income, just put it there for safe keeping until they need it. Fifteen minutes later, he comes out of the bank and puts his cell phone up to his ear after he punches in the number. He is waiting, closes his phone, and taps his fingers on the dash board like he is counting. Two minutes later, he tries it again; this time whoever it is answers. He takes a tablet and starts writing; it must be the address and directions. He pulls out of the bank and drives about four miles and pulls into a parking lot for a Pancake House, parks, and goes inside. I remembered to bring the telephoto camera this morning; so I sit there fiddling with the lens trying to get it to focus. I look through the lens, and Buranski is talking to Radko. Right, he asked to call him last night on his cell phone; I never thought he would meet him here this early. I guess he wants to fill him in on the job and when it will start. Oh wait, he told them as soon as he got the money, he would put the wheels in motion. What other talent does Radko have? He doesn't look like the electronics type. Thirty minutes later, he walks out of the Pancake House by himself and gets in his car. He flips his phone and punches in a number and makes another call. I am thinking maybe it's the electronics store. He backs out of his space and hesitates a little like he is trying to place my car or something. I go, this is not good. He shakes his head, rolls down his window, and waves at Radko who just walked out the front door. He says, "Get in." Radko starts to say something, but Buranski gives him that "right now" look, so he gets in. I'm like I wonder what that is about. I breathe a sigh of relief.

  I pull out of the Pancake House to follow Buranski. He is heading toward the jobsite in Palos Heights for some reason. Maybe that was the other call. They get to the jobsite. Buranski and Radko get out and walk over to the foreman. The foreman looks at Radko and shakes his hand. I am wondering what is going on; the foreman knows him too; maybe Buranski is going to use them both on this job. He calls the crew over and they take ten. Buranski talks to the group. I am looking to see if the guy that was swiping stuff is around, and I don't see him with the crew. Maybe the foreman had second thoughts about taking him back. They talk for about ten minutes. Buranski says something to the foreman. I hear "Pronto!" The foreman nods his head and holds up two fingers. Buranski looks at Radko, and they get back in his car. I guess they settled that. Two days to finish this job. Buranski drives back to the Pancake House and drops Radko by his car.

He flips his cell phone and plugs in a number. They answer and he talks for a few minutes and then heads toward 55. I waited until Radko left and follow at a safe distance. Buranski takes the ramp to go east on 55, and Radko stays on 45 south toward Orland Park. I follow Buranski on to 55. We are heading toward downtown. This really has me puzzled, like where is he taking me. He gets off at Cicero Avenue and heads south toward Midway Airport. I am really wondering now. He pulls into the parking area for short-term parking and goes inside. I figure I should follow him, but then I'm thinking I don't want to be too obvious. I decide to sit in my car; he can't be in there that long, they will tow his car. Fifteen minutes later, he walks out of the airport with an elderly lady. It must be Ana's mother coming for a visit. He puts her suitcase in the trunk. She thanks him and gets in the front seat, and he pulls out and heads for home. Forty-five minutes later, he pulls in the driveway and walks her to the door. Ana opens the door and is surprised. She gave Karl a big kiss and a hug and started to cry. She was saying, "Thank you for my birthday present." Her mother hugged her, and they walked inside. Karl went back to get her suitcase and took it inside. He looked at his watch, took out his cell phone, and made another call. He doesn't get an answer. He looks at the business card and redials the number; this time it goes through. He doesn't look happy. I read his lips, "Tomorrow, 9:00 a.m." He backs his car out of the driveway and drives away.

I follow him; he is heading to his office from the looks of it. I guess he figures he better go talk to the boss to bring him up to date. He gets to the office; it is almost two-thirty. The boss looks at him; he shrugs and walks into his office. Grozdan comes in and asks "What's wrong Karl?" Karl says, "First I can't get a hold of the guy to see the building today. I met Radko at the Pancake House and we had to go to the jobsite to get them to finish this job by Friday; then I get a phone call that my wife's mother was coming in around noon. So I had to free some time go to the airport to get her. It was my present to Ana for her birthday; tonight Elisia has a big game that I promised I would go to. Then I finally get the guy; he asked to meet him at nine tomorrow morning, and he will take me to the house to walk through it. Other than that, life is a bowl of peaches." His boss says, "Don't worry so much. You'll get old soon enough." Karl laughs, "Always with the sayings." Karl walks over to the project board, puts Friday's date on the board for completion of the Palos Heights job, and goes back to his desk and sits down.

The phone rings and he answers it, "KBW Construction, Karl speaking. Yes, I got the message, tomorrow morning at nine. Why? Security clearance required, do I have documentation clearing me to go there? What kind of clearance? I'll talk to somebody at the consulate tonight." His boss goes, "What was all that?" Karl says, "I have to talk to the consulate. I can't get within five blocks of the place without special clearance through security." Grozdan says, "That could be a problem; our friend was recalled to Bulgaria yesterday afternoon. He called me to tell me to keep an eye on you guys and don't let you get into trouble while he was gone; otherwise all of you will be on a plane back there." Karl says, "I have to leave, my daughter has a game tonight. They are playing York; they are the top school in their division; her school is trying to make the playoffs, so her school needs a big game if they are going to make the cut." Grozdan says, "Go enjoy the game. When is Ana's birthday?" Karl says, "Tomorrow, but we are celebrating on Friday; some more family is coming in then."

I look at the clock; it is only four-fifteen and Buranski is going home. I plug in York High School on my computer. Sure enough, they are the number one team in their division. His daughter goes to Willowbrook. That will be a tough game for them. They are outmanned or should I say "outgirled." York is always one of the top teams; they are like Marist, and they always seem to get good players every year. Those girls get recruited for some of the best colleges for volleyball. They send scouts to watch them play a couple of times every year. You look at the top female players, and you see where they are going; it boggles your mind. I mean, when I went to school, I don't even think they had female volleyball teams. That all started in the late seventies or mid-eighties. Before, it was just track, swimming, and maybe softball; most schools couldn't get enough girls to field a basketball team back then.

I follow Buranski as far as his street and decide I will go home. I called McCray to tell him the day was a bust; he picks up the phone, and I proceeded to tell him about my day. He said, "My day wasn't too productive either. I called my contact at the sheriff's department. He was in court today; so I was told by the secretary in his department. She said he would be in tomorrow after eight. I should try him then." I said, "I am just going to relax tonight unless you want me to go to a high-school volleyball game to keep an eye on Buranski." McCray says, "No need for that; tomorrow will be busy. If he gets to see the building, at least we will know where the job is." I think he needs some kind of security clearance; he said something about not being able to get within five blocks of the place. I start thinking about various buildings that are off limits to the general public; after the events of 9-11, they have tightened security almost every place. Think, Jim, think; it has to be somebody real important like the mayor or the governor; they both have homes in Chicago. What kind of information is Buranski trying to get and who is he doing this for? I'll be damned; I think I just figured it out. It isn't either one of them; it is the commander and chief. McCray is going to flip out when I call him back. I call McCray and said, "I figured out who they want to spy on, are you ready?" He says, "OK, I'll bite, who?" I say "Who has a home here and he comes back every few months for a couple of days and sometimes only overnight?" He says, "Holy S . . . , I'll bet you are right. Why else would Alfonso and the Bulgarian organized-crime guys want to know what is going to happen over there in that neck of the woods? Good work Jim, now we have to keep our eyes and ears open for any talk of him coming back here for a short visit. Maybe that was why this job had a real critical deadline." I said, "I swear I was just going through options and all of a sudden it was as clear as the nose on my face. Talk about getting into the middle of something big, this takes the cake. In all my years in this business, I have never once been a blink away from the big man." McCray says, "I was in a security detail once when Bush was the man in charge after 9-11; talk about being in a pressure cooker, that was it. That was why I jumped when they offered me this job. I like to figure things out and eliminate problems, but I don't want to be in there if bullets start to fly."

After I get off the phone with McCray, I fire up the computer. Now, at least I have an idea what they wanted to do, so I figure I will pull up some information about houses around his. I know they have the whole area patrolled, and there are FBI guys around there all the time. Nobody goes in or out without clearance. Now,I have to figure out which house is the target to set up the spy hardware. I look at the clock, it is almost six. I think I can drive down there and get a closer look. I'll need my IIA badge and a reason to snoop around. I'll figure that out on the way down there. Traffic should be slacking off by the time I get there. I put on my official black jacket with the IIA logo and grab my baseball cap with the same logo embroidered on it. If I get lucky, one of the FBI guys will remember me from a visit there when they had a big doing, and McCray thought we should get known by the security-detail guys. I'm pumped now. I get in my other car, a black Crown Victoria, with an antenna on the back, all official looking, and drive down there. Five blocks away from the house, I am stopped. OK, now let's see who is working this end. I show the dick my ID. He takes it to his car, runs it through security, and then comes back and says, "Agent Huggins, this is an unexpected surprise, what brings you down here tonight?" I said, "I need to do a little leg work; I hear the big guy is going to be in town in a week or so, and we got a tip that there might be something planned. So I need to look around to satisfy my boss." He says, "I called Lt. McElroy; he will be here in a couple of minutes to give you a walkthrough of the neighborhood tonight. You'll have to leave your car here. I'll watch it for you." I said, "Thanks, I didn't know how you guys operate here." He asks, "You carrying anything?" I said, "Just my cell phone." He says, "Leave it in the car when McElroy gets here." I said, "Roger!"

About five minutes goes by and here comes Lt. McElroy, all six feet four of him. Bald head, wearing his blue uniform with a 45 holstered on his right side, a walkie-talkie on his shoulder, and a cell phone in his hand. He says, "Huggins, follow me." We walked to the house, and he is telling me how they keep an eye on everything. Nothing comes in or goes out without being gone over with a fine tooth comb. I am impressed with the thoroughness they devote to their job. I see an FBI guy on watch by the front gate. McElroy nods to him, and he walks over by us. McElroy introduces me to Agent Simpson, "no, not Bart," he says, "Lawrence is my first name." We continue to walk another five blocks, and I said, "Thanks for showing me around here, I don't really see any way that somebody could try to get too close to the big guy. My boss will be pleased." We turned around, and McElroy walked me back to my car. I thanked them both and drove away. I grabbed my cell phone and called McCray and told him I just checked out the area. He was like, "Why did you go there tonight?" I said, "I needed to look at the houses on either side to figure out which one they are looking to bug. I think if they are going to try something, it would be the one north of their house; it seemed to fit the bill." McCray says, "Tail Buranski in the morning just to see where he goes. I'll put some extra guys down there. I still have contacts with the bureau; they will clear our guys." I said, "I am heading back to my place after I stop to have dinner; it just dawned on me I haven't eaten since my cinnamon roll this morning. You said it wouldn't stick with me enough." McCray says, "You are running on adrenaline." I said, "We'll talk tomorrow."

I drive back toward my place and go, "Do I really want to go to Maple Street Café again tonight?" Nah, I opt to go to the Olive Garden on Cermak Road. Tonight, I am in the mood for Italian; oh wait, it's Wednesday anyway. I order the linguini with clams and a salad and a glass of Chablis. The dinner was very good, but I did miss Val coming by every few minutes to check on me. Darn, I am wondering if all of her talk is starting to get to me. I tell myself I'm fine without a lady in my life and with her it would have to be the altar. I can tell she is not into one night stands; I see all the CPD guys that try to get her to go out with them. I know they are only looking for some action. Hell, I think every one of them that go there are married. I don't think there is a single guy in the lot. I know I'm not ready for that scene at least not in the foreseeable future. I walk out of Olive Garden; it is almost ten and I think, "Well today was not a bust after all." I drive home, take a shower, and hit the sack.

Chapter 4

Thursday morning, I am up at five-thirty, turn on the computer, and enter the address for the house north of the big guy's house. I pull up the information about the house. It recently sold for a little over a million dollars. No way, I think. What makes that house worth that much money? Wait, how much did they pay for their house, was it 1.5? Boy, I should have gotten into real estate in the nineties. I could have made a killing. Right now houses sit on the market eighteen months without a nibble. We need to find out who bought that place; it might give us a few clues. It is a big house that is for sure. I can imagine they would need to update the bathrooms and even the wiring, since a lot of those big old houses never had any updates added to them. Half of them probably haven't even put central air in. I didn't see a compressor but it could be in the back. The listing agent that sold the house might still have a page on the house; a lot of times, it takes a while to clear them out of the system. I enter the realtor, Baird and Warner. I browse through the listings, and they have a sale pending over it. But I can print out a detail page; I guess they keep it in case the deal falls through or somebody has second thoughts and decides that isn't really what they want. The house has an updated kitchen and a bath on the first floor, the second floor has five bedrooms, 2.5 baths, and a master suite with walk-in closets with their own bathroom and shower. Pretty nice digs if you ask me. The third floor, I am thinking attic, has three rooms and a bath up there. There were three fireplaces, two on the first floor and one in the master suite. How sweet it is! There is a multicar garage and a storage building in back. There are hedges and fencing around the entire lot. The lot is like a double lot, not the normal lot size you find in the city. These older neighborhoods all had big houses on big lots. The house didn't impress me; it looked like it needed updated windows and a good paint job. If I spent that much, I sure wouldn't want to have to spend a ton of money fixing those things. That's just my cheap side talking. If I had that kind of money, maybe I wouldn't worry about things like that. It's the house, not the way it looks or anything else, just that particular house. Who, What, Why, and Where, isn't that what journalists try to convey? Now I am asking the same things.

I look at the computer, and I see I have been on the computer longer than I planned. I am going to hurry if I am going to tail Buranski from his house. He was supposed to meet somebody this morning to go see the house at nine, but he had a problem. He needed security clearance to get into the area. He was going to contact someone at the consulate, but his contact was recalled to Bulgaria. I wonder who had a hand in getting that done. I get dressed and decide I'll take the Crown Victoria today. I don't know where I'll be heading but if I wind up back down there, at least my car will blend in. I leave my place at seven, and I should get to Buranski's place by seven-thirty, if I don't get stuck by a slow freight. I park a block away from Buranski's house. A few minutes later, his daughter comes out to wait for the bus; she looks happy this morning, maybe her team beat York last night. A few minutes later, Karl backs out of the garage, waves to Elisia, and drives away. I wait until he turns onto the main street and then follow. He is heading toward his office, but I don't really think he is going there this morning. I follow a few cars behind, so I will be ready in case he turns unexpectedly.

Instead of turning to get on 294, he goes straight. I follow as he gets to 45 and turns right and goes south and turns left on Cermak. I am thinking where are we headed? We get to Cicero, and he pulls into a parking lot next to a family-style restaurant and goes inside. I am getting curious now; I could go in and look around but then think I better sit tight. I can't see inside; the windows they have aren't full store-front windows. They are more like picture windows with venetian blinds, so they can close them to keep the sun out of customers' eyes. I really do need some coffee and a bagel or something. I look and two doors away there is a small bakery, and they have a sign that says coffee. So I get out of my car and walk to the bakery; I am wearing a baseball cap, White Sox, today. I go in and get a large coffee, and they have cinnamon raisin bagels; they toast it and butter it for me, and I walk back to my car. As I walk past the restaurant, I look in and Buranski is talking to an older gentleman at the counter. About ten minutes later, he walks out and gets in his car; he takes out his cell phone and punches in a number. He gets an answer and heads toward downtown. I have no clue where he is going, so I follow just to keep him in sight. We get downtown, and he heads for a parking garage around the corner from Michigan Avenue. I follow him on foot and look at the building he went in. The Bulgarian Consulate office, damn, he is going to talk to someone in the office to get security clearance.

Thirty minutes later, Buranski walks out of the consulate office with a folder. I am guessing he got what he came for, so now I figure he has to call his contact about seeing the house. He goes to the parking garage to get his car; luckily I found a spot on the street somebody just pulled out, so I took the spot. One hour maximum parking and I was only there for forty minutes. That was luck; I did leave my official business sticker lying on the dash, just in case I needed to park longer than an hour. In Chicago, you never know if that will work; most times they mark the tires and come back an hour later. They might look at my car twice, since it is official looking. Buranski pulls out of the parking garage and heads toward the expressway. I pull out of my spot and follow. He goes south on the Dan Ryan to the exit for 55 and heads west, and I am thinking why is he going back out southwest if he is going to see the house in here. He keeps going on 55, until the exit for Countryside, and he gets off and I follow. He goes right to the bank; I guess he needs to spend some of the 100 grand. Payment for his security clearance I would guess. While he is in the bank, I call McCray. He says, "I talked to my contact at the county sheriff's office, no luck with the guy. He must be invisible, nobody knows him. How does he have contacts with the permit department? Is it all about money and who they can pay off? Maybe he is just one of Mariano's henchmen, nothing more. Even the known associates of Alfonso, this guy doesn't come up. I said, "I'll stay with Buranski and see where he heads from here." McCray says, "I did get a couple of guys to go down to Hyde Park to keep an eye on what is going on there. I talked to one of my old partners in the bureau, and he cleared them to work in the neighborhood. Call me when you know something." I said, "Will do."

Buranski comes out of the bank and flips open his cell phone to make another call. He is talking for about five minutes and writing something down on a piece of paper. After he gets off the phone, he heads to the pancake place where he met Radko the other day. It is almost one, so I think either he is hungry or he is meeting Radko again. Maybe he needed money for him too. He pulls in the parking lot, and sure enough Radko is there waiting for him. He parks and they go in to get something to eat. My stomach is saying feed me, that bagel was ok but I need more food. I look around for a fast food joint; I can get a polish sausage, fries, and a coffee and eat in my car. Across the street, about half a block away, I see the sign. Ah, that will work, plus I need to go to the bathroom; my kidneys feel like they are about to burst. I drive over there, go in and get my food, and drive back to the pancake place. Twenty minutes later they come out; Buranski goes to his car to get something. He gives Radko an envelope. I am guessing cash to get things moving. Radko drives away; Buranski is on the phone again. I am like, it's his wife's birthday today and if the day continues like this, he is going to have a problem at home.

He closes his phone, looks at his notes that he wrote, and then pulls out. Back to 55 and heading to the city. He gets off at Cicero Avenue and goes south to 55th and goes east. I follow him and almost lose him a couple of times, but catch him at a light. He drives all the way east to Lake Shore Drive and goes south to the Museum of Science and Industry. He pulls into the parking lot and looks around like he is looking for somebody. He finds a place to park and walks toward the entrance. He is almost there and a black Escalade pulls up and motions for him to get in. He gets in the back seat, and the guy that was at his office is sitting inside. The driver drives away; so I read the plate to make sure I don't lose them and follow. Zip right over to Hyde Park; they stop by the security detail. Buranski hands them his papers; they look at him to make sure he is who it says it is and wave them through. They drive to the house. Buranski and his contact get out but the driver and the sidekick stay put. His contact takes him into the house. They are inside about thirty minutes, and they come out, get back in the Escalade, and head back to get Buranski's car.

I am thinking he must already know what he needs, and if it will work to get what his customer wants. The distance between this house and the big guys' house is about 300 yards tops. With the listening devices that are available right now, they can probably hear what they want to hear. I know the security team at the big guys' house sweeps the area for bugs every day; I don't know how they are going to do this unless they can jam the signals. That is why they wanted this house, it is the closest one. I follow them back to get Buranski's car. I am like how is he going to get his guys in there with this much security or is he going to tell them it will not work. He wants the job, and the money there has to be a way to do it. He is a professional from what I gathered, listening to his conversations with Grozdan. The guys that hired him also were told he is very good at what he does. If the Bulgarian organized-crime guys and Mariano is high on him, he must have some talent. Buranski gets to his car, flips the cell phone open, and makes a call. I look at my clock, it is almost four and traffic out of here will be slow going now. He pulls out and heads back the way we came 55th street to Cicero, and then he jumps on 294 north to head home. I call McCray and told him everything I could to this point. McCray says, "You can call it a day. If it's his wife's birthday relax tonight and we'll see what tomorrow brings." I said, "Thanks boss, I need a night off."

After I got off the phone with McCray, I continued to follow Buranski just to make sure he wasn't going anywhere else. He stopped at a florist after he got off of 294, went in, and came out with a nice bouquet of flowers for his wife's birthday. Ah, the good husband. Then he stops at a jewelry store a little further west, parks his car, and goes inside. A few minutes later, he comes out with a small package, something special for her birthday, I assume. From there, he goes straight home. I am thinking if he did those things for tonight, what about dinner? He told his boss, they were celebrating her birthday on Friday since more family was going to be here. I think, well, maybe he will take her out tonight, just the four of them. I know when I was married, it didn't matter if the celebration was another night; I needed to do something about dinner on her night, regardless. I am parked about half a block from his house and wondering about the matter at hand. About thirty minutes later, they come out the front door. Karl backs the car out and Ana, her mother, and Elisia get into the car. Bingo, I was right; he did plan to take her out for her birthday. I feel better. After he pulls out, I follow them from a safe distance. They go to an upscale restaurant on Butterfield Road in Oakbrook. I decide it is time for me to go have some dinner myself. He will not be doing anything else tonight that I need to follow him for. I leave and head to the Maple Street Café. Val will be pleased I am going to eat dinner at a reasonable time.

Chapter 5

Friday morning, I get up at six, throw on some clothes, and go pick up my coffee and cinnamon roll and drive back home. I turn on the computer to see if McCray sent me anything. Last night after dinner, I came back here, put the hockey game on TV, and promptly fell asleep. I didn't even see ten minutes of the game. I woke up about one and went to bed. I was completely exhausted. McCray was right, I was running on adrenalin. I look nothing from McCray, so I decide I will look for some information on spy gear to find a local shop. I couldn't believe all the different sites that came up. I didn't think there would be that many different options. I browse through some of the sites just to look at what paraphernalia they have to offer. Most of the sites are pretty much the same, and the prices seem real low, so I am thinking they can't really be all that good. The stuff is not like the things you see in James Bond movies; it's more conventional stuff but things that an amateur sleuth would be interested in. Not in Buranski's league, I figure he only wants top of the line stuff. Finally, I find a site that has more of the sophisticated surveillance equipment. The prices are three or four times that of the equipment on the other sites; now we are getting somewhere. I look at the address, and I go I bet this is the place he will contact since he is going to need to get his stuff if they are starting the job Monday. Then I think, how can he start the job without clearance and the permits. I figure today he will be very busy. At seven-thirty, McCray calls me and says, "I think we found out who the mystery guy is. He is a bail bond man part-time." I asked, "How did you find that out?" McCray says, "I was talking to a guy from the criminal court building and showed him the picture, and he ID'd him. Mariano sure has a lot of contacts in unusual places." I told him what I found out looking for surveillance equipment. He said, "Just stick with him today, from the sound of things it will be a very hectic day." I said, "That was what I was thinking too." I shut down the computer and head to Buranski's house.

Like clockwork, he is backing his car out of the driveway. I look for Elisia, but I don't see her standing outside waiting for the bus. Maybe she is not going to school today; I am ready to pull away to follow and here she comes out the door, whew. I look and the school bus is a block behind me. Talk about close timing; I think she has it down, pat. I follow Buranski since I don't know if he is going to the office or contacting the guy about the permit to get the job started. He doesn't take his normal route this morning; it is like he is heading toward the city. So I stay four cars behind to keep an eye on him. He drives to a truck rental place on 45 and pulls in the lot and goes inside. I guess he will need a truck to haul the supplies and material. A few minutes later, he comes out with an employee and they look at a couple of small trucks. He picks one that you could haul four rooms of stuffs in and tells the guy I need this Monday for a special job; the guy looks it over and says no problem. He talks to Buranski for a few minutes and tells him, "You can take it anytime you like; I just need to mark down the mileage and fill out some paperwork." He disappears into the office and comes back out with a folder and hands it to Buranski. That was easy.

Then Buranski gets in his car, flips his phone, and punches in a number. He talks for a few minutes and then pulls out of the truck rental place. I follow he goes south on 45 towards Countryside. I am thinking, "What, the bank or the Pancake House?"—The Pancake House—Radko is outside waiting for him; they go inside, breakfast time. About thirty minutes later, they walk out. Buranski says something to Radko to which he nods his head. Then Buranski makes another call. I wait; he is getting agitated. I think, tell me his guys aren't going to finish the place in Palos Heights today or maybe it's his contact about the permit. He backs out of his parking space and pulls out to go south on 45 again.

He drives past the exit for 55, so I think he must be going to the jobsite now. Sure enough, he drives right to the jobsite. The foreman and his guys are standing outside like there is a problem with something. Buranski walks up to the foreman; all the guys stop talking. He looks at the house and at the foreman. The foreman shrugs his shoulders and says, "We can't get in?" Buranski says, "Why?" The foreman says, "See for yourself." There is a sign on the door "Crime Scene, Do Not Enter" and a yellow tape stretched over the door. Buranski goes "What happened?" His foreman says, "We got here this morning a little after eight, and the police were here carrying out something; they told us not to leave. So we stand here waiting; the one officer starts talking to everyone in the crew, one at a time. I send one of the guys to call the office, no answer. Grozdan's not at the office this morning." Buranski goes, "So why didn't you call me?" He says, "They took our cell phones." Buranski asks, "Where is the officer now?" He no sooner says this and the officer comes up from behind him. He says, "You must be Buranski." So Karl says, "Yes, what happened here?" The officer said, "There was a robbery here and the people were assaulted and both of them are in the hospital." Buranski looked at him in disbelief, like you have to be kidding me. With everything else that is going on and now this. Buranski asks the officer, "Can my guys leave now? We'll have to finish this job after the people get out of the hospital." The officer says, "There was another guy on this crew, and there was a problem with missing materials as I was told. Do you know where that guy is?" Buranski said, "No the foreman told me the guy was going to replace what he took, and he hasn't seen him since." The foreman says, "I gave you his name and address. I don't know where he lived, can't you find him?" The officer says, "The address was phony or he gave you an incorrect street number."

Buranski says to the officer, "Here is my business card, please call me when you know when the people will be out of the hospital. We were supposed to finish this job today, so we could get paid. I have another job that they need to start Monday, and I don't want to push that job back." The officer says, "I would think they will only keep them twenty-four hours, but you will not be able to get in here until after the crime lab does their investigation. I am thinking two or three days. Sorry, but there isn't anything I can do to speed that up." Buranski says, "Thank you officer." Then he writes down the officer's name and badge number on one of his cards and sticks it in his pocket. Buranski tells the foreman, "We'll pay the guys for today. It isn't their fault they can't work. Send them home and meet me at the office later after three to talk about the other job. We'll have to finish this next week one day, right?" The foreman says, "Maybe, we don't know what happened in there." Buranski goes, "You are probably right. I'll see you later." Then he goes to his car and makes a call. No answer. I figure, the office: still no answer.

Buranski leaves, I follow, but lay back a little further than usual. I think he is going to the office. I'll just go there; this way I can go get some coffee and a sandwich. Sure enough that is what he does. It is after eleven when we get to the office. He walks next door to see Dragan. I guess he wants to know if he knows where Grozdan is. They talk for a few minutes, and Buranski unlocks the door and goes into the office. He walks through the building and I hear him start to rant, "Those no-good hoods broke in here and stole some stuff." I look through the camera lens, and I see all the drawers were opened and stuffs strewn everywhere. This is a fine mess. He goes to the company phone, it still works. He calls his wife, "Ana, be careful today, somebody was in our office and went through everything. I don't know where Grozdan is. I talked to Dragan, he didn't see Grozdan last night at a meeting they were both going to, but he just figured he forgot. He said he didn't see anything out of the ordinary this morning when he came to work. Grozdan wasn't here but he thought maybe he had something to do this morning." Ana says something to Karl, and he says, "I am not going to call the police. I'll call Radko now; he will send a couple of people over here." She says something else, and he says, "Yes, I will be home on time. What time are your brother and his wife getting here? Seven, that is good." Then he calls Radko and tells him what happened here and at the jobsite. Radko says something, and he says, "I hope you are wrong. Who else do you think would do this?" Buranski starts cleaning up the mess, trying to figure out if anything is missing. He looks at the schedule board, and there is a big red X over the Palos Heights jobsite. He says, "Damn, I bet whoever was in here went there to get money or something."

Twelve-fifteen, Radko and a couple of guys I am guessing from the gym show up at Buranski's office. He opens the door and lets them in. Radko walks beside Buranski and surveys the situation and tells the two guys what they need to do. They go into Karl's office and start to talk. Radko says, "I told you I didn't like that guy when we went to the jobsite. I smelled trouble and what do you have now?" Karl says, "You were right, but what about Grozdan and the office. I don't think that guy even knew where the office was." Radko says, "How do the guys get paid?" Karl says, "Cash. Grozdan goes to the bank, takes the money out, and gives it to the foreman. It is easier since a lot of the guys don't have bank accounts. This way they don't have to get ripped off by a currency exchange." Radko goes, "When is payday?" Karl says, "Today." Radko says, "I rest my case." Karl says, "I didn't even think of that, so where is Grozdan?" Radko says, "Good question, can you call your bank to see if he showed up to take the money out to pay the guys?" Karl says, "Yes, I will call them after one, the bank is too busy during lunch time." They continue talking; the guys come into Karl's office and start picking up the stuff, and one of them sees a small box. Karl looks at it and says, "My gun is missing. Oh great, I buy the thing to use it to protect Grozdan and myself and they take it." I am thinking, well, now I know it was a real gun, not a prop. Radko says, "I will leave these guys here for a couple of hours, in case our friends want to play games. I need to get back to the gym for a little while. Once Kurt shows up, I will leave." Karl asks, "Is that you manager?" Radko says, "Yes, he likes doing all the other stuff, I don't like being social to the members, I let them think I only instruct. It's better." Radko tells his guys, "You watch the front, you keep an eye on the back. I'll be back around two-thirty." Karl picks up the phone to make a call but then decides he better use the cell phone. So he goes out the back door. I can't hear who he is talking to, but I think it has to be his contact.

He comes back into the office, and like clockwork, at one he calls the bank. I hear him ask, "Was Mr. Grozdan there today to cash a check for payroll? What time? Nine, thank you." Now he is really getting agitated; his boss is missing, his gun is missing, the payroll is missing, the house they were working on was robbed, and people were hurt. Was it some neighborhood hoods or the missing worker? Interesting dilemma; why would Mariano's guys get involved in something like this? To me the missing worker is the most likely candidate but he wouldn't have the tools to get into an office like this without busting a window or something. Radko said something about someone else to Buranski. But he didn't repeat who Radko thought it could be. What about the Bulgarian organized-crime guy, he knew something about what this special project was all about. He might have the tools and the men that could do this, but even that doesn't make sense. There has to be a different reason. I mean, a 100Gs is a tidy sum of money.

Then it hits me just like what Buranski's project is all about. I call McCray and tell him what has happened so far today. He says, "What do you think happened?" I said, "The missing employee came here last night, tied up Grozdan, ransacked the office, found the gun, put the red X on the jobsite, went there for whatever reason, I am thinking money, didn't find it, came back here and kept Grozdan tied up all night, then went to the bank this morning; Grozdan got the money, since if he didn't the guy would use the gun on him. If we are lucky, Grozdan is alive, maybe unconscious but alive. The guy took the money and maybe Grozdan's car and is on the run." McCray says, "You might just be right, what is Grozdan's license plate number?" I look at my notes and read him the number. He says, "I'll call the state police and the local officials, make it an All-Points bulletin to locate a missing person." I said, "Good thinking, now if I could find a way to let Buranski know it's not his fault." McCray asks, "What did you say?" So I told him and he said, "Jim, I think we can get Buranski to work for us." I said, "So wise one, what should I do?" McCray says, "Call him and tell him you have some important information to give him but it needs to be returned in kind." So I said, "That might just work; we stop something from happening that we don't want to happen and find out who is behind this, and he gets the satisfaction of knowing we helped solve his problem. Hopefully, Grozdan is still alive." McCray says, "It's our best shot."

So I call Buranski at KBW Construction. He answers the phone and I tell him, "My name is Jim Huggins; I need to talk to you in private about a matter of great concern. Can we meet at the Gyro place in twenty minutes?" He says, "Who are you with?" I said, "This is a personal matter, I will tell you when we meet." I wait a couple of minutes, and finally he asks, "Why would I want to talk to you?" I said, "Grozdan." He says, "Twenty minutes. How will I know you?" I said, "I know you. I will introduce myself there." He says, "OK." I wait until he leaves. He says something to the two guys from the gym about going out. The one guy says, "Radko said keep an eye on you." Buranski goes, "I'll be back in thirty minutes." And he walks out back. I follow him to the Gyro place; he pulls in and parks and goes inside.

I walk in two minutes later and walk up to him and say, "Karl, my name is Jim Huggins." He looks at me like he remembers seeing me someplace before. We both ordered Gyro's and sat down at a table in the far corner. I said, "I have some important information to give you but we need to trade information. I have a theory on Grozdan, but I need information from you about a project you are supposed to do for Mariano." He looks at me completely puzzled like asking, "What the heck are you talking about?" I said, "To put you at ease, I work for IIA, which probably doesn't mean anything to you. But I have been following you for the past month. We need to know why this project is so special. In exchange I will tell you what I think happened to Grozdan, the robbery and assault in Palos Heights, the missing payroll, and your missing gun." He listened to me and then said, "You were at the arboretum right, the gym, and by my house, parked down the block in the black Crown Victoria?" I said, "Yes, that was me." He says, "Talk." I said, "This is what I think happened yesterday afternoon" and I laid out everything the way I did to McCray. He asked, "Any word yet on Grozdan's car?" I said, "My boss just called the state police and contacted all the local authorities. Hopefully your boss is still alive, and they find the missing employee with the payroll and whatever else he stole from the house in Palos Heights."

Buranski says, "I was contacted about doing some electronic eavesdropping and setting up twenty-four-hour audio to computer to record everything that will be discussed at a very secret meeting taking place in a few weeks in Hyde Park. That is the extent of what I know; they didn't tell me who was going to be at the meeting, but I figure it was someone real important once I saw the security detail the other day." I asked, "What else were you supposed to do there?" Buranski says, "I was told to install satellite dishes like for cable TV and use those to jam any devices they might have in the house next door. That way the neighbors would think the people were getting dish rather than have cable. I had to add some new windows with heavy duty glass and remodel two rooms for electronic equipment to use again later if this mission was a success." I said, "If we recover your missing employee and your boss, you do your job but keep us informed so we can get whoever is behind this." Buranski says, "Nikoli Filchev in Bulgaria, this is a favor for him." I said, "I heard that before, but who is he doing it for?" Buranski says, "My guess, the Russians." I said, "You are one smart spy." He said, "You are even smarter, you got me." We shook hands and I told him I would call him as soon as I heard anything. I called McCray and said, "You got a deal." McCray says, "Good work Jim, let's celebrate." I said, "Why we haven't done anything yet?" He says, "Yes we did, we turned him to help us."

Spy One—case file KB001; 10-16-10

Friday, 16:00 hours. Buranski is sitting in his office awaiting word on his boss Grozdan. The phone rings, and he answers it. "KBW construction, Karl speaking, how can I help you?" He listens for a minute. Then he says, "Sorry I could not call you but we had an emergency; the owner of the business was kidnapped last night and the police have been trying to find him." He waits until the caller asks another question and then replies, "Your job will need to be postponed a couple of days until this matter is resolved, the police hope to find him today but everything is in such a mess it will take a few days to get things back in order. Call me on Tuesday afternoon." A minute later Buranski hangs up the phone and says, "Done." I take that to mean the job is still on, and the delay was not a problem with Mariano or his customer. Buranski calls his wife on the business phone to tell her what has happened so far. I listen to his conversation with her. He does not say anything about our meeting, and the fact that he will be helping us find out who is really behind this whole project. He has an idea that it could be the Russians but only because of Nikoli and his past connection with the Russian leader. He asks her, "What time did you say your brother and his wife were going to be at our house? Seven, that should be OK, I hope they find something out soon. I will call you as soon as I hear anything." Twenty minutes pass, the phone rings. Buranski answers, "KBW Construction, Karl speaking. Yes, you have information on Grozdan? You found him? Alive? Thank God, where is he now? Mercy Hospital in Oak Lawn, thank you." He calls his wife, "Ana, they found Grozdan alive; he is in Mercy Hospital in Oak Lawn. I am going to go there now and then I'll be home."

While Buranski is getting ready to leave, McCray calls me and says, "They found Grozdan alive but in bad shape; his kidnapper used him as foil when the police caught up with him. He took a bullet meant for the kidnapper, not fatal; he was lucky the cop missed his vital organs by mere inches. They recovered most of the money and a box of jewelry from the couple the guy beat up in Palos Heights." I said, "I heard him on the phone, and he called his wife to tell her he would be home after he goes to the hospital." McCray asks, "Any slipups?" I said, "No, he is a pro, he never mentioned his meeting with me or what we proposed." McCray says, "Maybe we just got real lucky and will have a good informant to help us with catching whoever is really behind this. I figure Mariano is just doing this for the dough; he doesn't have to do anything or dirty his hands, and he collects a sizeable amount of money for the job. Stick with Buranski until he gets home, we need to see if anybody is tailing him besides you."

I said, "OK Boss. What are the plans for the weekend?" McCray says, "I am going to Washington. I figure Buranski is not going anywhere this weekend; he will have a houseful of family. So try to relax and get ready for Monday; I know that is a tall order for you, since you have been working six days a week for the past month. Why don't you go out on a date with that waitress this weekend?" I said, "What waitress?" He says, "Valarie." I am thinking has he been spying on me! I don't remember mentioning her name or anything to him. I know he is not physic, so how did he come up with that. Then I think maybe he talks to Tony. Didn't McCray say something once about Elm Street Café and knowing the owner? That has to be it. McCray is a sharp cookie, if I ever saw one. How he finds things out still amazes me. Then I said, "This Washington trip business?" McCray says, "Partly, I need to spend some time in McLean with my wife and kids. It's a big weekend for the oldest one, first-date stuff." I said, "I can relate, my daughter is fifteen and I know how she was; my ex drove me crazy with all the drama. Me, I told her, remember Natalie, this is only your first date, there will be lots more and with other boys. My ex wasn't pleased with that comment; but I know how these girls are; there is a new love in their life every other week." McCray says, "I will call you Monday afternoon sometime. My flight doesn't get to Chicago until three p.m."

I follow Buranski to Mercy Hospital while he goes to see Grozdan. I wait in my car until he comes out and follow him home, like McCray said. I did not notice anybody else tailing him. He gets home shortly after seven; there is another car parked in his driveway with out-of-state plates. I figure it must be Ana's brother and his wife. I park in the next block to watch; he said they were celebrating Ana's birthday Friday night since more family was going to be here; he didn't say if they were going out, but my guess would be that they would. Eight o'clock, a limo pulls up in front of his house. They all walk out the front door and get in. Everyone is dressed in nice looking clothes; even Elisia is in a dress with her hair done up. Boy, she doesn't look fifteen. There is a boy with them; I think maybe it is Ana's brother's son, tall, muscular, and good looking. I am guessing seventeen, must play football from his build. The limo pulls away and I follow. They go to 83 and head south and turn to go east on Butterfield and go to the Drury Lane Theatre. They all get out and go in. I look at the time, eight-twenty-five; the play starts in five minutes from what the sign says. Talk about being on time; that was pure luck. I am like, well now my job is done until Monday from what McCray said. So I decide I will go have dinner and think about asking Val out. Let's see, the last time I went out with a lady was what? Five months ago? That was only dinner and drinks downtown some function at Navy Pier, with a lot of local politicians. McCray thought I should attend since we were working on something involving a higher up.

I drive over to the Maple Street Café to have dinner. Val asks, "What are you going for a record this week?" I said, "Nah, I just get the weekend off, so I thought I would come by here tonight." She says, "Tonight we have fresh trout grilled with lemon butter, and a hint of garlic, served with rice and vegetables." I said, "That sounds good, I'll have that." She poured my coffee and asked, "So, what is the big occasion that you are off?" I said, "We had a real good week and my boss is going to Washington for the weekend, so he told me to relax. There is more to this than I can tell you but that is the thing in a nutshell." She said, "So what are your plans?" I said, "It depends on your plans." She asked, "What, are you asking me out?" I said, "I guess I am. But you work tomorrow right?" She says, "I can get one of the other girls to cover for me if you really want to take me out on Saturday night." I asked, "What will Tony say?" She said, "He will say good for you, you need to get out once in a while. I guess I have become too cranky for him." I said, "I don't have your address or your phone number." She writes them down on a ticket from her order book and hands it to me. She says, "Now you do." I said, "Six o'clock, is that fine?" She says, "I'll be ready and waiting. How should I dress?" I said, "Nothing real fancy, I'll wear a blazer and slacks, no tie." She said, "Fair enough, I'll wear a nice dress and heels."

Tony comes out of the kitchen with my dinner and sits down across from me and says, "Glad to see you finally asked Valerie out. She has been driving me crazy. I told her one day you would probably get up enough nerve to ask her out. I know you are a loner but sometimes you need to go out and just have fun, no strings attached." I said, "That is pretty much what my boss told me." Tony goes, "McCray right?" I said, "Yes, I figure you know him." Tony says, "I have talked to him a few times over the past three years." I asked, "About what?" Tony says, "He comes in here once in a while when he is in the neighborhood and we talk business; he likes to make sure everybody is happy that works on his team." So I ask, "And how do I rate?" Tony says, "You are in good standing with him; he likes your attitude and dedication to the job and how you dig deeper all the time to find information. He said a lot of the other staff members don't pour themselves into their jobs like you do." I said, "It is probably because he isn't married." McCray said, "You are probably right." I said, "Well thank you for the insight, but I was the same way when I was married." Tony says, "How long did that last, three years?" I said, "Four really. But it was a mutual understanding. I loved my job more than being married. My ex still tells me everything our daughter does, even if I don't want to know. But really, I'm glad she does; I see my daughter usually every Sunday all day, and she tells me her mother doesn't understand her. I tell her, she does really but she forgets how she was at your age. That satisfies her for the most part, and I spoil her probably too much but that is my fault since she is still my little girl." Tony says, "I know. I do the same thing with my daughter. My wife tells me stop treating her like that, she needs to grow up and face responsibility; it's not like when we got married wives didn't work, didn't even think of it. Everything has changed, and I don't know if it is for the better." Tony says, "Have fun tomorrow and be a gentleman with Val." I said, "I always try to be." He said, "Then you will be OK." I ate my dinner, told Tony goodnight, and told Val I would see her tomorrow at six and then I left.

Chapter 6

Saturday morning, I am up at the crack of dawn. I couldn't sleep any longer. I threw on some clothes and went to the donut place to get my coffee and cinnamon roll and went back home to try doing some research on Buranski. I wanted to see how far back I could trace him. McCray was probably already running background and stuff on him to make sure he was who he said he was and see if there was anything that could set off red flags about this operation. Me, I wanted to check a lot of personal history, family ties, and education. I logged onto the computer to see what I could find. I put his name into the database and get a report. This file has been sealed; no information is available. I am thinking McCray did that but then I wonder why would he do that. I said OK, there has to be another way to get information. I try the Bulgarian Department of Immigration, since he needed a visa or documentation to come to Chicago. I find a link and put in his name. It shows his name and the town he was from in Bulgaria. It lists his sponsors name as Nikoli Filchev and what he is going to be doing in Chicago. I am like, well that explains the favor for Nikoli. The job was already setup with Grozdan, since his firm was listed as the proposed employer. I check education to see if there are any education details in his personal file. He attended the American University of Bulgaria to learn English. After that he was an engineering student in Sofia, majoring in construction. He maintained a high-grade-point level all through school. His parents moved to Bulgaria in the eighties from Poland; his father was an educator and got a position at the state university. His education background is pretty solid. Now, if I could find out whom he worked for before coming here. Nikoli seems to be the link, but there is no business listed for him. I'll try a different link later. I put all this information in a file and click print, so I can read it in black and white.

I try another link and think that if he was in the military, he had to get the electronics bug someplace. I put his name in, and bingo he joined right after graduation from college. I wonder if they have mandatory military service as part of being a citizen. He was in a construction unit for a while but was transferred to another unit a few months after he joined. He was in the communications pool, very interesting. Why would a construction major decide to join the communications pool? One very important thing to remember, he studied English and spoke it almost all the time from what I gather. He even took his structural engineering in English. He must have known at some point he would be moving to America. Was it just a fluke that he studied English or part of a plan? I should try digging up information on his father. He was a professor of some sort. I'll dig up his information later. Buranski served two years almost all in the communications unit. His post was right on the border, with Romania along the Danube River. They were probably spying on them and the Russians to find out what was going on there. He met Ana on a weekend pass, while he and some friends were scouting around the area. They were married a few months later. A little more than a year later, their daughter was born. He was discharged from the army in July of '95, right after his daughter was born. Then he went to work in the private sector.

From what I can find on his working after he got out of the military, he concentrated on the construction part to learn all he could from his employer about how to rehab and do additions. He worked for the same company for almost seven years. Then he moved to a company that was more into building commercial real estate, maybe to add that to his list of qualifications. The firm was used to renovate and do additions to the American University of Bulgaria, the school he attended to learn English. Then they built the Sofia campus as an extension of the main campus in Blagoevgrad. It opened in 2003. After that project, I find no employer information for him until right before he applies to immigrate to the United States. Then he is listed as a construction superintendent for a multinational company, with offices in Moscow, Berlin, Warsaw, and Sofia. How could Buranski just vanish from public record for three years and then turn up again as a construction superintendent prior to wanting to relocate to the United States to seek a better life? This case is taking more turns than a roller coaster, zooming from one fantastic loop to another. The file for those three missing years was sealed by Bulgarian Department of Defense. I would think our recruit was doing high-level spying for somebody. That must be the time he was learning his other trade as a spy for Nikoli Filchev. There must be a connection someplace.

I look at the clock, and I am like, where did those five hours go? I have some errands I need to take care of before going to pick up Val for our date tonight. While I am out, I figure I should stop by the barber shop and get cleaned up. It's been at least six weeks since I paid them a visit. I think about tonight and where I should take Val. There is a real nice steak house in Melrose Park; they serve only aged steaks, with broiled onions and mushrooms, great baked potatoes, and salad. The staff is very considerate; if you want to talk for two or three hours, they will not bother you. They keep the water glasses full and make sure you are happy with everything. Their prices are a little higher than the chain places, but the food is much better and they don't rush you to leave. You reciprocate by tipping more than you would at a chain, so it is a trade-off. If you dress like I am going to dress, they know you are there for a nice, relaxing dinner; so that works for me. If you order drinks with dinner or just drink coffee, they don't mind. I stop by the cleaners and pick up the stuff I dropped off a few weeks ago and drop off the next batch of shirts. With my schedule the past month, I lost track of those things. I take the Crown Victoria through the car wash to get the dirt and grime off it and vacuum the interior, toss all the scraps of paper and napkins that accumulate under the seat, and spray the inside with Febreze, to give it a fresh scent rather than the smell of leftover pizza or something. I get back to my place, take a shower, and get dressed for tonight.

The phone rings, it is right at five o'clock. I look at the caller ID. It's my daughter, so I answer it. "Hi, sweetheart, how was your week?" She answers, "Not too bad, I had a big test Thursday in Algebra and I think I did real good on it. I am finally starting to understand it." I said, "That is good, I know you are smart." She says, "Thanks, Dad, I was having my doubts about learning that, I don't know why I need that but it is required, so I took it." I ask, "What time do you want me to pick you up in the morning?" She says, "I was hoping you could pick me up right after church; I am going to the nine o'clock mass; we get out about ten to ten. I'll tell mom you will pick me up there, so she won't get upset when you show up." I ask, "Is there something special you want to do tomorrow?" She says, "I'll be hungry, we could go for crepes at the place in Elmhurst; they make the best ones. After that I need to go find some new athletic shoes; I am going to try out for basketball. I need to do some extracurricular stuff. I have been practicing outside after school with some friends, and they think I can make the team." I say, "You really surprised me with that, I figured you just wanted to be a brain all the time. You keep taking all those advanced courses." She says, "Yes, I like those; but in order to have a more rounded education, I need to do something else too." I said, "I guess if you make the team, I'll have to make some of your games, if your mother won't get upset." She says, "Are you kidding, if I make the team, she would love you to go to the games; she said she can't stand the smell in the gymnasium. She asked why I couldn't wait until spring and play softball. I told her I might try that too." I said, "OK, I'll pick you up after church and I will look nice for a change." She said, "Thanks, Dad, I'll see you then. I love you." I said, "I love you too, sweetie."

    I leave my place promptly at five-thirty. I look at the address Val wrote down and go. Damn, I didn't think she lived in Park Ridge, a pretty upscale area. I guess you can't judge a person by where they work. I drive to her place. She has a condo in a real nice building. I park and go ring the bell. She answers and asks, "Do you want to see the place or do you want to see it after our date?" I am like, "I made reservations for six-thirty; I'll look at it later, if that is OK with you?" She says, "Sure, I might invite you in after our date for coffee and dessert. I made a pie today in my spare time. The apples are great this year, and I don't like the pies at the store; I load mine with cinnamon." I think to myself, she knows my soft spot. I say, "That sounds like a plan, I figure after we eat we will not want dessert right away. Besides we might go dancing after dinner." She says, "Are you kidding me? I haven't been dancing in years." I said, "Neither have I, I don't dance very well but I can move around the dance floor a little. This is a date right?" She says, "Yes, it is, but I didn't expect that too." I said, "We'll see how it turns out, we might not even find a place to dance unless we crash a wedding." She laughed and said, "There is a banquet hall on Harlem Avenue, and there are always wedding parties going on there. We could sneak in and grab a dance and split before they chased us out." I go, "Val, you sure are a surprise to me. If I knew you were this much fun, I would have asked you out a long time ago." She asked, "Where are we going for dinner?" I said, "Melrose Park, the steak house." She said, "Really?" I said, "Yes, really." She said, "I can't wait, let's go." I take Cumberland, south to North Avenue, and go west, right to the restaurant. We get there right at six-thirty. Perfect timing, I should have played the lottery today. I asked the hostess to seat us in the next room, away from the noise. They are having a big gathering for a family celebration. She says no problem.

We have a very enjoyable dinner and talk about our lives a little to try to get to know each other a little more. I mean, I have seen her at Maple Street Café for years, but we only talk typical conversation between waitress and customer. Tonight, we are talking to each other one on one, no Tony to interrupt or other customers wanting some attention from her. I tell her about my daughter and the plans for tomorrow. She tells me that she was engaged to be married before, but the man she was going to marry turned out to be no good. He lied to her about the fact he was never married. Well, it turns out he was married and had three children. His wife found out he was seeing Val, and she confronted her and said, "If you want him so bad, you can have him and the three children; they are a package deal. I thought he was cheating but didn't know with whom." So Val said, "No, you can have him. I don't like liars." The wife said, "He is CPD; they are all liars. All they want is some action on the side." Val continued, "I thanked her and swore off cops from then on." I asked, "What about me?" She said, "You are not CPD, you are something else hush-hush I've been told by Tony. He said you are not like those guys; you are an honest, hard-working man that works too hard. I swear sometimes Tony thinks I'm his daughter, and he tries to give me advice. I tell him I'm a grown woman. He says, 'I know that but you need a man in your life.' I ask, why? He says, 'You just do and that is the end of the conversation.'" The waitress comes back every so often to check on us; we are talking more than we are eating or drinking. I look at the clock, it is almost nine. I couldn't believe my eyes. Val and I talked for two and a half hours about everything we could think of talking about. We finished our dinner; I gave the waitress my credit card to pay the bill, she came back, I left her a nice tip, and we left.

Rather than go the way we came, I went east to River Road and then went north on River Road. I remembered from a few years ago, there was a club on River Road that had dancing on Friday and Saturday nights. Sure enough the club was still in operation. Most of the customers were from Europe but the dancing was still there; they only played music to dance to, not nightclub singers and that type of venue. I think all the songs they played were all for dancing. We were there for about two hours; we each had two drinks since there was a two drink minimum. Neither one of us drank our second drink. Then I took her home. She invited me in for coffee and pie. She was acting like she was going to ask me to spend the night but then she said, "Jim, I really had a good time tonight. Thank you for dinner and dancing, you made my week." I said, "Val. Thank you. I can't tell you the last time I enjoyed myself this much." She said, "I hope we can do this again, when both of us have a free Saturday night." She walked to the front door with me and kissed me and said, "Have fun with your daughter tomorrow." I said, "I'll try." I get home; it is just past midnight. I go to bed, and I'm out like a light.

Sunday morning I wake up and look at the clock radio. It is seven-thirty. I'm like, did I sleep through the alarm or what? I look, oh yes, I didn't flip it to alarm last night. Well I have a couple of hours until I have to pick up my daughter. I go to the kitchen and look in the fridge, hmmm . . . , nothing in here. I look at the coffee maker; nah, I toss on some clothes, drive over to the donut place, and get some coffee and a cinnamon roll. I know I'm taking Natalie out for breakfast but I need to put something in my stomach. I get back home and turn on the computer to try looking up something before I go pick up my daughter after church. I am really stymied as to why I can't find out any information about Nikoli Filchev. Then it hits me, maybe I'm not searching in the right country. I'm like maybe he is Russian not Bulgarian; they were part of the Warsaw Pact; some ties are hard to break, and some strongmen still run things.

Bingo, I find what I am looking for. No wonder he wanted Buranski to do the job since he has connections with the Russian mafia, the Bulgarian crime bosses, and Serbian underworld. When Buranski wanted to move to the United States, Nikoli was actually running the Bulgarian office and had been there for ten years as a diplomat on Russian affairs and has diplomatic immunity. They may be a democratic state, but they are still concerned about the Russians. I still can't figure out why Nikoli would sponsor Buranski to move to the United States. Another thing that puzzles me is if Nikoli is not Bulgarian, how can he sponsor somebody? Then I think about his connections with the Bulgarian leader, that could explain some of it but wouldn't the United States question who the sponsor was? More questions than answers. I look at the computer screen, see the time, and decide I need to shut this down and go get Natalie. I can finish this later.

I get to church right at nine-forty-five. Thank goodness, I remembered the shortcut and missed the freight train. Natalie and her mom walk out of the church; she sees my car and waves for me to come over. So I get out and walk over to where they are standing. I tell my ex, "Rachael, you look really good this morning." She says, "Thank you Jim, you look pretty good yourself. No jeans and a blazer, I'm impressed." We exchanged small talk for a few minutes, and I told her I would have Natalie home before eight. Then Natalie and I walked to the car, and I drove to Elmhurst so we could have breakfast. Natalie says, "Thanks Dad, mom was driving me crazy; so I told her you would pick me up after church so we could go to breakfast for a change." I said, "I figured it was something like that after you told me you wanted to try out for basketball. I think your mother would like it better if you tried out for cheerleading." She asked why I didn't and I said, "All those girls are stuck up and think they are going to get to go out with all the football guys. I'm not into that scene. I don't like jocks for the most part; they only care about sports." I say, "That's my girl, I knew you were smart."

The restaurant was busy but not jammed, so we got a table. Natalie ordered the crepes with strawberries and extra whipped cream and hot chocolate with whipped cream. I ordered a Denver omelet with an English muffin toasted and coffee. We ate our breakfast and talked about her studies, and I asked how her piano lessons were going. She said, "Dad, I don't really like the piano any more. I want to play something else, but mom said I have to stay with piano. Can you talk to her?" I said, "So what do you think you want to play?" She says, "Really, I want to play violin; I saw this one girl on Celtic Women, and she was fantastic." I say, "That is a huge challenge to play like that. I know the one you are talking about. I saw their special on TV. That is a commendable desire but do you really want to commit that much time and effort?" She says, "I already did some research, and there is a school in Chicago. I know I would have to give up something and the classes aren't cheap." I said, "You think it over real good. I can probably cover the costs but what about the chasing to get you there, and I don't think your mother would be too fond of that idea." She says, "Dad, you are probably right but that is my desire, maybe I'll wait until I get my license so I could drive myself." I ask, "Where in Chicago? If you are talking Old Town School of Music you would need a chaperone with you all the time. I know that area, they prey on young girls. I wouldn't want you going there alone, ever." She said, "Dad, you are too protective." I said, "I know sweetie and that is never going to change." We finish our breakfast and head to Yorktown Mall to find her athletic shoes. It feels nice spending the day with Natalie.

We go into a Footlocker store at the mall. I am floored by the prices on the athletic shoes. Me, I buy New Balance or Reebok tennis shoes. These things are unbelievable, Air Jordan's, Nike, and thirty different brands, all around two hundred bucks a pop. What happened to inexpensive lace-up, high-top basketball shoes? Don't tell me, I know it's been twenty some years since those were popular or the only kind you could buy. After trying on six different ones, she finds a pair that she feels comfortable in. On sale, 179.50; ouch, oh well, if she is going to play, she needs the support and so I pay the price. I ask, "Do you need anything else clothes wise as long as we are at the mall? I'll buy you a couple of new outfits if you want them." She says, "Dad you don't have to buy me clothes, mom and I go shopping all the time. I'm glad you offered but I am fine; my closet is full and I need to clean it out to get rid of things I don't wear anymore." I asked, "What would you like to do the rest of the day?" She said, "We could go to the arboretum. I like to look at the fall colors, and they are already turning. I think we can rent bicycles there and ride one of the trails." I ask, "Do you want to go to my place to change? Since if we are doing that, I don't want to ride in this outfit." She says, "Sure, you have some of my sweat outfits there and tennis shoes. Then you can put on your jeans and a sweatshirt and be comfortable too. I liked seeing you in slacks and a blazer for a change, you look nice in it." I said, "Thank you sweetie, I figured I needed to look like a gentleman once in a while."

So we drive to my place. I turn on the computer to check if they have bike rental. I saw an ad for a bike shop in Lisle that rents bikes. I am like OK, one way or another, we can bike ride together. I decide I'll take the SUV just in case. If we have to rent the bikes in Lisle, I can put them in the back. We drive down 53 to the arboretum. I ask at the gate if they rent bikes, and the guy says yes. We go over to where they rent them and we ride for two hours; we then go to the main building to get something to drink. That was a workout but it was fun. I need to do this more. We take the bikes back to the rental place. I ask, "Do you want to eat now or are you up to bowling a couple of games?" She said, "Bowling and I don't need kid bumpers." I said, "I might." She laughs and says, "Really dad, I heard how you bowl. If you don't get 200 on your first game, you get upset." I said, "That was the old me. Now if I bowl 160, I'm happy. Back then, I was bowling three leagues and two of them were for scratch bowlers. I haven't bowled league for twelve years." She says, "That was when you and mom split up right?" I said, "Right around there, I couldn't afford to bowl and pay your mom too, and so I gave it up. Now my job keeps me so busy, I only bowl if I have nothing else to do and it's just for fun, no money games." We bowled three games. Natalie was pretty good. She actually beat me one game. I couldn't figure out the lanes. I bowled this place a few times before, and it was always hard to figure the lanes. The way they dress the lanes now is different than when we bowled here. Boy, does this bring back memories. Now I'm bowling with my daughter; back then Rachael and I would bowl Scotch doubles with other couples, Candlelight Bowl for New Years before the big New Year's Eve bash. We would get home at three in the morning or go for breakfast at one of the all night joints on North Avenue. We sure had a lot of good times. I really don't know what happened and when things changed; but they did. I haven't really thought about it until now. Why? I'm not sure. Natalie says, "Dad, are you OK?" I said "Sorry sweetie I was just thinking. Bowling with you brings back a lot of memories about your Mom and I before you were born. You look like a natural out there." She said, "Thanks dad, you did beat me two games after you changed bowling balls." I said, "Just luck." We left the bowling alley and headed back toward my place.

We get back to my place. Natalie says, "Dad, can I take a shower before we have dinner?" I said, "Sure, I think I need one too between bike riding and bowling. What do you want for dinner?" She asks, "Do you have spaghetti and meatballs or chicken breasts? I could make us something here." I say, "I think I have that stuff, there are some mesquite chicken breasts in the freezer." She says, "I think I can make something from those if you don't mind my cooking." I said, "I'll let you know after I eat it." She takes her shower and puts her dress back on. I take my shower as she gets busy in the kitchen. I come out of the shower and put on slacks and a polo shirt. I walk out toward the kitchen and smell the cooking and say, "It smells good." She says, "You can't peek, I'll bring it to the table when it's ready." I ask, "Can you fix me a coffee please?" She says, "Coming right up, I made a fresh pot, the other looked gross." I said, "I figured you did, since I smelled the coffee too." She brought my favorite mug "Superman," a gift from her a few years ago after she and Rachael went to Metropolis for the Superman festival. I turned on the TV; the football game was over. The Bears lost today; they lost to Seattle in a squeaker 23-20. I'm sure Tony wasn't too happy about that outcome. I think he was going to the game today. He got tickets from a friend from CPD, if I remember correctly. I turn off the TV before something else comes on. Natalie says, "Dinner is ready." I go to the table, and it looks really good. She said, "I found linguini and black olives and stewed tomatoes, so I cooked the chicken breasts added garlic and olive oil and some spices. You didn't have garlic bread, so I made this pseudo garlic toast." I tasted it and said, "This is very good, where did you learn to cook like this?" She says, "I like experimenting and Mom doesn't mind; it saves her from planning meals." I said, "You can cook for me anytime." She said, "Thanks, Dad," as she is blushing with pride.

After dinner I cleaned up the kitchen and put everything away. She got on the computer to play a video game. I came out of the kitchen and was watching her as she played the game. I really miss having her around. I know I could not have her here all the time, but I do like her company. She really is smart and pretty much knows what she wants to do with her life. I mean in the summer, I get her for two weeks but that time is so hectic. It is like we are trying to squeeze everything into those two weeks. We go to the ball game, the museum, the beach, and catch a few movies and the two weeks are gone. I start thinking about Rachael again. For the life of me, I don't know why. Maybe since I saw Buranski and his family and the fun they were having and I think about McCray home in Virginia this weekend for family stuff, maybe I'm just feeling melancholy. Natalie says, "Dad, do you have any dessert?" I said, "No I don't keep them here. I don't need to eat that stuff since I go overboard and I need to watch my weight." She said, "Can we stop for ice cream when you take me home?" I said, "DQ?" She said, "That is good, I like their Blizzards." I said, "We can do that." Seven o'clock we leave so I can get her home by eight. We stop at the local DQ. I ask, "Do you think your mom would like something?" She said, "Are you kidding, she rags on me about my eating that but she really likes one special one they make." I said, "So we'll surprise her and take her one." Natalie goes, "Cool." So we go in and I order mine and Natalie orders hers and then orders her Mom's to go. We eat ours, and then she gets the one from the girl at the counter, and I take her home. I walk her to the door. Rachael comes to the door. Natalie hands her the DQ. Rachael goes, "For me?" We say, "Yes, for you. We ate ours there." She says, "Thank you, I wanted something but didn't want to go out." I said, "You're welcome. We had a real good day. Natalie even made dinner for me." I said, "Natalie I'll see you next Sunday. Call me if anything changes and good luck with your tryouts." Natalie said, "My shoes?" I go get them.

I go home and figure I'll finish my research and get ready for tomorrow. McCray said he would call me late on Monday since his flight didn't get in until after three in the afternoon. I turn on the computer and go to the site I was in before looking for information on Nikoli. I find a link that gives me some more information. He has been in Sofia since 1984; before that he was in Moscow for ten years, learning his trade as an assistant on Russian affairs. He would get sent to the other embassies to get a feel of how he was supposed to conduct himself with the press and answer questions only to the extent he was allowed to. He was friends with the former director that was recalled from Bulgaria so he got the inside scoop on what was going on there. Bulgaria was part of the Warsaw Pact after 1946 until 1989, when the communist party allowed multiparty elections. After 1990, Bulgaria transitioned to a democracy. So Nikoli was pretty much the man in charge as far as Russia was concerned. They had no reason to call him back to Moscow; his reports were always to their liking. He got along well with the people in charge in Bulgaria, and when they needed information on one of Bulgaria's neighbors, they always got it. Nikoli recruited people to go to Russia to learn things they couldn't learn in Bulgaria. He had a keen eye for finding talent. His superiors in Moscow acknowledged his commitment to creating stronger ties with the Bulgarian leader. The current leader calls him in periodically just to update him on what they are planning so as not to upset anybody. There is no mention of corruption in regard to his agency.

I print out about thirty pages of research and go to the kitchen. I look at the coffee Natalie made, it is cold. I had two cups with dinner and there are four cups left. I pour some coffee in my favorite mug.

I zap the coffee, add some cream, and one sugar and then take my reading material to the study to go through the stuff again. I reread everything I printed out and highlighted a few dates. There are no names in the stuff I printed out; it was more background information about Nikoli and how he got to be the man in charge in Bulgaria. It is almost like somebody is building him up to move up in the Russian political family, as a trusted diplomat who served his country well for the past quarter of a century. Right now, all of this is just supposition on my part. There is nothing concrete to connect him to Buranski other than that he sponsored him and it gave him a contact in this country. Why Nikoli would contact him about doing a job for Mariano is beyond me. There has to be a link somewhere. Does the Chicago organized crime have dealings with Bulgaria or Russia? McCray should be able to find out that information. I am trying to find a connection; on paper he looks clean. He has never been reprimanded for anything he has done. I look at the clock, and it is after eleven. I put the papers in a folder and mark it "N." I get ready and go to bed. I am lying in bed, and my mind is running in circles; this isn't going to work. I get up and go to the living room and turn on the TV. I find an old James Bond movie on and figure that should do it. Normally, I put something on and within ten minutes I go to sleep. I am watching the movie, and I think maybe we are looking at this all wrong. Nikoli might only want information he can use to further his career. If Buranski manages to unearth a tidbit of information from his surveillance, Nikoli can move up to a higher post. What Mariano hopes to gain from this is still a mystery or was he hired only as a go-between since he has the contacts to get the permits and get Buranski access to the house to set up this mission. To my way of thinking, I can't see any other reason to do this. I write some notes on a legal pad and put it with the folder. I need to read all the stuff I sent to McCray again; there might be a clue in there that I overlooked.

Chapter 7

Two o'clock I go back to bed; finally I can catch a couple of hours of sleep. My mind stopped going in circles or the caffeine finally gave out. I think I need to try decaf, especially if I'm going to drink it at night. I check my alarm, yes it is set for 6 a.m. I fall asleep and the next thing I hear is the darn thing going off. I rub my eyes and get out of bed. I look at my mug still half full. I drank the rest of the pot last night. I never drink that much coffee unless I'm out. Oh! Well, the body sure isn't the same as it once was. I'm only forty-five, what am I going to be like at sixty-five? I do need to get on an exercise program; I know I was out of shape riding with Natalie yesterday. I was thirty when she was born; it doesn't seem possible that she is fifteen already. Next year she will be driving, she already has that in her mind. I should look around for a car now, so that it doesn't surprise me when she asks for one. I know her mom will not get her a car or pay the insurance. That will fall on my shoulders. I get dressed and drive to the donut place to get my coffee and a cinnamon roll. I figure I should go by Buranski's place to see what is going on this morning.

I park in the next block, so that I can see him when he backs out of his garage. I look a few minutes; after seven-thirty his daughter comes out to wait for the bus. A few minutes later, he backs his car out and waves to Elisia. I watch him pull away. I look in the next block, there is a Black Escalade parked there. I can't see the plates, it is too far away. After Buranski drives past, they pull away from the curb to follow. I drop back a little and think let the game begins. I follow about six car lengths behind. Finally, at a light I read the number on the plate and then I look at my log. That is the same one that picked him up to take him to Hyde Park. What happened over the weekend? Buranski told his contact that they would not start the job for a few days due to what happened to his boss. I figure something must be up for a change in plans or something. I keep both of them in sight and try to figure where Buranski is going this morning. He doesn't take his usual route, instead he gets on 83 south bound. I follow him; he drives past the Cal-Sag Canal and stays on 83 going east. He goes to 43 and heads to Worth. The Escalade follows, so I turn to follow. He drives to the Village Hall and parks in the lot and waits until they open and then goes in. The Escalade parks in front of the building so they can keep an eye on him. A few minutes later, he walks out carrying a bunch of papers and a folder. He pulls out and goes south to 159th Street and goes left to his office. The Escalade follows and parks in a parking lot, half a block away so they can watch his office. I find a spot where I can see them and keep an eye on Buranski. I turn on my audio feed so I can hear what is going on in Buranski's office. This new equipment is nice; I can be further away and still hear everything he says. All I need to do is to set the frequency and I get it like I am in the next office.

Buranski makes a phone call. He says, "I picked up all the information. I need to fill out all the forms and take them back to the office tomorrow. They said they didn't see a problem getting the permit. We just have to plug in some dollar figures and write a description of what we are going to do. I don't normally do these, my boss does but he is in the hospital for a few days. I will go visit him later, that way I know the forms will be right. Yes we will get the shell finished before Thanksgiving, you know Chicago weather a month from now, we could have a heavy snow. And that pushes everything back. I will call you tomorrow." I think somebody must have needed another job done, he doesn't normally handle those, but with Grozdan not there. Where did he get the job? He has been off since Friday.

I am watching the guys in the Escalade; they seem to be getting bored. One guy gets out and says something to his partner. He walks about half a block to a service station, he goes inside, and then comes back out in a couple of minutes and walks around to the side of the building. I figure he must have had to use the bathroom. He goes back inside and comes out carrying a bag and a cup of coffee.

They have been sitting in the same spot for almost two hours, just talking and watching Buranski's office. I have been watching them and listening to what has been going on in the office. Buranski is working on the plans for the job he went to get the papers for, so that they can get the permit. I can see him at the drawing board against the back wall drawing things out and then looking at it to make sure it is right. I look at the clock, it is eleven forty-five, I am wondering what happened to Dragan today, he didn't show up at his usual time. From where I am parked today, I don't have a good view of his used-car lot. With having to watch the guys in the Escalade, I needed to position myself differently. The phone rings, Buranski picks it up and answers, "KBW Construction, Karl speaking. Hi Boss, How are you feeling today? That's good. I went to pick up the paperwork we need to fill out for the new project in Worth. Yes, I got the message, this is for a close friend of yours and we need to push one of the projects off to take care of this job. I understand. I will be over to see you about four. I just drew up the plans, I want to write everything down so we can put the costs down for the building permit and go over the application with you to make sure everything is the way it needs to be. I will see you then."

Twelve-fifteen I hear Buranski say, "Hey Dragan, when you coming over. Yes, I'm hungry, you want to go have lunch? OK, I'll come over there in ten minutes. I am working on a drawing." So Buranski and Dragan are going to have lunch, maybe I can follow them and get something at a drive through. I wonder how the guys in the Escalade will like following him to have lunch. A few minutes later, Buranski locks the door and goes out back to meet Dragan. Dragan is driving one of the cars from his lot. I watch to see if the guys in the Escalade notice Buranski with Dragan. Yes, they do and one guy threw his coffee cup out of the window. His partner said something. He got out and picked it up. I follow after they pull out and go; I have no clue where they are going. They drive past the Gyro place and go to a burger joint and bar. They park in front and walk in. The guys in the Escalade drive past the bar and turn at the corner so they can park and keep an eye on the car. I go damn, I did want to get something from the Gyro place. I think what the heck they went in there for lunch; it will be at least thirty minutes. I turn and go around the block and go back to the Gyro place, go inside to use the restroom, and get an order to go. I order a burger, fries, and a large coffee with easy sugar. Then I drive back to where Buranski and Dragan are having lunch. The bar has a side parking lot, so I pull in there to eat my lunch and keep an eye on them. One-fifteen they walk out and get in Dragan's car. I watch as Dragan pulls a U-turn and heads back to the office. The Escalade follows and then I pull out.

We get back to Buranski's office; the guys park in the same lot. I park where I was parked before to see what is going on. I am watching; one of the guys in the Escalade gets out I think to stretch his legs. He walks around the car and takes out his cell phone and makes a call. He walks toward the service station talking all the while. He goes inside and then comes out and goes around the side. A few minutes later, he walks inside. He is still talking on the cell phone. He comes out with another bag and coffee. He walks back to his partner and hands him the phone. The other guy talks for a few minutes and he motions for the other guy to get in. They pull out of the parking lot and drive to Buranski's office and park in front. One guy gets out and walks up to the door and rings the bell. Buranski comes to the door and the guy says something to him and turns around and walks back to the Escalade. They drive away and Buranski goes back inside. When he gets inside, he picks up the phone and makes a call. He asked, "Radko, you busy later tonight? Good we have something to do tonight, a small favor for Dragan. Call me when you are free." I think that is why Dragan wanted to go out to eat, so that they could talk in private. That probably explains why he didn't show at his usual time for coffee and to chat. Buranski picks up the phone, "Ana, I have to go out tonight later after dinner, a favor for Dragan. Radko is going with me. No, I'll be home for dinner. I have to see Grozdan at the hospital at four and so I'll be home by six." Buranski clears off his desk, lays out a bunch of papers, and reads each one in detail and places them in a stack. He writes a bunch of notes on his yellow tablet and gathers all the stuff up and puts them in an attaché case. I look at the clock, it is almost three. He goes over to the project board and makes a couple of notes. He goes back to his desk and picks up the phone, "Mr. Wojowski, please. This is Karl Buranski from KBW Construction. Hello, we have a bit of a problem, we need to push your job back a week or two. Yes, I see the date on the schedule board. To be completed by November 1st can we change that to November 15th? Thank you, I will tell Grozdan."

Three-thirty Buranski locks the place and goes out the back door. He has his attaché case along with another bag. He gets in his car and drives over to Dragan's car lot and says something to him. Then he pulls out and I follow him to Oak Lawn to Mercy Hospital. He parks in the lot and takes the attaché case with him. I park and walk inside to see if they have a cafeteria and a washroom. He will be with Grozdan for a while, so I can relax a little and stretch my legs and walk around a little. I have my cell phone with me just in case McCray calls me. I walk around for about twenty minutes and get a coffee from the cafeteria. They have Dunkin and Starbucks both. Boy, even the hospitals are into what people are drinking. I walk outside, drink my coffee, and then head back to my car. The cell phone rings, its McCray. I fill him in on my day. He says, "Sounds like you had a fun-filled day." I said, "Yes, and now it looks like I will have a fun-filled night." He asks, "What do you think they are up to?" I said, "I have no clue, something about a favor for Dragan. Buranski didn't give any details to his wife, only that he was going out later after dinner with Radko." McCray says, "It might turn out to be nothing." I said, "I agree but I figure I better tail him just in case." McCray says, "Call me in the morning; I have to meet with the Chief tonight to go over the information we have on Buranski." I said, "I was digging up information about Nikoli over the weekend." McCray asks, "Didn't you take any time off?" I said, "Yes, I even took Val out on a date and spent all day Sunday with my daughter." McCray asks, "So when did you sleep?" I said, "At night." McCray says, "Funny."

Buranski comes out of the hospital a little after five and gets in his car and I follow him. I figure he is heading home since he told Ana he would be home for dinner and he is going out later to meet Radko to do a favor for Dragan. He didn't say what time later, but I know Radko is usually at the gym until almost ten. I wish Buranski had said the time just to hear him repeat it then I wouldn't be wondering. I should go have dinner since I know where Buranski is going now. I follow him home and look for the Black Escalade to see if they decided to watch him tonight. No sign of the Escalade. Buranski parks in the driveway instead of pulling in the garage. I guess since he is going out later, he figures no sense putting it in the garage. There is a family restaurant not too far from Buranski's, I decide that is where I will go. It is a typical family place with a list of daily specials and a menu that takes about fifteen minutes if you read the whole thing. I look at the daily specials and see what a couple of people ordered and make my choice. They have pepper steak served with rice and some vegetables, it comes with soup or salad; I choose neither, the waitress says you can have fruit or cottage cheese. I said pass the dinner will be plenty. She pours my coffee and turns my order in. The food was decent, not great but it was a good choice. I guess I'm spoiled by Maple Street and the way Tony cooks. I pay my bill and leave the waitress a tip. I drive back to Buranski's to wait.

Eight o'clock Buranski walks out the front door and gets in his car. I am watching from the next block. He backs out and starts to pull away, and Elisia comes out carrying a present. He stops in front of the house; Elisa hands him the present. He leans over and kisses her to say thanks. Then he drives away. I am thinking this is why he is going out to a party of some sort. I follow him since I don't know where he is going. He heads toward the office; at least he took the ramp to get on 294 south like he does in the morning. I keep him in sight and try not to get too close. He gets off at 159th Street and goes west to Harlem and turns right. I think he is going to pick up Radko at the gym. Sure enough, he pulls in and parks. About ten minutes later, he and Radko come out and get in his car. I follow them to a restaurant in Midlothian; they park in the parking lot and go in. Buranski takes the present with him.

I wait for a few minutes; I park and walk in. There is a private room on one side that they use to hold parties. I grab a table, so that I can see the door. I order a coffee and look at the menu. I'm still full from dinner, but figure I best order something. I look and they have a dessert page so I order Apple Pie Ala mode with caramel sauce. I hear Dragan yell something to Buranski. I think he is happy that he and Radko showed up. The party is pretty loud and then I hear a band start to play. It sounds like a band you would find in a bar in Germany, I can't understand the words but the people in there are having a good time. I finish my pie and my coffee. From the sound in there, the party has quieted down a little. I look at the clock, it is almost ten. I pay my bill and go outside to wait. Eleven o'clock Buranski and Radko come out; right behind them is Dragan and a lady friend. Dragan walks up to Buranski and Radko and gives them both hugs and kisses them on the cheek and says thank you, my fiancée is glad you could make it tonight. So that's what it was, Dragan finally found himself a wife to be. Is that why he and Buranski went to lunch so that he could tell him about the party tonight?

You have to hand it to Buranski. He does everything he needs to do. He is taking care of the business while Grozdan is in the hospital; goes to an engagement party for a fellow countryman and even brings another of Dragan's compatriots to the party to show support. I don't know any of my friends that would do all the stuff Buranski does and I never hear him complain even once. He just does what needs doing. No wonder that Nikoli told Mariano that he is the man you need, nothing fazes him. He is smart and has a good eye for detail. He sees things that others wouldn't even think of looking for. I follow him to take Radko back to the gym; I know both of them probably had a few drinks but nothing you could detect from their actions. Buranski drops him off and gets out and shakes his hand and says something like you are next. Radko shakes his head, "Neyt, not me." Buranski laughs, "Ja you soon, watch!" Radko goes inside and Buranski gets back in his car to drive home. He stops at a Krispe Crème donut shop, goes in, buys a large coffee and a box of donuts, and heads home. I follow him until he turns on his street and then I go home. Whew! what a day. McCray you owe me one. It is almost one when I get home.

Chapter 8

Tuesday morning I hear the alarm go off; it's six-thirty already. I get up, get dressed, and head for the donut place. McCray said to call him this morning; I wonder if he is up yet. I try his cell phone, no answer. I don't leave a message. He will call me back. My number will show up as a missed call. I head over to Buranski's place to see if he is going to be followed today. I park in my usual spot in the next block; people probably get the idea that I have a job to do, I'm there every morning for at least an hour, maybe longer, and then they don't see me again until the next day. So far no sign of the black Escalade, but it is still early. Like clockwork a few minutes after seven-thirty, Elisia comes out to wait for the bus. A few minutes later Buranski backs his car out, waves to her, and drives away. I follow him and he goes past the ramp for 294; I'm like I wonder where he is going. I follow him; he goes to the truck rental place on 45 and goes inside. A few minutes later, he comes out with the guy he talked to last week, they walk over to a truck, Buranski looks at it, and shakes his head. Right, he was supposed to get the truck Monday, but with everything that happened on Friday the schedule got changed. The guy shook his head and shrugged. Buranski says something the other guy looked at him and nodded. They go inside; I figure to do some paperwork. Buranski comes out, takes out his cell phone, and punches in a number. He waits, OK, and then he starts talking. He gets out of his car and goes back inside; I figure he called the foreman about the truck. Buranski comes out and takes 45 south to Cermak, goes east to Cicero, and goes to the family restaurant he went to last week. He waits outside for a couple of minutes. Then I see his foreman walk up to his car. He gets in and Buranski is talking to him. I guess he is telling him where he needs to go to pick up the truck and the place to pick up the stuff for the job. The foreman gets out, gives Buranski a thumbs up sign, and goes inside the restaurant.

Buranski backs out and heads west on Cermak, I follow, and he turns on 43 to go south. I am like, right he has to take the paperwork to the Village Office in Worth to get the permit for that project. Sure enough that is where he goes. After that, he heads straight to his office in Orland Park. We get to Orland Park at nine forty-five, after two hours of chasing. I look and there is a black Escalade parked in front and three guys are inside it. The two guys from yesterday plus the contact guy; Buranski parks in back and goes to the front door to unlock it so that his contact can come in. I turn on my radio and tune in the frequency. Buranski says, "My foreman is picking up the truck and the supplies for this project this morning. We need to deliver the stuff to the house today so they can start work tomorrow. Can you get the clearance for them to get in the house today?" The contact guy says, "I will call to set it up, my guys will be waiting here until your foreman comes to get you. You can only have three men on this project. The boss doesn't want too many guys walking around." Buranski says, "That will work, there isn't anything real heavy to carry in there. Tell your guys my foreman will be here at two loaded and ready." The contact guy says, "You will all have security tags that were cleared to work on this house; the security guys will scan the cards and check your IDs with the tags. The information you gave me checked out so I was able to get them approved. My guys will provide escort service and will stay there until you guys leave." Buranski says, "Understood." He walks his contact to the front door and locks the door and goes back to his office.

He picks up the phone and makes a call, "This is Karl from KBW Construction. I need to talk to the order department. Yes, we have an account with you, hold on I'll get the number. Account number 68772. Yes, that is correct. Can I email my order form to you rather than read all of the stuff? Yes, I have computer access and your email address. I got it, thank you. The order is on its way. Please let me know when that stuff can be delivered to the jobsite so my crew can be ready to start. Thank you." Buranski goes over to the project board and writes the new project on the top of the list. Project #1 Worth second story frame out & shell to be completed by Nov. 22. Project # 2 Palos Heights finish job???? Project # 3 Wojowski Finish 2nd floor bathroom remodel and new master bedroom knock out wall from other bedroom to expand room. Nov. 1 Start Project #4 Pending no contract yet 2nd story house in Midlothian Call next week. I hear Buranski talking, "Dragan, you coming over? Yes, I'll make strong coffee. How's your head this morning? Ten minutes." I'm like, I didn't hear the phone and he didn't call through the company phone. I look through the telephoto camera; he has a Bluetooth in his ear. When did he get that?

Ten minutes later, Dragan walks in through the back door. Buranski asks, "Did you sleep last night?" Dragan says, "We went back to her place and talked until three this morning. Sophia was really happy you and Radko showed up. I told her you both are my oldest and closest friends from the old country. So she wanted to know about both of you. We talked all night about you two. She asked why Radko wasn't married. I told her he wasn't ready yet. You, I said got married in the old country and have a teenage daughter. She was impressed." Buranski says, "Thank you, I told Radko he was next, he laughed and said Neyt, not me. I said soon, he shook his head." Dragan says, "He loves the gym and all the muscle stuff, I think he is too thick between the ears." Buranski says, "Grozdan told me you were smart. I have to agree. We need to find a gal for him." Dragan says, "Lady wrestler maybe." Buranski laughed, "No, somebody slender like Nadia." Dragan laughed, "You're funny today Karl, Nadia was in gymnastics. I remember her, very talented, too skinny no body." Buranski says, "That was then you should see her now, vavoom!" Dragan goes, "You got a picture?" Buranski says, "I'll get one tonight. I'll show you tomorrow." About thirty minutes pass and Dragan says, "Thanks for the coffee, I needed it. Do you need any help later?" Buranski says, "No we will be good, my foreman and Radko will be here. That project gets started today."

My cell phone rings, it is McCray. He asked what was going on, so I brought him up to speed. He asks, "You said they are getting an escort to the jobsite and they were sitting with them until they leave?" I said, "That is what the contact told Buranski. He knows how tight the security is there, so I don't think it surprised him. The way I see it, I think it makes the whole project even easier since the guys in the black Escalade already have clearance to be in the neighborhood, and with the ID tags for Buranski, his foreman, and Radko they will not be subjected to questioning every time they go there." McCray asks, "How long did Buranski say this would take to setup?" I said, "I don't remember the exact number of days, but I think less than two weeks. He knows they need to be finished and have everything tested before the beginning of November since that whole area will be off limits until after New Years'." McCray says, "There may be a glitch in the plans, I found out last night he may be in town at the end of October something about a benefit." I asked, "Is that public news yet?" McCray says, "Not that I am aware of. There was a memo for all department heads to check their security details and have them on alert just in case." I said, "I am planning on following Buranski to Hyde Park just to keep an eye." McCray says, "I have two guys over there working with the FBI, once they get in the area you should take a break, I will have my guys on the lookout. They will call me when the truck and the Escalade leave and you can get back to Orland Park." I said, "If they leave here at two, they will be in Hyde Park by two forty-five." McCray says, "Thanks, I'll call you later. The FBI is aware there will be some work being done in that house. I started to tell them that was why I needed two guys there, but they already knew about the permit and who would be coming and going during the next couple of weeks. Whoever owns that house must be in real good with Mariano. Why else could he get clearance for his thugs to be providing escort service?" I asked, "No word on who bought the place?" McCray says, "Not that we can find out, the buyer supposedly bought the place as an investment, the owner thinks in a couple of years he can turn a nice profit." I said, "Yes, if the real estate market ever recovers from this recession." I said, "I can't see somebody buying something like that to sit empty for a couple of years." McCray says, "After the work is done somebody is supposed to move in, so there will be people living in it. That was all we could find out." I said, "That is real convenient." McCray says,

"I was thinking the same thing. Keep your ears peeled for any hints from Buranski's contact."

Buranski is busy in the office taking care of details and calling suppliers for the project in Worth, trying to get everything to arrive by the beginning of November. So his guys can get started on that project. The boss said the shell had to be completed before Thanksgiving, so that they wouldn't be interfering with the holidays. Satisfied, he goes over to the project board and marks Ordered after the Project. Buranski takes a large folder out of the lateral file and puts it on his desk and starts going through it, I think this must be the folder for the special project. He looks at the clock, it is twelve-thirty, he hasn't had lunch nor have I and he is supposed to be ready to leave here at two. He goes to the phone and makes a call, "Radko, what time you coming over? Fine. Can you stop at the Gyro place and bring lunch? I have been tied up all morning. That will be great. Yes, two o'clock we are supposed to leave. What time does Kurt get there? Good, we should be back from Hyde Park before seven. Did you talk to Kurt about filling in for you for two weeks? Yes, we'll be done on time. We'll talk when you get here." I am like, well he is going to eat, he isn't going anyplace, the escort guys are due back here at two, and the foreman will be here with the truck. So I decide I will go and pick up a coffee and something to eat at the burger joint a few blocks from here.

I get back from the burger joint feeling much better; I went inside, used the restroom, got my lunch, and so I am good for the afternoon. Five minutes after I get back, Radko shows up and parks in back by Buranski's car and goes in the back door. Buranski says, "I thought you got lost." Radko says, "They were busy, five people in front of me." Buranski says, "Here take this for the lunch." Radko says, "You always buy." Buranski says, "It's a write off, it's business." Radko says, "Fair enough." Buranski says, "This project we need to concentrate and get everything done, our timetable may change. I got an inside tip, we might have to run a test earlier than I wanted to." Radko says, "You are the electronics guy. I just install the stuff. Ivan and I do the grunt work and you play with the electronics." Buranski says, "How long do you know Ivan?" Radko says, "He came over the same time

I did, ten years. Grozdan put him to work like you. Why you ask?" Buranski says, "I just wanted to be sure he is good for this project." Radko says, "You pay him, he keeps his mouth shut. He works hard, this job gets done and you get more jobs. I think we need one more guy but you said only three, so we make do." Buranski says, "Those guys have you all wrong. They think you are just muscle, but you are smart too." Radko says, "You are the smart one. I only help you, this is your project not mine. You asked me to help, I help." I listen to their chatter like players on a team, bantering back and forth. Buranski says, "When we get to the job, talk only in Polish, I don't want those guys listening to us talk. Understood?" Radko asks, "How about Bulgarian or Russian? "Buranski says, "Let's wait for Ivan, see if he knows Polish."

At quarter to two, the black Escalade pulls up in front of Buranski's office. Five minutes later, the foreman shows up with the truck and parks behind the black Escalade. The foreman walks up to the door and rings the bell. Buranski goes out and opens it, so that he can come in. They walk into the office. Radko asks, "Ivan, how's your Polish?" Ivan says something, I can't understand. Buranski and Radko both laugh. Radko says, "Not that, your speaking Polish." Ivan says something else. Radko says, "When we get to the job, no English only Polish. We don't want those guys, he points to the street listening to us talk." Ivan says, "No problem." Buranski says, "Here are the rules. Nothing goes in there that hasn't been checked by me and those guys in the Escalade. Cell phones stay here, no weapons, knives or anything else, no drugs not even aspirin, no alcohol, cigarettes but not in the house, in the truck only. Understood?" They both go, "Really strict rules!" Buranski says, "That was the deal. We are cleared, so we have to wear security tags they get us in and out of there. We get back here they go in the safe. We have almost two weeks but that may need to be pushed up a day or two. Tomorrow we go there at eight and work until four and leave. Any questions?" Ivan says, "Are we leaving from here everyday or can we meet some place else closer?" Buranski says, "Here, I will be here at seven. It should take us thirty-five minutes to get there, but we can't go until our escorts get here. They don't even have to stop for security checks, they are in the system, we go with them no problems." Radko says, "Sounds good to me, but how are you going to get the other stuff there?" Buranski says, "That is being taken care of, I have a truck from Dish Network coming tomorrow with all the electronics gear. Our contact Mr. Giovani has all the details of the stuff we ordered, they pick it up and bring right in, and they stop by security and check off the list. All the labels on the materials will be switched, so they only show up as Dish Network installation stuff. OK guys let's go."

The black Escalade pulls out and they follow right behind. Ivan is driving, Radko in the middle and Buranski riding shotgun. I pull out and follow them. Boy, did I get an earful of information from his briefing! McCray will be impressed by Buranski sticking to details. I hope that bug has a recording devise hooked up to it, so that we can recover the whole conversation. I flip my cell phone, but then I think better of the idea. I'll wait until we get on the expressway and then I'll call McCray and tell him where we are. We get on 55 and I call McCray and tell him, "Alert your guys. We just got on 55, we should be there in twenty minutes unless there is a backup." McCray asks, "How did it go?" I said, "Wait until I call you back after your guys relieve me. Can we meet some place close to your office?" McCray says, "Sure, I know a restaurant a few blocks from my office. Meet me there, it is on Halsted and Madison at three-fifteen." I said, "OK, I'll be there."

The drive to Hyde Park went smooth, no traffic. We get to the security check. I fall off and turn to take Halsted north to Madison Street. Traffic is heavy down here; I don't know how McCray deals with it everyday. I like the burbs, a lot less congestion. Down here, parking is at a premium; the lots charge by the day and they are all jammed. Street parking if you can find one you have to feed the meter, but you can only park two hours max; they boot it and tow it if you don't go move it. I wouldn't want this hassle all the time. Two hours costs almost ten bucks. I remember when parking was a quarter for fifteen minutes. Two bucks for two hours, I could handle that. McCray will probably walk; he tells me he walks everywhere down here. He only drives when he has too. Can't say, I blame him in that respect. I wouldn't want to walk in the snow or rain, but that's me. I get to the restaurant early and find a spot on the street. My lucky day, I guess. I look at the sign. No parking between five and nine p.m. I think why then and go damn United Center is right up the street, no wonder. The Bulls and the Blackhawks both play there. I'm like, who is playing tonight, are they home or away? I mean the season just started. Baseball is over, football is in full swing. Chicago is sports crazy. There is always something going on. I get out of my car and find where to pay for parking, and pay my fee. I have to be out of here by five or they will tow it, that's for sure. I see McCray walking up the street, so I wait until he catches up to me and then we go inside the restaurant. The waitress sees him and shows us to a booth in the back. I guess he comes here often.

They bring us coffee and I look through the menu; I'm not real hungry but figure I should order something. McCray says, "The pies are great here. They make their own, not like most of the places." I said, "In that case I'll have triple berry." The waitress takes our order; he orders the same. Then I tell him how Buranski laid out the rules and how this was going to be done. I told him I was impressed at all the details Buranski thought through and how his contact Mr. Giovani was getting the electronics gear there, pretty slick if you ask me and using a Dish Network truck to haul it all in there. McCray listens to my recap and says, "I'll get our mole to recover the tape from today. Normally they just erase everything the same night, but this sounds important." I was going to ask who the mole was, but figured it's better if I don't know. I said, "Buranski is sure a pro, he knows all the stuff and Radko was a surprise too, I didn't figure him to do this sort of work. The foreman Ivan is just to work." McCray says, "So he laid out the schedule that was real nice too. It looks like you will enjoy some time off based on what you said. Your days will be pretty free until five and only if Buranski is going somewhere other than home." I said, "Thanks boss, I can do research or try to figure out what the big picture is." McCray asks, "You can't just relax can you?" I said, "Well, I have been baby-sitting him for a month now so I would like to be involved. This throws a huge monkey wrench into the plans since I will not be able to watch him and his guys." McCray says, "You could come downtown a couple of days and work on putting a complete dossier together on each of our subjects and fill in the missing blanks. Our computer here has a lot more search engines than your personal computer." I said, "That is more or less what I have been doing on Nikoli and Buranski." McCray asks, "Why don't you start on it tomorrow since you know Buranski and his guys will be tied up from seven until five everyday on this special project?" I said, "Ok, I'll drive down in the morning after the rush. I'll make discs on everything I have so I can transfer the info." McCray asks, "Why not just do a USB Zip?" I said, "How much data can they hold?" McCray says, "1G, that's more than you have on your computer." I said, "I'll see you around ten." I look at the clock, it is five minutes until five. I said, "I need to move my car or they will tow it." McCray says, "That they will. I'll have a parking pass for you, so you can park in the lot next door to the office."

After my meeting with McCray, I drive back to Orland Park to see what time they get back. I get to Orland Park about ten to six. Buranski's car is still in back along with Radko's car. Well, I guess they aren't back yet, there are no lights on in the office. So I find a spot where I can watch and not be spotted. Six-thirty the rental truck pulls up in front. Buranski and Radko get out. Ivan stays in the truck. The black Escalade is right behind them. Buranski and Radko walk to the front door and the guy riding shotgun in the Escalade yells something. Buranski turns around and walks over to him and leans in to talk to the driver. They seem satisfied and make a U-turn and head back toward the expressway. Ivan waits and Buranski walks over and holds up seven fingers. Ivan nods a drives away. Buranski and Radko go inside; he flips the lights and tells Radko, "Good job today. Those meatballs don't have a clue of what we are doing." Radko says, "I hate to run but I told Kurt I would be there by seven, so I'll be a couple of minutes late." Buranski says, "See you in the morning." After Radko leaves, he calls on the company phone, "Hi Ana, long day today, I need to go see Grozdan before I come home. Yes, I'll be home before nine. We'll talk then." He checks messages on the answering machine and writes a couple of notes, then locks the place up, and heads to Oak Lawn. I follow him, I guess out of habit. I know he is going home after he sees Grozdan, but I figure I'll stick with him until he gets home. He drives straight to Mercy Hospital, parks, and goes inside. I walk in to get a coffee from the cafeteria and use the restroom. About eight o'clock Buranski walks out and goes to his car. His cell phone rings, he answers it. He is talking and I can tell he is not happy. He gets off the phone, gets in his car, and makes a phone call. He talks for almost ten minutes and then he closes his phone and backs his car out. I follow and he is headed home. That is good; I was worried he was going back to Orland Park for something. That means in the morning I best follow him to make sure there are no changes in the plans. He pulls in his garage and I go home.

I set my alarm for 5 a.m. and then go into my study to copy all the data onto discs, I didn't get to the electronics store because I have plenty of discs. I load all of Nikoli's information on one disc. Then I load all the information I found on Buranski onto another disc. I look at some of the background info I gathered and put that on another disc. My phone rings, it is Natalie so I answer it, "Hi sweetie, how are you? Did you try out for basketball? Great, so now what is your schedule? Practice everyday from four until six. Saturday afternoon two hours. That sounds like a lot of extra things for you to tackle. That is for two weeks, then you start to play. Sounds like you are going to be real busy." She says, "Yes Dad, I'll be busy but I still have my Sunday's for you free." I said, "I'm glad of that. So when do I get to see you play?" She says, "The coach said our first home game is in three weeks. I'll have the schedule on Sunday. Mom's not happy since she will have to pick me up after practice everyday and take me on Saturday." I said, "I might be able to take you on Saturdays for practice, that way I see you twice." She says, "That would help Mom and me a lot." I said, "Call me Friday, I should know then if I can." She says, "I love you Dad." I said, "I love you too sweetie." I take a hot shower and go to bed to be ready before dawn to follow Buranski.

Chapter 9

Wednesday morning five o'clock the alarm goes off, I rub my eyes and think why did I decide I needed to follow Buranski this morning? Oh! well, I set the alarm I may as well get up and get moving. I'm like, I need to find out why he was upset at the hospital, maybe following him this morning will give me a clue. I get dressed and load all my stuff into an attaché case, so I look professional rather than throwing all the stuff into a shopping bag. I stop at the donut place and get an extralarge coffee and a cinnamon roll. I get to Buranski's about twenty to six. Five minutes later, he backs his car out and drives away, so I follow. He doesn't get on 294, he goes to 45 so I follow; he goes south to Justice and pulls into an auto repair shop. Ivan is standing there waiting for him. I look the truck rental that he was driving yesterday is sitting there. It has a flat tire and some damage to the right front fender. So that was why he was upset. I don't see anyone in the repair shop; Buranski and Ivan are talking, about five minutes go by, and a guy shows up. Buranski asks him a question. The guy says something. Buranski shakes his head. The guy says something else and Buranski says, "OK, how soon?" The guy says, "Two hours, maybe less." Buranski says, "OK" and leaves. Ivan stays at the shop. Buranski drives to the office in Orland Park. Radko is waiting in his car. Buranski parks and they go inside. Once they are inside Radko asks, "So what happened, you were upset last night when you called me?" Buranski says, "Ivan was pulling out of the gas station and somebody pulled out of a parking place right into the truck, there was an auto repair shop close by so he parked it there and called me. I said go home get some sleep I'll go there in the morning. The man at the garage said maybe two hours and he can drive the truck. We only need it today and tomorrow after that we can go there in the van."

Radko asks, "Did you call Mr. Giovani?" Buranski says, "Yes, I called him, he wasn't happy. I said, neither am I but things happen." Radko says, "So what is our schedule today?" Buranski says, "I told him I would call him and give him a time for his guys to be here since I didn't know anything else last night. Right now we can't do anything. Ivan has to pick up the bathroom fixtures and tile before we can go there. If you want you can go get some sleep or go to the gym, I need to make some calls, so I'll be busy for a few hours." Radko says, "Call me when Ivan calls you for picking up the bathroom stuff, I'll go sack out for a couple of hours. I trained a couple of hours with a new fighter last night, he is looking real good. We might sponsor him in competition." Buranski says, "You keep trying to find the next gold metal, don't you?" Radko says, "Why not, that's my thing. I love to see these guys compete." Buranski says, "That was what they use to say about you. You knew your stuff. How many metals did you win?" Radko says, "Two gold, one silver, and one bronze." Buranski says, "Get some sleep, I'll call you." I call McCray. His cell phone goes right to voice mail, so I leave a message. I look at the time, it isn't even seven-thirty yet. Why do I feel I have been up for hours?

I hear Buranski talking to himself I guess, mumbling something I can't understand. He sets up the coffee maker and spreads out a bunch of papers on his desk. About ten minutes later he gets up and walks over to the coffee maker and pours himself some coffee. Then I hear Dragan as he comes in the back door. He says, "You really should lock the back door, anybody can just walk in." Buranski says, "I see you just walked in, so it's too late to lock it." Dragan says, "You are in a good mood this morning." Buranski says, "Just a little problem with the truck, Ivan was hit last night. They will fix it this morning." They talk small talk for twenty minutes. Dragan says, "Thanks for the coffee. I could smell it next door. Strong, like a good woman which reminds me you have picture of Nadia?" Buranski says, "Come see her now." He flips on the computer and pulls up a picture. Dragan says, "No way not skinny Nadia." Buranski says, "See caption." Dragan says, "Wow! She's not married?" Buranski says, "No, she trains gymnasts, like Radko trains wrestlers." Dragan asks, "Where does she live?" Buranski says, "Bulgaria." Dragan says, "She is right for Radko. The two of them could train Olympic contenders." Buranski says, "That was my thought, Radko has one right now real promising and I think she has one or two good athletes too. But it takes money and talent." Dragan says, "And dedication." Buranski says, "This job will get us some money but we need more for a program like that." I think that is why he took on this project to get money to build an Olympic stable of talent to compete in world games? I am thinking, what did that report say about Nikoli and having an eye for talent? Maybe it wasn't for spies but athletes to win gold metals. I better read that information again.

My cell phone rings, it is McCray. I said, "Today is pushed back a few hours. The foreman was in a minor accident last night. The truck is being fixed this morning. Then he has to pick up the bathroom fixtures and supplies before they head to the jobsite. I got some more information that might prove useful. I'll tell you all about it when I get to your office later. I'll call you when they leave here." McCray says, "That will be fine. I have to go to another meeting about the timetable for the big guy." I said, "I should be there before lunch time." McCray says, "When you get here see Ramon, the parking attendant, he has your pass." I said, "Will do boss." McCray says, "You can drop the boss stuff, call me Rusty if you want. When you're in the office don't call me boss. We try to be informal since we spend so much time together there."

I am sitting there watching Buranski and listening to the two of them talk. I open my laptop and turn it on. I need to check something to satisfy myself. I go into the site I was in before checking on Nikoli to see what that said about him having a good eye for spotting talent to read it again. There is no mention of athletes, but I seem to recall reading something about him in that respect, where did I read that? Maybe in his duties the diplomat in charge of Russian affairs he was involved with athletes, I look and sure enough. Over the years, several of the top Bulgarian athletes have gone to Russia for more training to hone their skills and compete in competition to go to the world games. I am thinking that must be his second love, spying first, Olympic contenders second. That is kind of like Buranski and his feelings about putting together a team with Radko and Nadia. He is smart enough to know you need money to pay for all of that. In the old days, the governments paid for everything since it was for national pride but that isn't the case any longer with all the specialized training and the costs associated with doing that, most of them have cut back on funding that is where private individuals with money can get into the game. Some do it just for the joy of seeing their picks win metals; there is no money in winning but in endorsements after the fact. My thoughts are interrupted by Dragan saying to Buranski, "Be careful today, I'll be around later if you want to talk more." The phone rings, Buranski answers it, "KBW Construction, Karl speaking. Yes, Ivan we will be ready, what time will you be here? Twenty minutes, I'll call Radko." He calls Radko and then calls his contact and says, "Tell your guys we will be leaving here in twenty minutes. OK, yes we can drive to Hyde Park, they will meet us at 55th Street so they don't have to drive out here. Yes that is fine, we will watch for them."

Ivan and Radko get there almost at the same time. Radko parks in back and Ivan sits in the truck. A few minutes later, Buranski and Radko walk out of the office. Buranski locks the door, they get in the truck, and drive away. It is about ten-thirty, so I figure they will be in Hyde Park by eleven-thirty. I follow them until they get to 55th Street and their escort is waiting for them. Buranski sees the black Escalade and waits for them to pull out. I follow until I reach Halsted Street and head north to McCray's office. I pull in the lot next to his office and see an attendant wearing the name Ramon. I tell him who I am, he looks sure enough there is a permit for me to park. He tells me where to park and I park, grab all my stuff, and walk to McCray's office. He isn't back yet, but the secretary said he told her I would be there around noon. She takes me into the office; there are about ten walled off cubby hole offices, she shows me to one and shows me where the break room and the restrooms are, and then goes back to the reception area. I get busy and turn on the computer and there are instructions from McCray how to access certain data. I start loading the info I have on disc in and head to the break room and use the restroom. I go to the coffee area, see they have regular, decaf, tea, and all the fixings. I fix a cup and go back to the cubby hole to finish loading the data. I am working away and look at the computer, it is one-fifteen and then I hear McCray. He walks to the cubby hole I am working in and says, "Glad to see you made it and found my instructions, I told Vicki that you would be OK. I put you in this cubby hole since it is not used very often." I asked, "How was the meeting?" McCray says, "I'll fill you in shortly as soon as the rest of the staff gets here."

At two, McCray comes by and says, "Follow me." I follow him to the break room and there are six other people in there when we walk in. McCray introduces me simply as Jim. He introduces each member by first name only. They are all wearing their IIA badges. There are four men and two ladies in the group. McCray says there are two other members but they are on special assignment. McCray says, "I just came from a meeting with Schaunessy about a matter which concerns our department. The big guy will be making a quick trip to Chicago to attend a benefit next weekend. We need to be on our toes and keep a close eye on some people that may be in attendance at the benefit. I have an outline of the benefit and a list of people that are scheduled to attend. This is a high-ticket benefit for IIT to benefit the science wing. I will give each of you a few names to research from the list. We are only looking for associates that may have contact with known left wing or organized crime figures. We will have our work cut out for us since time is short. Thank you." I go back to my cubby hole. No wonder Buranski said there may be a rush on this. How did he find out? I am working away and McCray says, "I have some time now if you want to share some other information you discovered. Have you eaten lunch yet?" I said, "No I got here about a quarter to twelve but wanted to get this stuff loaded into the computer." He says, "Grab your coat we'll walk over to the restaurant." So I grab my coat and we leave.

We go to the same restaurant we were at the other day. The waitress leads us to the same booth and brings the coffee with her and pours us each a cup. She tells us the specials and the soups of the day. We are making small talk, she comes back, and we give her our orders. Then I tell McCray my findings about the connection with Nikoli and Olympic contenders. He said, "That is interesting but I don't think that is what all this high-tech surveillance is about. I think from what Schaunessy said it has more to do with his feelings about what is going on in Iran and that country's activities in developing nuclear power, I think that scares the hell out of Russia and Bulgaria and everybody in that region. I am wondering who they think the big guy will talk to about that while he is in town is of greater concern." I said, "I know, I was trying to figure that out too. He does have some mighty influential constituents that he talks to about certain special interests to get their feel about things and if he is proceeding in the correct direction while looking for alternatives. While he may have his own ideas he likes to ask for input from trusted advisors before moving ahead with any plan." McCray says, "You surprise me with your insight on this, Jim." I said, "I have a lot of free time to think." McCray says, "No, I think you are more intelligent than you let on and analyze each situation." The waitress brings our lunch, we eat it, and head back to the office. McCray says on the way back to the office, "Do you like hockey?" I said, "I watch it from time to time but that is about it." He said, "I can get tickets to the Blackhawks game." I said, "What game?" He says, "Tonight." I said, "How much?" He says, "On the house." I said, "You have to be kidding?" He says, "No, I know one of the assistants. We were in the Marines together. We talk all the time but I never take him up on the tickets." I said, "Only if I can get the night off, my boss has me working a special detail." McCray laughs and says, "I think I can fix that."

We get back to the office at three-thirty. McCray goes to his office and I go to my cubby hole to work on my research. I can hear some of the other workers talking, I look at the time it is almost six. Wow, I was lost on the computer for over two hours and have very little to show for it. Six-thirty McCray stops by my cubby hole and says, "Buranski and his crew just left Hyde Park. They will be back there tomorrow morning before eight. If we are going to the game, we should be leaving soon." I back everything up and shut down my computer. McCray says, "You can leave everything here. We will walk since it is nice out and then after the game you can get it and your car. Ramon knows we are going to the game so the lot will still be open." We walk to the stadium; he stops by will call to pick up the tickets. We find our seats right behind the Hawks bench up about six rows. The place is really loud as the fans cheer after the national anthem. The game starts at seven-fifteen, the Ref drops the puck, and the action begins. Wow, this is a lot different than watching it on TV as Keith gets slammed into the boards. The game was great; final score Hawks 2 Canucks1 in a shootout. After the game we walk back to the office. McCray says, "Glad to see you got into the game." I said, "It is contagious, all the fans cheering and yelling, it doesn't take much to get involved. Thanks for getting the tickets. I enjoyed the game more than I thought I would." McCray says, "You're welcome, I enjoy the games too but I don't have anybody to go with on a regular basis so I don't go." It's ten when we get back to the office. McCray says, "You can go get your stuff or just leave it there until tomorrow since I figure you will be here again tomorrow." I said, "Yes, I will come around nine." McCray says, "Drive safe, see you tomorrow." I drive home and it is almost eleven, I take a shower, and go to bed.

Chapter 10

Thursday morning I am up at six, force of habit I guess. I don't have to be downtown until after nine. I toss on some clothes and go pickup my coffee and something for breakfast. I'm hungry this morning, then I remembered we had lunch at two and then went to the Hawks game. We only had soft drinks and nachos there, by the time the game was over and I got home I only wanted to shower and hit the sack. They have a steak and egg bagel on the menu, so I get that rather than my usual cinnamon roll. That should hold me longer. I go back to my place, eat, and turn on the computer to see if I can find anymore information that might be useful. Just out of curiosity I go to the Olympic Games from the mid-nineties. I check out the wrestling and sure enough there is Radko in the stats just like he said two gold, one silver, and one bronze. Then I put in Dragan's name to see if he competed. He was a sprinter and competed in several events, no metals as an individual but on the relay team they took the silver. I look at the judges listed and who happened to be the judge Nikoli Filchev. Talk about coincidence that takes the cake. Buranski is younger than them by about four years, perhaps he was a spectator and got hooked on the Olympic Games. I don't imagine in the mid-nineties there was a lot for a sixteen-year-old to get hooked on, not like today with all the electronic games and the choices kids have. If I remember something about the economy, then it wasn't a great time in that part of the world. It's just odd that ten years after Radko and Dragan come here, he comes here thanks to Nikoli. Grozdan knows Nikoli, but I have the feeling he didn't think too highly of him from the remark he made to Buranski about it's your neck. I'm thinking maybe Nikoli would sacrifice Buranski if things went sour for him. I wonder what Grozdan really knows about him, maybe Buranski could get him into a conversation where his name comes up. I'll bounce that around with McCray. I look at the clock, eight-fifteen, I better get moving, I know the drive will be slow. If I didn't need my SUV later, I would grab the train.

I get downtown a little after nine. I park in the lot and walk over to the office and go in. The secretary is there, I don't see any of the other people. She said they would all be dribbling in shortly, the Hawks played last night, and a group of them were going out to a bar to watch the game. I didn't tell her McCray and I went to the game. She said, "The chief will be here after ten; he wanted to check on something before he comes in." I walked back to the cubby hole I was assigned to and got to work. I clicked on the email I sent from home and added it to the database. After that I went to the break room to fix a cup of coffee. I am reading some of the information that McCray gave us about this benefit and the list of people that are scheduled to be there. One name pops out of there and rings a bell for me. I know that name from some place. I put the name in the database to see what it brings up. I am reading the information like that doesn't make any sense. This guy is not a scientist or a physicist. Why would he be interested in this benefit for the scientific wing except to rub elbows with the big guy. I flag his name on the list to do more research. Little by little I start hearing the other people start coming in to get to work. Shortly after ten, McCray comes in and walks back to my cubby hole. He told me, "Buranski and his guys got to the job right on time at eight o'clock. I went down there to brief our men there about next weekend. I would plan on following Buranski tonight since I figure he is going to meet his customer to discuss a change in plans. I am interested to see if anybody else shows up at the meeting. I heard a rumor from the FBI that Washington is getting nervous about the benefit and trying to cover him properly. They don't like the idea that there is too much access and not enough security. They don't want to surround him with ten agents at all times, since it is almost impossible to do in a setting like this."

I said, "There is a name on the list you gave me that doesn't make sense, I'm going to investigate it a little more to see if I can find out why." McCray says, "That's why I wanted you to look it over, some of those names don't mean anything at all to me but you have a keen sense of connecting the dots in a puzzle. Let me know what you find. I will talk to you before you leave to follow our man." I said, "Thanks for inviting me to the game last night, that was great. The staff here would be unhappy if they knew we went to the game. The secretary told me this morning a bunch of them went to a bar to watch the game." McCray says, "I knew they were going out and I told them don't drink too much, but I think that is a moot point. This generation is not like ours. It's part of their ritual, but on the other hand I guess ours did drink a lot too but the times were different." I said, "I agree, I know I use to be able to drink with the best of them, stay out until the bars closed, and get up and go to work. Now if I drink more than a glass of wine with dinner I am asking for trouble."

I get back to my research after McCray leaves. I plug in the name again to see what else I can find out about Mr. Steven W. Landholm. I know there is a connection some place. I remember reading his name in an article some place. After about an hour of digging there is nothing I find that would raise a red flag about his name. I am stumped; I can't find what I was looking for. I look at the clock and it is almost lunch time. I decide I'll take a break and go for a walk, maybe that will clear my head and I will find what I am looking for. I tell the secretary, "I am going out for about an hour if McCray asks." She says, "He left a few minutes ago and said he would be back around four." I said, "Thanks, I'll be back." While I am out I stop at a little place to grab a bowl of soup and half a sandwich on special. I walk back to the office and get back to my research. I figured out the connection. Mr. Landholm is a left-wing writer that wrote books about how things should be not how they are. I am like, is this just a thank you that he is planning on attending. The tickets for this benefit start at like 500 clams and go up from there, I guess it's a matter of how close you will be to the main table. That in itself is not an issue. I am just looking for some other connection. There are a bunch of big name politicians on the list too but none that would be anti the big guy; they are here to be seen and showing support the way they do in Chicago by spending bucks for a benefit for IIT.

I look at the time on the computer, it is almost four. Boy, the time flies when you are having fun. I look over the rest of the names on the list and I don't see any other names that strike me as strange at this benefit. Now the problem becomes how can Buranski get everything finished before next weekend? He told them two weeks, but this will shorten the timetable if they expect everything to be in place and operational by then. I know he said something about having to finish the job quicker than originally planned; how is he going to do that with only three men! Hopefully I will get some answers tonight if the meeting with his contact takes place as McCray thinks it will. I figure I'll leave that problem until later, right now I need to run my report for McCray on what I found; he might be able to add some insight about Landholm or have the Bureau do a background check to make sure he is not a problem. McCray gets back to the office and comes by my cubby hole to see what I came up with. He looks over my report and says, "Good work. I'll have the guys at the Bureau double check this information. I agree with you about him not making any sense at a function like this. We'll see what they come up with." I said, "I am leaving in about twenty minutes to get to Orland Park before Buranski and his guys get there." McCray says, "Tomorrow you might want to follow our man depending upon what happens tonight. I have a feeling there might be a change in plans. Our guys in Hyde Park said there was a lot of extra activity today. The Dish Network truck was there almost all day along with Buranski and his guys. They were installing dishes outside and running some other wires. There were a couple of guys climbing ladders all over the place." I said, "I remember Buranski saying that Mr. Giovani set that up and the guys were cleared to go in there. I didn't think they would get all of the equipment until next week." McCray says, "That's why I'm concerned, it's like everything got pushed up. How would they know unless there is a leak in some place?" I said, "Maybe Mariano has a man inside in Chicago or Washington." McCray says, "That is probably a remote possibility, I thought everybody was cleared and there haven't been any transfers." I said, "What about the CPD detail?" McCray says, "I'll check with my guy at City Hall." I said, "I'll call you later with an update on what happens in Orland Park tonight?" McCray says, "I'll be at the office until eight and then I have a dinner date with Schaunessy at eight-thirty." I said, "Don't you ever keep regular hours?" McCray says, "I could ask you the same question." I laughed and said, "It goes with the job."

I drive out to Orland Park and stop at the Gyro place to grab something to eat and use the restroom before heading to Buranski's office. I get to Buranski's office and position myself to get a good view and wait for them to get there. I see Dragan is still at the used-car lot. About twenty minutes later, Buranski and his guys show up. Ivan parks in front and they get out and go inside. A few minutes later I hear them talking. Buranski says, "Tomorrow we will have to work a lot harder. Now we have all of the electronics stuff in place; you two can concentrate on finishing the bathroom while I start getting the program up and running. I want to test it next week to make sure it is powerful enough to hear what they want to hear. If you guys make enough noise in there, our baby-sitters will not be snooping around, they will sit on their asses and play cards. Today they drove me crazy coming to see what the Dish guys were doing and why it was taking so long. I told them the wiring was too old and we needed to run new lines to support the office stuff we are installing. They are clueless on this stuff; they are just muscle men." Radko says, "We should be able to keep them away from you tearing out the old bathroom stuff and hauling it down to put in the truck. What about the new shower that was supposed to be ready when Ivan picked up the other stuff?" Buranski said, "There was a problem with one of the pieces of glass, they said tomorrow morning Ivan could pick up the replacement. That means we don't start until after ten but we should be OK." Radko says, "I'll see you about nine tomorrow. I need to go relieve Kurt so he can go home." Ivan says, "So tomorrow I stop at the plumbing warehouse, pick up the shower, and get here by nine. When do I take this truck back?" Buranski says, "Tomorrow night after we are finished, I don't want to keep it over the weekend. Next week we only need the van." Five minutes later Ivan leaves.

Buranski gets on the phone. I hear him say, "Hi Ana, how is Elisia doing? Yes, I know this week has been crazy. Tomorrow I will be home for dinner at six. Tonight I will not be home until after nine, I have a meeting here in an hour, then I need to see Grozdan. Tomorrow they are supposed to send him home. I will talk to Dragan about checking on him tomorrow." Then he calls Dragan, he says, "Tomorrow can you go keep an eye on Grozdan, he is supposed to be discharged from the hospital. I don't know what time or if his wife will be there. Does she drive? No, I didn't think so. Can you arrange to pick her up? I'll get the details tonight, that way she doesn't have to ask a neighbor to do it. Yes, I'll be here in the morning, we have a later start. Eight in the morning I'll make coffee and bring some baklava. See you then." Buranski is checking messages and then the phone rings. He answers it, "KBW Construction, Karl speaking. Yes, I am waiting for you. Ten minutes. OK, You alone? Good, ring the bell I will let you in." Ten minutes later he goes and unlocks the door. Mr. Giovani by himself, nobody extra, with his two guys are sitting in the black Escalade. He goes in and Buranski says, "We got all the electronics gear today, it drove your guys crazy all the time putting up the dishes and running new wiring. They kept coming in trying to speed the other guys up." He says, "They are just muscle, they get bored." Buranski says, "Next week I want to test the stuff, I am working on the program but we might have a slight problem. The computer is not right. I need more memory to run this program." He says, "How much more memory?" Buranski says, "Double." He says, "How about for the test will it work?" Buranski says, "Yes, but not the way it needs to after we leave next week." He says, "I'll get you what you need, just write it down I'll tell Al to clear it." Buranski says, "When is your pigeon coming?" Giovani says, "I heard through the grapevine next weekend, they have a big doing and he will be in town, one night, maybe not even all night just a few hours." I am like, McCray will be furious. How did they find that out?

After Giovani leaves, I call McCray. I told him what transpired once Buranski and his guys got back and what Giovani said. McCray says, "There has to be a leak some place. I know my team and none of them know anymore than I told you. I purposely didn't tell them anything more, just check the names and make sure they are all cleared. I'll talk to my contact at the bureau again. Tomorrow I'll have an answer from my contact at City Hall." I said, "Buranski is going to see Grozdan tonight; he is being discharged tomorrow and he asked Dragan to pick his wife up and take her to the hospital to take him home." McCray says. "They seem to watch out for each other and help each other a lot." I said. "Yes, it is a trait with them they seem to care a lot about their fellow countrymen."

Buranski makes a few phone calls about the other projects to make sure everything is still on track. He calls the couple in Palos Heights to see if next week a crew can get in there to finish up. I guess it was a go. He goes over to the schedule board and marks Monday down next to it. He calls Ivan, "We need to get the other men over to Palos Heights next week to finish the job. Can Gorgi handle the last part of the job with two other guys? Good, call him tonight, see if he has a van since we need yours on this project. Saturday morning you and I will go talk to the people and make sure we have everything so we can get paid by them next week. If we need a van I can borrow one from Dragan, he uses it to get parts. Tonight I am going to see Grozdan, he goes home tomorrow. Maybe next week he can come back a few hours a day. I'll see you in the morning." He is studying the project board, still no contract for the Midlothian job. He looks at the clock and makes another call, "Mr. Wojowski, yes your house is still on the schedule, I was just calling to assure you. Yes Grozdan is getting better. He might even be able to work a few hours next week. I'll tell him you were concerned. Thank you." He is pacing around the office I am wondering why; he goes back to his desk, picks up the phone, and calls another number. They answer the phone. He says, "This is Karl at KBW Construction. We talked to you about doing the second floor addition to your house. I was calling to see if you decided to wait on the project or somebody else beat our price. No, I was looking over our current projects and we will be able to tackle another project sooner than we thought. Thank you, I understand. Yes, money is tight everywhere; the banks have it but don't want to lend it. Maybe I can help you. Call Mr. Wojowski at the Countryside Bank, I think he can help you. Yes, give him my name." I think no wonder they use that bank, it is a two-way street. They use that bank for business and if people can't get a loan they send them to their bank. That is very smart business on their part. Buranski turns out the lights, locks the door, and leaves to go to see Grozdan. I follow him as far as the hospital and think well he is going home after he sees Grozdan; he told his wife he would be home by nine. I should just head home or go see Val and have dinner; I haven't been there all week. McCray said he had a dinner engagement after eight, I look at the time. No sense calling him. I go back to the hospital and wait. Twenty minutes later, Buranski comes out and gets in his car to go home. I am watching like he seems to be looking for somebody, and then I see Dragan walking out of the hospital. Buranski waits and says something to him and then drives away. Buranski goes straight home from there; after he gets to his street I turn around and head to the Maple Street Café.

Val says, "Hello stranger, where have you been?" I said, "Working downtown a few days." She says, "Today the special is Swiss Steak with mashed potatoes and tomatoes and onions. It's good, I had that before the rush came." I said, "You talked me into it. So how has your week been?" She said, "A little slow, it seems a lot of the regulars have cut back on how many nights they can eat out." I said, "With the gas prices the way they are they probably use the money to fill the tank." Val says, "I never thought about that, you are probably right." Tony comes out a few minutes later with my dinner and asks, "No big news yet?" I said, "In what regard?" He says, "You and Val, I know you won't tell me about your job." I said, "We only went out one time." He says, "That's not enough?" I said, "Hardly. We barely know each other. We had fun and want to go out again when we both have a Saturday free." He laughs, "I married my wife after our first date, no reason to look anymore." I said, "Yes, I know forty-five years of happy marriage, you got lucky." Tony says, "How do you know that long?" I said, "A little bird told me." He looks at Val she shrugs, "So, did I lie?" Tony says, "I gotta get back in the kitchen." Val says, "Didn't I tell you he looks after me like I'm his daughter." I said, "Yes, you did. He is something else." Val says, "Yes, I love him like a father but I can watch out for myself." I said, "I'm sure you can, he is like a mother hen in some ways. He wants everything a certain way." She says, "I agree." I eat my dinner and go home, I tell Val, "I'll see you early tomorrow if things go the way they are supposed to."

I get home, it is almost ten, I look at my answering machine and there is one message. I play it. It was Natalie. She wants me to call her if I get home early enough tonight. I call her house. Rachael answers the phone. She calls Natalie. I said, "I just got home. Why didn't you call my cell phone?" She says, "I dropped it after practice and it broke." I said, "The new phones aren't built like the old ones. I understand. What's up sweetie?" She says, "You said to call on Friday about Saturday's practice but I need to know if you can take me. Mom has to work Saturday and she's not happy." I asked, "What time is practice?" She says, "One until three." I said, "Yes, I can do that for you." She said, "Thanks Dad, Mom will be relieved, she didn't want me to go by myself." I said, "I don't blame her." She says, "Dad, I'm fifteen I'm not a little kid anymore." I said, "All the more for me to worry about." She laughs "Thanks Dad, I love you, I'll see you Saturday." I said, "Twelve-thirty OK? I love you too." She says, "Yes." I'm like, Buranski and Ivan are going to the house in Palos Heights Saturday morning so I should be good. I take a shower and go to bed.

Chapter 11

Friday morning I am up at six as usual. I get dressed, grab my equipment, and head over to get my coffee and a cinnamon roll. I drive over to Buranski's; he told Dragan he would have the coffee and some baklava at eight. I am like, where is he going to get that? I figure I'll find out on the drive to the office. I get to his place a few minutes before seven just to be on the safe side. Ten minutes later he backs his car out and pulls away. He heads in his usual direction, jumps on 294 South, so I follow him. Traffic was nice this morning, thirty-five minutes from his house to the office. He parks in back, gets out, and opens his back door to take something out. Then I spot it, it is a full sheet of baklava. Dragan is already at the used-car lot; he spies Buranski and walks over. He looks at the sheet full of baklava and smiles. Buranski hands it to him and they both go in the back door. When he gets in the office he says, "You are early, the coffee isn't ready." Dragan says, "I can wait for the coffee I'm going to taste one of these." Buranski goes and sets up the coffee maker and flips the switch and walks back over to where Dragan is standing and asks, "So what do you think of Ana's homemade baklava?" Dragan says, "Tell Ana for me these are better than my mother made and hers were delicious, these are superb!" Buranski says, "Ana will be pleased, I eat maybe one or two out of a whole sheet and she gets upset, she wants me to eat more but I have to watch what I eat more now than before." Dragan says, "Me too but for these I'll make an exception. Thank you Karl, you are a good friend." Buranski says, "You are a good friend too. What you did to get Grozdan's wife and then take him home from the hospital needed a reward." Dragan says, "We are countrymen, right?" Buranski says, "That we are."

About a quarter to nine Radko shows up, he sees the sheet of baklava and says, "What's the occasion?" Buranski says, "It is a thank you gift to Dragan, Ana made them at home. Try one." Radko says, "Thanks I will." He takes a couple of bites and says, "Tell Ana for me, if she bakes like this I'm surprised you don't weight two hundred-fifty pounds, these are great." Buranski says, "She loves to bake. I think she could run a bakery with her skills but not right now. Elisia keeps her busy with sports and other things." Ivan shows up at nine and walks to the front door and rings the bell. Buranski goes and opens the door and he follows him to his office. Buranski asks, "Did you call Gorgi last night about finishing the job in Palos Heights?" Ivan says, "Yes and he just bought a van, his car was giving him trouble so he talked to Dragan and picked one from his lot." Dragan says, "His car was shot, I don't know how long he had it but everything was bad on it. The junk guy wanted me to pay him a hundred to haul it away. I told him no dice, you pay me if you want it. A couple of guys from another junk yard out west came and got it and gave me seventy-five dollars so I took it." Buranski says, "I hate to cut this gab session short but we have a busy day, I need to be back here by five to be home at six, Elisia has a playoff game tonight." He calls his contact and tells him, "We are leaving now we should be at 55th Street in forty minutes." A few minutes later Dragan goes out the back door, Buranski locks it up, and they go out the front and get in the truck and head to the job.

I follow them and then turn on Halsted Street and go to McCray's office to fill him in on the latest. I get to his the office a few minutes after ten. The secretary says, "You just missed him, he said to tell you he would be back in a couple of hours, plus he put a folder on your desk that he wants you to look at." I said, "Thanks Vicki, where is everybody else?" She said, "They are all out chasing down information from what I gathered. McCray talked to them this morning and a few minutes later they all grabbed their coats and headed out. That's all I know." So I headed back to my cubby hole, looked at the folder, and decided I needed some coffee so I walked back to the break room to fix it. Vicki came back and said, "That's what I need, a break." I asked, "How long have you been here?" She says, "I started right after McCray was given this job three years ago." I asked, "So what do you think of our leader?" She says, "I like him but there are times I swear that what we do isn't enough he gets moody." I said, "It probably goes with the job. When we are all working on different projects his job can be real demanding and now like this job everybody is involved on the same thing because of timetable. It just gets crazy." Vicki says, "Thanks Jim, I never thought about it like that, you are probably right." She asks, "You like being the lone wolf out there don't you?" I said, "I guess I do, for some reason I like working alone. I mean I have had partners before on projects but not very often, I work better by myself I think since I don't have to watch out for somebody else just me." Vicki asks, "You're not married are you?" I said, "No, I was for about four years but my working habits drove her crazy, we are friends and I have a fifteen-year-old daughter, I wouldn't change any of that." Vicki says, "Thanks for talking to me; all the rest of the staff think I'm too nosy." I said, "I don't normally talk about my personal life to anybody here other than Rusty." She says, "Maybe we can get together outside of the office and talk some more sometime down the road." She walked back to her desk and I went back to my cubby hole.

One-fifteen I look at the time on the computer screen and think where did the last two hours go? I read the folder McCray left for me and I started doing some research on the computer and boom two hours are gone like that. McCray flagged a couple of other names that he had concerns about. I couldn't find anything on those two names either. They don't come up in any scientific search or political search. I entered the names into an alumni search to see if they could be related to people that attended IIT, still nothing. I am thinking there must be a reason they want to attend this function other than the fact that the big guy is supposed to be there. I am like, the names are fictitious. They have to be since there is no data on either of them anywhere. McCray ran it through all of his channels and they come up empty, I put them through all the databases I could think of and we get nothing. Everybody that attends this function needs to be cleared. They must know that and they might be thinking that since they don't show up on any of those searches they should be safe. I know security is not going to fingerprint everybody that shows up to be admitted; they are going to look at the list and if they are

OK they let them in. There are no pictures on file, only names and preliminary information. If their ID matches, they get in. Why are the tiny hairs on the back of my neck standing up all of a sudden? About three, McCray comes back and walks back to my cubby hole and asks, "Any luck with those names?" I said, "Nothing but the tiny hairs on the back of neck suddenly were standing up." McCray says, "Your hunches are usually pretty good, that is why I wanted you to do your search too. I am going to flag those two for security to detain them until we can run their prints or at least their photos." I gather up some stuff to take home with me and McCray says, "What time did Buranski say he needed to be back at his office?" I said, "He said five since he has to be home for his daughter's playoff game. Tomorrow he and Ivan are going to look at the Palos Heights job to make sure his other guys can get in there and finish it up on Monday and Tuesday. I figured I would follow them and then head home to take Natalie to basketball practice." McCray says, "I'll talk to you tomorrow afternoon. I should be in the office by noon."

    I went to Orland Park to be there when Buranski and his guys got back from Hyde Park. They were a few minutes late getting back to his office. Ivan parked in front and they all went inside. I heard them once they got in Buranski's office. He said, "Today is payday, we had a good week and next week we should finish this job and the one in Palos Heights. I put something extra in your pay envelopes this week for all the extra effort. Ivan, I'll see you at nine in Palos Heights. Radko, I'll see you at eleven if you are up for eighteen holes. Dragan said he can make it and he will bring a friend to make the foursome, we have eleven-thirty T time." Radko says, "I can use some easy money, who's the fish?" Buranski says, "Somebody from his club, he always talks golf to Dragan, so he thought why not we need a new guy since Grozdan can't play until next year." Buranski says, "Only ten dollars a hole, no crazy bets on the side. This is just for fun. OK?" Ivan left and Radko said, "Karl you already gave me extra money last week." Buranski says, "You deserve it, you kept those guys away from me so I could work on the program. I am glad you found something they were interested in and you gave them some pointers." Radko says, "A piece of cake, I heard them talking at lunch the other day. One guy wanted to be a boxer but couldn't get a sponsor. I think he is pretty good, next week after we finish the job he is going to come by the gym for conditioning. I'll have Kurt work with him that's his specialty." Buranski says, "See you tomorrow, I need to leave." Radko says, "Enjoy the game, wish Elisia good luck from me. Who are they playing?" Buranski says, "Glenbard West."

They both left and I followed Buranski home and then headed to Maple Street Café for dinner. Val says, "You were right, you do get to eat at a regular time tonight." I said, "Yes, I'm glad I haven't since breakfast. What's good tonight?" Val says, "The Orange Roughy with crumbled cheese or Lemon Pepper Catfish are both good." I said, "I'll try the catfish but can I get it broiled with lemon pepper cooked longer than usual with rice and vegetables." Val says," No problem, what are you doing tomorrow?" I said, "Busy in the morning, then picking up my daughter for basketball practice after that research." Val says, "Tomorrow night?" I said, "What time are you talking?" She said, "After six I'm working until three and taking the night off, this week was enough." I said, "I think I can do that." Val says, "I can cook if you don't want to eat out. That way you get home cooked and you can sample my cooking." I said, "If it is like your baking I'm sure you cook good." She says, "Thanks Jim. Would you like anything special?" I said, "Surprise me." She says, "OK, I'll try." About ten minutes later Tony brings my dinner and says, "Nice to see you two talking and getting together again." I said, "I had nothing going on tomorrow night so why not." Tony says, "I know she can cook up a storm, when I bought the place the other owner said she did a lot of cooking for him but didn't want to cook all the time, she liked being with the customers more." The dinner was good, I'm glad I ordered it. I told Val and Tony goodnight and left. I got home, it wasn't even nine yet. I put on the coffee pot so I could do some research and maybe find out what was going on with the hockey game. At midnight I turn off the computer and go to bed.

Chapter 12

Six o'clock Saturday morning I am up. I couldn't sleep. I guess my body is just used to this routine; even if I don't set the alarm I'm up at six. Sunday's for some reason I can sleep until seven but seldom any longer. I went to the kitchen to look for something for breakfast; I have some cereal but no milk; the coffee from last night would be OK, but there isn't anything here to eat and for some reason I'm really hungry this morning. I get dressed and go to a local breakfast joint in the neighborhood and order pancakes with four strips of bacon on the side. I drink three cups of coffee along with my breakfast and then head back home. I look at the clock and I have about an hour until I need to be at Buranski's house. I decide I'll go to the grocery store to pick up some things for the house. I mean I can't remember when I went shopping before. The milk at home is old, I have no eggs, and I really should buy some fresh fruit and vegetables. I best pick up a package of meatballs and more chicken breasts too. OK, so now I know what I need at the store. I stop by the local super market; it is just opening so I can zip in and out and drop the stuff off at home before I tail Buranski. I take the stuff home and put it away and head over to Buranski's house.

I get to his house a few minutes after eight. He said he was meeting Ivan at nine, that should work out OK. I figure it will take about thirty minutes from his house to Palos Heights. I am sitting in the next block so I can watch for him to back out of his garage. Eight-fifteen he backs out and heads toward Palos Heights, but he takes 45 rather than 294. I follow him to find out where he is heading. He drives to the bank in Countryside and goes inside. A few minutes later he comes out and gets back in his car. I figure he needed some cash for his golf game today. He drives to the job site in Palos Heights; I follow him and stay out of sight. Ivan is already there; they walk up to the door and ring the bell. The lady of the house opens the door and lets them in. About twenty minutes later they walk back out. Buranski is writing some things down on his tablet and hands it to Ivan. Buranski gets in his car and Ivan gets in the van and they both drive away. I follow Buranski; he goes to the office. I figure he has some time to kill before they meet at the golf course, so he might as well use this time to catch up on some paperwork. He goes into the office and the phone rings. He answers it, "KBW Construction Karl speaking. Yes, I understand. Next week we need to be out of Hyde Park Thursday night ready or not. Friday the whole area will be off limits to everybody except for emergency personnel. Yes, I am going to try testing everything and setup the phone line to feed the info from the computer to your computer so you can listen to what is going on in that house." I am like there it is again, they are getting inside information from somebody. McCray hasn't been able to find the leak. Then, Buranski picks up the phone to make a call, "Hello, this is Karl, I need to talk to Sergi for a couple of minutes. Yes I can hold, he'll know." A couple of minutes pass finally Sergi gets on the phone. Buranski said, "That special order high-frequency receiver/transmitter, is it ready? Yes, I know I thought we had more time but we need to get it ready to test next week. Yes I'll pay extra just make sure it is ready. Wednesday OK, I'll call you Tuesday night. Thanks."

A few minutes later Buranski is shutting things off and getting ready to head to the golf course; he said he would meet them there at eleven. I follow him so, hopefully I can get a photo of the new player. He drives to the Palos Country Club on Southwest Highway. It has an eighteen hole course; the other one they usually play is only nine holes. I guess before the season is over they want to get a full round in. He parks and looks for Radko's car. He gets his clubs out and walks over to Radko. They are standing there talking and Dragan and his friend show up. Dragan introduces his friend to Buranski and Radko and they head for the clubhouse to register and play their round.

I did manage to get a couple of photos. I don't recognize the face. He was well dressed looks like an executive type, well groomed, appears to be in his mid-forties. I load the photos into my laptop to send to McCray to look at too. I hang around for a little while fiddling with the computer; that way I don't have to do it when I go pick up Natalie. McCray said he would be in the office by noon. I call him on my cell phone to let him know I was sending a couple of photos and the info I heard from Buranski's phone calls. He picks up his cell phone and listens to what I have to say. He said, "I will feed the photos into the database and do a quick search and I'll let you know later if anything comes up. As far as the leak, I agree it has to be somebody inside but where. That is the sixty-four thousand dollar question." I said, "I'll call you after Natalie's practice. I figure I will be home after four." McCray said, "I might still be here. I have a mountain of stuff to review before Monday's meeting."

I drive to pick up Natalie and take her to basketball practice. I get to her house about twenty minutes to one and wait for a few minutes. She comes out with a gym bag and her purse, a cell phone up to her ear. I open the door for her; she tosses the gym bag and purse in the back seat and gets in. I hear her tell who she is talking to, "My Dad just got here to take me to practice. I'll call you later after I get home. I'll asked Mom if I can spend the night at your house or if you stay by me." I said, "Hi sweetie, who was that?" She said, "One of the girls in my class; we started talking and she invited me over to her house tonight. We take a few classes together and she is real nice. She doesn't really have a lot of friends at school but I think she is just too shy." I asked, "Why do you say that?" She said, "I see her standing by a lot of the other girls, but she doesn't really talk; just more or less stands and listens to them all chatting away." I said, "You could be right, I have seen people like that but they need to feel comfortable before they will talk to anybody." Natalie said, "I probably initiated the conversation when I started talking to her one day about what the other girls were talking about. I told her those girls all want to be cheerleaders so the football players will notice them." She laughed and said, "Not me." I said, "Me neither, that is not my idea of fun. So we just started talking from that point on." I said, "That was nice of you. I know you have some friends but you don't seem interested in be in a clique." She said, "Dad, you are so right. How did you know?" I said, "You are a lot like me in some ways." We get to her school and she goes to get in her uniform. She said, "I didn't ask the coach if you can watch?" I said, "That is OK. I don't want to seem like an over protective father and sit there and try to butt in if I don't agree with the coach. I have my computer and some work I can do while you practice. I'll stay in the car while you do your practice." She said, "We should be done by three or maybe a few minutes earlier depending on if the coach likes what she sees. Otherwise we will be doing laps in the gym." I said, "I'll be waiting for you; the weather is nice and if I get bored I can do a few laps around the outdoor track."

I turn on my computer to start doing some research on the new guy. I pull up his photo and said to myself, "Now where do I start?" I figure let's see business executives in Orland Park. Is there a photo file or newspaper photo of the subject? I plug in Orland Park Chamber of Commerce recent activities and stories on their website. They had a golf outing during the summer with a real good turnout; if this guy talks golf all the time and he is in Orland Park, his photo may turn up. I search the photos. They had forty foursomes that golfed. They have photos of almost every group. I take my time and enlarge each photo to look at them; the ones with ladies I just skip since I figure he is playing with just guys. I swear they must have had a great golf outing. The weather from the pictures was great; everybody seemed comfortable, no sweltering heat; at least nobody looked like they were dripping wet. After about twenty pictures I decide to rest my eyes for a few minutes.

I get out of my car and walk over to the track. It sure brings back memories. I remember my high-school days and having to run laps on the track after football practice since we weren't sharp enough for our coach. He was a real character; he had nicknames for everyone. I remember him yelling at our quarterback one time and telling him, "Hey Romeo, if you would leave the girls alone you would play better." He said, "Coach, I tried but they keep following me everywhere I go." The coach said, "I can bench you for a few games, how would they like that?" He said, "Don't do it coach. I want us to win our division this year, we came close last year." The coach said, "I'll make you a deal, you show up every day to practice without any girls tagging along I'll start you again." Romeo thought it over and said, "Deal." We won our division that year and he got recruited by Illinois and signed to go to school there after his senior year. Today, he is a coach at a small college in Michigan. Funny how looking at something like the track can conjure up those memories. I haven't thought of the coach or our quarterback until now.

I walk back to my car and start looking at the photos again. I look at the photo again to make sure that this is the same guy. He is the CFO for a local business in Orland Park; he moved here in the in the late 1990s from Bulgaria, finished his education in finance, and as they say the rest is history. He helped turn the company around since they were on the verge of filing bankruptcy. They made him an officer of the company as thanks for salvaging them from near disaster. He is married has three children, and is the pillar of success to his fellow countrymen. He is someone they all want to emulate. His team was next to last in standings, but that didn't stop them from winning a couple of prizes. One was the most improved foursome from last year and the other was for most balls in the water. The prizes were all given in fun, but they stood there and had their photos taken. Dragan was on his foursome. There is nothing about him anywhere as far as being involved in any political organization or any run ins with the law. He is squeaky clean in that department.

I look at the time; it is almost two-thirty. Just for fun I go do a lap around the track; I finish my lap and I see a gentleman standing by the bleachers. I stop it is my old coach. He said, "Hey Jim, you still look pretty good out there; of course, you would do better if you had running shoes and a uniform on." I said, "Thanks coach, I didn't think you would still hang out around here." He said, "I needed to run a few laps myself and I only live a couple of blocks away so I come over here if the weather is nice." I said, "My daughter is practicing with the basketball team." He said, "I know. I told the coach to put her on the squad; I know her father. You won't be disappointed. So far she is doing real good." I said, "I will probably bring her next week; maybe we can chat for a while then and I'll be wearing the right shoes and sweats." The coach said, "I'll see you then." And off he goes to do his five laps. Eighty years old and fit as a fiddle. I walk back to my car and Natalie walks out of the gym. She asked, "Who was that?" I said, "My old coach." She said, "You went to school here?" I said, "Not at this school; he used to coach at my old school but couldn't pass up moving over here. It is close to where he lives so he could walk to school." She said, "I didn't know that." I said, "Now you do." Natalie laughs, "Dad, you seem to know people everywhere." I said, "Only in certain places."

On the drive to take Natalie home, we stop by the DQ to get her something and I get a coffee from the place next door. We sat outside; she ate her blizzard, I drank my coffee, and then I drove her home. I said, "Call me about tomorrow so I know what time to pick you up and where." She said, "I hope Mom says I can spend the night at Susan's house. I would have to go home early so I can go to church with Mom. If Susan stays by me, her Dad would pick her up early. They go to church as a family every Sunday. Mom and I go, but it isn't like them. Their church is different; they have morning worship at nine-thirty and evening service at seven-thirty and she said they even have Wednesday night prayer meetings and Friday night teen club." I said, "It sounds like they are pretty religious." She said, "They are but I still like her and she needs a friend here at school." I said, "That's my girl. I'll talk to you later just let me know." She said, "Thanks for taking me and the coach said next week if you want to watch us, she is inviting all the parents to our last practice before we start to play for real." I said, "That would be nice, I told my old coach I would probably be here next week and we could talk more then." Natalie said, "Cool Dad, I love you." I said, "I love you too." She kissed me and went inside.

I drove home to get changed for tonight. I get home and jump in the shower and put on a nice shirt and slacks. Go turn on the computer; I have about forty-five minutes until I need to leave, correction about thirty-five. I best pick up wine or flowers for Val; she is cooking. I review the info on the new guy and make a few notes on the file and forward the info to McCray. I am just about to walk out the door and the phone rings. It is McCray. He said nice work on finding that guy. The photos didn't ring any bells. I said, "I just sent you all the info I could find on him and he looks like a stand up kind of guy. He even applied to become a US citizen and doesn't plan on returning to Bulgaria." McCray said, "The leak might be from the security detail in DC; it seems some of the men are being investigated for little slip ups. I know they were all screened and cleared but you know how things are, sometimes people get lax or say something that they shouldn't. That detail is super tight and those guys are under the gun all the time. DC will know by Monday who is suspected in this; at least that's what my friend at the Bureau told me not ten minutes ago. Have a good rest of the weekend, we'll talk Monday." I said, "You too Boss." He said, "What did I say about the Boss bit?" I said, "Downtown no Boss stuff." He said, "I know I said that." I said, "See you Rodger." He said, "That's better."

I stop by the local Dominick's store and pick up a flower arrangement and two bottles of wine since I don't know what she is making. I figure even if doesn't drink it I did my duty by bringing it. I get to her place at five to six and ring the bell. She comes to the door I hand her the flowers and the wine and she said, "Jim, you don't need to bring me flowers or wine, but thank you. The flowers are lovely; I'll put them in water. You can uncork the Red Wine; I made Prime Rib, I hope you like it." I smell and the aroma is wonderful. I said, "If it tastes as good as it smells, I'll tell Tony to put you back in the kitchen." She said, "In that case, I'll toss this out and order pizza." I said, "I'm only joking. I heard what you said to the old owner." She said, "Tony was telling tales again?" He said, "You were a great cook but loved the interaction with the customers." She said, "That part is true. I would weight two hundred pounds if I had to cook since I have to sample everything." I said, "I like you the way you are." She said, "Thanks Jim, I think I'm too heavy." I said, "Not to my eye, you look just right." She said, "I might have to keep you around, you make me blush." I start to follow her; she said, "I set the table in the dining room. There is a side board and you will find glasses and a corkscrew for the wine if it doesn't have a screw on top." I said, "I only buy wines with corks, none of the screw on tops taste that good." She said, "So you know a little something about wine, I'm impressed."

I open the wine and let it sit a little while; I get the glasses ready and Val said, "We will be ready to eat in ten minutes. I'm letting it set a few minutes so it is just right. I made baked potatoes and I have all the fixings for loaded baked potatoes and we have fresh asparagus al dente not soggy." I said, "My mouth is watering already." She said, "You can pour the wine anytime you like, I am not real fussy about wine. If you think it is a good wine that's good enough for me." I said, "This wine I had before and it was good with steaks so I think you'll like it. I don't like a real sweet wine or one that is like sour grapes this one is just right for my taste." She said, "Here comes dinner." I walked over to the doorway to the kitchen to help. Val said, "You can slice the prime rib if you like." So I carried it to the table and cut into it and it looked like it was perfect, nice juice red in the middle and tender enough you could cut it with a fork. Val brought the rest of the stuff to the table. I placed a slice on her plate and dished up mine. The potatoes and the asparagus were cooked just the way I like them. I think Val sure knows her stuff when it comes to cooking a good meal. I raise my glass and said, "To the cook, this meal looks fantastic." Val said, "I hope it suits your taste buds." I said, "I'm sure it will." We talked all through dinner; I swear we sat at the table two hours just talking, eating, and sipping our wine. I looked at the clock and it was almost nine. She got up and started to clear the table so I got up to help. I carried the platter with the prime rib; I did eat half of another slice and it was so good I couldn't refuse. She put things away and said, "I hope you have room for dessert. I made peach cobbler today so we can have that with some vanilla bean ice cream on top of the warm cobbler." I said, "That sounds delightful, but right now I'm so full I couldn't do it justice." Val said, "We can watch a movie if you like; I have all the movie channels and there might be something worth watching." I said, "I would rather just sit and talk if you don't mind. I usually fall asleep watching movies even action movies." She said, "That is fine with me. I might even learn a little more about you." I said, "I could say the same thing."

About nine-thirty my cell phone rings. I said to Val, "It's my daughter calling me about tomorrow, I won't be on long." She got up from the couch and went to put the coffee on. I said, "Hi sweetie, so where do I pick you up and what time?" She said, "After church, you can pick me up there. Susan is spending the night at our house tonight but her Dad is picking her up at eight-thirty so they can go to church." I said, "Have fun tonight, I'll see you about ten." Val came back and said, "I went to make the coffee so you could have some privacy, I didn't want to eavesdrop on your conversation." I said, "That was nice but you could have stayed. She was only letting me know a new friend of hers was spending the night but leaving early to go to church with her parents and that I can pick her up after church with her Mom, my ex." Val said, "I'm glad you get along well with your ex and that you spend time with your daughter. I know it can be rough on everybody." I said, "I try to be a good father and I don't butt in when they are having a disagreement. I just tell Natalie, your mother doesn't want to see you hurt or make dumb mistakes. You may not believe me but she is just concerned."

Val said, "You really are a good father then. I hear some of the CPD guys talk and I think, "How do their wives take that crap?" I said, "I know what you are talking about. I hear those guys talk but truthfully half of them it is just talk, they need to be macho with the other men." I smell the coffee and Val said, "Do you think you handle a small piece of the cobbler with your coffee?" I said, "Bring it on." She said, "We'll have it at the table. I try not to eat in the living room." I said, "No problem, I like sitting at the table and talking to you across from me so I can look into your eyes. They are really pretty; I never paid much attention to them before. Did you do something different to them tonight?" She said, "I did put on a little makeup and some eyelash stuff. I don't wear that much when I go out since it bothers me outdoors." I said, "Well whatever you did made me notice them more." She said, "Thanks Jim for noticing most of the men I have been out with don't even give my eyes a second look." I said, "It's probably because they are looking someplace else." Val said, "You don't seem to be overly concerned with the size of my bust or the shape of my derrière." I said, "No, I enjoy your company and our conversations. I don't even think twice about those things since to me they are all superficial. I am more into people than just looking for physical attraction." Val said, "You are quite a guy, Jim. I don't think I have ever met anybody like you before that will talk to me and not just to seduce me to get me into the sack." I said, "Val,

I figured from all the CPD guys that keep hitting on you that you are not into that scene. They keep trying to sweet talk you but you can see right through them. I didn't ask you out just to go to bed with you. I like you and enjoy your company and truthfully right now I don't think I could handle a serious relationship or to make a commitment to something that would alter my life. I am thinking after Natalie finishes school and gets into college I might be ready for a major change. If you want to see me on those terms when we can get together I would love spending more time with you." Val just looked at me and came over and kissed me full on the lips. She said, "Jim, I would jump through a flaming hoop to have a relationship with you. You are the most honest, upstanding man I have ever met; you never once patted me on my fanny when I walked by or tried to peek down my blouse when I was standing next to you. You have always been really nice to me; you remember my birthday and give me a gift at Christmas." After we had our dessert, Val said, "You can spend the night if you like, no strings attached. I am a big girl and I won't cry if you don't come back." I spent the night and I got up early Sunday morning kissed her and went home to get ready to pick up Natalie after church.

    I took a shower, shaved, and put on some slacks, polo shirt, and a sports jacket. I have no clue what we are going to do today since Natalie and I didn't discuss it at all. I haven't looked at the entertainment section of the paper in weeks. The Bears are on Monday night away from home. The Bulls might be home; maybe she would like to go see the big men play. We never talk about sports other than just in passing. Since she is going to play that might be an option. Tickets could be a problem. I know the season just started but the newsies are saying they look like the Bulls of old when Jordan, Pippen, and Jackson won those championships. I don't follow basketball until they get to the playoffs, by then football is a thing of the past and hockey should be finished too. I only watch sports if I have nothing better to do. I know people that get wrapped up in all the sports. I guess that is OK if that's your thing. I guess I'm a workaholic, I mean if I'm not working on a case I'm researching material to keep up with what is going on internationally and nationally since those are the areas I am most involved with. I should really try getting involved with something aside from my chosen field and improve my social skills. I look at the clock, time to leave enough of beating myself up.

I get to the church just as people start walking out. I park and walk over by the entrance. Natalie and Rachael walk out and see me standing there and do a double take. I am dressed nicely again this week; they are really surprised. Rachel said, "What is the special occasion?" I said, "Nothing special, it felt nice last week to be dressed up for a change." Natalie grabs my arm and said, "I'm starving, can we go eat?" I said, "Sure sweetie." Rachel said, "You two have a good time, I have shopping to do." Natalie kisses her Mom and said, "I'll be home before eight. Enjoy your day too." Rachael said, "I will try." Rachael walks to her car and drives away. I asked Natalie, "So how was your new friend, did you two have fun?" Natalie said, "We did, we played some games and talked about all the stuff going on at school. Susan thought I am trying to do too much with playing basketball too but I told her I can handle it, besides I like playing and running off some of my excess energy. I like the activity; it is different than just studying and going to the library and doing research or being on the computer all the time. Half the girls don't do anything except play with their phones and sit on the computer. To me that's boring." I asked, "What does Susan do when she is not studying and doing homework." Natalie said, "She helps her Mom a lot I guess with the housework and stuff like that. She doesn't really have any activities outside of school. I think she wants to go to theology school after high school to be able to help needy people in other countries and introduce them to their religion." I said, "It sounds like she is pretty committed to their religion." Natalie said, "I know, we talked about it some but we don't talk religion since her faith is so much different than mine. She just told me that was what she has always wanted to do so I started talking about things going on at school." I said "That was probably the smartest thing to do." Natalie said, "We can go someplace different for breakfast, I love the crepes but I had too much sweet stuff last night." I said, "How about Richard Walkers Pancake House?" She said, "Where is that?" I said, "On Roselle Road in Schaumburg, we'll have to wait but I don't mind we can talk about what you want to do today."

We drive to the Pancake House and it wasn't as crowded as I thought it would be. They took our name and said it would only be a few minutes before most of the breakfast crowd is starting to leave. Natalie and I are talking and they call our name so we go get seated. I haven't been here in a long time, but I remember some of the things on the menu and they are still there. One of their specialties is an apple stuffed waffle. The menu says allow forty-five minutes if you order it. I decide I'll order one to go and take it home to have for dessert or something. Natalie is hungry and I'm hungry, so we order some usual fare stuff. I ordered a bacon skillet with two eggs basted; Natalie orders a skillet with vegetables and cheese, no meat. We start talking about what we could do today. I said, "Are the Bulls home today?" Natalie said, "I know the Hawks played last night. I don't know; I didn't see the schedule." I said, "It was only a suggestion." Natalie said, "We can go to see a movie after we eat, I would like that." I said, "We will look after we eat and see what is playing." Our breakfast came and we were both pleased with what we ordered; the food was very good. The waiter brought my Apple Waffle; it was hot out of the oven and smelled delicious. I was tempted to open it up and sample it right then but figured I was full enough. We drove to the cinema to see what was playing when and decided on watching "Life As We Know It." It was lighthearted and I figured I could sit through that. The other options were "Social Network, Red, Paranormal II, and Secretariat." There were a couple of other movies playing but none that I could sit through.

After the movie Natalie said, "We can go to your place, I don't really have anything special I want to do today. I can challenge you to a game of Checkers, I know you use to beat me all the time but I am older now and I have been trying to learn to play chess so I should be more of a challenge." I said, "Chess, I am surprised you really have to concentrate and think a lot more moves ahead." Natalie said, "So I found out, the first few times I played it was like five moves and I lost already." I said, "Where are you learning Chess?" She said, "At school, it is an afternoon after school activity in the resource center. Before I started practicing basketball I would go try to learn how to play." I said, "After basketball, chess will seem too tame." She said, "I know that Dad. I might try it again after basketball season; I did like having to think about planning moves." I said, "Warn me if you keep at playing Chess; I'll have to hone up my Chess skills." Natalie said, "That would be cool."

I drive back to my place and remember to bring the Apple Waffle in with us. I turn on the oven and put it in to heat a little. Natalie said, "I'll make your coffee, was it OK last time?" I said, "It was, I finished almost the whole thing." We go in the living room and Natalie is looking for the checkerboard; finally she finds it and said, "Are you ready?" I said, "Sure, you can go first." She made her first move and I countered. This went on for about six moves and I thought, "This is Fun" and then I looked at the board and said, "I think you have learned a few things from your Chess classes." She looks at me shyly and said, "Why do you say that?" I said, "Seven moves and I haven't taken any men yet, but that is about to change." With that being said I do a triple jump and she said, "Oh! Dad, you are just too good." In doing that I left myself vulnerable and she took two men in one move. I said, "I think we have a good game on our hands." I did win the first game, she won the second, and I won the third game since I had her cornered with no place to go. She said, "You're still the champ."

We went out to the kitchen and we had some of the Apple Waffle with Vanilla Bean Ice Cream on top. I had my coffee and she had chocolate milk. It was about five and Natalie said, "Do you want to go shoot some hoops?" I said, "I need to change." She said, "I do too." We both changed and we drove over to a park by my place to play. We pretty much had the court to ourselves. She is doing real good sinking shots that I know I couldn't make. We play a game where you have to shoot from the same spot the other person shoots from and shoot until you make it. Then we move to a different spot and shoot hook shots. After about forty-five minutes we are both working up a good sweat. We get back to my place and she goes and takes a shower before I take her home. After her shower I take one too since I stink. She said, "Thanks Dad, that was fun." I drive her home and tell her, "Call me during the week, my schedule will be crazy but let me know how things are going." She said, "I will Dad."

I walk her up to the door and Rachael opens the door and said, "So what did you two do?" I said, "We ate, we went to a movie, and we shot hoops." Rachael said, "In those clothes?" I said, "No, we changed and then showered after." She said, "There is still hope for you. You have learned a lot in recent years." I said, "Thank you Rachael. I am trying." Natalie kisses me and said, "I love you Dad." I said, "I love you too sweetie." Rachael and Natalie go inside and I drove home. All in all today was fun, no set plan but it turned out OK. I look at the clock and thought should I call Val? Yes why not. She said "How was your day?" So I told her what Natalie and I did all day. She said, "Are you tired?" I drove over to Val's and wound up spending the night. I knew I would have to get up early, so I told her, "Tomorrow morning I'll be gone when you wake up; I need to get home and get ready for a call from my boss and then get to work." She snuggled up closer to me and said, "That's fine. Just hold me for a while longer." I did and finally we both fell asleep.

Chapter 13

I woke up at a little after five, got dressed, and drove home. I am thinking to myself; I don't want to make a habit of sleeping at Val's every night. I enjoyed my night, but I know I can't do this every night. I get home take a shower, turn on the computer, and wait for McCray to call. I am waiting and looking at the clock; it is almost time for me to leave and get to Buranski's house. I am thinking he is going to the office and then they are going to Hyde Park and then I figure I'm heading to McCray's office again this morning. What was it McCray said? He had a big meeting with Schaunessy this morning and he had a lot of stuff to get ready for this meeting. I stop on the way to pick up coffee and a cinnamon roll. I get to Buranski's at six-thirty. Not bad. I look around and I notice a black Escalade in the next block. I'm like what a change in plans. He has been meeting them at 55th Street after they drive from Orland Park. I guess I better be alert today. Like clockwork Buranski backs out of his garage and heads to the office. I wait a while until the black Escalade pulls out behind Buranski and then I follow them. He drives straight to the office and gets there about seven-twenty; traffic was a little heavier this morning. He parks in back and goes into the office. Seven-thirty Radko shows up and they are waiting for Ivan with the van. Buranski said, "There is fresh coffee in the pot, I made it in case Dragan comes by. How was your weekend?" Radko said, "Pretty good the guy I am training had a competition Saturday night and he finished first. So I'm happy."

They are talking and waiting for Ivan and the phone rings. Buranski answers it, "KBW Construction Karl speaking. Yes, I saw your guys tailing me this morning, what gives? No, I think we will be OK. Did you get the other computer yet? Today, that would be good. How are we going to get it into the house? Yes, the Dish truck will bring it, they will have to show a packing list or something. I see a defective Dish that they need to replace; it's not picking up any signals. The other equipment will be trickier getting it in. I talked to my guy Saturday. It is supposed to be ready Wednesday morning. You have a plan, let me hear it. Yes, that should work. We will be finishing up the new windows on that side so yes set it up." Radko said, "What was all that about?" Buranski said, "I ordered a special piece of electronic gear that is almost top secret stuff, since they want to listen to everything that is said in that house this gadget will do the job and it will feed all the communications direct to the receiver unit and transmit it to our clients computer. It is almost like a live feed from a TV reporter except it is only audio feed. I almost flipped when they gave me the price but they said do it. So we do it."

It is almost eight when Ivan gets there. He parks in front and goes to the door. Buranski lets him in and they go into the office. Ivan said, "I had to go with Gorgi to pick up the materials for Palos Heights. I told him you figured I would have to do that since he hasn't picked up stuff there before." Buranski said, "We should get moving. Our escorts are waiting." They go out the front; he locks everything up and follows them. They are just about ready to pull away and he gets out of the van and goes back inside. I'm thinking maybe he forgot something. He calls on the phone, "Hi, it's me, we are heading into the city, Nine-thirty OK call this number. 773-770-4666, Yes, I checked the phone it is working. That is the line we want to use for the feed. Unlimited access it was already set up. I'll remove the jack and we will bury the line inside the wall. I'll hook it right to the equipment Wednesday you do your test today." Buranski goes back outside and shakes his head like I forgot something gets in the van and they drive away. The black Escalade pulls around them to lead and they follow. I wait a couple of minutes then head toward the city. I write down the phone number so when I talk to McCray I won't forget it.

I get to McCray's office park in the lot and go inside. The place is real quiet; I asked Vicki, "Where is everybody?" She said, "Mr. McCray called me this morning and said he was taking everyone from the office to an on-sight walk through so everybody knows where they will be Friday night. He wanted me to have them all meet him at IIT at ten-thirty and if you got here in time to tell you. He tried calling you but didn't get you. He figured you were in Orland Park." I said, "So, where at IIT are we supposed to meet him?" Vicki said, "The auditorium." I said, "Thanks, why didn't he call my cell phone?" She said, "He tried it but it went to voice mail and went dead." I said, "Thanks, I'll check my phone." I ask myself, When did I last charge the thing? I check and sure enough no bars, I dig around my SUV for the charger and plug it in. I drive to IIT and find parking close to the auditorium and walk over to the entrance. Lo and behold everybody is standing there all waiting for McCray to show up. A few minutes go by and here he comes with a very attractive lady at his side. He introduces her as Director of Special Affairs at IIT; I didn't catch her name but I will not forget her looks. We follow them into the auditorium and she gives us the fifty cent tour and shows us where Security will be setup to screen people coming in for the event and then she takes us around back. This is where the big guy and his staff will be until they are ready for him to make the presentation and then go to the Dining Hall for the dinner afterward. She is very thorough in her details. McCray lets her do most of the talking about what IIT is doing to make sure the night follows a real tight schedule. After the tour and seeing all the various places people need to be stationed McCray said to all of us, "You just saw Ms. Sullivan's take on how Friday night should be, now we will take it a couple of steps further in the event we have trouble on our hands. This where we come in, we need to monitor the activities of several people and keep them in our sights. You will each be assigned one individual to watch. Don't let them out of your sight the entire evening. Is that clear?" We all nodded in agreement. McCray thanked Ms. Sullivan and told the crew he would see them all back at the office this afternoon. He motioned for me to come with him. He said, "I will talk to you before I talk to them but right now I am going to lunch with Ms. Sullivan to go over some of the other details for Friday night." I said, "I'll see you at the office." Then I left.

It is almost noon when I get back to the office. Vicki is ready to go out for lunch; she asked, "Do you want to do lunch?" I said, "Sure but we need to be quick, so we are here when Rusty gets back." She said, "I know, the others were talking when they came in, they were all talking a mile a minute. I need to get out of here for forty-five minutes." I said "So where are we going for lunch." She said, "A little bistro around the corner, they have some nice lunch specials and we can get in and out fast." I said, "Lead on." She was right; it was a little bistro, the food was very good for a small place like this and it was sort of cozy. We ate our lunch and were back at the office before one. That in itself downtown is a trick. I thanked her for inviting me. I would have never gone there on my own. I offered to pay and she refused. She said "Next time." I said "I'll remember that."

 I go back to my cubby hole and start putting information into the computer. About thirty minutes later I hear McCray when he walks in to the office. He checks with Vicki about his messages and then walks back by my cubby hole. He said, "You want to talk here or in my office about what you found out." I said, "Maybe your office it is quieter." He listens to the buzz going on and said, "You're right." So I follow him to his office. He closes the door and I tell him everything that was said this morning. He writes down the phone number and said, "I'll check this out, it sounds like somebody planned this escapade for a while." He tells me. "The two other names that you believe are phony. Everybody else agrees they must be. So they are Red Flagged and will be detained until they get cleared. Schaunessy said, "Thank Huggins for me, he really has a nose for this sort of thing. Nice work on your part plus he wants to bump you up a grade in pay thanks to all your hard work." I told him, "I thought you deserved the bump up in pay before this project." He agreed but couldn't justify it, now he has something to tie it too. "So congratulations Jim. Now we can go have the meeting with the rest of the crew. You will be on Landholm." I said, "I see I need to do more research then." McCray said, "I just thought you would be the best man for the job."

 McCray gathers the rest of the crew and gives each one a name. He switched the names he had originally given each of them and said, "New eyes sometime find things old eyes didn't see. We actually have a few photos of some of the people but there are a couple we have to play by ear, when they show up. We could not find photos but we are still checking maybe we'll get lucky and everyone will have a drivers license, a state ID or a passport photo." I think to myself maybe our two mystery guests have passports and that's why they don't show up on any searches, even though the names sound American. After McCray briefs everybody on the time frame to have the final analysis of our subject I walk over to him and said, "Passports." He nods his head and said, "Yes, we have some foreign dignitaries attending that I just found out about this morning. There are a couple from Sweden, Denmark and Britain. It has something to do with physics or science." I go, "Great, now we have to worry about them too." McCray said, "No they have their own security people and they are all legit." I said "It looks like we will have a busy week." McCray said, "Sure looks that way, my wife wanted me to come home Friday I said no way, this case is coming to a head." I said, "It sure appears that way." I head back to my cubby hole to look for more information on Steven J. Landholm. After two hours my eye balls feel like they are going to fall out. I take a break and go get coffee. I walk up by Vicki's desk and she said, "Your eyes are all red, starring at the computer too long?" I said, "I guess so." She said, "I'll get you eye drops they will help get the red out."

She gets the eye drops and put them in my eyes and said, "Now blink your eyes a couple of times and then dry them with the tissue." I said, "Thank you Nurse." She said, "You're welcome Jim." I swear I could feel my heart pounding a little faster from her touch when she was putting the drops in my eyes. She has a real soft touch and her hands are really smooth. I never paid much attention before, but then again I never had the occasion to have her touch me. I see her in the morning and said good morning or said goodnight when I leave. Even when we had lunch I wasn't aware of her hands. I go back to my cubby hole and look at the information that I was able to find. At least with the system here I did find some current history on what he has been doing. He is an assistant professor of Political Science at a small state school in Minnesota. He finished his doctorate at UIC and was offered a position at the small state school so he took the job. "Well," I thought, "it isn't Berkley, but I guess everybody has to start someplace." He is married and they have two small children ages eight and ten. He met his wife when he was studying in Chicago; she was studying at UIC. The info on her is she was born in Serbia; her parents moved here about ten years ago while she was in high school. For the life of me I don't see any reason for him to be attending this except to listen to the man who embraces some of his father's ideals. I don't picture him as a threat I think it is more for self-satisfaction. I hear some of the troops getting ready to leave for the night and I look at the clock. It is almost five. I should cut out too if I am going to be in Orland Park when Buranski gets back. I tell Vicki I am leaving and head to McCray's office. Vicki said, "He said he did not want to be disturbed I'll tell him you left." I said, "Tell him I charged my cell phone so if he needs me call that number if it's before eight after that I should be home." Vicki said, "Have a good night Jim." I said, "You do the same."

    I drive to Orland Park and I don't see Buranski, there are lights on in the office so I look. Grozdan is sitting in the office looking at the Project Board. I didn't see his car; I wonder how he got here? Then I think Dragan probably picked him up since I didn't see him here this morning either. It is almost six and here comes Buranski. Ivan parks in front and Buranski said something to him. Then he and Radko go inside; he sees Grozdan and said, "Welcome back chief, we missed you around here." Grozdan said, "I called Dragan to rescue me from home, my wife was driving me crazy with all her shows. I tried to hide in my office but she would drag me out and say, I can't watch you in there, you heard the doctor no drinking, no smoking for three weeks, it would be better you quit doing both but I know you will never give up either of them. Only when you are dead will you quit. That was the last straw I called Dragan to bring me here." Buranski said, "How are you feeling otherwise?" Grozdan said, "Not too bad, I can't drive for another couple of weeks but I can do some things so why not come here and do them." Radko looks at clock and said, "We are running late I need to get to the gym. I'll see you in the morning at seven." Buranski said, "No make it eight, Ivan will be late again in the morning, he is going to pick up the new windows at seven. I want them there so we can start putting them in. The bathroom is finished so now we can concentrate on the office. Wednesday will be real busy so anything we can get done tomorrow the better it will be." Radko said, "That should be a piece of cake."

After Radko leaves Grozdan asked, "How's the special project?" Buranski said, "They put a rush on everything. It seems our quarry will be in town Friday for some sort of benefit at IIT and our client wants to be ready even if everything isn't finished. Thursday we are out of there for a few days that whole area will be off limits to everybody." Grozdan said, "So what do you think, will what you are doing work?" Buranski said, "We tested the phone line we are going to use for the feed and that will work, I even sent some phony info just to see if it worked. Tomorrow we get a better computer with more memory and a new piece of electronics gear. so we should be good. I told them I need to go back there next week just to button up everything and make sure they won't have any problems with the system." Grozdan asked, "When is somebody supposed to move in? I gather right now nobody lives there." Buranski said, "Giovani said right after we are finished, a new Doctor will be living there while he finishes up some special training at UIC on Michigan Avenue. He needed a place and Mariano told him he could live there free. He was thrilled to get the offer, He said he didn't need that much room but he was told the people that own the house are out of the country until May. They are in Australia of all places. Mariano said they saw the house so they bought it, they told him treat it as your own until we get back. If you know somebody that needs a place to live let them live there, they would rather somebody be living there so it doesn't get vandalized."

Grozdan and Buranski are talking and I hear Dragan when he comes in. He said, "Hey Chief you ready to go home to the little woman?" Grozdan said, "Not really but I know I have to, they said five or six hours two or three days this week, don't overdo it." Buranski said, "You have to listen to them, I am glad you are back, we will be real busy after this week. I think I got the job in Midlothian. I sent the guy to see Wojowski at our bank. He couldn't get a loan anywhere. Next week we start your special job in Worth and then we have Wojowski's house so the men will be busy. Once the shells are finished all the other will be inside work except for the windows

123

and we only need a few good days and those can get done before the snow flies." Grozdan said, "Then I am not really needed, you have everything lined up." Buranski said, "You are needed you talk to the suppliers and get better deals, me they know from nobody." Grozdan said, "So I am good for something. I'll see you Wednesday afternoon."

After Grozdan and Dragan leave Buranski picks up the phone and makes a call, "Hi Ana, I'm running late today, I should be home around nine I need to take care of a few things in the office and tomorrow I will not have time. Grozdan was here when we got back. He is looking pretty good. He can only work three days this week five or six hours but I'm glad he is back. After this week things will get back to normal for the most part. I'll see you in a while." My cell phone rings; I look it is McCray so I answer it. He asked me what is happening tonight so I told him about Grozdan being there and what Buranski said about the Hyde Park job and the fact that the owners of the property are out of the country until May. McCray said, "That is real convenient for Mariano, I wonder what the relationship is with the owners." I asked, "No luck on finding out who bought the place." McCray said, "The realtor said the whole deal was handled by the lawyers and the bank since the lawyer had authority to sign the papers." I asked, "Doesn't that seem strange to you?" McCray said, "Not really a lot of these type deals are handled by lawyers." I said, "I'll follow Buranski home. They have a later start tomorrow but he feels they will be OK since they are making good progress. Tomorrow the new computer comes and Wednesday his new piece of electronic listening device is supposed to be ready." McCray said, "I'll see you at the office then. Have a good night." I said "I will."

Buranski finishes up the stuff he was working on a little after eight. He shuts everything off, locks the door, and goes out the back door to get in his car to drive home. When he pulls out I wait a couple of minutes to follow. He heads right to 294 gets on northbound so I follow not getting too close. He gets off at his usual exit. No change in plans, he told his wife he should be home by nine. The traffic was not too heavy so he will actually be a few minutes early. He turns on his street; I drive to the next block and go around the block and head to the Maple Street Café for dinner. Val said, "Hi Jim, you hungry?" She brings my coffee and starts to tell me what today's special is and I said, "Just have Tony make me a steak omelet with rye toast, no potatoes." She gives Tony my order and comes back and sort of gives me a look. I said, "This week is going to be really hectic. I will most likely not see you until Saturday sometime." She said, "That's OK, I didn't expect to see you until Saturday. I already talked to Tony about getting one of the other waitresses to work Saturdays until after the New Year. That way we maybe can see each other more if you want too." I said, "Yes I want too but with my job I can't make any promises." She said, "I know but I felt I needed to change one of my days off and have the weekends off for a change" Tony brings my order out and he said, "You two seem to be getting along pretty good, Val is not as crabby as she was before so I say you are good for her." I said, "That is nice to hear." Tony said, "Don't play her along, if it doesn't feel right end it. I don't want to see her hurt." I said, "We are getting to know each other and I told her my feelings. So we are working things out." Tony said, "Good" and heads back to the kitchen. I eat my dinner and tell them goodnight and head home.

Chapter 14

Tuesday morning six I am up and getting ready for work. I think I don't have to leave yet I still have an hour since Buranski said they weren't leaving until around eight. I turn on the computer to check on something that was bothering me all night. I look to see if there is anything about the big guy's upcoming short visit to Chicago. There is a little blurb that security in Chicago has been beefed up pending a special presentation Friday night at IIT. That is all the clipping said. It was posted on Huffington Post news link of upcoming events. That means there will be a lot of press around Friday night to deal with too. Maybe that is what the two mystery guests are banking on; they may not even attend, they just want to be sure there will be a lot of coverage for the event. They might have something else in mind but what. I look at the computer and the time; well I best get a move on. I forward the link to the computer at the office downtown so I can pursue it a little more. I have a sneaking feeling that Landholm is tied in with this somehow. I thought, "I'll work on that angle when I get to the office."

I drive to Buranski's and follow him to Orland Park. We get to his office right at eight o'clock. He parks in back and goes inside. A few minutes later Radko comes in followed by Dragan. Dragan said, "What, no coffee?" Buranski said, "Hold your horses, it should be ready any minute; I set it up to start at eight." Dragan has a box he is carrying. He puts it on Buranski's desk and opens it and asked, "What do you think?" Buranski looks inside and said, "Who made these?" Dragan said, "Sophia." Buranski said, "They look delicious, what's inside?" Dragan said, "Fruit peaches and berries with a light honey glaze on the outside." Buranski said, "I'll have a berry one with my coffee." Radko said, "Make mine Peach." They all fix their coffee and Ivan shows up. He said, "What's the occasion?" Dragan said, "My fiancée made these last night so I brought them to share." Ivan said, "Congratulations, you are finally getting married. Radko you next?" Radko said, "Nyet." Buranski and Dragan both said to Ivan "We think so." They have their coffee and fruit-filled treats and get ready to head to Chicago. They all told Dragan, "Tell your fiancée they were delicious." Dragan said, "I will, thanks." They all go out the front door after Buranski locks everything up and head to Chicago. I follow them until 55th and they pick up their escort. I head to McCray's office. I get there at nine-thirty, park, and go in.

McCray comes in around ten and walks back to my cubby hole. He said, "This piece you sent what are you thinking?" I said, "Last night this whole thing was bothering me about the connection with Landholm and our two mystery people. I think Landholm wants to be sure this will be a big event so he can use it to promote his new book. If Huffington Press is posting it, then they will get the attention. I think the two phonies may try something to make the news more interesting. What I haven't figured out yet but I have this weird feeling it will be a mess. I am trying to research Landholm and places he visited recently to find the connection." McCray said, "I can have the Bureau send over his last couple of months activities that they compiled based upon your initial reaction as to why he would be here. Maybe that will speed your search." I said, "That definitely would." McCray said, "I'll go call them, you'll have in shortly."

Eleven-thirty and I don't have the info from the Bureau yet, then I remember they are an hour different. McCray probably got them as they were about to leave for lunch. I can use a break myself. I walk up by Vicki and asked about McCray. She said, "He left about twenty minutes ago to meet Ms. Sullivan at IIT to talk about a change in plans." I asked, "Are you ready for lunch? I am at a break point and I'm waiting for some stuff from DC. My treat." She said, "I'll get my sweater." So we went to the small bistro that we went to the other day, again the food was very good. I asked, "How did you find this place?" She said, "One day I was in a hurry to get something to eat and I noticed a menu in their window. I was surprised at how good the food was and the fact that I could get in and out in about forty-five minutes. Most of the other places around here within walking distance you need a little more time. We get an hour for lunch even though we don't have to punch in and out I try to get back early. The phone starts ringing before one o'clock almost every day." I said, "Thank you for sharing it with me, the place Rusty goes I know we couldn't walk there and get back within that time frame." She said, "I know, I have gone to lunch with Mr. McCray enough times. He likes my company once in a while just to get out of the office and away from the phone." I said "I think he misses being out in the field like I am, then for the most part you don't have to worry about the phone. That is somebody else's problem." Vicki said, "You are probably right. I know Mr. Schaunessy drives him crazy with phone calls. I swear sometimes he wants to rip the phone out of its socket and unplug it." I said, "Then they would just call his cell phone. You can't escape it in his job." We had a nice lunch and got back to the office by twelve forty-five.

I walked back to my cubby hole and behold the info I was waiting for came through. I printed out all the information and began studying it. I don't know what I am looking for but hopefully something will click. In the past two months Landholm has made several short trips, I am figuring to line up promotion of his new book. It comes out November 9th, that is two weeks away. Boy if he could get some extra publicity between now and then demand for his book would go up. There must be a review of his book someplace. Even though it doesn't go on sale until the ninth, most reviewers get advance copies. I check the Washington Post for reviews. Bingo there it is, the review said it was pretty much along the same lines as his late father's books were. He is exploring the path of socialism in America and how close we are getting to the point of no return where our only choice will be to socialize everything, between the high level of unemployment and the increased public assistance required to keep the citizens fed, housed and provide them with health care. He feels we are not very far from turning this country into a socialist country. He figures given the amount of unrest within the country and the power that the executive branch has at its command it is not that far-fetched of an idea. After reading that review I said Damn, that is probably why he was making those other trips. I bet he enlisted some underground help to stage a demonstration to coincide with this "Fund Raiser/ Benefit Dinner" It is not going to happen inside but outside once all the dignitaries are inside and seated. That would disrupt the whole affair and he could come outside and get up on a stage or get cornered by a TV reporter and talk about how right his book is. Look at the crowd all chanting anti-administration slogans and waving banners. A throw back to the Vietnam War protests, that was during his father era. So we have the father and son almost fifty years apart, traveling down the same path to glorify socialism in one manner or another. I hope I am wrong in my feelings about this, wait until McCray hears this, he will flip.

McCray comes back to my cubby hole after he returns from his meeting with Ms. Sullivan to find out what I came up with. He listens to my theory and asked, "Do you have anything to back this up?" I said "Only that gut feeling of mine that tells me Landholm is planning on using this Fund Raiser for his benefit. I doubt he even cares one way or the other about other implications of doing this. If he can show unrest and bring protesters to upset this whole program he will be in his glory." McCray said, "And what do we do to thwart his plan if indeed he has a plan?" I said "I would arrange to have a National Guard unit called up and stationed around IIT, call it a matter of principle or a learning exercise so they learn about crowd control first hand while we have visiting dignitaries in Chicago. I know none of them are Heads of State or any high-ranking political figures but it might be a way for us to force Lindholm to think twice about doing a demonstration." McCray said, "I see your point but on such short notice I don't know if we can do something like this." I said "We could always ask the Mayor's office to call in all the off duty personnel to beef up CPD presence since this is going to draw a huge crowd outside the event." McCray said, "That we would probably have a better chance of doing. It is the Mayor's City." I said "I could be way off base on this but with the two mystery guests and no information that is about all I could come up with. Guys like this need an event to do their dirty work and this seems tailor made for him." McCray said, "I'll talk to Schaunessy and see what he thinks. This is going to be a big night for everybody involved."

I go back to work looking for anything that might add credibility to my feelings about this whole affair. I was born in 1965 so anything about Vietnam I would not remember. There are scores of books about that era but I am only interested in what Landholm's father was writing about to find a correlation. I guess I will need to make a trip to the library to find some things written by his father. I try a search on the computer but that doesn't really help me. I look at the clock it is almost five and I think I guess I could go there first thing in the morning just to look. I head to McCray's office, his door is open and he is on the phone so he holds up his hand five minutes. I nod and go talk to Vicki for a couple of minutes. After he gets off the phone I tell him what I decided. He said, "That might give you a little better understanding in light of the fact you feel his son is starting to become more of a spokesperson for socialism. I don't know anything about his father I was only in grade school during the 60's and that stuff was all so foreign to me. We played Army games but it was more like GI Joe stuff not like Vietnam. We grew out of that pretty fast with all the rock music and we switched from playing soldier to playing make believe guitars." I said "I missed all that fun, I think we were into Saturday Night Fever or something like that and anything country." McCray said, "I talked to Schaunessy and he will talk to the Mayor and express his concern based on your hunch. He will let me know what His Honor thinks." I said "I'll see you after I go to the library in the morning." He said, "Have a good night."

Out of habit I drive to Orland Park and get there about six. Buranski was already back from Hyde Park, Ivan and the van were gone and I didn't see Radko. I turn on my receiver to listen to what was going on in the office. Buranski was on the phone, I think Tuesday right he was supposed to call about his special piece of electronics gear. I listen to hear if I can get any information about where he is getting it from. He is talking to somebody, What was the guys name? I heard him a week ago asked for him, what was it? He said, "What time tomorrow? Ten, any chance earlier? I'll tell my man to see you OK? Yes the Dish Driver I just have to give him a time. Don't let me down. I'll pay you Friday in cash after lunch. Your place? Sure."

He hangs up the phone and goes to the project board. Palos Heights he erases them from the board. The Worth project is next up. He looks at the clock picks up the phone "This is Karl from KBW Construction is Mr. Grozewski home? Yes I can hold. We are calling to make sure somebody will be there Thursday so they can deliver the wood and materials to put your addition on. They wanted me to call today so I can give them an answer tomorrow. Thank you." He goes over to the project board writes "Material to arrive Thursday" on the board. The phone rings, he answers it "KBW Construction, Karl speaking. Yes, I talked to Sergi the equipment will be ready ten tomorrow morning, have your driver ask for him, no there is no paperwork just get to me so we can install it. Yes I will test it once I install it." He hangs up and makes another call "Ana, yes I am leaving real soon. I have one more call to make. Yes I can pick up the pizza, order it from Malinati's, yes the one by the house. Eight o'clock that will work. See you soon." He picks up the phone "Hi chief, yes I called Grozewski somebody will be home Thursday so the lumber company can deliver the wood. You call them tomorrow to set it up. Gorgi finished the house in Palos Heights today. Ivan will bring the check in the morning. Yes I will see you tomorrow before I leave, Elisia has a another game tomorrow night. No I think this will be their last game. They made the playoffs and won the first game, this round I don't know they are all tough schools. Yes, I'll tell her Uncle Tad is rooting for them."

He shuts everything off, locks the doors and goes out the back door. I said to myself Pizza that sounds good, I haven't had one in over a month. I think it was before this project. Natalie was over and nothing sounded good so we went out for Pizza on that Sunday afternoon. From a new place that opened on Roosevelt Road. It was very good, a little pricey but I am used to the pizza joint in the neighborhood, it is only carryout but it is decent pizza. For me it's OK if I'm in the mood for pizza after working all day or watching football on Monday night. They don't open Sunday, I guess they need a day off too. Now do I go see Val or order a pizza after I follow him home? Pizza wins tonight. I think I still have a couple of brews in the fridge in the garage. That will work. I look at a menu I have in the glove compartment to decide what I want and call on my cell phone to order it. I tell them eight-thirty just to make sure it will be hot when I get it. Buranski pulls out and I follow him, I am like I don't remember seeing Malinati's around his house. There are a couple that I know of but not close to his house, I guess I'll find out. He gets off at North Avenue and goes west to York Rd and goes south. He goes across the railroad tracks and sure enough there is a carryout location. He parks goes in and picks up his order and heads home. I'll have to remember that if I am in the mood for deep dish. Buranski goes right home and I go around the block and head home. I get to my neighborhood joint at eight twenty and walk in Rocko said, "Hey Jim, long time no see." I said "Working crazy hours I haven't had your pizza in what six weeks at least." We talk for a few minutes and I said "Things should get back to normal soon so I'll be here on Monday night's for my pizza when they do." He said, "Good, I miss your smiling face."

I get home at eight-forty five, grab a cold brew from the fridge in the garage and go to the kitchen to eat my pizza. I am on my third slice and the phone rings. It is Natalie so I pick it up and say "Hi sweetie how is your week going?" She tells me "The coach said don't forget Saturday's practice your parents are invited." I said "Tell your coach I plan on being there to watch." Then she said, "The coach said I am the most improved player on the squad the past two weeks." I said "Congratulations sweetie, I knew you could do it." She said, "I wanted to tell you, Mom could care less, I mean I guess she is happy for me but I don't know if she will come and watch me practice or play in our home opener. Our first three games are all on the road." I said "I will mark the dates down for your home games hopefully I can make most of them." She said, "That would be awesome Dad." I said "Remind me to pick up a schedule Saturday from the coach." She said, "OK, Dad, I will. I love you." I said "I love you too sweetie, I'll see you Saturday twelve-thirty unless something changes." She said "Goodnight Dad, glad I called you. I feel better." I said, "Me too. Goodnight sweetie."

After I get off the phone, I go mark my calendar for Saturday and then I think. Friday night is the big night. I hope everything comes off without a hitch. I think about what we are looking at Friday night. Let's see almost a thousand people are scheduled to attend the Fund Raiser Benefit Dinner. Of those one thousand we have the Mayor, the Governor plus ten or twelve foreign dignitaries plus their security people. They have security setup to screen all the regular guests attending the function using scanners like the airport uses and they use in the court house downtown. Twelve stations per 75 people. Then we will have the media covering the activity and then if I am right the protestors start showing up to turn it into a real circus. Waving banners and carrying signs and shouting things to draw attention to their group. This thing is supposed to start at seven and run until ten. Dinner is scheduled to be served at eight, tables of eight or ten. The first hour is speeches about the science department and how important science is in light of the energy issues we are facing. The big guy is supposed to present an award for work on wind power to an Illinois Wind Farm corporation, whose CEO is a graduate of IIT. Then everybody moves to the banquet facility.

Chapter 15

Wednesday morning I am up at the crack of dawn and ready to head out the door and my phone rings. It is McCray. He said, "Are you going to the library this morning after you follow our man?" I said, "That was the plan. What's up?" He said, "I had a heated meeting with Schaunessy last night and we went over all the information that you put together and he tends to agree that there might be more to this whole night than meets the eye. He has a meeting with the Mayor this morning about calling in more manpower. He was debating about calling the Governor but is holding off on that until after talking to the Mayor." I said, "I gave this whole thing more thought again last night after I got home and had a pizza and a brew and I think this is tailor-made for Landholm and some sort of demonstration. If you get all of those people in one place at the same time you know the media will be out in full force. I don't remember the three of them being together for anything. The Mayor was instrumental in getting a Solar Power Facility built In Chicago and endorsing going green with gardens on high-rise roofs. McCray said, "You have been doing a lot of research." I said, "Some of this stuff I follow since I think we need to find other energy sources, we can't rely on oil forever." McCray said, "Don't get lost at the library. I know you and your penchant for details, besides the Hawks play at home tonight. I talked to my buddy and we can use the seats tonight I have first dibs." I said, "Are you inviting me to go again?" McCray said, "With all the stuff going on tonight might be a nice aversion." I said, "Count me in." I head to Buranski's to follow him to Orland Park.

The drive to Orland Park was uneventful. Buranski parks in back and goes inside and makes his coffee. A few minutes later Dragan comes in, followed by Radko and the three of them are drinking coffee waiting for Ivan to get there. Dragan asked, "Did you show

Radko Nadia's photo?" Buranski said, "No I haven't I forgot all about it and he turns on his computer and pulls up the photo." Radko looks "That's skinny Nadia?" Buranski said, "See the caption and what she is doing." Radko looks at it and reads. He said, "Wow, I should have stayed in touch with her. I thought she was just a skinny kid that would get married right after her competing days were finished. I guess I was wrong there." Buranski said, "Why don't you call her to talk sometime?" Radko said, "After we finish this job I might just do that." Dragan said, "You two would be good together, you both love training future Olympians." Buranski said, "That would only be a connection not a reason to get married, there needs to be something more." Dragan said, "Put the two of them together and I think they would find it." Radko said, "What are you two up too?" Buranski said, "We are only trying to look out for you when you get older." Ivan shows up and comes in. Buranski said, "We have a busy day I need to be back here by five, Elisia has a game tonight. It is probably their last game so I need to be there." Dragan goes out the back door, Buranski locks everything up and they go out the front door and head to Hyde Park. I follow to 55th and they get their escort and I head to the main library. I stop to get a fresh coffee. The library doesn't open until nine. I find a lot close by, drink my coffee and head to the library. I walk in and I'm impressed. My local library is only one floor and all spread out. This place is enormous, I know why McCray said, what he did, I could get lost here.

After three hours of reading material looking for a connection I think I find what I was looking for. During the '68 convention in Chicago there were anti-war demonstrations and protestors of every breed. Landholm's father was one of the leaders of a group of demonstrators that was arrested and held overnight. The next day he wrote a piece that was picked up by the press and he made the front page of the Tribune. Perhaps that is what his son is banking on. Here he is in Chicago with the son of the old man the man in charge in Chicago. The notoriety of it all, if he can get the coverage he can put his newspaper photo alongside his father's in the museum he started in his father's name. I am like could this be all it is about? Some people trying to live up to the likes of their father. His father was forty-eight years old in 1968 and he is forty-eight now. Is that a coincidence or is just the way things work out? His father continued to be involved in left wing organizations up until a few years before he died. That was all most two years ago and his son started getting more actively involved in the left wing movement shortly after that and he penned his new book that hits the streets next month. I can't find anything real concrete but from the sound of it, he is just following in his father's footprints to tout the benefits of socialism to anybody that will listen or read his views. Other than that one arrest in '68 he was never arrested for anything else. All of the other members of his father's organization would be in their seventies at least since he was twenty years older than most of them, sort of the senior spokesperson at that time.

I leave the library, pick up my car from the lot and head to McCray's office. It is almost one when I get there. Vicki said, "You just missed him, I think he walked to the restaurant for lunch." I asked, "Did you eat yet?" She said, "As a matter of fact we were real busy all morning and I never thought about it." I said, "If you can leave we could go to your favorite place, I'm famished but don't want to walk over there." She said, "I will ask one of the girls to listen for the phone, I have done that before and it worked out OK." So we went to the little bistro around the corner. I had half a Ruben sandwich and a cup of soup. She had Turkey Breast on a Kaiser Roll. We ate our lunch and were back in the office before McCray got back.

He came back by my cubby hole to find out what I came up with on my research. I told him what I thought while I was gathering all the information at the library. He listened intently and said, "If that is all Landholm wants to accomplish he should get his wish since I know all the media will be there taking photos. I can see the headline now "Son of Left Wing Agitator arrested for staging a demonstration Friday night at IIT!" I said, "The headline is too long, I think it should read "Son Like Father." and show a photo of the two Mayors with Father and Son below it." McCray said, "I like your thinking, maybe we can make that happen." I asked, "Anything new on our guys in Hyde Park or about the leak." He said, "No nothing new, they did say they were surprised the Dish Network truck showed up again to exchange one of the dishes, they thought they did that the other day. The driver showed them the request, that one of the dishes was defective so they let them in. The FBI guy called me I told him let them do it. No sense upsetting things now since the job is almost finished." I said, "Buranski said he was going to run it through its paces and do a full-fledged test tomorrow to make sure everything is operating the way it is supposed to before they close up the place. I wish I knew what kind of a test, I would think there would have to be people in that house in order to actually find out if they can hear everything." McCray said, "I might be able to talk to my guy at the Bureau and ask him to do a walk—through of security to sweep every room for bugs and report directly to him on a room by room basis. That way when he runs his test he will know if they are picking up everything." I said, "Wait I remember Giovani saying something about doing something to cause them to be talking inside the house. He only said it once."

McCray said, "Are you sure about that?" I said, "When he and Buranski were talking about what they needed to do, Buranski was concerned if the unit would do its job since there is never any talking going on inside the house. They always talk outside on the grounds and on the front porch. If anybody goes inside the house to check things they go in alone and do a walkthrough and come back out and report All Clear." McCray said, "I wonder what Giovani has up his sleeve." I said, "That was my thought but that might also let us know who the leak is since we haven't been able to uncover anything in that department." McCray said, "I would sure feel better if we knew who that is." I said, "Tomorrow morning I will call our guy and remind him of our deal, we have left him alone to do his job now we need the pigeon." McCray said, "It's worth a shot, he is probably getting nervous with the deadline tomorrow and making sure his system will work. Reassure him we will bail him out if something goes a miss and he sets off all the alarms." I said, "We still on for the game tonight?" McCray said, "Yes, I picked up the tickets while I was out for lunch, it should be a good game for the Hawks. I'll be in my office, I gave the rest of the staff the night off since I know they are going to the bar again and we will all be working our tails off Friday night." I said, "I want to finish up this report and make a couple of phone calls. Just let me know when you are ready to leave."

I finish up writing the report from the information I gathered at the library and filed it under Landholm. I called Natalie on her cell phone just to say Hi and see how she was doing. She was happy I called her today since it was a crazy day at school. Tonight she has to study for a test tomorrow and she is so wrapped up in basketball she can't concentrate on the other stuff. I told her "You can do it, the basketball is a diversion, the studies are what is important so you get the grades for college." She said, "I know you are right Dad. I'll try this subject is boring but I know I need it. So I'll study honest." I said, "I love you sweetie, I'll talk to you tomorrow to see how you did." She said, "I love you too Dad and thanks." I call Val at home since she told me she was taking tonight off. I forgot that when McCray asked me about going to the game. I think Val was hinting that I could stop over after work tonight. I tell her I'm tied up downtown and it will be eleven o' clock when I leave here.

Am I ready for a relationship like this right now? It would be like when I was married to Rachael, I couldn't really tell her when I would be home on this job you do what you have to do. I think to myself all this time Rachael and I have been divorced she hasn't latched onto somebody else, she is still extremely attractive, she didn't let herself go on put on a lot of weight, she works out at the gym Curves if I remember what Natalie said. I don't think she has been out on a date in over a year. Natalie said, she is always working at her job and spends every night at home. Once in a while a couple of the ladies she works with will call her to join them for dinner but never any guys. I mean I have gone out with probably six ladies since the divorce but they were more social affairs where I needed to have a date to attend a function. I was happy with no female involvement and then Tony and McCray planting the seed to ask Val out. Heck I even like talking to Vicki, I am not interested romantically but she is interesting to talk to. She lives downtown because she works down here and there is always stuff going on. I never asked if she was seeing anybody, we only talk because we are both working here. If I ran into her on the street, she wouldn't even look at me twice. She is a downtown girl through and through. Heels, nylons, makeup, and dresses sharp every day. Me I am a suburban Dad with all the failings of a suburban Dad. I am a divorced male with a teenage daughter, two sets of wheels, child support to pay and a house in the suburbs. Lord knows I am not a flashy dresser but I do get dressed up once in a while on a whim. I am comfortable in my sweatshirt, jeans and tennis shoes with a baseball cap on my head. Yep I fit the bill. McCray calls my name and I snap out of my train of thought. How did I get in this situation again?

McCray said, "We should be heading to the stadium." I said, "Let me shut this down and grab my jacket, I'll be right there." We walk to the stadium and it looks like it will be a full house again. After winning the Stanley Cup this past season, these are the hottest tickets in town. Tonight they play the Kings. We grab a couple of sodas and some Nacho's and get to our seats so we will be there during the National Anthem. Jim Cornelison sings the National Anthem and the crowd is on its feet the whole time cheering and yelling. The crowd seems like they will be a rowdy bunch tonight hungry for a win. It seems the year after a team wins the Stanley Cup everybody is gunning for them and they take great joy in beating the champs. Tonight though belongs to the Hawks they get the win 3-1.

McCray and I walk back to his office and he said, "Jim, you looked like you were in another world when I said we should be leaving for the game." I said, "I was just mulling over things in my life, I think Val wanted me to come by her place tonight after work since she took the night off. When you asked me this morning about the game I didn't even think about what Val said last night so I took you up on the offer. I really don't think I am ready for a heavy relationship right now. Natalie is fifteen and still has three years of high school and then probably college. I don't know how I can balance all the stuff." McCray said, "I see your dilemma, take it from me a good woman is really hard to find and one that will put up with the life we lead that is another matter entirely. My wife hounds me all the time to get home more, I tell her I'm in Chicago you could be with me, she said, "The kids need to finish their education in Virginia." So we go round and round about that. You want my opinion? I would wait until everything is settled with Natalie." I said, "That is pretty much what I felt from the git go, I enjoyed her company and we have a good time when we are together, I just don't think I can do it twenty-four sevens and give Natalie the attention she needs." McCray said, "Think it over real good first and maybe talk to her a little more and just keep it an occasional thing for a while. Sometimes these things work themselves out without any outside intervention. Sounds like she is ready and you're not." We get back to the office building I tell McCray "Thanks for the game it was a great. I'll talk to our guy in the morning. He gets to the office early so he can make coffee before they head to the city. I'll call him before the other guys get there." Then I head for home. It is eleven-fifteen when I get home park my SUV and go inside. I am bushed tonight and tomorrow will be loads of fun, I take a shower and hit the sack.

Chapter 16

Thursday morning six I am up, got dressed, and walk out the door at twenty after. I drive to the coffee shop, get a large coffee, and give them my thermos to fill. I figure I'll need more than a large coffee this morning. I almost walk out and the gal said, "Don't forget your cinnamon roll!" I turn around and go back to the counter as she said, "You never forget that." I said, "Too many things on my mind I guess. Thanks." She said, "Come by when you have more time and we can talk." I said, "Thanks." I looked at her name tag. She said, "This isn't my name. I don't like guys hitting on me so I use another girls tag. My name is Barb, by the way." I said, "I'm Jim. It's nice to meet you and know your name. I'll remember." I walk out and get in my SUV and I think, "I have been coming here almost every day for what three years, isn't that when they opened here, and I have seen her almost every day but we never talk. I just give her my order or I should say she sees me and gets my coffee and cinnamon roll ready before I even get to the counter unless they have a few other customers in line. We say Good Morning, maybe talk about the weather, but no chatter. Is there a full moon tonight or something happening with the planets that is causing all this mayhem?" I drive to Buranski's and get there just as he is backing out. Talk about timing it close, that was close. I follow him to Orland Park and park my SUV and take out my cell phone and call him.

I said, "Good morning Karl, how are things this morning?" He said, "Huggins right?" I said, "Yes, I wanted to find out if you knew what sort of diversion Giovani has planned for today so you can test the equipment." He said, "He didn't tell me precisely what he was planning but I think it will involve the two legmen that get us in and out of there. He told me not to worry and that there would be plenty of conversation going on inside the house." I said, "My boss said to assure you if your equipment sets off all the alarms, we will bail you and your guys out. So you won't have to worry about getting sent back to Bulgaria." He said, "I was wondering when I would hear from you again. I am living up to my part of the agreement, right?" I said, "Yes you are, I think you have been straightforward and you manage to fill me in on what stage you are, so we can be ready if we need to get you and your guys out. We don't want your customer to get suspicious about your activities. We are giving you free reign as long as we know what's coming. Have you heard anything about who they think will be having a meeting there with?" He said, "Not a word, strictly hush-hush. That's all I was told." I said, "Monday we need to sit down face-to-face and try to put this mission out of commission so we can find out who is really behind this whole thing." He said, "Call my cell phone, I'll give you the number, we can meet for breakfast." I said, "The Pancake House on 45? Eight-thirty?" He asked, "You know that place?" I said, "I saw you and Radko there twice." He gave me his number in case there was a change. I was like I never expected him to give me his cell phone number and I put it in my phone right away, Under the initials KB. I said, "Good luck today." He said, "We'll be OK."

Ten minutes later Radko shows up and a few minutes later came Dragan. They start jabbering away in something I can't understand. Then Ivan comes in and interrupts their discussion. Buranski said, "Dragan, you are getting married Thanksgiving weekend. Why?" He said, "Sophia wants us to get married when all her family is together so they don't have to come again later. So I said, 'What about my family?' She asked, 'Are any of them coming here?' I said, 'No we could go there.' So now, what do we do?" Buranski said, "Have the wedding here and go home to see your family for a honeymoon. That way you both get to spend time with family." Dragan said, "You are the smart one, what about money?" Buranski said, "The money you get from the wedding. I'll make up the difference." Radko said, "Wait I'll contribute too." Dragan said, "You guys are too much, Sophia will be thrilled." I think Buranski can fix anything, isn't that what Mariano said?

At seven-thirty they head for the city. I follow to 55th Street and their escort is waiting. I drop off and go to Halsted Street and proceeded to McCray's office and park. I walk in there is only Vicki there. She said, "You're early today." I said "Busy day. Is he in?" as I pointed to McCray's door. She said, "I think he spent the night here, I got here early and he was walking out to see Mr. Schaunessy about a possible problem. He said he would be back later but no idea what time. He said, if anybody asks, he is out of the office, period." I said, "I wonder what that is about, since I talked to him late yesterday and told him all the information I put together." She said, "He sure looked disheveled, like he hadn't slept much, his clothes were wrinkled like he slept in them on the couch in there. He had shaved, I will give him that much. I know he usually keeps a change of clothes in his office so if he has to go see somebody he looks good. I guess he used those before and didn't replace them yet. It's just not like him." I said, "I know what you mean. He always tries to look good. Well, I guess we will find out when he gets back. What time are the others supposed to be here or are they off until tomorrow?" She said, "I didn't hear anything about them not coming in today so I would guess around nine-thirty they will start showing up." I went to the break room to get a bottle of juice and then went to my cubby hole to get to work.

I was going over what Buranski said about Giovani planning some sort of a distraction so he could test the equipment without fear of setting off the alarms. If he is planning on using his two escort men to provide the distraction that is surprising, since they are Buranski's ticket in and out of that area. I am wondering what trick he has up his sleeve. I reassured Buranski if anything went sour we would bail him and his crew out on McCray's word. Those agents didn't know anything about our deal and the men in blue sure didn't know. Two of our guys are there but I didn't think McCray told them of the plan. They are only there as extra eyes. Their job is to keep us abreast of any changes or unexpected visitors in the area. They have been there eight days and no reports of anything unusual. Why do I get the feeling that today will be the day that something will happen? Those tiny hairs on the back of my neck are sticking up again. I hear talk in the other part of the office. Vicki was right after nine-thirty, the other team members start moseying in. I can hear them talking up previous nights' game and how much fun they had at the bar. About eleven, I walk up front and tell Vicki, "I'll be back! I need to go check on something." I didn't tell her what, I just have this weird feeling that something is amiss. McCray would probably be upset but if he is concerned about a possible problem, I should be too. So far this project has gone really smooth and to my way of thinking, maybe too smooth. Sure there were a couple of minor setbacks but nothing of any major consequence. I head to Hyde Park just to satisfy my curiosity. I don't have my jacket or baseball cap only my badge and my ID, plus I am driving my SUV. I get down there and I am stopped by security five blocks from the house. I ask who is in charge today. The dick asks me, "Why do you want to know?" I showed him my badge and he said, "Agent Huggins, wait here. I'll call my boss." I stand there and wait. He goes and gets in his department-issued Gray Crown Victoria and calls his boss. A few minutes later he comes back and says, "Captain Robinson will be here shortly. There is a melee going on a few blocks from here. He said something about a couple of security personnel getting into a fight with some workmen working on a house. They broke up the fight. Now they are trying to figure out who started it." I said, "I'll wait, I just need to talk to him about tomorrow's plan for the Chief." The dick said, "Suit yourself, it could be a while." So I walk back to my SUV and try calling McCray's cell. Nothing! It was dead.

Shortly after noon, I see a CPD Captain walking in my direction. He stops by the dick and the dick points to my SUV. I get out and show him my badge. Captain Robinson said, "What can I do for you, Agent Huggins?" I said, "I was asked to come down to talk to you about tomorrow and if you are going to need extra security for tomorrow's visitor." He said, "I think we have enough man power here unless you know something we don't. You guys don't usually come snooping around with no just cause. Maybe I should be asking you why you are so interested. I took the liberty of checking, you were down here about two weeks ago snooping around. Lt. McElroy jotted your name down in the log so if you came back around we would know who you are." I said, "I am glad to see you guys followed procedure." I asked, "So what just happened over there?" He said, "It was all just a big misunderstanding. Two of the security people thought that the guys at the house having some work done on it were mixing it up, so they went to break up what they thought was a fight and they got right in between them and both took shots to the head. It seems one worker was giving one of the thugs, pardon my term for the guy, a boxing lesson. They apologized for hitting the security guys but they got right in between them. Neither of the security guys were hurt, maybe their pride but one guy was all muscle and the other guy was a scrappy kind arms flailing everywhere." I think to myself Radko giving the aspiring boxer a lesson. That was a pretty nice diversion. I said, "Thank you, Captain Robinson. I'll tell my boss you are fine." I drive back to McCray's office; it is almost one-thirty when I get back.

I walk in and Vicki said, "Have you eaten yet?" I said, "No, too busy." She said, "McCray called and said to tell the crew to take the rest of the day off. He expects them here tomorrow at three rested and ready to go since he figures it will be a late night tomorrow." I asked, "Did he say what time he would be back?" She said, "Around four." I said, "Let's go eat then, I tried calling him but his cell phone was dead." She said, "I know it is on the charger in his office." So we go have lunch at the bistro around the corner and we knew we didn't have to hurry back, so we chat a while longer. I asked her, "So why is it that an attractive gal like you has not been snatched up by some handsome single man down here?" She said, "Most of the men down here are either career motivated, trying to move up in the corporate world or sports junkies that spend all their time and money on pro sports going to the games and trying to be big time jocks. They are not my type. I'm more into the intellectual type of men but they are few and far between and even some of them their work is all they are concerned with. Why do you ask?" I said, "Curiosity. Mostly because you are very attractive and have a real gentle touch from when you put the eye drops in to get the red out." She said "Thank you, Jim. That is the nicest thing I've heard today." We finish our lunch and head back to the office.

After we get back to the office I go write up a report for McCray about today's events so I will not forget anything. Vicki said he would be back around four. I look at the clock; it is just after three. I am sitting there reviewing some of the reports I put together and I take a folder and browse through it again. I am looking at the report from a week ago and something strikes me. Why does that seem out of place like with Landholm? I read the thing again and I go, "Damn, I think I know where the leak is. It has to be at the Bureau since they were the only ones that knew what we were doing." It is like they wanted to have something to go wrong so that they looked good. I think to myself, is it possible that one of the agents has some sort of tie to Mariano? Maybe a family member that is in hock to a loan shark for gambling debts that is tied to Mariano in some way heck maybe even a family member married into that family. It wasn't like the old days, the wives were pretty much chosen by the boss. Marry an Italian woman from the neighborhood. Today, everybody is marrying whomever they please; the old taboos are gone. Perhaps, there are still some throwbacks to the old ways but not as a general rule. I'll talk to McCray so that he can probably get his contact to do some background checks to see who has relatives or ties to Chicago.

McCray comes in and walks back to my cubby hole. I gave him a copy of my report of the antics in Hyde Park. He said, "I heard all about it. My FBI contact told me what was going. He called Schaunessy when he couldn't get me. Schaunessy handed me the phone so he told me what was going on." I asked him, "Do you have men inside the house?" He said, "Yes, I have two guys inside checking everything for tomorrow and they are giving me an all clear as go room to room." I said, "Bingo. How did Mariano know they would be doing that today?" McCray said, "I see your point. I'll call my friend at the Bureau and see what he comes up with." I asked, "What is the schedule for tomorrow for me?" McCray said, "I told Vicki I wanted the rest of the staff here tomorrow by three dressed and ready to roll. I have a small shuttle bus that will take them to IIT so they don't have to worry about parking or anything like that. You and I can go together or you can meet me there at three-thirty. I figure you will be watching our man to see who he pays for the equipment. In the morning you can relax and catch some extra sleep." I said, "Like I'm going to do that, like you are going to do that." McCray said "Touché!" I said, "I'll call you later. I am curious how the test went and I'm sure Giovani will call him tonight at the office before he heads home to give him feedback if it worked."

When I left I didn't see Vicki at the front desk. I think maybe McCray told her she could leave early since there wasn't anything else for her to do today. I walk over to the lot to get my SUV and I see her standing by a bus stop. I asked, "Where are you headed?" She said, "I have a converted loft over on South Michigan. A friend of mine was transferred to DC and asked if I wanted to move in. He didn't want to put it on the market in this economy. So I pay him what I was paying for my one bedroom on Wells so he isn't losing too much. He said he didn't need the money but I told him I would rather pay. I didn't want to feel like I was taking advantage of him. If he gets transferred back I would find another place. He is just a close friend I went to school with, we actually roomed together for a while. We became friends and would do what we could to help each other through difficult times." I drove her over to South Michigan and jumped on the expressway from there and headed to Orland Park.

I get to Buranski's office early, it is only five-thirty. I look around. Buranski's car is in the back. Radko's car is parked next to it and Dragan isn't at the used-car lot I go. I might as well go get a coffee and something to nibble on. My energy level right now is like zero. This day was strange in more ways than one. So I drive over to the Gyro place, get an extra-large coffee, and a Gyro to go. It will be a little messy but I grabbed extra napkins, that way if I don't eat until late it is no great worry. I get back at five to six and a couple of minutes later they arrive. Ivan parks in front and they all go inside. Once they get in Buranski office, I hear them talking. Ivan said, "That was some show Radko and Dino put on for the cops." Buranski said, "That diversion allowed me to run the tests on the equipment, everything worked the way it was supposed to. I don't know who was behind getting the agents to go room to room and give the all clear but I know we picked up almost everything. There was one area that I couldn't pick up anything but that could be a steel-walled room for security. If he is in there, nobody will hear anything. I did what I could in the time we had. Next week, I may need to adjust a couple of things if we can get back in there otherwise they live with what they have." Radko said, "I hate to run but I need to get to the gym." Buranski said, "Tomorrow after three, it's payday. I have to see Sergi for lunch and pay him for the other equipment and Grozdan will be here tomorrow if Dragan picks him up on time." Radko said, "I'll be here." Ivan starts to leave and Buranski said, "Ivan, you did good on this project. I was concerned you might not be able to do this kind of work but you did good. I know you would rather be knocking down walls and building new second stories but this was a money job flat out. Tomorrow we will go over next week's schedule for the Worth job. Have a good night." Ivan said, "Thanks boss. I tried to do everything you wanted, I am glad you were pleased." Then he left.

Buranski picks up the phone and makes a call. "Ana, I will be home in a little while. I have a guy coming by in a few minutes. It shouldn't be too long. I'll call you when I'm on my way." He was fiddling with stuff on his desk like he is getting nervous about something. About ten minutes later the phone rings and he answers, "KBW Construction Karl speaking. Yes, I am waiting for you. Ten minutes that is fine. Ring the bell I'll let you in." Ten minutes later the black Escalade pulls up in front, there are two guys in the back seat. One I figure is Giovani and my guess would be the boss man himself Big Al. The shotgun guy gets out and opens the door and I was right the one is Giovani. I look at the other guy; six—feet-two at least and two-hundred and fifty plus pounds. It has to be Big Al. I didn't bring the camera with the telephoto but for him I don't need it, I have seen pictures of him in the paper. There is no mistaking him, the suits he wears, the mammoth diamond ring he wears on his right hand, his fedora, and his ever-present cigar. He doesn't smoke them anymore; he just chews on them and thows away when he is done. Buranski lets them in and doesn't look surprised. They go into his office.

Big Al said, "I told Vito not to tell you I was coming, I wanted to surprise you. I wanted to tell you I'm impressed by the system you setup. The test today was right on the money; I heard the all clear from every room except one." Buranski said, "I figure they have a steel encased security room, nothing can penetrate that room." He said, "That is pretty much what I figured but the conversations we are interested in will most likely take place in the library or his office. Those jamming devices you setup confused the hell out of the security detail. I guess they shut the system down two or three times. By the time you did your test, they got the system back up and running. I think they figure there was an internal problem with the system." Buranski said, "You seem pretty well versed on their system." He said, "It's almost the same system I have at home. I can tell by what they talked about." Buranski said, "Next week I need to get back in there for a couple of hours just to make sure the backup system is working properly. As I understand it, somebody will be moving in there for a few months and we will not be able to get in there again until he leaves." Big Al said, "Yes, the doctor moves in Thursday. He will be there until the end of April when his classes will be over. We will pay you the rest of the money after you check the backup system. I will need an access code to open the backup system and retrieved the data am I correct?" Buranski said, "Yes, you are correct. The backup unit will be in between the wall in the closet and the new bathroom. There is a dummy panel you must remove and then you can retrieve the data once you enter the code. I will give you that when you pay me." I think Big Al is not the only shrewd one. Buranski can keep right up with him.

 Big Al said to Vito, "Make sure your guys don't mess anything up in there after he leaves. That gets sealed off, and the doctor was told the new office and bathroom will be off limits. The doctor said, you can lock off the whole second floor for all he cares. Everything he needs is on the first floor." Giovani said, "I already told them what you said." Big Al said, "Tell them again, I don't want any slip ups." Giovani said something I didn't understand and Big Al said, "It has been a pleasure doing business with you, maybe I can use your services on another matter after this one runs its course." Buranski said, "We'll see, it depends. I don't like having to restrict myself to limited manpower but in this case I know it was essential." A few minutes later, Buranski walks them to the front door and lets them out. He goes back to his office and makes a call. "Ana, I am leaving now. Do I need to pick up anything? Yes, I should be home by eight-thirty. See you soon." He locked the place up and heads for home and I follow him.

He drives straight home no stops and gets there about eight-twenty. I go around the block and head home but decide I should go see Val at Maple Street Café since tomorrow night I'll be downtown until past midnight I'm sure. I walk in and Val said, "Hello stranger." I said "I figured I better come here tonight since tomorrow night I'll be downtown real late." She said, "Later than last night. I tried calling you until eleven and then went to bed." I said, "I was tied up and couldn't even call you, the day was just unbelievable. I'll tell you all about once this thing is finished." Val said, "I know you and your job, you warned me. It comes first." I asked, "What did Tony cook up special today?" She said, "Homemade cabbage rolls." I said, "That sounds good to me, are there any left?" She said, "If there aren't, I can get you some Stouffers frozen ones." I said, "I'll pass and have a burger if nothing else." She said, "Of course there are extras. Have you ever known Tony to not cook enough of his specials?" I can see she is in a playful mood tonight. I said, "What are you doing when you get off tonight?" She said, "Why do you ask?" I said, "I have a late start tomorrow. I get to sleep until seven." She said, "Really that late?" I said, "Yes really." She laughed and said, "You are funny tonight aren't you Jim." I said, "I didn't think you would notice." She said, "I noticed now. If you had told me you didn't have to get up until nine or ten, I might have said something else." I said, "I wish I could but after next week things should be back to a somewhat normal schedule." She said, "With you that's almost impossible. Do you even know what a normal schedule is?" Tony comes out carrying a plate filled with cabbage rolls. He said, "How many do you want?" I look at them and say, "Three. They are huge." He puts three on a plate, hands it to me, and said, "She was a little upset you didn't see her last night." I said, "I gathered that. Does she get this way often?" Tony said, "Only when she has a night all planned and it goes bust." I said, "Thanks for the tip, I'll try to remember." I wondered, who said,

"Hell hath no fury like a woman's scorn?" I'll have to look that up. Whoever it was, he was right as rain. I ate my dinner, said goodnight to Val and Tony, and go home to get some sleep.

I am home a little after ten, and put the news on and fall asleep in my chair. I woke up at about two in the morning and decide I should go to bed. What an exhausting day this was. I was going to write everything down that transpired last night at Buranski's office, but when I got home I passed out in my chair. Damn, I'll go write it now otherwise in the morning I will forget something. I go to the kitchen and make a cup of coffee, it's instant but right now I need to shake the cobwebs from my brain to write this stuff down. If I made a pot, I would be up all night. I take my coffee and go to my office and write the report. At last it's done and I think I remembered everything. That way when I talk to McCray I have it in front of me. I go to bed and set the alarm for seven and promptly fall asleep.

Chapter 17

    Seven a.m. the alarm goes off, I roll over and turn it off. I am thinking wait what was Buranski doing this morning? Wait he said he was going to the bank to get money to pay Sergi, Radko and Ivan. Then he was going to meet Sergi for lunch at his place. I don't even know where Sergi's place is. I thought Sergi was the electronics wizard guy that he ordered the new piece of electronics from. Why would he go there for lunch unless I missed something? I think back to his conversation. I'm sure he said something. I guess I should follow him to the bank and see where he goes after that. He told Radko and Ivan he would be at the office after two and that Grozdan would be there if Dragan picks him up on time. I am supposed to meet McCray at IIT at three-thirty. I better tell him I will most likely be late. I'll call him while Buranski is in the bank. I get dressed and go to the donut place to get my coffee and cinnamon roll. I remembered my thermos to have them fill it too. Barb said, "You're late this morning." I said, "No, I had a late night and later start this morning." She said, "You don't seem groggy this morning." I said, "Thanks, I did get some sleep." I leave and think to myself, she was talkative again this morning. I know it was later than usual for me and she didn't have five people in line. I drive to Buranski's office and get there a little after eight. I figure he will leave for the bank at about twenty after; so I park and drink my coffee and eat my cinnamon roll.
    Eight twenty-five Buranski backs his car out of the garage. He closes the garage door and then goes to the front door. Ana opens the door and he goes back inside. A couple of minutes later he is carrying a box that looks like a cake box and puts it on floor in the back seat. He goes back and kisses Ana and gives her a hug. Then gets in his car and drives away. I follow him to the bank, we get there

a little after nine, he parks and goes inside. I figure now is a good time to try calling McCray since he will be in there for a while. I try McCray at the office, no answer so I call his cell it goes right to voice mail. I leave him a message to call me. Fifteen minutes later Buranski comes out carrying a small bag, I figure that must be some cash. He pulls out and heads toward his office in Orland Park. I follow him and sure enough that is where he goes. He parks in back, takes the bag from the bank with him, then he comes back out and gets the cake box and takes it inside, then he comes out again and opens the trunk and gets another bag out of there and takes it inside. After a few minutes I see him in his office hanging a banner. It says, Happy Birthday Uncle Tad. I am thinking it has to be from Elisia and it's Grozdan's birthday. He sits the cake box on the unit where he makes the coffee and makes his coffee. A few minutes later here comes Dragan and Grozdan. Grozdan looks at the banner and sees the cake and says, "This is why you wanted Dragan to get me early today? Thank you, I almost forgot it's my birthday."

They have coffee and Grozdan cuts the cake and takes the first slice and says, "This is homemade." Buranski says, "Elisia baked it and decorated herself just for you." He says, "Tell her I said it is delicious. I am not supposed to eat a lot of sweets but I can't pass this up." They sit and talk for about thirty minutes and Buranski says, "I'll be back in a while I have to go see somebody. Radko will be here around two and Ivan should be here too." He goes out the back door and drives away. I follow him, I still haven't heard from McCray but if he calls I call him back. He drives toward the expressway but doesn't get on, I follow him and he takes a road that I don't remember him taking before. It winds around and we wind up on County Line road he takes that to another road and all at once we are on 83. I am like this is a roundabout way to get to 83 me I would have just taken the other road. He goes north a little ways and turns right back into an area where there are some factories. I am like this must be Sergi's place. He pulls up in front and parks and walks to the front door. A guy opens the door, I think I saw this guy before someplace but where. Buranski follows him in, so I am sitting there racking my brain trying to think. Wait that guy he was at the restaurant in Midlothian when Dragan made the announcement he was getting married. A few minutes later they both walk out, Sergi gets in the car with Buranski and they drive away. I follow them. He goes two blocks makes two turns and they pull up in front of a restaurant called "Sergi's II". I'll be damned, he opened another place. His electronics business must be good.

I am sitting there and thinking to myself. This guy must be crazy opening a restaurant here, how are people going to find it. I look and there are only three cars there. I look at the clock it is about eleven-thirty and then little by little a few cars start coming there. At twelve fifteen there are twenty cars in the lot. I think the food must be good or something. I mean there isn't any other place around here that I know of. The factories when we turned off of 83 those people probably don't have a lot of choice. I'll have to check this out sometime I don't want to interfere with Buranski and his contact. The phone rings and it is McCray. I said, "I am following our guy, he paid the electronics guy and now they are eating lunch at a place called Sergi's II, I guess he owns this place and the one in Midlothian too. The electronics business must be good if he can operate two restaurants too." McCray says, "I'll do some checking, I think Mariano might be involved in those places. I seem to remember the name from someplace." I said, "I might be late getting to IIT. Buranski has Radko and Ivan coming to the office at two to pay them." McCray says, "You know where I'll be park in the lot by the CTA stop. It is only a short walk from there." I said, "Do you want me to tell you about last night at Buranski's?" He says, "No it isn't necessary we got the whole thing on tape." I ask "How?" He says, "We cleared the backup out last night after Buranski left. After next week, we shouldn't need to tape everything he will be on our side. Right?" I said, "That is the plan." He says, "I'll see you later for the big night."

One-fifteen Buranski walks out alone gets in his car and heads back the way he came. This time he gets on 83 and heads toward Orland Park. I wonder why he came here the way he did. Was he shopping for something or what? I'll have to check something later. That area looked pretty exclusive. All the houses are set back off the road nobody is right next to each other, good sized wooded lots, I am guessing three acres each a couple of mil per house. That's way too rich for my blood. I am following him and think that is where Big Al lives, I'll bet any amount you want. He was just casing the neighborhood I wonder how he found that out?

We get back to Orland Park a few minutes before two parks in the back and goes in. Grozdan says "Was I right?" Buranski says, "I would say yes but I want to ride by there again just to get a better look. I couldn't slow down or pull over to take photos. Next week I'll take a my Canon with the attachments." A few minutes later Radko and Ivan show up, they see the banner and tell Grozdan Happy Birthday, How old are you?" Grozdan says, "Old enough." Buranski says, "I'll tell you he is sixty-eight today." They look at the cake. Grozdan says "Help yourself, I'm not cutting anymore." They look at the coffee and Buranski says, "It's from ten o'clock it should be fine." They help themselves and Buranski says once they eat their cake and drink their coffee "I told you today was payday," he hands all three of them envelopes. Grozdan said, "I didn't do anything?" Buranski said, "You didn't need to I owe you more than that for letting me handle this operation. He wants me to look at another project once this one runs its course I told him I would let him know. I don't like being too restricted. I did this for Nikoli since I owe him, but I won't know until after next week if they will even get anything worthwhile out of this project." Grozdan said, "You did what they wanted you to do. It's not your fault if it turns up empty." Buranski said, "You can say that Nikoli might not be as nice. If he doesn't get what he wants somebody will pay for it one way or the other." Grozdan said, "Take your wife away this weekend and go to Wisconsin Lake Geneva forget about this job. Next week will be a different story." Buranski said, "I might just suggest it. Do you still have the place up there?" He said, "Why wouldn't I. I love the place right on the lake, it's peaceful it reminds me of home." On that note, I figure I can leave and go join McCray.

I drive down to IIT and find the lot by the CTA station park and walk over to where I'm supposed to meet McCray. He is talking to the rest of the staff making sure everybody understands their assignments. He nods to me in recognition that he sees I made it. He tells everybody to go relax for about an hour since he doesn't figure anybody will start arriving until after five-thirty. They will not even open the doors until six so that they can start screening the guests. Each member has the names and some have photos of the people they are assigned to shadow. The news media has just started to arrive to setup their equipment. The TV networks are all scattered for different vantage points, the newspaper guys are all wandering around wondering if there will be anything to write about that will get them a headline. I watch those guys and I think this is like a huge chess game, each one trying to get a move ahead on the board. About five-thirty the first group of demonstrators start to arrive, they are waving banners and carrying signs. They are directed by CPD to line up on the opposite side of the street, to stay out of the street so as not to impede traffic. They don't like that but the men in Blue are not going to give in to them. As long as they are peaceful they can stay there. At about ten to six some early arrivals start showing up. They line up by the doors to be first in line when they open the doors. The crowd starts building, since this is only by ticket benefit in the auditorium seating is first come first seated but when they adjourn to the dining hall that is by table and ticket to get closer to the head table. I look at the crowd of demonstrators and it is growing in size too as more people start arriving. At six-fifteen I spot Landholm he walks over to where a group of demonstrators are and talks to them for a few minutes. I figure he is giving them last minute instructions on what he wants them to do. As he turns to walk toward the hall, they start yelling slogans and raising banners to make a show for the press. Landholm smiles and waves to the camera crews that were testing their equipment.

    He walks across the street to go inside so I follow him to see where he is going to sit during the speeches. He goes through security screening and walks to the auditorium and goes inside. He takes a seat in the very last row so that he can get out easily once the speeches are finished. Pretty smart I figure. Also if the demonstration outside gets rowdy he can head outside to be there to put on a show. By six forty-five the auditorium is pretty full, there are a few empty seats but not many. On stage most of the people making speeches are already seated with the exception of the big man himself. He will come in right before his five minutes and then he will make the presentation they will escort him off stage and everybody will head to the dining hall once they are all seated he will be escorted in for the benefit dinner. Then and only then can we breathe a little easier. I find McCray and ask about our two mystery guests, still no sign of them but security is still on alert. Seven o'clock the Dean of the Science Department is introduced along with various people up on the stage. The foreign dignitaries from England, Denmark and Sweden, the Governor is announced he comes out and takes his seat, then the Mayor is announced he takes his seat next to the Governor on the right side of the stage. There is an empty seat between the Mayor and the Dean for the recipient of the award to sit. The speeches start once the introductions are made. After the first three speeches there is a disruption outside in the lobby. Everybody was on edge wondering what was going on It seems some of the demonstrators wanted to crash the function to make their voice heard. CPD in their shields and helmets stood their ground and sent them back across the street. No blows were exchanged only heated words. The camera crews were rolling the whole time and McCray and our team gave a big sigh when no one needed to use force to move them back.

At seven forty-five the Dean announces that the president will make the next speech and present the award. Hail to the chief begins and here comes the president with six bodyguards around him. He goes to the podium and thanks everyone for their applause and says "Tonight is not about me or my job, I am here tonight to talk about science and how important it is in our lives and to present an award to a distinguished graduate of IIT." He talks for about five minutes and makes the announcement. The recipient comes out from behind the curtain and walks over to the president to accept his award. The applause is loud and the president waves and is escorted away by his bodyguards. The Dean thanks everybody for attending the award ceremony and tells them dinner will be served in the dining hall at eight-thirty. So everybody starts leaving to get to their tables. Meanwhile outside the crowd is getting larger and noisier we can hear them as everyone heads to the dining hall. It was like as soon as the president left the stage it started. I look where did Landholm disappear to? I go out into the lobby he is watching security like he is waiting for somebody. McCray walks up behind me and says, "Our two mystery guests showed up, they have been detained until they get cleared." I said, "Landholm is in the lobby like he is looking for someone, I wonder if it's them he is looking for?" He says, "We'll know soon enough. So far security hasn't cleared them they are still sitting." Landholm walks over to security and talks to one of the people and comes back to where McCray and I are talking. He is watching us with some interest and walks over to us. He asks, "Are you two involved with security here?" McCray says, "In a way, why do you ask?" He says, "I was waiting for two associates from Vancouver whom I invited to attend tonight so they could see our president in person."

McCray said, "Mr. Landholm, I presume you knew security would be tight for tonight's function. So why would you invite two guests to attend?" Landholm said, "I am an associate professor of political science and I spoke at a seminar in Vancouver during the summer to a group of students and we have a mutual interest in this President. We feel he is moving in the right direction on certain matters. When I found out, he was going to present an award I ordered three tickets. One in my name and two using other names, they were supposed to pick up the tickets when they arrived but I haven't seen them yet." McCray said, "Come with me." I tag along to see what happens. They go to security and sure enough they are his two associates. McCray said, "We still need to clear them through security to make sure they don't pose a threat." Landholm said, "Call Professor Wiermach in Vancouver he can tell you what you need to know, this is a research assignment for them. Their passports should be good since they flew in today." McCray asked, "What about the demonstrators outside where to they come into play?" Landholm said, "This is free publicity for me I have a new book coming out in about ten days. I talked to some students at a few schools and they made the trip here. They are just carrying banners and waving signs to show support for me." McCray said, "Let's check these guys out." A few minutes later we all walk to the dining hall. Landholm and his guests are escorted to a table. McCray and I find the rest of the staff all seated at one table and we join them. McCray starts to ask a question and they strike up Hail to the chief so we all stand and wait for the president to come in and be seated. He says, "Ladies and Gentlemen thank you for the applause, it has been a very busy day and I'm hungry so let's eat." That drew another round of applause, he sat down and they started serving the meals.

At nine-thirty the president stood up and said, "Thank you all for attending this benefit tonight, the proceeds from tonight's benefit will go directly to the Science Department Foundation to encourage young men and women to pursue a career in science and to purchase new equipment for the department. Thank you all for allowing me to be your guest." Everybody applauded as his security detail came in and escorted him out the back way. McCray gave a thumbs up to our crew and we headed outside. The demonstrators were still hanging around and there were a few camera crews there to capture a few photos of prominent people that attended tonight's benefit. Landholm and his two friends walked across the street to talk to a group of demonstrators. He was greeted with a few cheers and he waved to the camera crews again. He was at home in his element. I said to McCray, "Sorry chief I felt there would be a problem here tonight. Things just didn't seem right to me." He said, "Jim, We were here only as a safety precaution, we would have been here anyway since we are part of national security. Besides it was good training for the rest of the staff." I asked, "Where was the big guy heading?" McCray said, "Hyde Park he was going to entertain a few friends and then head back to DC early tomorrow. He does his weekly Saturday morning address from the White House." I said, "Well at least we will find out if Buranski's equipment worked. Mariano isn't going to pay him the balance of the fee until he gets the code to retrieve the data from the recorder he setup there. Buranski said he needed to get back in there next week to verify that the backup worked. He wanted that in case the computer failed." McCray said, "Good work Jim, take the weekend off, I'm catching a plane to DC in two hours to appease my wife plus Sunday is Halloween night so I best be home.

I'll be back late Monday I'll call you when I get back." I go get my car and head home exhausted.

On my drive home, I have all these thoughts running through my head. Saturday I have free until I need to pick up Natalie for practice and spend some time with my old coach. Then Saturday night with Val, I really need to talk to her about our relationship and slow it down. Buranski was going to take his wife and daughter to Wisconsin for the weekend if they agreed to it. If Grozdan owns the place up there why not enjoy it. Pretty soon the snow will be flying and unless you are into winter sports that's not the place to be. Then Sunday is my day with Natalie. I wonder if she left me a message. I look at my cell phone and there isn't anything on it, I try to make a call and the phone is dead. Oh, well, I'll put it on the charger when I get home. I get home it is almost one. I check my answering machine and there is a message from Natalie about tomorrow. So I will call her before I call Val. Then I go to bed.

Chapter 18

Seven a.m. I wake up, I didn't set the alarm but I am awake so I toss on some clothes and head over to the donut place to get coffee and a cinnamon roll. My regular gal isn't working this morning, I look they have all sorts of Halloween decorated donuts, I figure what the heck I'll buy two dozen and take them for Natalie's practice as a treat. I go back home to drink my coffee and eat my cinnamon roll then look at the clock. It's still too early to call Natalie or Val. I go turn on the computer to see what is going on in the world. I would turn on the TV but Saturday mornings the local stations all cater to the youth with programs they would enjoy.

On the computer the local news feed has some topics to look at. Last night's fund raiser benefit dinner gets top billing. The lead headline, Together at the same function, The president, the governor, and the mayor all on the same stage and seated together at the head table for dinner. The president was all charm and thanked everybody and he was all smiles the whole night. After that he made a short visit to his house in Hyde Park for a gathering with some staunch supporters and personal friends. He flew back to DC at about five a.m. Chicago time. Demonstrations last night at IIT were staged to coincide with the release of a new book by Stephen J. Landholm the son of a noted left wing writer during the Vietnam War era whose writing is similar in content. He praises the current President for his effort to socialize the country with Health Care for everybody and his taking over the auto industry by saying they are too big to fail so we will shore them up. Landholm predicts his next move will be to provide free housing to all the homeless and make it so the unemployed don't lose their homes since they aren't working. It is the government's responsibility to help those that can't help themselves. In his opinion that would be the next logical step toward socializing this country. I think boy in the press will have a field day if he makes a suggestion along those lines.

I go to the kitchen and call Natalie first and tell her I was tied up all night. She said, "I only wanted to remind you about the practice and to find out what you thought about me going to a Halloween party with a couple of friends." I asked, "What did your Mother say?" Natalie said, "She said I think you should stay home or the two of us go out for dinner and a movie." I said, "I like your Mom's thinking." She said, "Aw Dad, It would be fun." I said, "I'm sure it would but it's your Mom's rules not mine, if you were with me that is what we would be doing too." She said, "You two are so much alike, I can't believe you didn't stay married to each other. Ok, I'll do what she wants to do." I can picture her sticking out her bottom lip pouting. She was so cute when she would do that when she didn't get her way. Then I call Val to find out if she has any plans tonight. She said, "As a matter of fact I do have plans tonight. I didn't hear from you so I was invited to a Halloween party at the VFW hall for the senior citizens in the community. Do you want to join me?" I said, "I was hoping we could go out to dinner and maybe see a movie and then talk for a while." She said, "The party for them is from seven until nine, I'll be free after that then we could grab a late dinner and talk." I asked, "Do you want me to pick you up at home or the hall?" She says "At home nine-fifteen." I said, "I'll see you then." I am like How come things have to be so complicated?

I go pick up Natalie to take her to practice. Good thing I left the donuts in the car this morning I would have forgotten them. She looked at the boxes. I said, "A treat for after practice. Do you think your coach will mind?" She says, "Not at all we are all usually hungry after practice. These will help." We get to her school and I see my old coach and tell him we can watch them practice. He says "Where's your change of clothes?" I said, "To tell you the truth I forgot. I had a late night last night downtown." He says, "Let's go watch your daughter play. We can do that next week." So we go inside to watch the team. I was surprised there were about twenty parents there to watch the practice. After the practice the coach thanked us all for attending. The girls play their first game next Tuesday at

Glenbard East in an Invitational game at six p.m. to any of you that are interested in watching them in their first game. There first real game that counts is Friday the 19th. I wrote that down, not that I know where I'll be or what I'll be doing. My old coach says, "You have a fine looking daughter and she has a good eye for when to take a shot." I said, "Thanks coach. I'll tell her what you said. I'll see you next week and I'll be ready to run, I need the exercise." He says, "We all do but most find other things to do. I did it for so long so it's easy for me to exercise. It is part of my daily routine." After practice all the girls grab donuts and eat them before they head to the locker room to change. Natalie comes out and says, "Thanks, Dad, the girls were glad you brought the donuts." I drove her home and asked her "So what did you and your Mother decide to do?" She said, "We are going to dinner and then we are going to bowl I told her I beat you one game. She said there wasn't anything good at the movies and she wants to see if she can still bowl." I said "Have fun, I'll pick you up tomorrow after church OK?" She says, "Yes, I'll tell Mom I know that is easier to pick me up there. I love you Dad." I said "I love you sweetie. Have fun and take it easy on your Mom, I know she has to be rusty."

I go home and decide I'll take a nap. I don't have to pick up Val until nine-fifteen. I put a college football game on for noise and fall asleep on the sofa. I wake up about six and I'm hungry. I'm not picking Val up until after nine, I best chew on something to hold me over I haven't eaten since breakfast. I call Rocko at the pizza joint and order a small special well done and go pick it up. He says, "On Saturday night you are getting a small, I said I haven't eaten since breakfast and I am going out with a lady friend later." He says, "I can dig it." I go home and eat the pizza then get dressed to go out. I get to Val's a little after nine so I figure I'll wait, she said nine-fifteen. I ring the bell and she said, "Come in I need to change, I just got home." She was wearing some make up and wearing a "Cat in The Hat" hat and she had cat whiskers on her nose and a cattail on her butt. I said, "I didn't know you liked Dr. Seuss." She said, "It's just an easy costume to make and the seniors don't care it was just for fun. They all wanted to eat and drink. Most of them didn't even dress up."

We went to a restaurant not too far from her place. They are open until midnight on the weekends. Neither one of us had a taste for anything special so that was why we picked this place. I ordered a chopped steak with a baked potato she had Chicken Divan and a cup of soup. We talked for a while about our day. I told her about Natalie and her practice and she told me about her day. She said, "Tony was getting on her nerves prying again." I said, "I sort of figured that. He really does like to keep an eye on you." She said, "I know he means well but he drives me crazy." I said, "I'll talk to him." She said, "He won't listen, he has his own ideas about you and me. I told him you were not ready to settle down yet, you are too concerned with your daughter and the next few years to even think about anything else." I said, "You were reading my mind. I wanted to talk to you about our relationship but you figured it out before I could tell you." She says, "I told you no strings, I do enjoy your company, I don't expect anything from you, I mean I would like to see you more often but I understand. Don't beat yourself up over it. I'm a big girl. Just call me." So I said, "Fair enough." I asked, "What do you want to do now?" She said, "Go back to my place, I'll put on a pot of coffee and we'll have apple cobbler for dessert after." I said, "Sounds good to me." So we went back to her place. I stayed all night and left at eight to shower and change to pick up Natalie after church.

I picked up Natalie at almost ten at church. Rachael asked, "What are your plans today?" I said, "We never even talked about it. We will wing it today." Natalie said, "Did you have breakfast yet?" I said, "As a matter of fact no, I did have coffee but that was it. I wasn't really hungry." Natalie said, "Do you want me to cook and we can just goof off today?" I said, "If I had eggs, bacon, and milk that would probably work, with my schedule I haven't been shopping for anything." She said, "Oh! Dad, how much trouble is it to stop at Jewel or Dominick's once a week?" I said, "Probably not too much if you enjoy doing that. I only go when I am out of coffee then I pick up things that I might need." She said, "OK let's go someplace different, I was reading about an omelet place where you can order anything you like. It's not too far from here it's called EggsCetra I think." I said, "I remember seeing an ad but never checked it out. We'll go there and then we can go shopping, I'll let you plan our dinner." She said, "Deal." We found the place and it was pretty good, Natalie was happy since she could order it loaded with veggies. I was not that adventuresome I had a Denver omelet. After breakfast we stopped at Dominick's and bought a bunch of things and headed to my place.

Natalie challenged me to a few games of checkers after we got home. We played five games I won three but it was a struggle, she is getting better. I looked at the schedule for the Bears, it is their bye week, the Hawks play the Rangers in New York Monday night. The Bulls played last night. Boy for a sports town there is nothing going on today. I don't want to just watch football for the sake of watching football. Natalie heads to the kitchen to plan her Sunday surprise. I asked her what she was making and that was what she told me. We did pick up the Sunday paper for a change so I started leafing through it. It has been ages since I sat down with a Sunday paper. I used to read the Tribune religiously for years. It was chocked full of interesting sections not like the New York Times or the Washington Post but close. Then with computers and instant news everywhere the paper changed plus management changed and the paper needed to change. In my opinion, it wasn't for the better but that's only my opinion. There are only a few places you can get the New York Times now, years ago you could pick it up at a bunch of places. I enjoy reading it from time to time since they always have so much content I think the last time I picked one up it took me a week to read every section. Now you can subscribe to it online but to me that isn't the real deal, the heft of the paper and all the sections, there is no way I could read that on line.

I am sitting there reading and the smells from the kitchen are getting stronger. A few minutes later Natalie brings me a fresh cup of coffee and asks, "Does my surprise smell good?" I said, "It sure does." She says, "We still have an hour or so until it's ready, do you want to go shoot some hoops with me?" I said, "Sure sweetie let me change to my sweats." She says, "I am going to change too." So we go shoot hoops for about forty-five minutes and head back to my place. Natalie says, "I get the shower first, so I can finish dinner." I said, "No problem, I can wait." Before she heads to the shower she fills my coffee cup and says "No peeking." Whatever she made I can smell the garlic the aroma is unmistakable but a smell I enjoy. After her shower she says, "The shower is all yours, by the time you are dressed dinner should be on the table if it turned out right." I said "It sure smells good." She says, "Thanks, Dad, I read this recipe and was itching to make it so we'll find out if it's any good." I took my shower and put on my jeans and sweatshirt and went to the table. Natalie says, "This is an easy version of Chicken Tetrazzini and Garlic Bread." I tasted it and said, "I give the chef four stars." She beamed with pride and took a bow. After dinner, we sat and talked until it was time to take her home.

I asked, "Do you need dessert?" She said, "Not today I am stuffed, are you sure you won't eat what's left?" I said, "Take it home you and your Mom can eat the rest tomorrow, I'm sure she will enjoy it as much as I did." I drove her home and walked her to the door and Rachael opened it. Natalie was carrying the glass dish with the rest of the dinner in it. Rachael asked, "What's this?" I said, "Natalie made a new dish and I told her to take the rest of it home since I never know when I'll be home for dinner. It was delicious trust me." She took a smell and said, "I might dig into it when we go inside if it tastes as good as it smells." I said, "Natalie I'll try to make Tuesday's game, no promise but I'll try." Natalie said,s "Thanks Dad, I love you and thank you for letting me cook dinner." I said "I love you too sweetie and thank you for making that dish. It was terrific."

Chapter 19

Monday morning six o'clock I am awake and think wait what do I need to do this morning. I need to meet Buranski at the Pancake House on 45 at nine for breakfast and tell him what McCray wants him to try doing when he sees Mariano on Wednesday to collect the rest of his fee. Today, I think his guys were starting the project in Worth at eight. I guess, I should cruise by his house to see if he is going there before we meet for breakfast. I calculate the time from his house to Worth and figure I should be at his house before seven-fifteen. Knowing him he wants to make sure his guys are on time and to tell Ivan anything he may have forgotten. Sure enough he backs out of the garage at seven-fifteen so I follow him. We get to the house in Worth about ten minutes to eight. A few minutes later Ivan and his crew show up. There are four guys in one car, Ivan and two other guys in his van. Buranski looks at the men and asks Ivan a question and then goes and rings the bell. Mr. Grozewski comes to the door. Buranski shakes his hand and talks to him for a few minutes. In the driveway there is a load of wood and stuff for the second floor all covered with plastic so in case it rained it wouldn't get wet. Ivan tells a couple of guys what he wants them to do and then Ivan and Buranski follow Mr. Grozewski inside. About fifteen minutes later, Buranski walks out gets in his car and drives away. I look at the clock it is almost eight-thirty. I follow him to the Pancake House for our meeting.

We get to the Pancake House at five minutes to nine. He walks in and I follow him. We get a booth in the back away from the windows so we can talk. I asked, "How was your weekend?" He said, "Pretty good we went to Lake Geneva and just relaxed." I said, "I'm glad to hear that." I told him mine was pretty good too and then got down to the matter at hand. I said, "McCray would like you to try getting a little more detail from Mariano if you can. We are trying to figure out who his real customer is and if they were able to get any information Friday night from the big guys visit." Buranski said, "I will try but he doesn't like to talk much. He is suspicious of everybody even Giovani, the way he treated him I was surprised. To him it was just another job, he didn't want any slip ups." I said, "McCray was impressed how you didn't let anything slip out and that you followed Mariano's instructions to the letter. Now if we could just figure out where the information is getting transferred too he would be even happier." Buranski said, "I might be able to put a trace in the system that will follow the info from Hyde Park to where ever he is sending it too as long as he just forward it. If he edits it and reposts it then we are out in the cold no clue." I asked, "You sure that you can do something like that?" Buranski said, "I remember something we did in a class in Russia for an exercise on tracking things that were sent so I think yes, we should be able to do it. I will need to tie in another line but there is another dead line there so I'll hook it up to the system and feed it to a different number that we can monitor."

I said, "McCray wants a sit down meeting with you after you fulfill your obligation to Mariano and Filchev." Buranski said, "We can work that out, this week I have a lot of things to clear up since I was tied up with that project." I said, "Let me know what works for you and I will set it up, McCray usually likes these meetings downtown in his office." Buranski said, "That should be OK, I will arrange my schedule and let you know what works for me." I said, "Here is my cell phone number." Buranski said, "I'll write it down for later use, I don't want it in my phone when I meet Mariano." I said, "Good thinking, you never know what is going to happen next." We talked for about an hour at least and covered a lot of information. Buranski said, "Tomorrow I will find out if I can get in the house to finish things up. It will just be Radko and myself since my foreman is running the other job. I only need a little help and he is cleared." I said, "Then the next day you meet with your client and turn over everything. The ID's, the code, and then he pays you the balance of your fee if I recall what you said before." Buranski said, "Then I'm done with him until April when the doctor moves out, then we need to retrieve all the equipment before the owner returns and finish the remodeling that we were doing." I said, "Stay on your toes around Mariano and his kind, they can get nasty if things aren't to their liking." Buranski said, "No more difficult than Nikoli, I'm sure. People just disappeared no questions asked." I said, "Call me with a day and time." Buranski said, "Call me Karl that is what my friends call me." I said, "OK Karl, call me Jim." We shake hands, I pick up the tab and we leave the restaurant. He heads to Orland Park and I head downtown to write my report for McCray. I get downtown at eleven-thirty and go to the office. Vicki said, "Hello Jim, how was your weekend?" So I told her about it but left out spending the night with Val.

I go back to my cubby hole to start writing and it is really quiet in the office. I write my report and print out a copy to read before I save it for McCray's eyes. I walk up by the break room fix a cup of coffee and go ask Vicki," Where is everybody today?" She said, "Mr. McCray said they had today off since he wouldn't be back until late and they all did a good job Friday night and needed to be rewarded." I said, "How did he do that?" She said, "He called them all Saturday when he got home and found out he had to attend a meeting in DC this morning before he could schedule his return flight so it will be late when he gets back." I said, "Thanks for the update Vicki, I am going to go finish this. I'll keep you company so you aren't sitting here alone." She said, "That's nice of you Jim, I figure I'll stay until around three and I'll skip lunch then leave early and eat then." I said, "I'll join you I had a good breakfast so I'm good until then." I write my report and make sure everything is in there, make a disc and label it for McCray and put it in his bin of things to review with a hand written note. That says to call me if he has any questions.

I walk up by Vicki about three, she turns everything off, switches the phone to record and we leave the office. I get my car and say, "Let's eat someplace a little different, I have a taste for a good steak." She says, "Morton's is always good and they won't be jammed at this hour. I'll warn you it's pricey." I said, "I have heard of them and I know it will cost more than our usual lunch but that's what I have a taste for." So we drive over to Morton's, they have valet parking, so we get out and go inside. I look at the menu. Yes indeed it is pricey, no backing down now. I think I have what two hundred with me, in my emergency fund in case my car breaks down or whatever. I'll just replace it later in the week when I go to the bank. We eat our meal and talk for about two hours I look at the clock and it is already six. I think WOW we just had a great meal and we talked for over two hours, no interruptions. The place is starting to get crowded, I guess we should free up another table for them, not that they are looking at us wondering when we are going to leave. Vicki smiles and says, "Jim, I really enjoyed having dinner with you, I never thought you and I could just talk like this for this long and we never talked about work or the boss or sports." I said, "I feel the same way; I find your company and our conversation scintillating if I may use a three dollar word." She says, "Jim, you contributed as much to the conversation as I did." We talked about everything under the sun, I told her about my fascination with New York Times or the Washington Post and she told me she has the boss bring her The Washington Post every time he comes back from DC. She is truly the intellectual type I could tell that just from our lunch conversations I just didn't realize how well read she is. We get our bill and I pay for dinner with my American Express card, then go out front to get my car. I tip the valet attendant and drive her home.

She asks, "Do you want to see the place?" I say, "Sure, I don't have any plans for tonight." She says, "There is parking on the side, I have access to a parking spot but I never bought a car, I don't need one since I am always downtown." We park and go up to her converted loft. It is pretty neat, no space is unused, I think I should remember a couple of these things for my place it would be a lot neater. She shows me her bedroom and says if you look just right you can see the lake. She brushes real close to me and pulls the curtain and points see there and I look just a little glimpse but you can see it. She turns and we kiss, it wasn't planned but it sort of just happened. I think why did I let that happen? She looks at me as if to say, Is that the best you can do buster? Then I feel I best call it a night but she takes my hand and I stay all night.

Chapter 20

The next morning I am awake at six and I look at her sleeping so peaceful, I hate to disturb her but I need to get going if I'm going to keep an eye on Buranski. I look at my cell phone, there is a message from McCray from last night eleven thirty. I listen to the message. McCray says, "Call me in the morning after nine I just got in town and I'm going to get some sleep." Vicki is still sleeping, I tiptoe around the room and get dressed and figure I should write her a note, I am looking for something to write on and she gets out of bed and wraps the sheet around her and asks "Leaving already?" I said, "If I was home I would already be gone getting my coffee and a cinnamon roll before starting my day." She says, "I have something better." I look at her and say, "Yes you sure do, I did enjoy my dinner and our night. I didn't plan for this to happen" She says, "I know but I did." She pulls me toward her and gives me a big kiss and says "Will that keep you all day?" I said, "It'll have to, I'll call you once I know what I'm doing later." I walk to my car and I think to myself. Now Jimbo you have a real problem, do I need to lay this out in black and white. I do that from time to time talking to myself. Especially when I do something really stupid and this falls into that category.

I look at the clock, I'm like I might as well just drive to Orland Park no sense driving all the way out there to turn around and go there. I'll stop on the way and get some breakfast. I drive to a pancake joint in Orland Park and go have breakfast and drive to Buranski's office. I get there a few minutes to eight, he isn't here yet. I park in a good spot to keep an eye on his building. He was going to see if he could get in there today but I don't know if that happened. A couple of minutes later Buranski arrives and parks in the back. He goes inside and sets up the coffee pot, a few minutes later here comes Dragan. He says, "What are you running late this morning?"

Buranski says, "No this is my normal time, you got spoiled when I was getting here at seven or a little after." They talked for a while, the coffee was finished and they fixed their cups and talked some more. Buranski says, "So how are the Wedding plans coming along?" Dragan said, "Sofia and her girlfriends were writing invitations last night. They are going to mail them today. It is all set for Friday night after Thanksgiving and then Saturday we leave for Bulgaria. I talked to Grozdan, he said he will help my guy if he has any problems while I'm gone. Eight days what can happen?" Buranski says, "Your guy, do you trust him?" Dragan says, "Yes, Why do you ask?" Buranski says, "Call Radko he has a couple of guys that can sit with your guy to make sure he doesn't try anything foolish. As insurance." Dragan says, "I'll think about it." He finishes his coffee and leaves.

Buranski picks up the phone and makes a call "Hello, what did you find out? Can we get in there today for a couple of hours? Yes, call me back at this number. Thank you." Buranski gets busy with projects on his desk. Goes over to the schedule board and makes a few notes and goes back to his desk. Twenty minutes later the phone rings he answers it "KBW Construction, Karl speaking. Yes, we can get in there after lunch. Three hours tops. No just two, myself and Radko. Your guys coming here or meet them at 55th? 55th OK, One o'clock got it." Buranski picks up the phone. "Radko, yes we can do the job today be here at twelve-fifteen, bring a van." Buranski is working in his office, I can hear him as he moves around mumbling to himself. I can't understand what he is mumbling about, maybe he is trying to recall the training exercise so he remembers all the steps when he tries setting up another line to trace the original one. He goes back to his desk and turns on the computer, I don't know what he is looking for but he is sure concentrating on the computer for one solid hour.

A few minutes after twelve Radko shows up with a U-Haul van and parks in front and rings the bell. Buranski was still concentrating on the computer and jumped when he heard the bell. He goes out and unlocks the door for Radko and they go into his office. Radko said, "You look nervous. Any problems I should know about?" Buranski said, "I was trying to find some information about something I want to try when we get to Hyde Park to finish the job. It is complicated but I think it will work. I need you to keep the two guys away from me while I set up the backup and run a test to make sure everything will work right, then we need to seal up the one wall so nobody sees the other phone lines. You paint the wall after I'm done and we install another jack and plug in the computer and we are done." Radko said, "That shouldn't be a problem, I can give the one guy another lesson about an hour and his buddy will watch." Buranski said, "That should give me enough time to check everything and test it so we know the backup is working properly. Mariano is driving me crazy with all these little details. He said it is only in case something happens to the feed he can recover the backup. I told him he doesn't have anything to worry about that the system is good. But he worries." Radko said," Can you blame him the money he is paying you, how much is he charging his customer?" Buranski said, "I know what you mean, he gets a big fat fee and doesn't get his hands dirty. We do the work, take the chances and he sits at home and turns on the computer to listen to idle chatter or just forward everything to his customer to decipher. OK I'm ready let's go." Buranski locks the back, turns the lights out and they go out the front and head to the city. I follow them to 55th and then head to Halsted and drive to McCray's office.

    I get there about one-fifteen, park and go in. Vicki looks extremely good this afternoon. I point to McCray's office. She says, "He went out to lunch with Mr. Schaunessy about an hour ago. He will be back after two." I ask, "Where is the rest of the staff?" She says, "Lunch they will be getting back shortly." I head back to my cubby hole to write today's report. A few minutes after two, McCray gets back and he comes back to my cubby hole to talk. I told him what I heard this morning and he says, "Well after tomorrow and then when we can set up the meeting with our guy we will be able to put this case behind us for the most part." I said, "Buranski seemed nervous this morning like he wasn't sure if this dual line he is going to hook up will work." McCray says, "I can imagine he would since if it does work and his customer finds out there could be unpleasant repercussions. Mariano is no slouch in that department he has plenty of options." I asked, "So what was the meeting in DC about if I might ask?" McCray says, "They want me to think about Schaunessy's job, I guess he is approaching retirement age and they want somebody they can count on and my name was presented by Schaunessy. I told them I would let them know. My wife wants me to transfer back to DC in January so I have a bit of a dilemma." I ask, "How much different would it be if you took the job, you could still commute like you do now." He says, "My wife thinks the children are at the age where I should be around a lot more and be involved in their lives more." I went "Ouch, that is like playing a trump card in bridge, you need to follow suit." He says, "Exactly and that is what she is banking on." I said, "I wouldn't want to be in your shoes with that decision." I said, "Buranski and Radko are in Hyde Park right now finishing up the job. Tomorrow he has a meeting with Mariano to get the rest of his fee and to give him the access code and their security ID Cards. Mariano is sure a stickler for details, no wonder that Filchev decided to use him. Plus he knows Buranski's work ethic." McCray says, "We'll talk more later."

 I worked until about four and figured I should head back to Orland Park to find out how everything went. I stop by Vicki on the way out to tell her I had plans tonight. My daughter has her first game today at Glenbard at six. I said, "I will call you after her game to talk." She says, "I'll be home alone all night." Then she hands me one of her keys. On my drive to Orland Park, I am thinking to myself. I am really in for a big problem here. I don't want to hurt Val, I do enjoy her company but with Vicki it is so different. I know I haven't known her as long as I know Val, yet the vibes are there. The touch, the feel, the scent all encouraging me to go back again tonight to find out for real if it is the right thing to do. I don't even have anybody I can talk to about this situation. I know if I let Val down Tony will be hotter than hell about it since he told me outright, if it's not right cut it off with Val don't play her along. How did I know I would wind up in this situation? I get to Orland Park and Buranski isn't back yet so I think I should run over to the Gyro place real quick and grab a sandwich since I am going to try to make Natalie's game at six and

I should eat something first. I go pick up a sandwich and drive back to his office.

They get there at five o'clock and Radko leaves Buranski out in front and drives away. Buranski goes inside and makes a phone call. "Hello this is Karl, Yes, I'll hold. We have a problem with the equipment, It isn't working right. I checked all the connections, yes I checked those too. We aren't getting any feed. I checked the backup it is working fine but the main feed was dead. Where do you think the problem is? No I didn't see any loose wires anyplace. Check your signal to see if you get anything. You have a signal, then the problem has to be there. Tomorrow nine a.m., yes I can be there." I think it must be Sergi and a problem with the new equipment. Buranski makes another call "Hello, yes I know there is a problem, I just talked to them about it, I am going there tomorrow at nine to solve it. We need to get back in there tomorrow after lunch one hour tops. Ok I'll talk to you after we fix the problem." Buranski looks at the clock and makes another call "Hi Ana, Yes I am leaving as soon as I lock the place up. I'll be home by six." I am like good I might just make it before the game starts. Buranski leaves and I follow until I get to Roosevelt and head to Glenbard HS.

I get there just as the teams take the floor, I see Natalie and wave. They played a pretty good game. Glenbard is a stronger school in basketball than her school is. This was an invitational game to get the squads use to playing in a game like situation rather than just practice. They only lost by four points. I saw Natalie after the game before she got on the team bus. I told her I thought she played good and she made some clutch shots. I said, "This is only a warm up game." She says, "I know but I wanted us to beat them." I said, "Wait until they count, don't show everything you have in these kind of games, save it for when it counts." She says, "Thanks Dad for coming I didn't see any other dads a couple of Mom's made it." I said, "I love you sweetie, call me later." She said, "I love you too, and I'll try later." I go outside to drive home and I think. Do I dare go to see Vicki? Besides, I ask Natalie to call me later. I could call Vicki and apologize and say I had a prior commitment that I forgot about . . .

Nah, she would know I was lying. McCray said we would talk more later I look at my cell phone. He called while I was watching Natalie play basketball. I call him and it goes to voice mail. So I leave him a message and head downtown. I might as well face the music. Tomorrow is another day.

Chapter 21

Wednesday morning I am up at six o'clock. This morning I am not as quiet as I was yesterday morning but Vicki doesn't stir. I get dressed and fix myself a cup of coffee. Vicki set up the coffee pot last night so it would perk and be ready for six. We talked until after two I think. I got here at a little after eight. She asked, "Have you eaten?" I said, "I had a sandwich at about five." She asked if I like Chinese, I said sometimes. So we ordered from a place and they delivered. The food was good. We started talking and the next thing I know it is after one and then we talked a little while longer and went to bed. I don't know if it was me or the aroma of the coffee that woke her up. She wraps the sheet around her and joins me at the table. She asks, "How does the coffee taste?" I said "Pretty good." She says, "I don't usually make coffee but I know you, you live on it so I figured I should set it up so you have it. Sorry I don't have any cinnamon rolls." I said, "That isn't a problem. You are sweeter than any cinnamon roll." She leans over and kisses me and asks "Still sweet?" I said, "Yes, very." We talked for about thirty minutes and I said "I hate to but, I have a job to do." She gives me another big kiss and asks "Will I see you later?" I said, "Sometime. I don't know when or where." Then I head to Orland Park since it is already seven-twenty. I know Buranski has to meet Sergi at nine but I think he will go to the office before he goes there since he has other things to take care of. Today is going to be very busy I think and then tonight there could be a late meeting if everything turns out OK.

I get to Orland Park at ten after eight, not too bad considering I stopped at a donut shop to get a large coffee and a cinnamon roll. That will hold me until lunch time. Buranski is in the office and on the phone. I listen and try to figure out who he is talking to but not having much luck. At eight-thirty, Dragan and Grozdan both walk in the back way. Buranski holds up his hand as if to say quiet. They go to Grozdan's office so Buranski can finish his conversation. I am thinking maybe it is Mariano about another problem. Buranski says, "Ok, I can talk now." And Dragan and Grozdan come into his office. He says, "Sorry but the connection was bad and I could barely hear Nikoli. He wanted to know if I finished the job in Hyde Park, I guess his customers want to make sure before they transfer the rest of the funds. I asked him if he received anything over the weekend. He said, "Only a little bit but it was enough to know the system worked. There will be more meetings in a few weeks. I was told." Grozdan says, "Well now you can stop worrying about Nikoli, you only have to worry about getting the rest of your money." He said, "That should not be a problem, I have something Mariano needs he doesn't get it until I get the rest of the money. Tomorrow at the latest." Then he picks up the phone and makes a phone call "Hi this is Karl, tell him I will be ten minutes late. Thank you." He grabs a folder and heads out the back door and says, "I'll be back in about two hours, if Radko calls tell him to be here at noon with the van."

I follow him but I know where he is going and decide I should run home to check on things there. I haven't been there since Monday morning besides I need to grab a couple more changes of clothes. I don't want to wear the same jeans another day. I better run by the bank too, since my funds are almost gone. I never checked my messages at home, I know I should be able to get them, I just need to find the instruction sheet and remember my ID number. Too many numbers and ID's to keep straight. I miss the old days, no computer, no cell phone, we just did our job, blind to a lot of things but it always worked out. How did we get so dependent on these electronic gadgets? Sure, we have instant access to a boatload of information but that doesn't necessarily mean we are smarter. Half the time you spend trying to find where to get the information you are looking for, there is so much wasted time as far as I'm concerned. Just put me in the field tell me what you want me to do no tools, no electronics, I'll do the job. This stuff is mind boggling for sure. Oh well we can't stop progress, if it weren't for computers and technology we would have never landed on the moon or sent spacecraft deep into space to send photos back from Mars. But I do miss the mystery and the digging it took to do what we do.

I get home check my messages. Natalie called me late Tuesday just to say thanks again for watching me play. McCray called too and said he would talk to me this afternoon. He wants me to meet him at the restaurant about one for lunch. I am like why either of them didn't call my cell phone. I look at my cell phone it is dead again. I think when did I get this phone? Maybe the lithium batteries need changing, I look at the time and think I can probably stop by the phone store and get an upgrade, they should be able to transfer all my numbers. I think how many numbers do I have of people I call ten at tops. I think I bet I can't remember more than three numbers. I look at the mail grab some clothes and put them in a duffle bag. I am like tonight I should call Val at least and apologize for not calling her since Sunday. I don't really know what I am going to tell her. Truthfully I should go see her and explain this is not going to work and tell her that did enjoy our times together. No further explanation, just kiss her on the cheek and leave. Then I'll have to go tell Tony that I broke it off, I didn't want to hurt Val so it was better just to end it now before we got too far in. I can hear him rant but I'll just have to listen. I feel better already, now I just need to follow through. I stop at the phone store to get a new phone, I have had this one four years already. They were surprised I didn't come back in every year for a new phone, since it is part of the deal. Me I use it as a tool not for playing games or texting. I download things on my laptop and send photos. Then I head downtown to talk to McCray. I'll go back to Orland Park after lunch.

I park real close to the restaurant and wait for McCray to walk up to my SUV. He gets there right at one and we go inside to his favorite booth in the back. He says, "I missed you last night, were you out?" I said, "Yes as a matter of fact I was. I went to watch my daughter play her first game and then I had another commitment to attend too. My cell phone died and I didn't know it until today when I went home to check on a few things. I just picked up a new phone so I should be good for a couple of years." He said, "I am not prying, I just wanted to talk about my situation. Since I couldn't get you I called my wife and we talked everything through. I told DC I would take the job but I needed more weekends at home. They asked me who should take over my job and I said you were the most qualified but I think you would miss the field work too much to take it. What do you think? It would be a big step up for you. You would have to deal with me and put up with all of DC's whims. However, it might make it easier for you to decide what you want to do with your personal life. Monetarily it would be easier to pay for Natalie's schooling with a substantial increase in pay plus perks like a car, parking, and expense account just to mention a few." I said, "Rodger I don't know anything about your job, I am a good field agent period. The reports and dealing with the mucky mucks that's your thing." He said, "If you remember I was a field agent before I took this job. You learn quickly and I would have about six months to groom you if you are interested." I said, "I'll have to think this over real hard and talk to a few people before I give you my decision." He said, "Fair enough." We eat our lunch so I can head back to Orland Park. I tell McCray "I will talk to you later I need to find out if our man has a meeting tonight to get paid or if it is going to be tomorrow. Oh! by the way he talked to Nikoli this morning the system worked. I'll write it all down in my report for tomorrow."

    I drive back to Orland Park and get there around three-thirty. McCray and I talked for two hours over lunch. I didn't think we could talk that long. I can't get over him telling DC I am the most qualified to fill his spot. Boy, what would Rachael think if I was still married to her? Why did that just POP into my head? It is like when Natalie and I were bowling and I kept thinking about Rachael. This is really weird. I get the feeling that somewhere deep down inside of me I never really got over her. We got divorced so I could live my life and do my job and she could have her career and raise Natalie. What was that Natalie said, "I can't believe you and Mom still aren't married to each other, you are so much alike."

    Four o'clock Buranski and Radko get back from Hyde Park. They park in front and go inside. Grozdan says, "I thought you said this would take an hour tops." Radko says, "That's what he told me too." Buranski says, "I just wanted to make doubly sure that the system was working properly. Did you get the feed on the computer?" Grozdan says, "Yes if you can call it that, just some buzzing and dial tones." Buranski says, "That was the best I could do, nobody was inside the house so I sent some signals to jam their electronics that started the buzzing until they switched it off. Whenever somebody is inside and starts to talk the machine will start recording and then transmit the info to the computers. His and ours." Grozdan asks "Any way they can find out you did that?" He says, "Not without tearing the system apart, I buried the other feed inside the wall and the other jack leads to a dead phone. Somebody would have to knock the wall down to find it." Radko says, "I need to get the van back and get to the gym. I'll see you tomorrow after three." Buranski says, "Any change I'll call you." A few minutes later Dragan comes in and says, "You ready? I promised Sofia I would be at her house early she wants me to go with her to pick out stuff for the tables and sample the food." Grozdan says, "I know, you just go keep her happy and agree to everything. I was like you just get it done. For them it is a big deal, they worry about the food and the decorations." They leave and Buranski is alone. He is fiddling with stuff on his desk. Five o'clock the phone rings he answers it "KBW Construction Karl speaking. Yes, tomorrow at eleven. Where? I know the place. Yes, I was there once. Yes for a play. Go to the dining room. Got it." He picks up the phone and makes a call "Hi Ana, Yes I'll be home the meeting is tomorrow. I'll tell you all about it when I get home."

 I don't know who is happier this project is all but done him or me. Maybe I can get back to some sort of a regular life after tomorrow. Yes I know we still have to do the face to face with McCray more formality than anything else. By my estimation the big guy will be in Hyde Park five or six times between now and April when everything gets ripped out. That is a lot of money for so few opportunities to listen to some high-level conversations. Maybe they are anticipating more high-level talks during the holiday break. He said something about in a few weeks there would be more meetings. I don't know where he gets the inside line. McCray said they thought they found out where the leak was but I'm not so sure based on what he said. That information could only come from somebody in the security detail in DC, since they have to do advanced planning. They would know before the information becomes public. Buranski leaves at about six and I follow him. I follow him home and then head to the Maple Street Café to talk to Tony, my mind is made up and then I'll go talk to Val.

I drive to the Maple Street Café and walk in and Val is working. I said, "I thought you were off tonight I was going to call you and then stop by to see you after I talked to Tony." She said, "So talk." I said, "I really wanted us to be alone." She said, "Let me guess, you want to stop seeing me Right? So you wanted to tell Tony so he wouldn't get too mad since you know how he is." I said, "I wanted to tell you how much I enjoyed the times we were together and I didn't want you to get hurt." She said, "I figured Sunday morning when you left that you were not going to come back, maybe intuition but I had a feeling. I told Tony I thought we were through since Saturday night was not like the other nights." I said, "Val you are a very special lady and I hope that you will find the right guy for you." Tony comes out of the kitchen and said, "Is what I heard true, that you and Val are through?" I said, "I wanted to talk to you before I talked to her but she was here not at home." Tony said, "She has a sense when things aren't going to work, she can feel it or something. So are you going to eat or just drink coffee?" I said, "I'll eat, fix me a special." He heads back to the kitchen. Val comes over and talks to me like nothing happened. She is her usual happy person. I eat my dinner pay my bill and tell them I'll see them most likely later in the week. I look at the clock it is already eight-thirty. I head downtown to see Vicki.

I get to her place after nine and go to her loft. I started to put my key in the door and she opens the door and says "I was wondering if you would be here tonight or not and she plants a big kiss on my lips." We go inside and she has food on the table. I looked and she had two places set, a bottle of wine, some bread, and I smell pasta cooking. She said, "I hope you are hungry I don't usually cook but I was in the mood for some Italian food tonight, I hope you don't mind." I said, "No I don't mind it smells delicious." She dishes up the food and I opened the wine and poured two glasses. She made homemade meatballs and spaghetti with a light marinara sauce. I could tell the meatballs were homemade they were twice the size of the ones that most restaurants use and the flavor was fantastic. She said, "I mix the beef and sausage together with some chopped onion and garlic and brown them in olive oil and then cook them in the oven for about thirty minutes first." The dinner was extremely good, I probably ate more than I should but it was that good. It was almost eleven and we were just talking about things in general, she didn't ask me about my day or anything. She had the movie review section from the Sunday paper lying on the buffet table, I looked at it and she said, "I was looking at what is opening this month. Do you want to see the latest chapter of Harry Potter? It opens the 19th some places might even do it on the 18th after midnight." I said, "I think I only saw the first one with Natalie. Why do you ask?" She said, "I enjoy the writing and thought it might be fun to go with you to the movie when it opens." I said, "I'll think about it." Then we talked until after one and went to bed.

Chapter 22

Six o'clock and I am awake, I smell the coffee and think this is really nice. My coffee will be ready before I am out of the shower. Vicki is curled up and has the sheet half covering her head. I go take a quick shower and get dressed. I pour my coffee and she stirs and looks at the clock and completely buries her head. I sit there drinking my coffee trying not to laugh. Finally I bust out with a laugh she turns and says "What's so funny?" I said "You were bound and determined to cover your head and you pulled all the covers up but your feet and behind were totally uncovered. You were so cute doing that I couldn't help myself." She wrapped the sheet around her and joined me at the table. She asks, "Did you sleep OK?" I said, "Once we went to sleep. Yes. Thank goodness I don't have to punch a time clock or have a boss standing over my shoulder I might need to grab a nap later." She says, "You are the one that started it." I said, "I know but I was just getting even with you for last night." She says, "It was fun, besides I can sleep for a couple of hours before I need to go to the office." I said, "Lucky you." I kiss her and say "I'll see you later, today will be hectic from the way things are shaping up." She holds me and says, "You know where I'll be." And then she kisses me again before I leave then she goes back over to the bed and covers her head.

I drive to Orland Park and get there at almost eight. Buranski is there already he is sitting at his desk talking on the phone. He hangs up the phone and goes over to the schedule board and makes some notes. A few minutes later, Dragan comes in and pours some coffee, Buranski gets up and refills his cup and they start talking. He asks, "How was the food last night?" Dragan says, "It was good but I told Sophia we don't need so many different things." She says, "That is tradition we need the appetizer, the soup and the entrée, and then desserts with the cake." She says, "Not everybody likes cake." I just went along, she was going to have her way. Buranski says, "That was smart on your part." Dragan asks, "Did your invitation get there yesterday?" Buranski says, "Tell her yes we got it and we will be there." Dragan says, "Did you tell her I asked Radko to be best man?" She said, "That's good since she didn't want me to be standing up there with all those single females. Maybe Radko will find a lady." I told her, "We already found a lady for him, he just doesn't know it yet." Dragan says, "Who are you talking about Nadia?" Buranski says, "Yes when you are there for your honeymoon go see her. Nikoli will arrange it, she can come here for a month, she will be on holiday until after the New Year the students go home for that month." Dragan says, "You have been busy."

Buranski stays in the office until shortly after ten and then heads for his meeting with Mariano. He takes an attaché case with him and locks the place up. I follow him, I know where he is heading, I figure he will be tied up for at least an hour so I drive by my place just to check on things. So much for my taking a nap I really feel fine I'm not tired right now. See me in two hours I might be. I drive over to Drury Lane and park, I see Buranski's car and two black Escalades parked together. I figure Big Al and Giovani but then I am thinking maybe it is the mystery man from the original meeting. McCray was never able to put a name with either of those guys. Maybe I'll get lucky when they come out and I can get a good photo. I guess I need to be on my toes. Just because this is payoff time doesn't necessarily mean the job is over. At twelve-thirty, the drivers and the shotgun guys come out and start the cars and pull over by the front door. A few minutes later Buranski walks out with Big Al and the mystery man. I look at the guy like I have seen him someplace. I just need to remember where. Was it on the news a few months ago? Boy he is familiar. I take a picture maybe I can load in the computer and do a search. This time I got a clear image so that should make him easier to find. Buranski shakes hands with both of them and goes to his car. He takes the attaché case out of the trunk and holds it out for Big Al. Big Al motions for his bodyguard to get something from his car which he does. They swap attaché cases, neither of them open them.

Trust is a great thing. Me I would be opening the case and double checking the contents.

Big Al gets in his car, Buranski gets in his and the mystery man gets in his. I am trying to figure out whom to tail. My cell phone rings it is McCray so I tell him my dilemma. He says, "Follow the one we know nothing about just to see where he goes, it might get us a clue as to who he is." I say, "That was pretty much what I thought about doing. I did get a clear picture of him and I swear I saw he someplace, maybe the news or something." McCray says, "I'm heading back to DC tomorrow night and I talked to my friend at the Hawks, the tickets for Sunday are available I need to call him, can you use them?" I ask, "What time's the game?" He says, "Six o'clock why?" I said, "Sunday I spend with my daughter. Let me ask her, she might get a kick out of going. I'll let you know after she gets home from school I'll call her." McCray says, "I am heading to a meeting with Schaunessy, he has some things he wants us to cover with our new guy when we have our sit down. He found a couple of discrepancies in some of the data we gathered, that he wants cleared up." I said, "What the three years where there is no record of him?" McCray says, "No I think it is something else that has him edgy."

I tail the mystery man. They head to Chicago and go to Hyde Park, not too far from where the job was. The driver pulls up in front of a big old hotel and the mystery man goes in carrying the other attaché case. He holds up his hand and gives the driver a signal five and five. I figure he is saying ten minutes, I don't know if that means if he doesn't come out in ten minutes, come look for him. The sign in front says No Parking the doorman goes over to the car and says something to the bodyguard. The guy says something and then hands the guy some money. The doorman goes back to his post and sticks the money in his pocket. About ten minutes later, the mystery man comes out no attaché case. Must be another payoff for something I am thinking I wish I knew who he saw in there. I am waiting for them to pull away and I see a guy I recognize come out of the hotel by the side door. He is dressed in a black suit, dark glasses and wearing a hat. I go to myself that is Agent Simpson, I'll bet money on it. No wonder they got passes for Buranski and his guys, Simpson signed off for them.

The mystery guy motions for the driver to drive and so I follow them. Wait until I tell McCray what transpired here. The driver turns around and heads for the expressway, I follow them. He goes to Cicero and heads to Midway Airport. They drop him off at the entrance and drive away. I go now what happens, this guy is flying where. I decide I better park and go inside just to get a look. There was some short term parking where Buranski parked when he picked up Ana's mother so I parked there and went inside. The guy has no luggage maybe he flew in this morning and is going back, his part is done for now. I look at the flights leaving in the next thirty minutes. One to DC at two forty-five, Gate number 7, I watch sure enough the mystery man is flying to DC. I walk out and get in my SUV and head to Orland Park. I figure Buranski has been to the bank and should be at his office. I get there about three-thirty and think why didn't I stop for something to eat. I have been on the go all day. I look Buranski is in his office, I don't see anybody else, Grozdan isn't there, Dragan I don't see him at the used-car lot. I decide heck I'll go pickup something and get right back.

I get back to Buranski's office at almost four. Radko is there talking to Buranski. I listen to what is being said. Buranski said, "I was as nervous about my meeting with Mariano, we talked and I gave him the code information, returned our security tags and then he gave me the balance of my fee. I didn't open it until I got to the bank. It was there in full. I put the bulk of it away. I kept out enough to pay you, Ivan and Grozdan. The rest will sit for a while since I'll need some cash for Dragan's honeymoon. Radko said, "Don't forget I'm contributing too." Buranski said, "I know you said you were going to but with you being his best man isn't that enough. You will have to pay for his bachelor party, your Tux and all that stuff." Radko said, "I put money aside already so I am good." Buranski said, "Ivan is supposed to come by tonight after working in Worth all day, I was going to stop there to check progress but the meeting took longer than I figured. I had to eat lunch there with Mariano and the man from DC." Radko asked, "Did he ever introduce him to you?" He said, "No, I thought he was going to in the dining room but then the waiter brought the food right away. So we ate. That guy can eat no wonder they call him Big Al." Radko said, "You going to be here tomorrow morning?" Buranski said, "Yes, I'll be here by eight, a big day I have another job to get setup. It's a construction job in Midlothian." Radko said, "I'll come by then we can talk more. My guy is fighting tonight."

Buranski gets busy with stuff on his desk. I look at the clock and call Natalie to see if she wants to go to the Hawks game Sunday. She says, "Are you kidding, those are the hottest tickets in town. Yes I would love to go but I have to ask Mom, since I know we will not be back by eight." I ask "Is she home yet?" Natalie says, "No she doesn't get home until almost six tonight." I say, "Call me after you ask her. I told McCray I would let him know tonight. I'll talk to you soon sweetie." Buranski picks up the phone and says, "Ana, I am leaving in a few minutes, tell Elisia I will be home tonight. I think things will get back to normal for a while now." I think Yes I know what you mean, getting back to normal sounds good to me too.

Then I think wait what is normal for me these days. I think about Vicki and how this week has been. I can't remember being this taken with anyone, since Rachael and I were together. We were high-school sweethearts and we each did our thing after high school, she went to a local university, I went to Illinois. We would see each other over breaks and then once I finished college I went into the service and was recruited for security after six months. I served almost four years and then got a job with IIA. Rachael and I got married in April 1992. Natalie was born in August 1995 and then Rachael and I split up in the fall of 1998. I have been with IIA almost twenty years all as a field agent. Maybe that is why McCray said I was the best suited for his job. Most of the men I worked with when I started were ten years or so older than I was so I learned a lot from them. Two of them retired after twenty-five years to do other things, two transferred to DC since they thought the Midwest was too calm. I have been assigned to jobs in Minnesota, Missouri, and Kansas in the past as the need arose since I was willing to go wherever they needed me. After my divorce, I was more or less a lone ranger, I didn't mind working alone, and I wasn't tied down too much. When Natalie was little, I would only see her on holidays and her birthday for four hours at a time. That changed about three years ago. Rachael said she needed some relief and I needed to have a larger role in her life. Now I thoroughly enjoy our Sundays and watch her grow into a remarkable young lady. My cell phone rings it is Natalie. She said, "Dad, I asked Mom and she said that would be OK just don't get me home too late." I said, "Thanks sweetie I'll call McCray and tell him we'll go." I called McCray and told him and he said, "I'll have the tickets tomorrow at lunch, meet at the same time. I'll need a break before I clear my desk for the weekend."

Buranski leaves his office a few minutes after six and I follow him to the expressway. He gets on 294 north, I drive to 55 and head to Chicago. Vicki will be surprised. I guess I should call her and warn her or ask her where she wants to eat dinner tonight. I call her on my cell. She answers and I ask, "Do you want to go out for dinner tonight?" She says, "Where are you now?" I said, "I just got on 55, I should be at your place before seven." She says, "I'll meet you in front and we'll go to a new place that opened a few blocks from here." I said, "I'll see you soon." So I drove to her place picked her up and we went to a restaurant on Wells Street. They had a lot of different selections on the menu, we both ordered the same thing and it was very good. Then we went back to her place. She says, "I was surprised you called so early, I was figuring it would be like last night after nine again." I said "No my guy went home early nothing extra going on tonight so I headed here rather than to my place." She asks, "What about tomorrow night, do you have plans?" I said, "Right now you are my only plan. Tomorrow hasn't gotten here yet. You know me and my job. I do what I have to do. I never know in advance what the next day or night will bring. I haven't even looked at my daughter's basketball schedule. It is stuck on the refrigerator and I meant to grab it." She says, "Look it up on line. I have a computer and I will let you use it." I said, "Why didn't I think of that?" She says, "You're a male, that's why." I said, "Ouch that hurt." She says, "You asked for that." I said, "I guess I did." I checked and yes they are playing another warm up game, it's Friday at five-thirty at York HS another invitational game. I should make that, then Saturday she still has practice and I told my old coach I would be there. Vicki and I talked until almost midnight and then we went to bed.

Chapter 23

Friday morning six o'clock and I am up go get a shower and get dressed pour my coffee and think. How did a guy from the wrong side of the tracks wind up with this classy city lady who is a complete opposite of me in more ways than one. I mean yes we talk about a lot of interesting subjects and share some of the same tastes in newspapers. It seems we can talk about almost any subject and carry on a decent conversation. There never really seems to be a lull while we are talking and even when we aren't talking we get along fine. If somebody would have told me you have to meet this lady I would have said, Yes sure me in my jeans and sweatshirt and her in her fancy dresses and heels. I swear she lives in heels all day long, I know I couldn't do that, there is no way those things can be comfortable. She always dresses nice at least that I have seen. Maybe she has some in old jeans and a flannel shirt she bums around in on Saturday. I am sitting there drinking my coffee and she says, "You are awfully quiet this morning." I say, "I was just sitting here marveling at our relationship, if I might call it that. I was thinking to myself how different we are, you dress up every day, wear heels and nice looking clothes, I throw on jeans, a sweatshirt and baseball cap and I'm set for the day." She wraps the sheet around her and says "I am not dressed up now and you like me this way don't you?" I said, "Yes I do as a matter of fact you are cute wrapped up like that."

We talk and kiss a few times and I figure I best get out of here before she entices me to go back to bed. It wouldn't really take too much but I know I have to be in Orland Park by eight. I kiss her again and say "I'll see you after Natalie's game. Do want pizza tonight for a change? I have a taste for one right this minute." She says, "From Lou Malnati's stuffed with sausage, mushrooms and black olives." I said, "That will work. I'll call you after her game you order it and I'll pick it up." She says, "Have a fun day." I said, "You too."

I drive to Orland Park and get there at ten minutes to eight. I stake out my spot and get ready for the morning. I stopped for coffee and a cinnamon roll that will hold me until lunch time. I am sitting there and I see Radko drive up and then he pulls around in back and parks next to Buranski's car. Dragan walks over from the used-car lot and they go inside together. Buranski says, "I see you made it this morning, how did your fighter do last night?" Radko says, "He won in about eight minutes, the other guy just gave up I think. This kid is strong and he has learned some good moves." Dragan says, "When are we going to see this prospect fight?" Radko says, "After your honeymoon if Sophia will let you out on a Wednesday night. There's a tournament in mid-December and he will be there." Dragan says, "Give me the date I'll write it on the calendar, I'll be there." Radko says, "December 15, seven p.m. at Max's gym in Cicero." They talk for about thirty minutes and Dragan says, "I have to get back to the lot, I have a couple coming by around nine looking for a van." Radko says, "Make 'em a deal they can't refuse." Dragan says, "I have this van that has been on my lot too long, it's a good van in good shape, but I can't seem to move it." Buranski says, "It probably gets lousy gas mileage, people don't like paying the price to fill it up." Dragan says, "No this one is pretty good I drove it for a couple of weeks and it wasn't too bad on gas. I think it is something else." Radko says, "Let me look at it before they get there." Dragan says, "Come look now then." Buranski says, "Go see what you think I need to call this guy anyway." Then walk out the back door and Buranski makes a call. "Hello, this is Karl from KBW Construction is Mr. Kowalski home? Yes, I can wait." After a couple of minutes he is talking "Yes, I heard your message, you got the loan from Countryside Bank. Yes, I can come over this afternoon to go over things with you. One that is fine."

Nine o'clock Radko comes back from the used-car lot. He said, "I solved his problem the van smelled like it ran over a skunk. Dragan couldn't smell anything. I took one whiff and got the Febreze and sprayed the whole inside, now it smells nice." Buranski said, "Now maybe he will sell that van and stop complaining." Radko said, "Only until the next one he can't sell. He buys some of these at auction for peanuts then tries to get top dollar and some of them should go to the junk yard but he sees a bargain and can't pass it up." Buranski said, "That will change once he gets married. I think Sophia will get involved in the business call it a hunch. I think she likes to be around him all the time. I'm glad Ana doesn't want to get involved in my work. She doesn't even ask or want to hear about the jobs. She just wants me home more but she understands when I need to work I work, we get our time so she is happy." Radko said, "How long have you been married?" Buranski said, "Sixteen years and we never fight. She listens to me when I talk and I listen to her so we communicate. I was lucky when I found her. We both never wanted anybody else. We met at a party and that was it, we knew it was meant to be." Radko said, "Yes you were very lucky, that doesn't happen very often."

Buranski said, "The reason I wanted to talk to you this morning is I have proposition that I want to discuss with you." Radko said, "I'm listening." Buranski said, "The money I got for the job, I want to setup a school to train Olympic contenders in wrestling and gymnastics here in Orland Park with you working with the wrestlers and I'm trying to get Nadia to come over here for a year to see if we can make it work. Are you interested?" Radko said, "I'll put up money of my own too since that was what I hoped to do with the gym but there is never enough extra to do that. How did you get Nadia to do it?" Buranski said, "It's not a done deal yet but I talked to Nikoli about making her the offer. When Dragan goes on his honeymoon, he is supposed to find out if she is agreeable. He knows her where Nikoli is just a way to make it happen for the red tape and everything." Radko said, "That would be great, I saw her picture and the bit about her working with gymnasts there, pretty impressive." Buranski said, "That's what I thought and when this job came up I started thinking about what to do with the money. This way it does some good to help aspiring athletes fulfill their dream. Those people won't miss the money to them intelligence is just a game." I was listening to their conversation and said, Wow, I knew he was smart but I never realized how smart he really is. Plus he has a conscious which is rare with a lot of the people I run into. Most of them are greedy or will do whatever for the money. He really thought this out. I'll put all of this into the report for McCray to go over with Schaunessy. Radko and Buranski were talking about the details and where to setup the facility and just trying to get a feel for what they need. They talked for over an hour and Buranski looked at the clock and said, "We'll talk more later, next week. I have to go to Midlothian to do the plans." Radko said, "Just call me when you want to check it out more. I'll look for a location we can get cheap. There are a lot of empty buildings, I'm sure we can get some help setting it up. I'll talk to some people too."

Buranski leaves to go to his meeting in Midlothian. That gives me a chance to go meet McCray. He said one o'clock, I'll be a couple of minutes early unless I get stuck in a lot of traffic. I drive to Halsted and Madison and go to the restaurant and get a spot two cars away from the front door. I should buy a lottery ticket tonight. I am watching for McCray and he comes up from the other direction with an envelope in his hand. He hands me the tickets and says, "I left early so I would have the tickets. I got tied up this morning I was going to go there before I went into the office but couldn't do it." I said, "I could have picked them up at will call." He says, "Yes you could but I needed to see him and thank him for his generosity. When I get back I'll introduce you to him." We go into the restaurant to have lunch and I tell him what Buranski is planning to do. He said, "That guy is something else, here I thought we hit the jackpot with getting him and all he really wants to do is setup the training center. It was just a way to get the bucks." I said, "He might still be good if Mariano comes up with another job after this one runs its course as he said." McCray says, "That might very well be true, but that will be on your watch not mine." I said, "Why so?" He says, "Schaunessy said he was going to step down earlier he went for some tests and his heart specialist said he can't take the stress of this job much longer. So he is moving up the time table to right after the New Year. Next week I have a meeting in DC to get you appointed as my replacement. The way I see it, resources are spread so thin they don't really have a choice it's my call. I help you at first but then it will be your baby." I said, "I was doing a lot of thinking and I guess I am about ready to get some kind of normal life for a change." McCray says, "You and Natalie have fun Sunday."

We finished our lunch and I dropped him off at the office and head to Orland Park before I go watch Natalie play at York. Boy talk about a bomb being dropped on you, No time to react just go with it and see what happens. I haven't talked to anybody about this whole turn of events. I don't even know who I could count on for some good advice and then I think the coach he is still sharp for being 80. I'll talk to him Saturday while Natalie practices. The only other person whose judgment I relied on in the past was Rachael. Why all of a sudden does she keep popping up in my mind? I get to Orland Park a few minutes after three, I don't see Buranski's car yet. I am playing with my computer and I put the photo in to try to get a name. I look at the photo again and I go now I know where I saw him. He was at a function in Hyde Park he came in from DC with some supporters of the big man. He works for one of the Super Pac lobbyists firms. No wonder they want to know who he is talking to and why. These guys front all the monies so they want to know what is going on over there all the time. Since it could impact the flow of oil and that means big bucks. They don't miss a trick.

Buranski gets back about twenty after three and goes into the office. Ivan gets there at almost four and tells Buranski what they finished this week. Buranski gives him an envelope and says that is for last week. Then he hands Ivan the pay envelopes for the men for this week. Ivan says, "I asked the men to work tomorrow for a few hours so I will pay them tomorrow, if I go pay them tonight two or three will not show up tomorrow." Buranski says, "Did you check with Mr. and Mrs. Grozewski?" Ivan says, "Yes, they liked the idea, that way we get a little bit ahead for next week." Buranski says, "Do they expect extra pay for tomorrow?" Ivan says, "No just regular pay." Buranski says, "We will be OK, I built some extra in for problems and you didn't tell me of any problems." Ivan leaves and a few minutes later Buranski leaves right after that. I look at the clock I should get to York with time to spare.

I get to York at five-twenty and head to the gym. I wave to Natalie and I see Rachael sitting in the stands. I go over and sit down next to her. I say, "What brings you out to one of these games?" She says, "I had a real busy week at work and I needed a break so I told Natalie I would come to her game and then we can go out for dinner." I said, "That is good, I don't imagine either of you would want to cook tonight." I said, "I had a real busy week too and I have a situation I need to talk about." Now for the life of me I didn't know why I said that it more or less just slipped out. She asked, "Anything I can help you with?" I said, "It is really complicated." She said, "You met someone and you don't know if it's right or not?" I think that would be the last thing I would want to discuss with her. I said, "No, it's about my job, they want me to take over McCray's job, he is moving up to Director since Schaunessy is retiring due to health problems." She said, "Mister Field Guy in suits and being downtown not a lone ranger. Do you think you can do it?" I said, "I have thought about it and I really do like being in the field but even that is changing so much due to technology. I use a laptop all the time to check things but I don't really enjoy that part of it." She asked, "What did McCray say?" I said, "He said he would guide me for a few months after that I would be on my own and that I was the most qualified for the job." She asked, "What did he say about your pay?" He said, "There were perks like parking, a substantial increase in pay and an expense account to cover incidental expenses." She said, "You have been with them what eighteen years?" I said, "Right about there." She said, "If you want my opinion I say take the job, the retirement benefits will be even better than being a field agent." I said, "Thank you Rachael, I guess I just needed to talk."

    We watch the game in between our talking and cheer every time Natalie gets the ball. After the game Natalie changes and tells her coach that she is going home with her Mom. The coach comes over to meet Rachael and sees me and says, "You are both here tonight. Remarkable, I wish I could get more parents to come together." Rachael started to say something I held up my hand and the coach was off to see another parent that was taking her daughter too. Natalie says, "You two seemed to be talking a lot." I said, "I was surprised your Mom was here since you said she wouldn't come to watch you play." Rachael says, "I did enjoy your game and it doesn't smell like I remember when I was in school." Natalie says, "You didn't have air conditioning." I say, "Bravo!" We talked for a few minutes and then went outside. Rachael and Natalie invited me to join them but I declined, since I didn't want to change their plans. I went by my place to check my mail and see if I had any messages on the machine and to grab some more clothes. Then I remember I am supposed to call Vicki to order the pizza when I was leaving Natalie's game. So I called her and told her I had to stop by my place to look at the mail and get a change of clothes. I said, "Tell them forty-five minutes at least under my name." She says, "OK I will do it, I'm hungry just thinking about it now." I said, "I'll see you in an hour maybe less." Then I drove downtown, picked up the pizza and went to Vicki's place.

    We ate the pizza and talked until after one. I still haven't told her about McCray and the fact that I might soon be her boss in January when Mr. Schaunessy retires. I was still trying to come to grips with the whole concept myself. Being with her right now is one thing with me as a field agent and her as a secretary. If I become her boss will that or would that change things? We haven't even talked about if this relationship is serious or whether it was just a fluke hooking up between us since we discovered we could talk and then we became lovers. I still can't figure out the attraction since I am so much different than the men she was dating before and she is certainly different than the ladies I have gone out with since I have been divorced. Mostly just casual affairs that would last for a few dates and then boom it would be over. Val was different and I did enjoy her company but it just didn't feel right. Now with Vicki there is something that I can't put my finger on there is a closeness and an energy. It is as if two worlds are going to collide and nothing can stop it. We seem to feed off of each other and find comfort in each other's arms. Like tonight while we were talking she was curled up by my side, I had my arm around her and we stayed like that for almost two hours. I could never do that with Rachael or Val. I guess, tomorrow night I will have to lay it on the line. Right now she is sleeping snuggled up next to me, I feel the warmth of her body and smell her perfume and then I fall asleep.

Chapter 24

Saturday morning I am up at six, I don't know why. Force of habit I guess I smell Ah the coffee is brewing. I could really get use to this service. I go take a shower and throw some clothes on and fix my coffee. About seven Vicki wakes up and says, "You're up early this morning." I said, "Force of habit I guess, the only morning I usually sleep a little later is Sunday but only until seven or seven-thirty then I have to get ready to pick up my daughter for the day after church." Vicki says, "You are a good father spending so much time with her and going to watch her play basketball." I said, "Today I take her to practice and this might be their last Saturday practice. I'll know after today." Vicki asks, "What time do you have to pick her up?" I said, "About twelve-thirty so we are at school by one." She asked, "Will you be back after that?" I said, "I have a couple of chores to do at home that will take a couple of hours and then if you want me to come back I will." She said, "Why wouldn't I want you to come back? I enjoy your company more than I thought I would, you surprise me with all the different things we talk about." I said, "Likewise, I never met anybody like you. You sure aren't just the usual secretary that only thinks about her hair, nails, and makeup that is for sure. You are intelligent and witty, not to mention that you are very attractive." By this time, she has wrapped the sheet around her and joined me at the table. She leaned over and kissed me and said, "You are the nicest man I have met in a long time. I was beginning to think I would have to settle for one of the sports jocks that I used to date but now I don't think I could tolerate one. You are pretty intelligent yourself. I didn't know a field agent could be so interesting." I said, "I like to dig for details so I think that is why I read all the stuff. You never know when it might come in handy." She asked, "Do you want to go have breakfast before you leave?" I said, "Sure do you have a place in mind?" She said, "If you give me thirty minutes to shower and dress I do have a place that we can walk to." I said, "No problem, I'll fix myself another coffee." She took her shower and got dressed and we went out.

We got back to her place a little after eleven and I left to pick up Natalie for practice. I get to Natalie's at twelve-twenty. A few minutes later, she came out and we headed to practice. I asked, "How was your dinner with your Mom last night?" She said, "It was good, it would have been better if you had joined us." I said, "I thought about it but I did have other plans." She said, "Mom told me what you two were talking about. I was hoping that you were talking about getting back together. That way I would have both of you all the time." I said, "Sorry sweetie, but I guess I just needed to talk to somebody about the whole deal to help me make up my mind." I took her to practice and my old coach was standing outside waiting for me. He said, "Are you ready to run?" I said, "Give me a couple of minutes to change."

So I get my small duffle bag from the trunk and go inside to change and then come back outside. He said, "Take it easy on me Jim I'm almost twice your age." I laughed and said "I should be telling you to take it easy on me, I'm the one out of shape." We do five laps and I'm keeping up with him barely, I think he was taking it easy on my account. I said "Thanks coach, I needed the workout." He said, "Anytime you want I'm here if the weather is nice." I said, "Coach I value your opinion and I have a decision or two to make, may I talk to you about them?" He said, "Fire away." I said, "I was offered a desk job as the Field Operations Manager since my boss is moving up to Director of the Chicago office. My problem is I don't know if I want to be corralled in an office, I know, I have the experience but I'm not sure about losing my freedom." He said, "You have been doing your job in the field for a long time, it would be a logical move for you to move up but I can understand your concern. I had the same problem when I switched schools and came here, I was comfortable, where I was but this was a challenge and I needed to see if I was up to it. I took the job and I learned a lot more by doing it." I said, "The other problem is I am seeing a really nice lady but I am having reoccurring thoughts about my ex Rachael, every now and then I am doing something and she pops up in my mind and I wonder what she would think." He said, "Jim, I don't know if I can help you on that. I have been married for fifty-five years and wouldn't change anything about it. We get along real good and she understood when I made the move and supported my decision. What would Rachael think about the move?" I said, "She told me take it. It's a good opportunity."

He asked, "What about this lady you are seeing, have you talked to her about it?" I said, "It's complicated, if I take the job I will be her boss." He said, "Jim you have a major problem on your hands. Even if you married her you would have problems keeping the two separate. Then you would still be wondering what Rachael would think or do if you two had a disagreement personal or job related." I said, "Coach, did you study physiology in your spare time?" He said, "I did study to be a therapist but got hooked on coaching. I figured that I could do more good building athletes." I said, "Thanks Coach, you helped me a lot." We are standing there talking and Natalie comes out and comes over to where we are. I asked "How was practice?" She said, "It was good after today I don't have to practice on Saturdays, we will practice three days a week after school if we don't have a game." We both tell the Coach take it easy and we leave. We drove to a fast food place to grab something to eat and then I take her home. I said, "Don't forget we are going to the Hawks game tomorrow." She said, "I know and my friends are jealous. I told them you got tickets from your boss and they were like. You know how much tickets are, that's awesome."

After I dropped her off I went home, took all my dirty clothes from the week and started my laundry. I cleaned the kitchen and the bathroom while the laundry was running. I think more to occupy my mind so I didn't have to think. I went through my mail and decided I should pay my bills. I haven't sat down to do that in over two weeks. I looked at the stack of bills go make a pot of coffee and go through them. I looked at my bank statement and my checkbook and go I didn't enter my last deposit. Our checks get deposited electronically and I starred at the figure for my deposit. I remembered McCray said, Schaunessy bumped me up a grade, I figured it would only be a hundred dollars difference it was over five. I paid all my bills and felt elated I have more money left than I thought I would. Then I thought about what McCray said about me getting a substantial increase in pay when I took his job. I never really gave it much thought, I figured out how he makes a couple of grand more a month than I make but he has all the headaches. Is that enough to compensate for the loss of freedom? Even if I knew how much money I would be making, is it worth the money. I mean I really enjoy being in the field. I know McCray would not be happy if I told him they need to transfer somebody in to take over his job. I think about what the coach said about being married for fifty-five years and what he said I would be looking at if I stayed with her and became her boss. I am like why can't things be simple like they were twenty years ago? Now I have more questions than answers and no clear decision. I finish my laundry and call Vicki to find out what she wants to do tonight. I call her number but don't get an answer. I think that is strange she said she would be home. I look at the clock and it is almost six, I know I told her I would be taking care of chores for a few hours after Natalie's practice. I figure I might as well head downtown. At least the place is clean and I have money in the bank.

I got downtown to Vicki's and ring the bell, I know I have a key but I didn't want to walk on anything. Vicki answers the bell and I said, "It's just me." She said, "Why didn't you just use your key?" So I went in and said, "I thought you might be busy I called but didn't get an answer." She had a towel wrapped around her and said, "I was in the shower so I would be clean when you got back, Smell." I smelled and she asked, "Do you like Lilac?" I said, "Is that what you are wearing?" She said, "Yes, it is a new body wash and I love the smell." I said, "On you anything would smell good." She said, "Hold those thoughts until after dinner." I said, "Speaking of which, that was why I was calling to find out what you want to do tonight." She said, "We can stay home or we can go out it's your call." I said, "Let's go to Gene & Georgetti's Restaurant." She said, "You know how much that costs?" I said, "I know it's expensive but I feel like treating you tonight. This past week was brutal besides I got a raise." She said, "You did when?" I said, "McCray told me Schaunessy bumped me up a pay grade and I just looked at my bank statement, I didn't think it would go through until next month." She said, "On a Saturday night we'll have a long wait unless you know somebody. People make reservations and still have to stand in the crowded bar for an hour before they get seated." I said, "It sounds like a scene from a movie." She said, "Wheeler Dealers." I said, "You saw that?" She said, "I love the old movies like that. James Garner, Rock Hudson, and Doris Day a whole lot of the old movies." I asked, "Come Blow Your Horn?" She said, "Love it." I said, "I thought I was odd liking old movies like that, I would rather watch those than most of the new stuff coming out all violence and special effects. I just like to be entertained." She said, "That is the way I feel for the most part." I called the restaurant to make reservations, I gave them a name. Vicki said, "What did they say, Mr. Crawford?" They said, "No problem we'll have your table ready."

We go to dinner and the place is packed. I give them my name and slip the guy twenty bucks. He says, "Follow me Mr. Crawford." So we got seated right away, other people that were standing in the bar looked miffed when we walked in and got seated. I heard about doing that from McCray, he even told me the name to use. He is sharp that is for sure. Vicki says, "Wow, I didn't think we could walk in and get seated, I have been here before and we always had to wait over an hour." I said, "Yes but you were with jocks and drinking. They like the money from the bar. Me I don't drink booze very often and wine on rare occasion." The steaks were wonderful that was why I wanted to go there. We had a really good dinner and we talked for two hours over dinner then headed back to her place.

We get back to her place and she says, "Those thoughts you had earlier about the smell of Lilac. Follow me." I followed her to the bedroom and she had a bowl of potpourri and some purple stones. The whole room smelled of Lilacs. She asks, "Do you like it?" I say, "Yes it smells very nice not too overpowering." She says, "I'm glad I wanted to change the room around some, I even cleared out two drawers if you want to bring some clothes." I say, "We need to talk but I have been putting off talking to you." She says, "I'm all yours nobody else even comes close to you. I did a lot of thinking today while you took your daughter for practice and did your chores. I want to meet her sometime, she sounds like a great young lady and if you and I are going to be seeing each other like we have I don't want her to be too upset because I'm stealing her father." I said, "I will see what I can do but I haven't told her about you just yet. Heck I don't even know how to tell her, she was hoping I would get back together with her Mom since she feels we are so much alike." She says, "I can see your problem. Teenage girls get like that, give it a couple of years and she will be over that. She will be going to college and she will understand." I said, "Do you really think so?" She says, "Trust me I was just like her, I wanted my parents to get back together. They did and they were miserable, after I finished high school and started college I understood, sometimes things like that just don't work out right. They got divorced and now they are friends, they couldn't be married to each other they were too much alike. You will get a chance to meet them Thanksgiving. I'm making Thanksgiving dinner and they will both be here." I said, "That might be a problem for me. I was invited to her house for Thanksgiving dinner." We talked until almost three about all sorts of things. Quirky things, like what bugs her or what bugs me. I'll tell you I have never talked to a gal as much as I have talked to her and about all sorts of things. We went to bed and Sunday morning I wake up at seven and think. How is this going to work? I go take a shower to get ready to go pickup Natalie after church.

    About eight Vicki wakes up and wraps the sheet around her and joins me at the table. I am finishing my second cup of coffee. She says, "You look nice this morning, is that how you normally dress on Sundays when you pick up your daughter?" I said, "No before I used to wear jeans and a sweatshirt and a few weeks ago I decided I needed to change my image." She says, "You look nice so I'm sure Natalie and your ex are glad you changed." I said, "Yes they both commented about the new look and liked it. It even made me feel better." She asks, "What are your plans today?" I said, "We don't have any definite plans except for later, we are going to the Hawks game." She says, "Really?" I said, "Yes, McCray called me and said his friend told him the tickets were available and ask me if Natalie would want to go. I called him back after I talked to her. So she is real excited about going." She said, "She probably wants to drool over Kane." I said, "I don't think so she is not into jocks or really any one guy in particular right now. She is more focused on her studies and basketball." I said, "It will be a late night for her I normally have to get her home by eight but the game will most likely not before until after eight-thirty and then getting out of downtown to drive her home. I am thinking almost ten." Vicki asks, "You coming back here tonight?" I said, "If you want me too otherwise I'll sleep at home for a change. I haven't slept there in what over a week. We have been inseparable except while we are working or other things we need to do . . ." She says, "I know and that surprises me too. So yes come back here silly."

I leave to pick up Natalie and decide what we will do before the game. We go to my place after breakfast and play a few games of Checkers. Then she says, "Let's go for a bike ride, this might be the last Sunday we can do it." I said, "I agree, it is getting cooler every night. I expect we will see snow pretty soon." We rode for about two hours and I said, "We should eat something before we go to the game." She said, "I'll make us something. It's cheaper than going out." I said, "Good luck on finding something to make." She said, "I always come up with something." We go back to my place she looks at everything and says, "You were right there isn't anything here." I said, "We'll go downtown I know a place not too far from United Center we can eat and then be there for the warm-ups." So we go to the place I meet McCray. They weren't real crowded so we ate and I drove over to park and get there early. We are walking through the place and she asks "Where are our seats?" I said "About six rows behind the Hawks bench." She says, "OOW I can see Patrick up close and in person. He is so HOT!" I say, "I didn't think you watched hockey?" She says, "I don't but he is in all the teen magazines too." We stop by one the stands and I buy her a Kane Jersey. She says, "Dad you don't have to buy that for me." I said, "I know sweetie but I want too." She took the tags off and put it on over her sweater. Then we head to our seats. A few minutes later the players come out for the warm up and she is watching every move he makes. We had a good time at the game, too bad the Oilers beat them 2-1. The Hawks played Atlanta

Saturday night in Atlanta and won. I drove her home and she had to call her Mom on the cell phone and tell her that I bought her a jersey. Rachael came to the door and asked, "Did we have fun?" I said, "A blast." I tell Natalie "Goodnight and I love you." She kisses me and says, "Dad you are the best, I love you too. I can't wait until Friday when I can wear this to school the other girls will drool."

I drive back downtown to Vicki's. She asks, "How was the game?" I said, "It was good but they lost." She says, "I know I watched the end of the game, I was trying to spot you two." I asked, "Did you see us?" She says, "No they only focus on the players on the ice once in a while they pan the audience but no I didn't see you." I said, "Tomorrow will be busy unless I miss my bet." We talk for about an hour and go to bed. She already has the coffee set to start at six I say "Thank you." She says, "For what?" I said, "For spoiling me."

Chapter 25

Monday morning I am up at six do my morning routine and pour my coffee. About a quarter to seven Vicki comes out wrapped in her sheet to join me at the table for a few minutes before I leave. She asked, "Will you be in the office today?" I said, "It depends McCray didn't give me any instructions about today. I know, he doesn't get back from DC until late again, he said, he had another meeting to attend. I need to go keep an eye on our man to see what is going on there. Once I find that out I'll have a better idea." She said, "He was in a rush Friday when he got back from lunch, he told the staff to enjoy the weekend. Then he said he would see them Monday when he got back and they could come in after lunch today." I said, "Sounds like something is brewing otherwise he would just wait until tomorrow." She asked, "Did he talk to you about any new projects? He was going over a bunch of stuff Schaunessy gave him but he didn't elaborate." I said, "No he didn't say anything except have a good weekend and we'll talk when I get back." She said, "I was just wondering he has been meeting with Schaunessy almost every day for hours on end." I was thinking to myself getting on the job training before he took over his job in January. Getting to know the staff over there on Michigan Avenue to make sure there will not be any unhappy campers when he moves over there. I told her "I will call you at the office once I see how my day is going to play out." She gave me a kiss and headed back to bed to catch another forty winks.

 I drive to Orland Park and stop for breakfast at a Pancake House not too far from Buranski's office. I figure he will not be at the office until around nine. He said things would get back to normal after last week. Then I think he might even stop by the project in Worth to see what Ivan and the crew got done Saturday. I take my time and enjoy a regular breakfast for a change. I drive over to Buranski's office and there are lights on inside but I don't see his car, then I figure it is probably Grozdan. He wasn't there Friday, so Dragan picked him up this morning. How long did he say it would be until he can drive? Nine-fifteen Buranski pulls up and parks in back and goes inside. He goes to his office and Grozdan comes in and asks, "So how are the guys doing on Peter's house?" Buranski says, "They finished the shell on Saturday, now today the guys can start laying out the rooms but he changed a couple of things. His wife wants the bathroom bigger with a shower and a tub plus a linen closet for towels and sheets between the bathroom and the master bedroom suite. So I need to revise a few things and I told him this would jack up the price some. He shrugged and said, "Give the lady what she wants, I'll pay the difference." Grozdan says, "That's the way he has always been, me I would have said forget an addition let's move to a senior community so we don't have to do anything. He told me his wife said, "I don't want to live with a bunch of old people I like it here in Worth, we raised our children now I want to make this place nicer." Buranski looks at plans and does some figuring and tells Grozdan this will add about four grand to the bill." Grozdan says, "I'll call him, he called while I was at the doctor on Friday, then I got busy and forgot."

Buranski gets busy with the plans and makes the changes. Then goes over to the project board and makes some notes. Next week start to Wojowski's house get the shell up before bad weather sits in. Then he puts a tentative start date for the Midlothian. He looks at the clock and sets up the coffee pot. Ten-fifteen here comes Dragan and he says, "Just like old times our morning coffee break, I missed our twenty minutes every morning." Buranski says, "I did too believe it or not. Did you and Sophia decide where you are going to live after you get back from your honeymoon?" Dragan says, "We talked about it some, her place is nicer than mine and we have a little more room but to me it is more a ladies house than mine. It even smells like a ladies house." Buranski says, "Is your place paid for?" He says, "Almost I think I have five years and it will be paid for. I thought of renting it to Igor my mechanic, since he wants to move here rather than drive twenty miles a day from Aurora. His wife says not until school is out." Buranski asks, "How old are his children?" He says, "Second and fourth grade." Buranski says, "Tell him to tell his wife at that age it doesn't matter plus they will make new friends they move right after Christmas, you rent the place to him and move in with Sophia and in six months buy a new house and sell hers." Dragan says, "That sounds good to me I don't know about Sophia but I'll talk to her." They finish their coffee and Dragan leaves.

Buranski is busy working on the plans and the phone rings he answers and says "KBW Construction, Karl speaking. Yes, OK I'll tell my foreman. I am working on your plans now. Next Monday is what we are planning. Will that work for you? Today, I am ordering all the wood and the materials for your addition. No changes from the original plans. Good. No we should be finished before Thanksgiving, tell your wife my men will not in her way." Grozdan comes in while he is talking. After he gets off the phone he says, "Wojowski, that guy can drive me crazy with questions." Grozdan says, "But he has been patient letting us do the job for Peter first. I'll talk to him if you like." Buranski says, "No I got everything figured out. We start his job next Monday, I send Ivan and three men there, I work with two guys in Worth we put the windows in add the siding and then there is only drywall and painting and their house will be finished. They will take care of the carpet and window treatments. Oh! Yes, I need to call the electrician too so he can work after we put the windows in and we can stop using extension cords for light." Grozdan says, "Why not get Ivan to bring in a couple of more men?" Buranski says, "Nah I can do the stuff, that way I'll keep my weight down for the holidays." Grozdan says, "Plus you work cheap right?" Buranski laughs and says, "Glad to see you got your sense of humor back. I was wondering when the old you would be back."

My cell phone rings it is McCray I answer it "Hello chief, where are you?" He says, "I'm still in DC at the airport so I thought I would call you about the meeting at my office when I get back." I ask, "What time is your flight?" He says, "I leave in fifteen minutes. I should be at Midway Airport at 3:15. Can you pick me up? We need to talk before today's meeting." I say, "Sure Chief, I am at Buranski's office, just trying to find out what is going on, same old stuff all construction jobs talk." He says, "I told DC you would take the job but I had to do some arm twisting to get you approved." I started to tell him I was having second thoughts but they announced his plane was boarding and he said, "Bye, I'll see you at 3:15." I think well this is not what I wanted to hear but I did tell him yes in a way.

I look at the clock and go. It's too late to go downtown and have lunch with Vicki and then have to be at Midway at 3:15. I call the office and she answers. I say, "I'll be at the office later, I am picking up Rusty at Midway at 3:15, he just called me and ask if I could do that and I said sure." She asks, "Is there a problem, he usually takes a cab?" I say, "Not that I know of, he said he wanted to talk to me before he has the meeting there." She says, "Schaunessy just called here to see if he was back yet, he seemed real nervous about something and he didn't sound like his normal self, like he was gasping for air and having a hard time breathing." I said, "Call 911 and send an ambulance over there!" She says, "Why?' I said, "Sounds like he is having a heart attack he has been warned by his doctor to take it easy." She says, "I'll call but what if it's a false alarm?" I said, "Better to be safe than sorry." She called 911 and requested an ambulance. She called me back about thirty minutes later and said, "You were right, they got there right before he blacked out. They took him to Northwestern Memorial Hospital on Huron Street to the ER Department." I say, "Good work on your part." She says, "Thank you, for all we know he could have died had you not told me to call 911."

I get off the phone with her and decide I'll go to the Gyro place for lunch. It is one-thirty and nothing going on here. I drive over and go inside to place my order and here comes Buranski not five minutes after I walk in. He places his order and sees me and says, "Fancy meeting you here." I say, "They have good Gyro's." He says, "Don't I know it. I come here all the time." We sat down and talked like pals. He says, "When do you want to setup the meeting with your boss?" I say, "I am picking him up at the airport at 3:15 I'll ask him and call you back. What works for you?" He says, "Tuesday night or Thursday I just need to tell Ana which night I'll be late." I said "I'll call you later, I have a meeting at the office after I pick him up." He says, "Call my cell phone even if I'm home I'll answer unless we are eating dinner." I say "I'll call you later." We walk out together and shake hands like long lost friends. He heads back to his office I head to Midway Airport.

I get to the airport at three so I park in the short term lot. You can't drive around and wait for somebody they keep you moving better to pay the fee and park. It's not a long walk plus I need to stretch my legs and move a little. That run with the coach on Saturday sure told me I'm out of shape. Then bike riding Sunday with Natalie my legs know it. I walk to the terminal and I get stopped. They say you can stand here if you are waiting for somebody to arrive but you can't go inside without a ticket. I am like things sure have changed I remember I use to pick up people and wait to greet them when they got off the plane. I just didn't realize how tight security was at the airports now. Heck I drove everywhere I need to go, even when I had to go to Kansas City I drove. They said, I could fly I said no I'll drive. McCray walked out at about three twenty-five I asked, "How was the flight?" He said, "Boring." I said, "Schaunessy called Vicki to see if you were back and she told me he sounded like he was gasping for air and had trouble breathing. I told her to call 911 she did. He had a heart attack and they took him to Northwestern Memorial." McCray said, "Will he be OK?" I said, "They had him in ER when she called me back. I haven't heard since. Oh! I had lunch with Buranski not planned we both wound up at the Gyro place to have lunch. He said, he was available Tuesday or Thursday for our sit down meeting." McCray said, Thursday sounds like the best option right now with Schaunessy in the hospital." I said, "I'll call him later and tell him."

McCray said, "I didn't want to put you on the spot in front of everybody today without talking to you first. I told DC I was sure I could convince you to take over my job, it will just take a little time to wean you off of being a field agent. When I go over all the projects Schaunessy has been sitting on you will understand why he was a mess. I thought he should have retired six months ago but the caseload kept growing and he thought he could handle more but he kept tabling projects to take care of the hottest things first. It will take six months to get things under control. DC said, they kept asking if he needed help he kept telling them no everything was being handled. So do you see why I said, Take the job Jim with your drive and dedication we can make this work." I said, "Since you put it like that I guess I don't have any choice." He said, "Welcome aboard the Train to Nowhere. Aside from a small group in DC most people don't even know we exist. Our funding is hidden from the general revenue audit we are a sub-department with no cabinet position. Ours is strictly hush-hush and on a need to know basis. That is why it is the train to nowhere. You want to be visible you go to the Bureau everybody sees them with their FBI field jackets with big bold lettering ours is the little IIA Agency logo that looks like the Nations seal." I said, "Thank you for all that insight. I never knew a lot of the things you just said." He said, "Now you do, I think you and I can make a real good team, they might even want us in DC after a year or two." I said, "I don't think that is for me." He said, "After you make a few trips there you'll change your mind. Heck, your daughter might even like going to college there."

We get to the office at almost four-thirty, I park and we go inside. He looks at the messages Vicki has waiting for him and says, "Vicki get everybody to meet in the break room. Give me about fifteen minutes and I will join everybody. I have to take care of a couple of things first. I could use a hot cup of coffee if it's not too much trouble." Vicki says, "I just made a fresh pot, I figured after the way day has been I better make one." She goes and fixes him a mug of coffee and takes into his office. Then she gets everybody to meet in the break room. I join them and they ask me "What is this all about are we getting canned?" I say, "I hardly think so after the past few weeks you should all be praised for your hard work." They talk in whispers trying to come up with why McCray wanted to hold a meeting late on a Monday afternoon. A couple of them get cans of juice or soda from the fridge, I fix myself a coffee. Twenty minutes later McCray comes in and says, "I called this meeting today since there are going to be a few major changes taking place. Originally they were not going to happen until after the middle of January but in light of what happened to Director Schaunessy today the time table has been pushed up. I just got off the phone with the head of our agency and told him what happened today. Effective immediately I will be moving over to Michigan Avenue to take over Director Schaunessy's job. Agent Huggins has been promoted to fill my job since he is the most qualified. I talked to him about it to feel him out and trust me he would rather stay in the field but he has a clear understanding of what was happening. Originally, I figured I had a couple of months to ease him into the job but after today he will be handing out the assignments and looking at the stack of unfinished projects sitting in Schaunessy's basket you will all be very busy. Thank you all for your hard work and I am proud of the job this department has done over the past few weeks. I congratulate all of you."

After about fifteen minutes of hand shaking and pats on the back he said, "I am going over to the hospital to check on Director Schaunessy after that I would like all of you to join me for dinner at Morton's Steak House. I called them after I got off the phone with Washington and arranged for them to set aside a few tables for us. I will see you all there after eight." The staff could not believe what he just said half of them were getting ready to leave to go visit a neighborhood watering hole to kick around what happened today. The rest of the staff already left, right after McCray left to go to the hospital. Vicki and I had thirty minutes to chat by ourselves. Vicki came over to me and said, "Congratulations Jim, I had no idea." I said, "Trust me, I was hoping Washington would shoot me down, I don't know anything about all the reports and the meetings he had to attend. I am like a fish out of water floundering to breath and not having much luck." She said, "I guess I'll be here to help you along, he didn't say anything about taking me with him. I typed a lot of the reports for him and know his schedule every week. So that should help." I said, "Thanks Vicki, a couple of times I wanted to talk to you about the job offer but chickened out both times." She said, "It will all work out, I know you after all our talks you will be able to do his job, maybe not the same way he did but you'll do the job I'm sure since that's how you are." I said, "Thanks for the vote of confidence and I'm sure I will need a lot of help making the transition." I asked, "Are you ready to go so we can be there when Rusty gets there?" She said, "Give me a couple of minutes to freshen up and fix my makeup."

I drive over to Morton's and we go inside to wait for McCray to get there. The host shows us to our tables. Most of the staff are there, only a couple of missing faces but the others say they will be here shortly. Most of them ordered beer and are talking about the Hawks next game. McCray gets there about ten after eight followed by our missing couple. I think perhaps we have an office romance blooming from all the close work they have been doing. I make a mental note to keep an eye on them after I take over. The waiter comes and takes our food order and the staff decides they want to toast McCray and congratulate him on moving up to Director. So they start and then each of them share a personal thought about him. I thought it was all very touching that in the three years he has been in charge that they have that much admiration for him. In my dealings with him he has always been fair and straightforward on what he expects from everybody. When it came around to me I said, "I will let you in on a secret if it weren't for that man there I would have left this job a few years ago I think I was almost burned out and he sent me to Kansas City to take care of a problem there and I came back rejuvenated since I learned something by the whole ordeal." Vicki was the last to speak and she said, "Mr. McCray has always treated me fair and never told me to do anything. He didn't expect me to be his gopher and chase to take care of a lot of chores that other Executives think their secretary should handle for them. He treated me the same way he treated each of you like we were members of the same team. He never made any passes at me or told off color jokes. He has always been a true gentleman. Thank you Rodger It has been a pleasure working for you." He said, "Just because I'm moving over to Michigan Avenue that doesn't keep you away from my wrath if things aren't going well at your office. Agent Huggins already knows he will have a hard row to hoe but I have all the confidence in the world that he can do the job. Thank you all for those thoughtful words about my influence on all of you. I know I didn't deserve all those kind remarks since I rode a lot of you real hard."

By the time, we finished our dinner it was already pushing eleven o'clock. McCray said, "I hate to call it a night but tomorrow will be very busy for me and for all of you I am sure. Thank you all for coming tonight." He walked out and slowly everybody else finished their drinks then headed for home. I drove Vicki home and went in so we could finish the conversation we started at the office. I said, "Vicki, I know we have been inseparable for the last eight days I think and I truly enjoy being with you all the time but now given the situation at the office I don't know how it will work out. Being your boyfriend is great I mean you spoil the heck out of me, we seem very compatible even though we are from different sides of the track. I have always been a field agent and enjoy that immensely, you are a well-dressed, intelligent, and attractive downtown lady. Now that I have been put in the position of being your boss, I don't know if I can keep my feelings under wraps at the office. I already think a couple of people suspect we are seeing each other but haven't said anything to me or ask me outright if I was seeing you. I don't know if what we have is strong enough to withstand all the office gossip that will take place if everybody finds out that I spend every night here. Then I have to think about my daughter and what effect this whole situation will have on her. I think I have fallen in love with you and that makes it even more difficult to do the right thing." Vicki said, "If I may say, a couple of things perhaps it will help." I said, "I relinquish the floor to the lady of the house."

 She said, "First and foremost I too think I have fallen hopelessly in love with you. I tried to tell myself this wasn't happening but then every night when you get here my heart starts beating faster. I start getting the jitters like what happens if you don't come back. While you were talking just now I had the feeling you were going to say, this was all a mistake. Well I have news for you Mister for me it has not been a mistake. You opened my eyes to the fact that people from two different worlds as you said can come together and fall in love. Love can't be planned it just happens and sometimes we don't even know it until BAM it reaches out and makes us take notice. As far as working together I can always switch with one of the secretaries over on Michigan Avenue. I'll talk to Mr. McCray about us and tell him that in all fairness it wouldn't be a healthy situation to have us working in the same office moral wise. I would love you to move down here and live with me, if you want to get married so your daughter won't feel left out I'm up for it. That way you could bring her downtown so she could get to know me on your Sunday's." Then she gave me a big kiss and started to cry. I held her in my arms and kissed her back and said, "Do you always hit this hard?" She said, "Only when I don't have any other choice." I said, "I'll have to figure out what to do with my place. The market is terrible and I still owe on the place." She said, "I could move out there because this place is only temporary unless I can convince Stuart to let me buy him out." I said, "It looks like we have a lot of things to figure out but at least now we both know how we feel and what we can do to make it work." She jumps into my arms and said, "I love you Jim more than I thought I could ever love anybody." It was after two when we went to bed.

Chapter 26

Seven o'clock I am awake, I do a double take at the clock. What happened to my normal six o'clock wake up? I smell the coffee and it smells like it is brewed. I go take a shower and look at Vicki sleeping away. After my shower I fix my coffee and sit there drinking it. Today is the beginning of a new chapter in my life. I am deep in thought and here comes Vicki wrapped in her sheet rubbing her eyes and says, "Good morning my love." I lean over and kiss her and say "I actually overslept this morning and I'm not even upset about it." She says, "Maybe love had something to do with it." I say, "How do you figure?" She says, "Since you were looking for it but couldn't find it because you weren't at the right place at the right time." I say, "You mean because we found it last night or early this morning." She says, "That would be my guess." I say, "I need to go out and take care of a few things I'll be at the office around noon. Tell McCray I will call him so we can go over what projects we should assign to which teams." Vicki says, "He is going to tell you, you're in charge figure it out." I say, "You're no help." She says, "I am going in early today so I can talk to him. I know he has a lot of things in his office that will need to be transferred over to his new office. I can help organize all that stuff and get the office ready for you and your new secretary" I say, "Send a young pretty one." She says, "She transferred since she knows how you are, you men are all alike." I say, "Thank you."

 I drive to Orland Park and call Buranski on his cell phone and ask, "Are you at the office yet?" He says, "As a matter of fact I had to stop at the bank this morning and I am running a little late." I ask, "Do you have time for breakfast at the pancake place on 159th Street?" He says, "Sure, I can meet you. Why?" I say, "I'll tell you when we meet." He says, "Twenty minutes I should be there." I say, "See you soon." I drive to the pancake place and park and then I call McCray on his cell phone. He answers and says, "Good morning Jim, where are you?" I say, "Orland Park to have breakfast with our man, I want to try something out on him." He says, "Already thinking ahead I see. That is a good thing. I will be at the office most of the day, I am at the Michigan Avenue office right now to brief all the employees here and then I will be over there to start boxing up things I will need transferred." I ask, "What time do you think you will be at your old office?" He says, "About an hour." I say, "I told Vicki I should be at the office by around noon I have a bunch of things to take care of this morning." He says, "She can manage the office for a while. I don't imagine any of the staff will wander in until around ten." I say, "That was what I was thinking after last night. Thanks chief that was really a good idea last night." He says, "You and I will be in a closed door meeting from one until four going over details and caseloads."

Buranski shows up and we go inside and get a booth in the back. He says, "This was not expected. I thought you were going to call me last night." I tell him about what happened. He says, "I can understand, I had to do the same thing when Grozdan got shot." I say, "I remember it well. But I wanted to talk to you about an idea. Let me know if you think this will work." He says, "What do you want to try?" I say, "I want to pass some phony information to see if we can find out who Nikoli is passing this stuff too." He says, "How are we going to do that?" I say, "That feed at the house is voice activated right?" He says, "Yes that was the way it is designed." I say, "I have two men down there and they can talk in different languages, I can get them inside and the one agent can help them since he sounds a lot like the big man. They start talking about what options we have with Iran and Syria to stir things up a bit." He says, "That would probably work. But how will you know where the information is going?" I say, "Call it an educated guess but I think it is more about oil than anything else. They want to jack the price up again." He says, "When do you want to do this?" I say, "Friday afternoon, by Monday we'll know who is talking to whom." He says, "It should work. I am game." I say, "Our sit down is Thursday at four downtown." He says, "I'll clear my schedule and tell my wife I'll be late." I say, "These usually take four or five hours sometimes less." He says, "Give me an address." I give him my card.

After my breakfast with him, I head to my house to try to figure out what is going to work best for Vicki and myself. I do a real good walk through. The house is big enough that we would each have enough room. I am not a clothes hog and the guest room that Natalie uses has another closet and extra dressers. The other bedroom I made into a study and my home office. The living room is nice not too large, the dining room and entry way are normal sized, the kitchen is large enough that I have a table that seats four and counter space. All the appliances are almost like new. It would be a shame to give all this up. Vicki's loft is very efficient, there is no wasted space yet I feel after a while we might get on each other's nerves since there is no room for escape. I guess I'll talk to her and give her my opinion. I could bring her out here this evening to see if she finds anything objectionable other than the fact we are not downtown and able to walk or grab a bus anywhere. This would be a huge change for her. Working downtown I can see the pluses of living down there too, I know I am spoiled out here since I have favorite places to go for different things. I look at all my bills and the mortgage payment do a tally and know how much I still owe. If the market was decent I could come out a little ahead but I don't see the market getting back to where it was for a very long time. How long do I want to sit on it, how much would I really get if I put it on the market? I change clothes to slacks and a sports jacket, no tie. Oh! Well, I may as well head downtown and get ready for my new responsibilities.

On the way downtown, I stop at the bank to replenish my spending money. I mean I splurged over the weekend that was for sure. Money doesn't last very long right now. I like paying cash and try not to use my credit card unless I absolutely have too, since I tend to forget about keeping the receipts. I know that will need to change. I get to the office around eleven-thirty and everybody is there waiting for their new assignments. McCray is in his office going through things and deciding what to leave and what to transfer to his new office. Vicki is in there helping him get things organized. I walk in and they both say, "Nice of you to join us." I say, "I need to give the staff their assignments but truthfully I don't even know where the files are for projects that need our attention." McCray says, "See that large file on top of the filing cabinet, those are all projects that Washington thinks we need to research. They are coded as to priority, the red tags mean first priority, blue are next level and yellow are when somebody has nothing better to do." I ask, "How many projects are in that file?" McCray says, "Right now twenty but that number will grow significantly after I weed through Schaunessy's folder." I ask, "Anything else I need to know right now?" McCray says, "Good luck and get the staff going." I take the file folder and go to the break room pour a cup of coffee and read through the Red Files first. Right off the bat I have four priority projects and think about the members of the staff and who seems best suited for each project. I call all of them to the break room and pass out folders for each team and say "These are the priority projects right now, by Thursday some of these may get shuffled when I get the new files from Director McCray. Read through them and see me if you have any questions. I will be in a closed door meeting for three hours this afternoon. So save your questions until tomorrow morning. I hope all of you will be here by nine since we are going to have a lot of work to get done. Thank you and good luck."

About a quarter to one Vicki came back to the cubby hole I had been using for the past few weeks and said, "I guess he is ready for you two to have your closed door meeting. I told him about us and he said he will work out the switch with one of the secretaries over at his new office. He agrees that if we are going to make this work it would be better if we weren't at the same office. He also asked if we were thinking of having any children. I said we haven't even discussed that or really even thought about it." He said, "You probably should before it happens, if you know what I mean." I said, "Something else to throw into the mix I guess. We'll talk later I want to tell you my thoughts on another matter too." So I headed up to his office for our meeting.

He said, "Congratulations and good luck with Vicki, she is very spirited and has some very strong opinions but I guess you already figured that out." I said, "Yes, last night as a matter of fact. We started seeing each other more or less by accident, we had lunch a couple of times and I was surprised by the variety of subjects that we discussed and one thing lead to another and we went to dinner one night and she invited me in to look at her loft, from then on we have been more or less inseparable except for when we are working." He said, "I noticed the change in you. This relationship has been really good for you since you don't seem as nervous as before." I said, "You're right and I didn't really notice it myself but I was able to talk to Tony and Val to explain that I knew ours was not going to work. Once I did that it seemed a huge load was lifted off my shoulders." He said, "Now getting down to brass tacks here are the things you need to know and what my recommendations would be."

We talked for over two hours and finally I said, "Did you notice that we seem to have one team that has gotten themselves into a relationship?" He said, "I thought that was happening and tried splitting them up at IIT but somehow they wound up together in spite of it." I said, "I noticed it too and I am wondering if it will affect their performance." He said, "Talk to them or split them up so they aren't together all the time, when relationships sour it can affect the moral of the whole department. I could always arrange to transfer one to DC for six months since they are clamoring for new people." I said, "I like that idea we switch one with them and see if that works. I'll talk to both of them and let you know which one would benefit the most by the swap." He asked, "Any questions on what we covered?" I said, "How long are you going to be available to help me make this work?" He said, "As long as you need me but I think in a few weeks you will be comfortable enough in your new position." I look at all the stuff in boxes and he said, "All that stuff will be transferred over to Michigan Avenue tomorrow morning. I will have our maintenance crew over here early to pick up the stuff. Vicki will be here tomorrow morning to get you setup and show Denise around and learn the routine here. Then she will be joining me at Michigan Avenue, she is like my right hand person she knows my quirks and can filter my calls better than anybody else I have known." I said, "Thanks Rodger for everything, I really do hope I don't let you down." He said, "Mark my words Washington will be looking to move both of us to DC within two years."

After we finish our meeting he left to go over to the Michigan Avenue office. I talked to Vicki for a few minutes and said, "I need to go take care of some things. I'll see you around eight if that is OK." She said, "He told you I would be working for him starting after tomorrow?" I said, "Yes, he told me." She asked, "Did you talk about us?" I said, "I told him how this all happened and that you have had a real impact on my thinking and made it easier for me to figure things out." She says "Thank you I didn't know that." I said, "We'll talk more later. By the way did any of the staff come up to you and ask any questions." She said, "No but some of them looked puzzled. They were grumbling about what you said about you expecting them here by nine to get things rolling." I said, "I want to institute a new policy, I think them coming in whenever is counterproductive, if we have a nine a.m. meeting that keeps them focused." She said, "He tried that before and it lasted about a month but then with the jobs they were working on that fell by the wayside for some reason." I said, "I'll keep that in mind." I kissed her and headed out to my house to take care of a few things."

I get to my house and gather my mail and go inside. I sit down at my desk and pay all my bills for the month. I look at the time and figure Natalie will be home but I am not sure what time Rachael gets home. I decide to wait a little while longer as I try to formulate my plan in my mind. I never intended for this to happen but like Vicki said you can't plan for it, it just happens. At six-thirty I call Natalie and say, "Hi sweetie, how are you today?" She says, "Hi Dad, this is a surprise I was going to call you after dinner to ask you the same thing." I ask, "Is your mother home yet?" She says, "Yes, she just got home a few minutes ago and we were trying to figure out what to make for dinner." I ask, "May I talk to her for a minute?" Natalie gives her the phone. I ask, "Would it be alright if I came over to talk to both of you for a little while?" Rachael says, "What time are you talking since we were going to get dinner started?" I say, "I could bring pizza if you like that way you will not have to cook." She says, "I'll ask Natalie if she wants pizza and what she wants on it." I hear her asking Natalie and she says from the place by him

I like their special, Dad knows what that is. So Rachael says, "Yes, that will be fine." I ask, "You still like your pizza with mushrooms, green pepper and sausage?" She says, "That is what I order if it's good pizza not cheap like Caesar's or Domino's." I say, "I'll see you in thirty minutes." I order the pizzas from Rocko and figure I better call Vicki and tell her it will be later than eight.

I pick up the pizzas and go over to Natalie's house. I ring the bell. Rachael opens the door I say, "Pizza Delivery." She says, "You don't look like the pizza delivery guy." She invites me in. Natalie comes up to me and gives me a kiss and says, "Hi Dad, how did you know I was dying for pizza?" I said, "It was an educated guess." We go into her dining room and I say, "I wanted to talk to both of you and explain a couple of things and rather than call you on the phone I wanted to talk to you both in person since what I am going to say has to do with both of you." I clear my throat and I feel like I'm standing up in front of an audience and I feel my stomach getting queasy. I say, "First off I was promoted to McCray's job since Director Schaunessy had a heart attack on Monday and is in the hospital. Washington told McCray effective immediately you are the new Director of the Midwest office and Huggins gets your job. That means I will no longer be a field agent and I will be downtown everyday. The other thing is I know this will shock both of you but I fell in love with a lady downtown. McCray's Secretary Vicki. I didn't expect that to happen but it did and I wanted you both to know it doesn't change anything between us. We haven't decided yet if we will be living downtown or at my place. Regardless, I will be there for you both if you need me and I will still make your games Natalie and we will still have our Sunday's together. Vicki wants to meet you and get to know you but I will leave that up to you to decide."

Rachael said, "Well congratulations Jim on three things, your promotion, your new found love and that you had the nerve to come talk to us face to face and tell us about it. You really surprised me with your straight forwardness and honesty. Have you set a date or anything like that?" I said, "I will most likely have that information tomorrow since we are going to hash it all out tonight. She told me she was having her family for Thanksgiving dinner and would like both of you to come too." She said, "Did you tell her I invited you here?" I said, "Yes, as a matter of fact I did but the invitation came while we were just friends. Right now we have more pressing issues to take care of other than a Thanksgiving dinner." Rachael said, "Tell her I will think about it, I guess we could be civil I mean if you two are going to be getting married." I said, "That was all I needed to hear. I will convey the reply. Now tell me what you really think of this unexpected turn of events." Rachael said, "Really Jim I'm happy for you. I think you will be a great husband for her, if you can give up being a field agent for her you must really love her." I said, "That wasn't even in the equation, I had no idea I would get the promotion and so fast. My head is spinning right now with my new responsibilities at work and the changes in my personal life. I really do love both of you more than you know. This just came like a thunderbolt." Natalie said, "Can we eat before the pizza gets stone cold?" I said, "Sure sweetie, let's eat." So I ate with them and then headed downtown.

I get to Vicki's and I tell her everything that I told Natalie and Rachael and their responses. She says, "Jim, I have never met anybody like you before in my life. What you just told me that you did further solidified that fact. How did I get so lucky as to find you?" I say "I am the one that should be asking that question." She says, "Perhaps it was just a matter of fate, I truly believe things happen for a reason, sometimes the reason isn't clear at the time but later it becomes crystal clear." I said, "I guess we will find out." Then we proceeded to talk about her loft and my house. Finally I said "Let's take a ride out to my place and I will show you what I mean and then you decide. I mean if you want to stay downtown I will agree to it but we will need at least a three bedroom two bath unit, since if Natalie spends the night on occasion we need a bedroom and a bathroom for her plus if we have out of town guests it is nicer." She says, "You have really given this a lot of thought." I say, "Yesterday when I went there before I came downtown I walked through my place critically to see if it would fill the bill. The only big difference is you can't walk everywhere or grab a CTA bus to get you there." She says, "OK I'll grab a sweater and I'll go look at your place."

We drive out to my place and give her the twenty-five cent tour. We get to my bedroom and she looks it over and says "We would definitely need to change this." Then she sits down on the bed. I sit down beside her and say "What do you mean?" She says, "This mattress will not hold up plus I would need a vanity and a dresser. I have them both at my Mother's house but never wanted move them to put them in apartments since I moved every few years. She would be happy to get them out of her place." So then I drive her around the neighborhood and show her the local pizza place Rocko's, where the Dominick's store is, plus the Catholic Church, since I found out she is Catholic. She says, "I am rusty on my driving. I have a license but haven't driven in like ten years since I walk or take the bus." I say, "That will not be a problem. You'll get plenty of practice if we move out here." She says, "I would like a church wedding if you want to go through the ritual but that means we can't get married right away." I say, "What makes you think I wouldn't do that?" She says, "Can we go by the church tomorrow to find out what we need to do?" I say, "Whatever you want love." She says, "You are not a member of this church are you?" I say, "I have been inside a few times with Natalie, since she and her mother are Catholic and during her two weeks I would go with her to church on Sundays." She says, "So you know what we are all about?" I say, "Yes for the most part, I don't understand a lot of the Latin but yes I guess I do." She says, "Originally I just wanted us to get married, I didn't even think about a church wedding but then I figured if I didn't have one that would break my Mom's heart. I think she really gave up on me finding the right man and getting married. I called her while you went out to take care of things and she was so excited I thought she was going to cry right then. She asked me, when she was going to meet you? I said, Friday night if that's OK with you." I say, "Friday night is fine." We get back to her place and it is almost midnight.

Chapter 27

Wednesday morning I am up at six-thirty I smell the coffee go take a shower and then fix my coffee. Around seven Vicki joins me at the table wrapped in her sheet. She says, "You don't have to leave this early you know." I say, "I know but I am an early riser and I have a lot on my mind this morning so I need to formulate my plan for the office. You can sleep for another hour and then we can go to the office together." She kisses me and goes back to bed. I flip on my laptop and start writing. After about thirty minutes, I put in the name of my church and copy down the information so I can call the priest later so we can talk to him about getting married. I look at my plan for the office and go I need to import all the staff's personal information and get familiar with each of them one on one, find out their quirks, their hobbies, etc. I guess I can pick Vicki's brain some since she knows a lot more about them. I fix another cup of coffee and look at the clock it's almost time to wake sleeping beauty. So I go in and kiss her and say, "It's almost eight we need to leave by eight-thirty." She shakes her head and says, "Five minutes more?" I sit there and finally she stirs and says, "OK I'll get up and she gets up goes and gets in the shower, fixes her hair and puts on some makeup slips on a dress and puts her heels on and says I'm ready." I look at the clock and it is eight thirty on the dot. I go "Wow! How do you do that?" She says, "Lots of years of practice." We drive to office and get ready for the day.

Around nine o'clock some of the staff start showing up by ten after everybody is there. I call them altogether in the break room and go over the assignments and ask if they have any questions. There are a couple of questions so I answer them and I layout my plan. I ask them all to think about this as a new challenge. I say, "I feel that if we have a weekly meeting as a team we can eliminate any problems before they arise. I know this is a change for you but it is also a huge change for me. Unlike you, I was pretty much a lone ranger and there are projects like I worked on thinking that being a lone ranger is a good idea. Hopefully, one of you will be a candidate to take on projects like that. I know Director McCray liked you working as teams since another set of eyes sometimes helps. We will see how this works. I am open to suggestions on ways to improve things but in our business there are certain things we can't change. As all of you know, the stuff we work on is highly sensitive and the information we gather is proprietary and not to be shared with others outside our agency. Over the course of the next month or so I will be conducting annual reviews on each of you for Washington. I will tell you right now they want to steal one of you and swap you with an agent from Washington. They like to do that on occasion since it keeps everybody on their toes. Thank you all."

Vicki was busy with the guys from maintenance to gather up all of McCray's stuff and showing Denise the operation here. The two guys from maintenance were here probably for an hour. They had a flatbed cart and a two-wheel dolly, and they loaded everything into the elevator and were done. Vicki showed Denise around the office and showed her the break room and where all the office supplies and coffee-making stuff was located. She made the coffee when we first got there, so it would be ready for my meeting with the staff. I thought only two drank coffee and the others drank juice or energy drinks. Vicki told Denise, "We supply the coffee and the other drinks, since we don't want vending machines in the office. We order all the supplies from a distributor who drops them off so nobody has to go shopping." Denise seemed to grasp all the details. I noticed she had a stenographers tablet and was making notes that looked like scribbling to me. Vicki then sat down beside her at the desk and went through the programs in the computer, then she printed out a list of the staff and all the details she had on them. She handed me one and said, "I figured you would want a copy since I know your inquisitive mind so you can evaluate them better. I know they are coming up for annual review since it has to be in before year end." I said, "Thank you I made a note to ask you for that but figured you would be real busy showing Denise how everything works here." Vicki said, "Give me another ten minutes here and I will go over the stuff in there and you can move your stuff into your office." I said, "No problem, I have a bunch of things to do back there before I'm ready to move up here. Take your time. Besides it's almost lunchtime. Why don't you and Denise go have lunch, I'll listen for the phone." She said, "Thanks Jim, we might just take you up on that. Can we bring you something?" I said, "A corned beef on rye, with Swiss and mustard, no lettuce or tomato and a small bag of chips." I handed her a credit card.

While they go have lunch, I fix my coffee go back to my cubby hole to organize the stuff to transfer to my new office. I guess I'll have to grab some stuff from home to make the office look homey. I'll put a couple of pictures of Natalie on my desk and maybe my Corvette model of my dream car after Natalie goes to college. It is a 1983 Stingray from the year I graduated high school. I wonder if Natalie had pictures taken in her basketball uniform yet. I'll call her tonight and ask. That would look great there. I look at the clock and make a phone call. I call the Catholic Church by my house and ask for Father Duggan. He answers and I say, "This is Mr. Huggins, I live in your parish and during the summer when my daughter spends her two weeks we attend your church. I wanted to see if my fiancée and I come and talk to you around six to find out about getting married there?" He says, "Mr. Huggins, are you or your fiancé Catholic?" I say, "She is." He asks, "Practicing?" I say, "I assume so since she wants a church wedding." He says, "Six o'clock is fine we eat at five so I will be available just come to the parish house and ring the bell. Sister Angeline will show you to the office." Well at least I took care of that, I'll tell Vicki later I called to set up an appointment.

Vicki and Denise got back at ten to one with my lunch and Vicki brought it to me in my cubbyhole. She said, "I figured you would already have your stuff moved to your new office." I said, "I wanted to wait until you got back. Besides, I was busy enough. The phone never rang by the way." She said, "Some days are like that. But usually during lunch, the only person who would call was Director Schaunessy looking for Rusty." She said, "I told Denise we are informal here and on a first name basis. She likes that over Michigan

Avenue and how formal they are." I said, "I like that. I don't want to be addressed as Mister. Jim is fine with me." She said, "That was what I figured." I said, "I am going to eat my lunch in the break room, I don't like eating at my desk and getting food on the computer keys." She said, "I'll get your office ready while you eat. Director McCray is probably wondering where I am since I told him I would see him after lunch." I went to the break room, and she set up my office.

After I eat I go to my office and look it over and go, "Why did he leave that stuff here?" She says, "That is personal memorabilia that he is trying to decide if he wants to ship home or just pitch since he has so much stuff." I look at the pictures on the wall and figure most of them can stay or go they don't bother me. I would like a couple of Chicago pictures but I'll have to find the ones I want. I tell Vicki, the office looks nice. She says, "Thanks, I changed a few things around since I figured you wanted to be able to look out at the skyline." I say, "You were right on that part even from this view I like the skyline." She says, "Here are the codes for the computer and access keys to get into the accounts which you will need. The keys for the file cabinets are here and the rings are coded with colors so you should be able to find files you are looking for. Other than that I can't think of anything else. Oh! Yes, this button here calls the secretary if you are having trouble trying to find something or if you want her to tell people you are unavailable." I say, "How do I get you?" She says, "You already did get me lover boy." I say, "I'll pick you up on Michigan we have a six o'clock meeting with Father Duggan." She says, "You called them about us?" I say, "I sure did." She kisses me and says, "I'll be ready at five-fifteen." I say, "You might want to put on fresh lipstick." She says, "You might want to clean your lips too." Then she leaves.

I am working at my desk and Denise calls me and says, "Phone Jim, it's the boss." I pick up the phone and say, "Hi Rodger or should I say Director?" He says, "Funny Jim, I was trying to find out where my secretary is." I say, "She just left, I ask her to take Denise to lunch and bring me back a sandwich." He asked, "How did your meeting with the employees go?" I said, "As far as I could tell, it went fine and I told them to be on their toes since Washington wants to steal one of them on a swap for six months. I think that will shake them up and make them think, plus they all have reviews coming up." He said, "You're right that will definitely shake them up." I said, "I also said I might be looking for somebody to be a lone ranger to do jobs like I did. That raised a couple of eyebrows, I saw a couple of the staff perk up on that." He said, "I didn't even give that any thought. But you're right. We might need another person like you." I said, "I was thinking about Buranski and recruiting him for special ops." He said, "We can talk to him on Thursday about that option." I said, "I think we can use him on some projects with his talents." He said, "First we need to clear him through Washington. They still have some doubts about his background." I said, "After Thursday, there shouldn't be any doubts." He said, "We'll talk again tomorrow before the meeting." I said, "I set the meeting for 4 p.m. here." He said, "That will work. I'll have Vicki arrange my schedule so that I am out of the office after three until Friday morning."

Around three, I go out to the break room and found some of the staff in there talking at one table. I asked "Questions or a problem?" They said, "Neither, we were talking about tonight's plans." I said, "Hawks and Coyotes right?" They said, "Yes." I said, "I'll take the Hawks. They lost Sunday night to the Oilers." They said, "Do you follow them?" I said, "I am a recent convert. Earlier I would watch them if they were on and I had nothing else to do. But now, I'm a believer." I said, "Just try not to stay out too late, this week is half over and I don't think we have accomplished anything concrete yet. I know our jobs are not like factory jobs where they measure performance by the number of units sold or manufactured. Ours are non-tangible costs, but it is a matter of how much useful intelligence we gather and can verify as real." They said, "We never heard our jobs described in that sense. We were always told it's a matter of national security. That is why we are in existence and what we do is strictly hush-hush." I said, "That part is true that what we do is hush-hush. But the reality is, if we don't provide useful tangible proof about a proposed threat or a matter that concerns our security, they can eliminate our agency and turn it back over to other agencies. Then we would all be out of jobs and I don't want to see that happen."

When I left the break room, I could hear them talking, which to me was a good sign. They have gotten out of their funk from McCray being promoted and giving me his job. I stopped by Denise, and she asked, "What time do I need to be here in the morning?" I said, "If you are here by nine that is fine, I will be here around eight every day so you can start earlier if you prefer. That way, you can avoid the five o'clock rush." She said, "That would be great! I mean I can be here at eight-thirty since the train lets me off right at Madison Street and I walk two blocks and I'm here." I said, "Today any time after four you are free to leave, I imagine this was a hectic day for you." She said, "Yes it was, but I would rather be busy. Over there, half the time we were bored and didn't have a lot to do." I said, "Well here you will always have plenty to do."

Around four forty-five, the staff starts leaving. I am by the front desk going over the call log and looking at messages that need to be returned. They ask, "You watching the game tonight?" I say, "No I have other plans I forgot about the game until I saw you talking. I will see the end of the game though I'm sure." They say, "Goodnight Jim." That really surprised me. I shut everything off and lock the doors and go get my car to pick up Vicki on Michigan Avenue. I pick her up and we head out to my house so we can go talk to Father Duggan at the church. We get there and ring the bell Sister Angeline answers the door. I say, "Good evening Sister Angeline, we are here to see Father Duggan." She leads us to his office and shows us in. He gets up and shakes our hand. I say, "This is my fiancé Vicki Sandquist." He says, "Here is what you two need to do if you want to have a church wedding here and he details everything about me taking a couple of classes to understand Catholicism and the fact we need to post the banns in the weekly. We usually need four month's but the time can be shortened if everybody is in agreement and all participants have fulfilled their obligations."

We said, "We would like to be married before the end of the year if that is possible." He looked at the calendar and said, "That is not a lot of time." We said, "We know but we really want to get married as soon as possible. We can go get married downtown and come here to have the marriage blessed." He thought about it and said, "We can work it out, it isn't like you two are twenty one and eighteen and I'm sure you are not going to take the marriage vows lightly." He looked at the calendar and said, "December 18th we have an opening at two p.m." I said, "Book it." He asked Vicki a bunch of questions and then he asked me the same bunch of questions. He said, "I think you two are well suited. We need you to fill out this request and then pay to cover the printing cost and I'll make sure they get posted in due time. You, Jim, will have to come here for the next three Saturdays for two hours each Saturday. Vicki, since you are of the faith you know what you need to do, then you need to get your marriage license from downtown and bring it before the ceremony." We thanked him and left. Vicki said, "I'm so happy! Let's celebrate someplace." I said, "I know just the place." I drove to North Avenue and went to my favorite steak place and Vicki said, "This is your favorite steak house. It's my dad's too."

After dinner we go back to her place and talk for a couple of hours before going to bed. Tomorrow while McCray and I are tied up in the meeting with Buranski Vicki is going to have dinner with her mother to tell her what we decided and when we are going to get married. Then she has to line up her bridesmaids and go try on wedding dresses. She has girlfriends from college that still hound her about getting married now she can get them off her back. She said every time they get together it is the same. They are showing her pictures of their children and how much they have grown. Me, I will be hard pressed to find some buddies to be in the wedding party. I mean I could ask Tony he would be thrilled in a way, I could ask McCray to be my best man since he is the closest thing to a true buddy I have. I guess that's one of the disadvantages of being a lone ranger you don't develop friendships. Maybe I could ask Rocko he might like having a Saturday night off. I mean all the guys I know are going to be ten or fifteen years older than her bridesmaids. The guys I went to college with are scattered all over the place and busy with their jobs. They don't even get back to Illinois to visit family anymore. I haven't talked to them in twenty years or more. My high-school buddies I still have two or three I talk to on occasion. I'll wait and see how many I need. I'll ask McCray tomorrow before our meeting.

Chapter 28

Thursday morning I am up at six-thirty go take my shower and fix my coffee. A few minutes after seven, Vicki comes out and says, "Are you happy Jim?" I say, "I most certainly am." She says, "I am too, I have never been this happy. I hope it lasts forever." I say, "I'll do what I can to keep you happy." She says, "In that case come back to bed for a little while." I say, "No fair pulling a shot like that, is that unsportsman like conduct or what?" She nibbles on my ear and says "Follow me." So I follow her back to bed. She helps me get undressed and pulls me into bed. After twenty minutes I say, "I have to get another shower I am supposed to be in the office at eight." She says, "You'll make it. I'll scrub your back." I say, "Oh, No you don't I fell for that before and we were in the shower for an hour if I remember correctly." She says, "OK tonight then." I say, "That sounds really good, but I better get moving." So I take a fast shower get dressed and drive to the office. I get there at five after eight. Ramon the parking guy says, "You have a new parking spot your boss told me to give you his right by the door since he doesn't need it any longer now that he is on Michigan Avenue." I go in and turn everything on and make a pot of coffee. Eight—thirty Denise shows up and a few minutes later the staff starts showing up. I go in my office flip on the computer to catch up on what happened in the game last night. Damn they lost again with a score of 2-1.

A few minutes after nine, I went into the break room and said, "Tough game last night! I really thought they would win that game." I said, "I'm glad to see all your smiling faces this morning. I talked to Director McCray last night to give him an update. I gave you all a thumbs up. Today I will start my reviews since there is a lot I need to cover with each of you. The reports don't get turned in until the beginning of December. So if something needs a little finessing, there is time to improve. I will start with Adam at ten in my office. Today I will most likely only have time for two of you and I haven't decided who will be next up. Let's get to work. Thank you."

I go to my office and took out the personnel folders and found Adams folder. He has been with the IIA since 2005. He had gotten good reviews each year, was a political science major in college, and was recruited by Schaunessy upon graduation. All the cases he had been assigned to were related to politics, and his reports were always extremely detailed. I went through the file to read a couple of them, and I was wondering why he hadn't decided to move into a job with one of the political parties. To me he was the right age to get involved in that. I made a couple of notes on things to discuss with him and put the files back. At ten Denise told me that Adam was waiting and I had her show him in. She closed the door and left.

I talk to Adam for about forty minutes and cover everything in his review. Then I decide to ask him some other questions just to see how he would respond. He is sharp and knows pretty much what he would like to do. He says in five years he wants to move to Washington to be closer to the political action and maybe work for one of the major contenders in the presidential race. Along the way, he hopes to be married and have two children and a house in McLean. I was surprised how well he thought everything out. I thanked him for his time and told him his report looked good. Well at least now I know why he is so involved in the political cases.

Denise calls me and says phone line one. I pick up the phone it is McCray and he asks, "Are you free for lunch at one?" I say, "I can arrange that, where?" He says, "Our usual haunt." I say, "OK I'll see you there." I go out and tell Denise I will be out of the office from twelve-thirty until two-thirty if anybody is looking for me. Then I think who would be looking for me. I'll be at lunch with McCray. Vicki is at the Michigan Avenue office and Buranski is in Orland Park. I go back in my office and try to decide who to review next. Perhaps, Erika she is very athletic, works out a lot and is paired with Mitch more often than not. I grab her file and read through it. She played Volleyball, Basketball, and was on a swim team and tried out for the Olympics but didn't get chosen. Her majors in college were Coaching and Law. She was recruited in 2006 by Schaunessy to add more diversity to the staff. She is five ten, one hundred and thirty pounds, blue eyes, dishwater blonde. For fun, she plays beach volleyball with some girls she went to school with and in the winter she plays on a girls basketball team. She is very active in her community and works on food drives during the holidays. Her reviews have always been extremely good and she impressed McCray I see his notes. She may be a candidate for a job with more responsibility. I keep her file out and make a couple of notes. Tomorrow morning at ten.

Twelve-thirty I leave to meet McCray for lunch. I decide I can use the exercise so I walk the four blocks to the restaurant. It is around forty degrees and a little overcast. So far we have gotten lucky no snow yet. We might get really lucky and not get any until in December that works for me. I get to the restaurant at five minutes to one. A cab pulls up and McCray gets out and we walk in together. The hostess shows us to his favorite booth and tells us the waitress will be with us shortly. We talk for a few minutes while we wait. I tell McCray, "I started the reviews and have a question about Erika." He asks, "What is your question?" I say, "I read your review from last year and you think she may be a candidate for a position with more responsibility. What did you mean by that?" He says, "She has all the makings of a lead investigator; she only needs the opportunity to prove herself." I say, "So in a year nothing worthwhile turned up to find out if she could do it?" He says, "Nothing I could earmark as a test. She did her job and always gave a hundred and ten percent on every project. Maybe in the new group of cases I am reviewing right now there will be one to move her up to lead." I say, "Just flag the one and I'll see how she does. I want to pair her with a different agent, one of the newer men for a change. Why does she always seem to be with Mitch?" He says, "They are one of the best teams, they complement each other nicely. She writes great reports. He is a digger like you and keeps digging to uncover things others might miss."

Then I say, "To change the subject. How would you like be my best man next month when Vicki and I get married?" He asks, "What day?" I say, "Saturday the eighteenth." He says, "I will have to check with my wife, but right now I would say yes. I know the following week I am on vacation until after the New Year. Washington wasn't pleased, but I reminded them I am always on vacation at that time. Besides, you know as well as I do, nothing gets done for those two weeks except paperwork to close out the year." I said, "That was one of the reasons we wanted to get married. That way, we get a honeymoon and don't have to work for a couple of weeks to boot." He said, "Your boss might not like you taking that time off while he is gone too." I laugh and say, "I know, we are taking a cruise in the Caribbean for five nights and coming home for Christmas and the New Year. I will be in the office to close out the year and Vicki will be doing your reports I'm sure." He says, "That's what I like about you. You plan everything in advance." I say, "It must be the training." We eat our lunch and I say, "Four p.m. our meeting with Buranski." He says, "I already told Vicki I would be gone the rest of the afternoon, I'll walk back with you and annoy Denise until our meeting." We walk back to the office. Denise gives me a couple of messages. I go make two phone calls and get things setup for our meeting. I get the staff together and say, "You can all leave at three-thirty today. I will see you all tomorrow bright and early and review some assignments."

Buranski arrives at ten to four. I ask, "Did you park in our lot?" He says, "I parked on the street." I say, "You might want to move your car. I'll tell Ramon to let you park in our lot. Your car will be safer." I call Ramon and tell him to give him my old spot. He walks back in a few minutes later so we can start our meeting. I make the introductions and he says, "Director McCray I owe you a lot for interceding and finding Grozdan like you did. Thank you." McCray says, "You have been very helpful and have lived up to your part of the bargain, I thank you for that." Then we start the full blown interrogation and cover some missing information in his bio that our sources could not verify. We asked about his relationship with Filchev and other contacts in Bulgaria. He told us outright that when he came here from Bulgaria, he never figured he would hear from anybody there since he wanted to start a new life for his family. He was surprised when Filchev contacted him about this project. He said there wasn't anybody else here in the States he could ask to handle this request. His construction job was a perfect fit to get access to the house. That was why he told Mariano to contact me personally and nobody else since he knew of my special electronics training in Russia for two years. The meeting lasted until after eight. McCray said, "I think I have everything I need. This should satisfy Washington. Now we want to ask you a question?" I asked, "What do you think about joining us for special ops jobs as the need arises? We were impressed by your thoroughness on this project, and you possess some highly skilled training that could be useful to us. We still need to clear this with Washington, but I think it is a win-win situation."

He said, "On what terms?" I said, "We would pay you as an outside contractor. We would make sure you were never in any jeopardy as far as getting sent back to Bulgaria. You would be well compensated for your time." He said, "I will think it over and talk to my wife and it can't interfere with my job at KBW Construction." I said, "Understood." He said, "Call me after you find out from Washington. Hopefully, they will approve me." McCray shook his hand and said, "Welcome aboard Karl." Buranski said, "And your first name?" McCray said, "Rodger." He said, "Thanks Rodger! In Bulgaria, everybody calls everybody by their last name. I don't really know why but that was what we were taught. In this country, friends use first names and bosses are usually 'Sir' or 'Madam'." McCray said, "We try to be informal. I don't like being called boss or mister and Jim follows in my footsteps. We will be in touch with you as soon as we know anything. Normally, Washington takes a few weeks to decide things like this." Buranski said, "Have a good evening," and he got up to leave. I said, "Can you wait a few minutes?" He said, "Yes I can." McCray said, "I will leave you two alone. I have a bunch of information to send to Washington."

After McCray left, I said to Buranski, "Remember that project I talked to you about to send some phony info to Mariano. The big man will be in town this weekend, so I just found out today. Monday morning, are you busy?" He said, "Not that I know of why?" I said, "I wanted to come to your office to review what is said in Hyde Park over the weekend. Say at seven." He said, "That will work. I can get there early." I said, "Ok! Then we can have our people track where the information went. I will know in a day or two if there was anything confidential in any of the conversations that sets off any alarms." He said, "That is good thinking and you will know who Filchev is sending it to by then?" I said, "We should, it is just a matter of what is discussed and with whom." He asked, "You like strong coffee?" I said, "Yes I do. I'll bring some cinnamon rolls. Do you like them?" He said, "Homemade ones?" I said, "Done! I'll see you Monday morning."

After Buranski leaves I turn everything off lock the place up and call Vicki. I get her voice mail and think, Oh! Yes, she was going to her mothers and then she and a couple of girls were going to look at gowns and a wedding dress. I call Natalie to tell her what was decided. She answers the phone I say, "Tell your mother Vicki and I are getting married on the 18th December by Father Duggan." She says, "Dad, really you want me to tell Mom, you better call her yourself. I can't believe you are getting married that soon." I say, "We didn't want to wait the four months so I made a deal with Father Duggan that he couldn't refuse." She says, "What did you say? Did you tell him she was pregnant?" I say, "No silly, I said we could just go downtown and get married at city hall then have the church bless our marriage." He said, "Let me see what we can do. So they had a two o'clock open so we filled it in. I know it is going to cost me extra money." She says, "I would never have thought he would go for that." I say "Marriage is big business for the church." She says, "Dad, you must really love her, I hope I like her when I meet her." I say, "Sunday is still our day I need a big favor from you." She asks, "What favor?" I say, "Can you steal your Mom's recipe for homemade cinnamon rolls and make a double batch on Sunday?" She says, "I know that recipe by heart I make them every other week it seems." I say, "After church we will go the store and get all the stuff OK?" She says, "That will be fun." I say, "Do I need to call you Mom or can you let her talk on your phone?" She says, "Hold on I'll get her, I love you, Dad." I say, "I love you too sweetie."

Rachael gets on the phone and so I tell her about our wedding plans. She says, "Jim, You still amaze me. Thank you for telling me about this. Do you expect Natalie and me to be at your wedding?" I say, "Why not, she's my daughter and you are her mother." She says, "Plus your ex?" I say, "So?" She asks, "Who is standing up with you?" I say, "McCray as things stand right now." She asks, "How many bridesmaids?" I say, "A Maid of Honor and two bridesmaids I think." She asks, "Who else are you going to ask if you need too?" I say, "Probably Tony and Rocko, remember I was a lone ranger no buddies after we got divorced." She says, "It was your job. You couldn't make friends because you only wanted to work all the time." She says, "Everybody needs friends even if only workmates to go out and have fun with, but not you your job was all you ever thought about." I say, "I realize that now more than you know but truthfully I never was interested enough to make friends. Hopefully, I can make amends and grow some friendships now." She says, "That would be nice." I say, "I could start with you as my friend, you know me better than anybody else. What do you say?" She says, "Jim, OK I'll try it but don't ask me any questions about your love life or advice on those matters." I say, "Deal. Saturdays I have to go for two hours of training at the church for three weeks straight." She says, "Lucky you." I say, "Thank you Rachael, I really need you in my corner." After I get off the phone I call the pizza joint and order a pizza to go and then drive to Vicki's place.

Vicki got home around eleven and said, "I saw you called. But we were getting fitted, and then we went out to eat. I was going to call you back but then figured you would be here sleeping." I said, "No I called Natalie and told her and her mom when the day was. Then I ordered a pizza and came here. I hadn't eaten since lunch with McCray." She said, "Did you finish it all?" I said, "No, I saved about half. I know you. You'll eat cold for breakfast." She asked, "Where did you get it from?" I said, "Lou's to go." She said, "It might not last until breakfast. The girls were being goody goody. We all had salads." We talked for about an hour and she devoured the rest of the pizza and said, "It was almost as good cold." I said, "I know it tasted really good to me tonight too." It was almost twelve-thirty when we went to bed. I swear we weren't in bed ten minutes and she said, "You promised me a special shower tonight." I said, "Are you serious?" She grabbed the sheet and said, "I sure am."

Chapter 29

I wake up at seven-fifteen and go I really need to get up. Why did I let her con me into that? I feel groggy this morning. I feel like I was out drinking with the staff at work. At my age, I can't do that stuff anymore. It's hell being over forty-five. Vicki is thirty-two, I don't know how older guys go out until two or three and get up at six-thirty, they must take vitamins or something. That is something else I need to do I am overdue for my annual check-up I saw a reminder from my doctor in the stack of mail. I should call him today and get in before the wedding. The doctor will be surprised. I haven't checked my blood pressure in months but I know I should. Vicki stirs a little I slip out of bed and pour my coffee, thank goodness for the timer on the pot. Every morning at six it perks. At least this morning I don't need a shower, I get dressed and pour a second cup of coffee and here comes Vicki rubbing her eyes. She says, "See I told you that you would get up this morning." I say, "Barely I didn't even want to move this morning." She says, "Thank you I enjoyed it." I say, "I did too my little sexpot." She smiled and says, "I can sleep another hour. My boss doesn't expect me until nine." I say, "I asked him to be my best man. He will let me know for sure once he talks to his wife." She asks, "You're home tonight right?" I say "I sure am, let's eat in tonight." She says, "I'll cook."

I get to the office at eight-twenty and go to the break room to make a pot of coffee. Boy I sure could use a cinnamon roll this morning, maybe once Denise gets here I can run out and pick up donuts for the staff. This week has been unbelievable in more ways than one. I wait for the coffee to brew and pour a hot cup and go to my office. Denise gets here about a quarter to nine, the one bus was late and she apologized. I say, "It's not a big problem besides it's Friday and I may let everyone off early today to enjoy the weekend."

She asks me, "Do you have any weekly reports I need to turn into Director McCray?" I say, "Yes, once I put them together but first I am going to pick up something. Do you prefer donuts, cinnamon rolls, or bagels? I thought I would treat the staff this morning." She says, "There is a bakery over on Halsted Street that has real good sweet rolls and everything, that way you could mix them up." I say "Thanks I didn't think of that. I'll be back in twenty minutes." So I go pick up a mixture and put the box in the break room. They even had good cinnamon rolls so I was happy. I tell Denise, "I am unavailable for the next hour or two so I can work on my reports." She says, "I'll take messages if anybody calls."

At eleven I tell Denise "I have the reports for you, from what I remember you only need to fax them over to Vicki and she will give them to Director McCray." She hands me a list of calls and I say, "When did I become so popular?" She says, "Some of the calls were for Director McCray but they were mostly people looking for donations or favors, I didn't think I should give them his new office number. He will get plenty of those calls." I go through the stack and there is one name I recognize so I call the person back. I say, "This is Deputy Director Huggins, what can I do for you Lt. McElroy?" He says, "What did you do get promoted Agent Huggins?" I say, "It wasn't my idea. I'm a field man like you. What can we do for you?" He says, "That doctor who moved into the house next door is pretty strange. We were told he would be living here for about six months while he finishes some special classes. He has had some foreign visitors the past few days. I thought you might want to check them out." I say, "I appreciate that, I haven't gotten a memo or a tip from anybody about any activity at that house. I'll check it out and get back to you." I call McCray and tell him about the conversation. He says, "Let me check with Washington, they were doing a check on this doctor and I haven't seen anything from them yet." I say, "We still have two of our staff there right?" He says, "By the way I told my wife about your request and she said I could do it as long as she gets invited to the wedding too." I say, "No problem, it isn't going to be a huge affair." He says, "Yes, there are two of the agency people there.

I borrowed them a couple of weeks ago, they will be heading back to DC on Monday."

Around noon, I tell Denise "I am going out for a couple of hours, please hold the fort down for me. If anybody calls I am out of the office and you don't know where." I go get my SUV and drive to Orland Park on a hunch. I call Buranski on his cell phone. He answers it and I say, "Karl. Are you free for lunch? I had a taste for a Gyro and I know a good spot." He says, "Give me twenty minutes." I say, "I just left downtown, I'll meet you there." I drive to the Gyro place and wait for him to show up. He parks next to my SUV and we go inside and order. I ask, "That feed you have, is there any way we can listen to what is going on in that house or is it only activated by the other house?" He says, "I think I can redirect the listening devices to listen to this house. Why do you ask?" I say, "I got a tip from the CPD that this doctor is having foreign visitors almost every day. So I told him I would check them out." He said, "When I get back I will try it. There is a way I know. I will check whether I can do it from here. If I was there, I could just manually redirect them. I'll check with Sergi. He'll know." I said, "I would rather not get more people involved." He said, "No involvement. I'll tell him I have another project coming up that needs to be controlled from a remote location. He is a tech geek. He likes challenges." I said, "If we uncover something here, Washington will approve you in no time." He said, "I'll call you after three. I have to check the house in Worth and then line up the crew for Wojowski's house." We walked out together and shook hands. I drove back downtown and Denise said, "Vicki called and I said you were out." I went to my office and called her. She said, "I know we are eating at home tonight. I just remembered I invited my mother to meet you tonight." I said, "Now that you mention it, yes I do vaguely remember." She asked, "You want me to reschedule it?" I said, "No, I don't want to get off to a bad start with your mother."

Three-thirty my cell phone rings. It is Buranski. He says, "I talked to Sergi he told me how those operate and so I redirected two of the microphones to this house and it works. The Doc had another visitor. They were talking in some dialect I can't understand." I say, "Do you have a tape recorder that you can copy the conversation to?" He says, "I can send you an audio now on the computer." I say, "Do that but if you can make a tape that might be easier." I go I wonder what this doctor is up to. Did Mariano even check the guy out? This is all too convenient to be a coincidence. The little hairs on the back of my neck start bothering me again. I hate when that happens I know we are in for something. I call McCray and tell him what Buranski said and that he was sending me an audio to listen to. McCray says, "Get Erika to come to your office I'll be there in fifteen minutes I want to listen to this. She is multi-talented and understands several languages, perhaps this will be her break." I say, "I'll have her here." I go out and tell the staff to have a good weekend, all of you are free to leave but I need Erika to stick around for a while to finish her review." I figure that way the others won't get suspicious. They all said, "Thanks for the treats in the break room, they were delicious."

McCray gets there at almost four. I am in my office talking to Erika and he walks in. She says, "Hi boss how is your new job?" He says, "It is more work than I thought it would be, it would be easier if Director Schaunessy was giving me three months of training but I guess we'll get through it. And please drop the boss stuff you know it irks me?" She says, "OK Rodge, do you like that better?" He says, "As a matter of fact yes. Now did Jim tell you why we kept you after telling the others they could leave?" She says, "He wanted to finish my review." He says, "That was part of it but we want you to listen to a conversation to see if you understand the language and what they are talking about." So I open the attachment and turn the volume up. She listens and says, "They are talking in Arabic about Iran and Syria and what needs to be done before the United States sends in special ops teams to bring about change. 'We need to talk to our friends in Saudi Arabia and Iraq to have a meeting of the ministers to work this out. Iran is a threat to all of us, if they keep pursuing nuclear power. Can you talk to your father about setting it up in Kuwait next month?' The doctor says, 'My father knows nothing about my work for the cause. I am here for additional medical training as far as he knows. Some other brothers have talked to me about this matter recently, and I told them I have a high-level minister who can arrange such a meeting. His fee is not cheap. But he is honest and keeps his mouth shut.' They said, 'Contact the others and set it up. Just let us know when and where the money is to be deposited'. He says, 'Leave me your cards with email addresses. I will not call you on the phone.'"

McCray said, "They talked to the doctor about those things. He must have a powerful father and the minister must be pretty high ranking to set up that type of meeting." Erika asked, "Do you want me to transcribe everything that was said into written form?" He said, "No I think with this and the tape recording, Washington can figure out what to do about this meeting. I think you just earned yourself a promotion little lady." She said, "I didn't expect that to happen for at least another couple of years. I still have a lot to learn." He said, "I have been keeping tabs on you. In fact, I made a note in your file, which Jim asked me about yesterday as to your qualifications for a lead investigator opening. I will approve his recommendation based upon what you did today." She said, "How soon will that happen?" He said, "I would say before the yearend, it will become official." She said, "Thank you for your confidence in me and your coaching so I could get better." He said, "Thank you for your hard work and your linguistics talent." She said, "My father was transferred to a lot of different posts while I was growing up and I learned something each time. So when we came back to the States, and I enrolled in college and I studied more." She left and McCray and I talked for a while. Both of us were overwhelmed by what happened at that house that day. I said, "If it hadn't been for Buranski's equipment already being in that house and his ability to reverse the microphones to pick up this conversation, we would have never found out about this." He said, "Washington will truly be surprised by this. If this turns out to be true and verifiable, it will definitely be a feather in both of our caps." I asked, "What are your plans this weekend?" He said, "I catch the night flight to DC and I'll be back Monday afternoon late." I said, "I have to meet my future mother-in-law tonight and tomorrow I have two hours of instructions at church." He said, "Sounds like fun. I'll call you Monday." I said, "Enjoy your weekend." He said, "You too."

After I shut everything off and lock up I head to Vicki's to meet my future mother-in-law over dinner. I get there and Vicki is setting the table. I ask, "How long until your mother gets here?" She says, "Thirty minutes or so why." I say, "I need to make a couple of phone calls and change clothes." She says, "You'll have time my mother is always ten or fifteen minutes late." I kiss her and she says, "What was that for?" I say, "Just because." I go call Natalie about Sunday to find out what she wants to do. She says, "We are making homemade cinnamon rolls per your request." I ask, "Well what about the other request of meeting Vicki?" She says, "Can we do it another day? I have a ton of studies to attend to plus I think I have two games coming up." I say, "Sure, I think Vicki and I will be at my place next week a couple of times, maybe we could have dinner someplace so you can meet her." I call Buranski on his cell phone and think about our plans for Monday since this turn of events overshadows what I wanted him to do. He answers the phone. I say, "That was a nice piece of work; Rodger is taking all that information with him since he will be in DC over the weekend. We have a gal in our office that speaks about six languages so she translated the audio you sent. Are you going to the office in the morning?" He says, "Yes, I have a lot of paperwork to do, plus I am meeting Radko for breakfast prior to that." I say, "That other project did you redirect the microphones yet?" He says, "No, I didn't hear from you and I told Ana I would be home by six." I say, "Leave them the way they are for now. I'm not interrupting dinner am I?" He says, "No we are taking Elisia out for a special dinner tonight." I say "Enjoy, I'll see you Monday."

I change clothes and join Vicki in the kitchen to find out what she made for dinner. She says, "If you must know Mister Nosey I made prime rib with asparagus and cheesy au gratin potatoes." I say, "It smells delicious. What can I do?" She says, "You can open the wine and let it breathe and put a fire in the fireplace. She likes that." So I go turn on the fireplace. It is natural gas but it looks like a regular fireplace without the mess. I open the wine and the doorbell rings. Vicki says, "I'll be right there." Then she comes to answer the door. Her mother comes in and says, "You must be Jim, I'm pleased to meet you." I say, "Likewise." She says "I can see why Victoria fell for you, you are a hunk." Vicki says, "Mother, please that's not why I fell for him and you know it. If I wanted a hunk I could have fallen for any of those jocks you set me up with. That's not my thing." She says, "I know I just like seeing you react." I think to myself Ah the mother daughter thing. Vicki says, "Jim this is my mother Margaret, her friends call her Maggie. Her business associates call her Mrs. B why I'll never know." Her mother says, "You know perfectly well why they call me that you are just being polite, I can be quite a bitch pardon my French if things aren't running smoothly at the office." I ask, "What type of business are you in?" She says, "Ladies apparel, high end negligees, brassieres, and fashion wear we sell to Carson's, Macy's and Specialty stores." We go to the dinner table and Maggie says, "The dinner looks delightful dear." Vicki says, "I hope you like it, I made it special since I know you love prime rib." She says, "If it tastes as good as it looks I'll be in heaven." The meal was delicious and Maggie was really impressed with the whole meal. She stayed until almost eleven and said she was looking forward to Thanksgiving and seeing me again.

Chapter 30

Saturday morning I am up at seven and go take a shower and pour my coffee. Vicki is still sound asleep. I turn on the computer to check a couple of things to get ready for the day. I am looking for some information on the doctor living in the house. I am trying to remember what Mariano said. This doctor was going to be here about six months for some specialized training at University of Illinois Chicago Medical. There has to be a record of his name someplace. I can't call Mariano but then I think Buranski can short circuit the computer so he has to go back there since the backup will fail. He said he would be in the office this morning after breakfast with Radko. What time is my training? One to three. This might just work out. I'll call him at ten. Without the doctors name there is no way I can check out his background or family. We don't even have a photo of the guy. Well at least right now we are a step ahead, given more information we can be even further ahead.

Around eight here comes Vicki wrapped in her sheet. She sees me working on the computer and asks, "What are you looking up?" I say, "I am trying to download a file on things non-Catholics need to know before getting married in the church." She says, "Father Duggan told you the other day." I say, "I know but I'm one of those likes to read about it rather than hear about it." She says, "You'll do just fine, just agree to everything and say Hail Mary and Thanks Be to God. Instead of Amen and pass the biscuits please." I say, "Very funny, I don't say that." She says, "I know that I was just trying to be funny, you're so serious this morning." I say "I have reason to be, I am entering into a whole new realm shortly and I'm not sure I can pull this off without a hitch." She puts her arms around me and says, "You'll do great. I am just so happy that you are actually going to attend those classes for me." I say, "My Ex converted to Catholicism after we were divorced, she was looking for something to help her and a friend of hers got her to start going to her church so she and Natalie joined."

I leave about eleven to go see Father Duggan for my first two hours of instructions. I get there early and figure I should go by my place and neat it up a little and get my mail. I see the reminder from my doctor and call his office. I get his answering machine so I leave a message for him about getting in to see him for my annual checkup. I give him my office phone number and ask him to call me Monday if possible. I look at the big stack of mail and decide to go through it since I have the time. Nothing really interesting mostly credit card applications, insurance offers and organizations looking for donations. There was one piece of mail that was worth opening it was from Tony at Maple Street Café. He wants me to stop by the next time I'm in the area to chat. He says he tried calling the house phone but nobody ever answers, he wants to make sure I'm still around. I guess I should go see him after I finish with Father Duggan. Do I really want to tell him I'm getting married next month? We'll talk and see what gets discussed. I go for my meeting at the church and then go to see him. I walk in and he says "Your still around I see." I say, "I am downtown everyday now due to a promotion." Then I proceed to tell him what brought that about. He asks "So are you staying down there all the time?" I say, "Yes, no more field work, I need to decide which one will make a good lone ranger." He asks about the case I was on and I say "Truthfully I don't know if that is finished yet." He asks, "Can you tell me anything about it yet?" I say, "Not really, it is just on a break right now but as soon as I can I will tell you all about." He says, "Val has a new beau." I ask, "Who is the guy?" He says, "She met him at a party the Legion had for the seniors and after you two were kaputz he called her and they have been seeing a lot of each other." I say, "I'm happy for her. It just wasn't going to work for us." Tony says, "Stay in touch and stop by more often." I say, "I will I promise." I drive back downtown to Vicki's to see what she has planned. She says, "Nothing special I just want to spend a quiet evening at home with you alone." I say, "That works for me."

Sunday morning I am up at seven. I get dressed and go out to pick up a Sunday paper. I went to Union Station and the newsstand there had the *New York Times* and the *Washington Post* so I bought both of them. Then I went to the bakery on Halsted and picked up a coffee cake and went back to Vicki's. I am drinking a second cup of coffee eating a slice of Apple Streusel and Vicki comes out wrapped in her sheet and says, "You were busy this morning." I say, "I thought I should go get something I need to leave around nine to pick up Natalie after church so I bought some reading material and went to the bakery." She says, "So I see. It looks good." I say, "It is very good. Denise told me about the place on Friday." I cut a slice for her and she says, "This is really good." We talk for about twenty minutes and I kiss her and say, "I'll see you tonight around nine." She says, "Have fun with your daughter." I say, "I will." Then I leave to go pick her up.

We go for breakfast at an *IHOP* in the neighborhood, then go to Dominick's to buy all the stuff to make the cinnamon rolls. She asks "Do you have cookie sheets and a mixer?" I say, "Yes buried in the room off the kitchen. I put all that stuff in there since I never use any of it." She says, "Then we should have everything we need." We drive to my place and she makes a pot of coffee for me and says, "I don't need any help but if you want to stay here and keep me company that is fine." So I grab a chair and watch. She is really good at this I think. I don't remember Rachael ever being that much of a baker. I wonder where she got that from and I think it must be from my side of the family, my mother and all my aunts could bake up a storm. I remember during Thanksgiving and Christmas and family picnics, there was always plenty of baked goods. Well, she comes by it honestly that is for sure. I wonder why I never got interested in baking. I like to eat enough of the stuff but never thought about trying to bake anything. Natalie looks at me and asks, "Dad, were you lost again?" I say, "I was just remembering my mother and all my aunts baking all the time and you fit right in." She says, "I never knew that. I know Mom doesn't really bake that much, the cinnamon rolls were her specialty though. I remember when I was little we would bake them all the time." I say, "That they were." She makes a double batch and puts them in the oven to bake and says "After I clean this mess up we need to play Checkers I'm getting rusty." I say, "I'll go set up the board." We play two games while the cinnamon rolls bake, then we take a break. She makes the icing for them. One she leaves plain and one she makes with caramel sauce. I lick the spoon and say, "That adds something to them." She says, "I like to experiment, I hope you don't mind." I say, "That's fine. I think they will both be great." She says "After they cool, we'll split one of each."

We play two more games of Checkers and I ask, "What do you want to do for dinner?" She says, "How about Friday's?" I say, "There is one not too far from here. That sounds good I haven't been there in a long time." She says, "I know, Mom and I go there every once in a while for something different." I ask, "What time do you want to go?" She says, "Anytime, I'm hungry now, we can sample the cinnamon rolls for dessert." I say, "That works for me." We go to Fridays and the place is packed, the TVs all have football games on them and it is really noisy. The hostess says "I can seat you away from the noise." I say, "That would be great if you have a quiet corner someplace." She takes us off to the side and sure enough we can talk without having to yell at each other. We order our dinner and enjoy our conversation. I say, "Vicki asked me again about meeting you and I told her maybe one night this week, we'll come out and take you out to eat. So you two can meet." She says, "It might have to be Thursday. I play basketball Wednesday and Friday. Friday is our first home game. Are you coming?" I say, "I marked that one down and I will be there." We go back to my place for a little while before I need to take her home. We sample the cinnamon rolls and both were very good. We put them in covered pans and I take them with when I drive her home. Then head back down to Vicki's.

I walk in and Vicki is laying on the floor reading the Washington Post. She says, "I like to do that once in a while, I used to do that all the time it makes reading the paper easier." I say, "Not for me. I get down there and I have trouble getting up." She says, "You're not that old yet." I say, "Sometimes I feel that old." She says, "Join me." So I get down there, she hands me a section and says, "Find five mistakes. I found them let's see if you find them." I read through the section and say, "I only found three." She asks, "Which ones?" So I tell her and she says, "The other two aren't as obvious until you find them." I read through it again and say, "OK, smarty where are they." She opened the paper and said, "One, Two." I looked and I saw the errors and felt that she was right. I said, "Since they do everything on the computer and nobody does proof plates anymore, they just go to press. Earlier, heads would roll because of things liked that. Now everybody just accepts the minor errors as part of the normal routine. Unless somebody complains, they don't even put corrections in the paper for a lot of the things. She asked, "How was your day?" I said, "We had fun. Natalie made homemade cinnamon rolls for me for a meeting first thing tomorrow in Orland Park. Then we went to Friday's for dinner, and it was packed and noisy but the food was good. She has a game on Wednesday and Friday. So we will take her out on Thursday so you two can meet." She said, "I am looking forward to meeting her. She sure has a lot of talent from what you have told me so far." We talked until after eleven and went to bed. I said, "I need to leave by six-thirty tomorrow." She said, "Don't wake me." I said, "I'll try not to."

Chapter 31

Monday morning I am up before six, take a shower and when I come out, the coffee is ready. I fix a cup and drink it and fix my travel mug to take with me. Vicki is all wrapped up and just the top of her head is sticking out of the covers. I kiss her and leave to meet Buranski at seven. I drive to Orland Park and pull around back and park. I knock on the back door and in a couple of minutes he opens the door. I carry the two containers with the cinnamon rolls in and he says "I can't eat all of those." I say, "I didn't figure you could but I didn't want to split them out." He says, "The coffee is strong, do you use cream or sugar?" I say, "Two creams and one sugar." He says, "You might want to double that my coffee is strong." I taste it and say "Wow! How many scoops do you use?" He says, "Five or Six that's our way Strong, put hair on your chest."

He turns on the computer and says, "The doc had more visitors this time it was like four or five all at one time. All of them came on Saturday afternoon. From Sunday nothing dead silence." He plays the audio and I can't understand anything more than a few sayings. I say, "Send this to my computer and if you have the tapes I will take them downtown so when McCray gets back we will listen to them again with a translator." He asks, "What about the other project?" I say, "Somebody looked at the schedule wrong he is in India and the Far East until Thursday." I ask "Is there some way you can create a problem on the setup there so Mariano has to get you back inside the place?" He says, "I turned off the backup so it wouldn't record what was going on in this house. He will probably call me today. Why do you ask?" I say, "I need to get the doctors name somehow to do some digging." He asks, "Something not setting right with you?" I say, "It is just too much of a coincidence for my liking." He says, "I know what you mean. I always get concerned when something like that happens. In this business that doesn't happen, it is usually well planned out." I say, "I thought Mariano was super cautious. How did he end up letting this doc use the place? If we knew that it might make me breathe easier." He says, "I'll talk to Mariano and feel him out." I say "Thanks. I hate to run but I have a busy day." He says, "So do I. Thanks for the cinnamon rolls, please take some with you." I say, "Thanks, I will. My daughter made those yesterday." He says, "Tell her they were really good." I say, "I will for sure."

    I drive downtown and go to my office. It is just after eight-thirty when I get there. I open up the place and Denise walks in about five minutes later. She asks, "Did you oversleep?" I say, "No, I had a seven o'clock meeting in Orland Park. I need to get you a key. I know Vicki had one since McCray was always out of town or in meetings so she could open up the place. Remind me later I'll go get a copy made." She goes and sets up things in the break room and makes a pot of coffee. I take the rest of the cinnamon rolls and put them in the break room. She looks at them and asks, "Homemade?" I say, "Yes, my daughter baked them yesterday for my meeting." She takes one and says, "These are good, my compliments to your daughter."

    After the staff gets there, I call Erika to my office and say "After work I need you to translate again." She says, "I am not working on anything important at the present time, I could do that now if you like." I think about it and say, "Write everything down for me or translate on the computer and print out the full text in English. I can always send him a copy on his laptop if there is anything important." She gets busy and I work on a report. The staff can figure I am finishing her review. After forty minutes and she says, "Finished." Then she hands me five pages of conversation. I say, "Thank you Erika, I'll read through this and see if I need to send it to him." I read through it the first time trying to make sense of what they are talking about and trying to remember what was said the other day. I look and I have a copy translated by Erika. I think to myself these guys sure don't hold back on anything. I figure they figure this house is pretty safe that nobody will be listening to them. It seems their biggest concern is whether the United States is going to send some spec ops units into Iran and Syria that could interfere with their plans to get some brothers working to start setting up cells in those countries. Now this conversation is a whole lot different than the one from Friday. They wanted a meeting of ministers from the other countries to discuss what pressure they could put on Iran and Syria to keep them inline. Is this doctor working both sides of the street or is he merely a messenger for somebody else? This has me baffled, who were these other guys and how did they all get clearance to be in the neighborhood? I tell Denise that I will be back in a couple of hours. I call Lt. McElroy and ask if he has a half an hour. I'll be there in fifteen minutes. He says "Yes, I have some time. Did you find out anything about all these visitors?" I say, "That's what I need to talk to you about." He says, "I have an office on Halsted, meet me there." He gave me the address. It was right outside the six blocks area.

    I get to Lt. McElroy's office and park in front. He comes to the door and invites me in. We go into his office. There is a large map of the area with flags denoting who lives where. I figure he has a bio on everybody in the area. So I ask him point blank. "Did your department get word about this doctor who was moving in for almost six months?" He said, "We were informed that somebody would be living in the house for a short term while they finished up some specialized training at UIC Medical. They gave us a brief history of him and that he had diplomatic immunity. So we were not to interfere with his coming and goings or an occasional visitor." I ask, "Who gave you the information?" He says, "The boys from Washington." I say, "Doesn't that seem odd to you? Here you have to clear everybody who goes into the neighborhood and they tell you not to bother this guy." He said, "I didn't think too much about it. The doctor seemed pretty quiet, getting up early, going to his classes, and then coming home. But then, last week all these visitors kept popping up. That was why I called you." I said, "I thank you for that and we have gotten some information. But it hasn't been verified yet as to being accurate. Do you have the doctor's name and nationality?" He gets the sheet and tells me what it says. I write it down on a tablet I carry with me. I say, "You have been extremely helpful and I think thanks to your curiosity we may be able to foil some plans they are making." He asks, "Do those plans concern this neighborhood?" I say, "No, all over in the Middle East.' He says, "We don't normally get a lot of Arab people in this area except when the big man is in town and having a fund raiser or something." I say, "I'll keep you posted, but my gut feeling is this guy will be leaving way before April."

I drive back to my office and Denise says, "Director McCray called while you were out. I told him I would have you call him as soon as you got back." I go to my office and call his cell phone. He answers and asks, "Where did you disappear too?" I tell him, "I went to see Lt. McElroy about the doctor and his visitors." He asks, "What did you find out?" So I told him everything I was told." He says, "Why would Washington tell them hands off this guy?" I say, "That was my exact thought too." He says, "The information that Erika gave us Friday was accurate and all verified. Now with this latest group that is really a puzzle." I say, "Precisely." He says, "I already gave the transcript to Washington and they are working to find out who these others represent." I say, "My guess is al-Qaida." He says, "Mine too." I ask, "What time do you get back?" He says, "My flight leaves Dulles at three p.m. eastern. I arrive at Midway at five-ten." I ask, "Do you want me to pick you up?" He says, "That's nice of you to offer. Sure we'll have dinner and talk." I say, "I'll call Vicki and let her know." He says, "Good thinking." I say, "I'll see you at the airport." Then I call Vicki to tell her about this evenings plan. She says, "That is fine I need to go to the salon with the girls tonight to try on our gowns and to make any changes." I say, "I'll see you at home after." She says, "Don't be too late." I say, "Ditto." I get back to work and look up the doctor and his family on the computer. His father is really high up in the Kuwait government. His son is trained as a doctor but wants to move into radiology and treatment of cancer patients or at least that is what it says. He was returning to Chicago to hone up his skills end of report.

About three-thirty Denise says "Phone call Jim." I pick it up it is Buranski. He says, "Mariano called today and wanted to know what happened to the computer it went dead? So I told him I need to get in there and he said tomorrow afternoon three p.m." I say, "Go ahead and pacify him, while you are there erase the backup tape so there is no evidence of the other spying." He says, "I told him maybe there was a short circuit or something." He says, "The doctor called and said the lights kept flickering, he told him to go to the basement and flip the circuit breaker to see if that worked. The doctor said everything shut off but came back on after he flipped it twice." So I told him, "That was probably why the computer shut off and nobody turned it back on and rebooted it. But I really should check it out. You are going to have about six weeks of no access." He said, "That's why I called you. You know what needs to be done. Just fix it. My guys will meet you at 55th Street with your ID." So I told him, "No problem and there will not be a fee for this, it is part of maintenance." So I said, "Just check everything and redirect the listening devices, I heard the big man will be in town this weekend and I don't think the doc will get any more visitors after Saturdays meeting." I said, "We got a lot of info from Saturday's audio. Washington was impressed." He said, "I'll call you after I change everything and make sure our feed is still working." I said, "Good luck and be careful."

I work until four-thirty and figure I should head to Midway to pick up McCray. I drive out there and traffic is a little slow but not too bad. I get there a little after five and park in the short term lot so when he gets out of the terminal I can just pick him up. About five twenty-five, he walks out and I pull over to pick him up. We head downtown and he told me what Washington had to say. He also said, "Washington is getting real nervous about something. One of the agents said something to his boss in DC about all the activity next door and then we set off bells with our activity." I say, "He is going there tomorrow, since Mariano said his feed wasn't working and he wanted him to fix it." He says, "I don't care what you tell our man, just have him shut it down. No reason to get those guys climbing all over our back." I say, "I'll think of something. Mariano knows the big man is supposed to be in town this weekend. I still don't know where he is getting his information. We thought Simpson was the leak but maybe there was more than one source. I know Simpson was reassigned so where is he getting the info?" McCray says, "That is the sixty-four thousand dollar question that everybody wants answered." I drop him off at his office on Michigan Avenue and go back to my office to check something before heading over to Vicki's.

I turn on my computer and look at the information about the doctor again. Trying to figure out how he came in contact with all these people. It has to be where he did his internship, why isn't there anything in his bio about that? I guess I better do some more research. After an hour I find what I am looking for. He did his internship in Dubai. That's where all the money is and all the activity has been taking place. Satisfied I shut down the computer and head to Vicki's and I think I haven't eaten since breakfast. I call Vicki's cell phone but don't get an answer. Then I call McCray to see if he has dinner plans. He answers his cell phone. I ask "Do you have dinner plans?" He says, "No I don't and I haven't eaten since early today." I say, "I'll pick you up in ten minutes and we'll go get some dinner." So I drive over to Michigan Avenue and pick him up. I ask, "What do you have a taste for?" He says, "Burgers are fine with me, if you know a good place around here." So I drive to Ed Debevic's on Wells Street. He says, "I've heard of this place but never managed to get here." So we went in and had dinner. He says, "How do you know this place?" I say, "I used to come here all the time when I came into the city but haven't been here for a long time. When you said burgers the bell went off." He says, "Thanks I enjoyed it. It's not all stuffy like a lot of the places around all trying to outdo each other." I drop him at his apartment and head to Vicki's. I walk in and she isn't home yet so I go fix a pot of coffee. Vicki gets home around nine and says, "Fix me a cup, I'm exhausted." Then she proceeded to tell me about the fittings and I told her about my dinner with McCray. She says, "I would have had more fun with you two than with the girls." We talk until after eleven and go to bed.

Chapter 32

Tuesday morning I am up at six and do my morning routine and think I really should start an exercise program. I'm getting a little thicker around the middle. I fix my coffee and think about what I need to do today. I drink the first cup and am fixing a second cup when Vicki comes out and says, "You are up early this morning." I say, "I have a lot to take care of today. Did you see Natalie's basketball schedule?" She says, "I thought you said she plays Wednesday and Friday nights." I say, "I think that was what she told me but I thought the date on the schedule listed it for today." She says, "The schedule was on the fridge at your place." I say, "Thanks, I better remember to bring it here. I have some errands to run after work, I'll be back before seven." She asks, "What would you like for dinner?" I say, "Surprise me. I have no clue, as long as it's home cooked, I will be fine." She says, "I'll dream something up." I say, "Thanks. Right now I can't even think about food or what I would like." I kiss her and tell her, "Have a good day. I'll talk to you later. I gotta run." She says, "I love you." I say "I love you too."

    I head to the office and get there before eight o'clock. I make a pot of coffee in the break room and go to my office and turn on the computer. Something just isn't sitting right in my mind about the doctor. How did Mariano find out about him needing a place while he finished some specialized training? Who is really behind this spying on the big man's house? Could Nikoli be tied in with this whole deal? Buranski said, "Nikoli is a man with many contacts throughout the Middle East. He deals with a lot of other people besides Russians or Bulgarians. He likes to keep his options open." How can I find out if he travels to Dubai? I say to myself, "Think Jim. Think . . . ." That's where the money is, right? Dubai is an adult Disneyland where anything can be had for the money. I don't think IIA has an office there, but we might have one in Saudi Arabia. I'll check with McCray. I call Buranski to tell him what I was told. He answers and I say, "Washington is getting nervous. We need to disable the feed as a precaution. McCray wants us to shut it down for a while until they figure out what is going on with the doctor. One of the agents complained to his boss in DC about all the activity at the house." He says, "I understand, I'll tell Mariano the computer got fried. That will buy some time." I ask, "That could upset Nikoli and his client." He says, "Nikoli will call me. I can handle him. He understands sometimes things happen and you need to wait. Mariano thinks money can get you anything, he doesn't understand. To him it's all about the money."

I call McCray to ask him about IIA in Saudi Arabia and he says "We had an office there, but we shut it down after 9-11. We still have an office in London, but nothing in that area." I ask, "How can we check on travel of a diplomat, from say Bulgaria to Dubai?" He says, "You can check with the visa department in Dubai, explain who you are and that you need to verify travel of a certain individual. They should be able to help you." I say, "Thanks, I'll try that. It is only a hunch, but I'm trying to tie things together. There are too many coincidences and in our business that doesn't wash." He says, "Let me know what you find out and if your hunch is correct." I check the time difference between Chicago and Dubai. They are nine hours ahead of us. The latest I can talk to anybody is probably five p.m. their time. I could try a Web site to find out the hours of operation or see if there is an email address for official inquiries. Why couldn't these people be from here in the States? I can call anywhere and get answers here. I check the Web site, and there is an official contact for visa information. I call the number and somebody answers. I try to explain who I am, the person says something and another person picks up the phone and speaks in English. So I ask them about checking on travel of a diplomat from Bulgaria to Dubai. The person says please hold and they come back and say, "You need to contact the director." They spell the name and give me a number and say, "Try tomorrow morning before nine our time." I write it down and say, "Thank you. You have been very helpful." At least, I have a contact name, now to call them before nine their time. That's midnight here.

The rest of the day was pretty much routine. I did another review, and looked at the new batch of cases McCray sent over via messenger service. I look there is a *hot* sticker on one file. I open it and inside there is a bio on the doctor, his family, and his contacts since last year and a handwritten note from McCray. "Washington thinks we need to pay real close attention to the doctor. It seems he upset somebody in Dubai when he left abruptly to come to Chicago. He still had six months to go on his residency requirement. I think he was sent here on a purpose. All of this other stuff is just a smoke screen to hide the true intention. Rodge" I read through the info. It has a little more detail than I found originally, but in essence it is no more revealing. I am like, "Who can I give this to without blowing our cover." We are already watching him not intentionally but in light of the tip from Lt. McElroy. Maybe I should pay him another visit to see if they have photos from last week and Saturday. I know they have cameras in the area supposedly for traffic control. But that area is off limits to general traffic. I call him and ask "Do you have twenty minutes?" He says, "For you, I have time. Be at my office at two." I say, "Thanks, maybe you can help me on this." I drive over to his office and go inside and ask, "Do you have any photos of the visitors from last week on the cameras you guys have posted for traffic control?" He says, "The photos from those cameras are not very good, but yes we did get some of them, I don't know how much good they will do you. With the garb they wear, they all look alike." I look at the photos and say, "I see what you mean." I ask, "What about cars and license plates?" He says, "They came in taxi and walked six blocks, since the cabs were not cleared to enter the area. They had some papers that gave them access signed by a consulate." I say, "From Dubai?" He says, "Saudi Arabia." I say, "Keep an eye on him, the big man is supposed to be in town this weekend. I have a hunch he may decide to try something. I think this other stuff is to send us on a wild goose chase. We may need your team to take him in for questioning and search the first floor of that house. He only has keys for the first level and access to the basement." He says "I would love to do that, but we were told to keep our hands off by the Bureau guys at the big man's house something about the guys father being a big shot in his country." I say, "That's true, but we think he got tied up with some of the wrong element in Dubai and he was sent here on a mission." He says, "Just give us the word or get the Bureau to do it." I say, "I'll let you know. We still have a few days. Just watch him for me." He says, "OK."

I drive back to my office. It is already three and I'm like "Damn!" I need to eat something but I don't want to ruin my appetite for dinner. I walk over to the hot dog place a couple of doors away from the office and get a double with fries and eat it before I go back to the office. I walk into the office and she says, "Director McCray was looking for you a few minutes ago. I told him you would be back around three-thirty so you can get your wits about you." I say, "Thanks, I better go call him. I need to tell him what I found out." So I go in my office and close the door to call him. He picks up the phone and says, "What did you find out from Dubai?" I say, "They gave me a number of the person I need to talk too. But I need to call him before nine a.m. their time." He says, "So that means late tonight you have to make the call." I say, "That is the plan, I don't relish coming back here at eleven to make a long-distance call and don't even know if I will get somebody that speaks English." He says, "The man you are calling will speak English. It is almost a prerequisite for department heads." I say, "I paid a visit to Lt. McElroy about the visitors. They have photos from the traffic cameras, but they don't help, they were all wearing typical Arab gear. They looked like they just arrived in town and all took taxi's and walked, since the taxi's weren't cleared to enter the area. Plus they all had access permits signed by the consulate for Saudi Arabia." He says, "That is really interesting that they would go through all of the effort just to visit the doctor there. Why didn't they just arrange to meet him outside the area to discuss whatever it was they wanted to talk about." I say, "I know, it really doesn't make sense to me either. The only thing I can think is that they feel that the house is the safest place to meet. Right under the radar, so to speak. We can't touch them and McElroy's men can't touch them since it would cause an international stir and the Bureau already told CPD hands off any visitors to the doctor." He says, "I'll call Washington."

About five p.m., McCray calls me back and says, "I think I ruffled a few feathers with my call. I bypassed our office and called the Director of the CIA and asked him point blank. What the hell is going on and why did the Bureau say hands off any visitors to the doctor living next door to the chief?" He said, "Those orders didn't come from my office. If you have reason to believe there is a threat to the Chiefs safety, do whatever you deem necessary to quash it." I say, "We don't know for sure, but there has been some unusual activity. I will send you a tape we recovered of conversations inside the house." He says, "How did you get the tape?" I said, "Through a person, we were told to watch since there was a big deal going on between Mariano and a contact in Bulgaria who we think was selling the information to the Russians." He asks, "What was his role?" I say, "To setup a listening post connected to a computer and feed the information to a remote computer. This system is voice activated by goings on in the Chief's house when he is in town." The Director says, "Your man set that up?" I say, "Yes. He was trained in Russia several years ago." He asks, "When did all of this come about?" I say, "About three or four weeks ago, we had been watching him for three weeks based on a tip and nothing. Then boom, here comes Mariano to talk to him about this project. We got him to join our side after a disgruntled employee kidnapped his boss and stole the payroll. It's all in my report." The Director says, "Send me the tape and do whatever you have to. I don't want anything happening to the chief on my watch." I say, "I feel the same way." He says, "I'll take care of the Bureau. Stay in touch." I say, "It sure sounds liked you did more than ruffle some feathers." He says, "I didn't really have any other option and we needed to resolve this before something bad happens." I say, "I'm with you all the way." He says, "I'll join you at your office tonight when you call Dubai." I say, "I'll call you when I leave to come back here and pick you up at your place." He says, "That would be great." After I get off the phone, I lock the place up and head to Vicki's for dinner.

I get to Vicki's and she says, "The boss was really in a mood today, I have never seen him so upset. He called Washington about something and they told him they would get back to him. You know how he gets when he gets agitated. I'm sure you have seen him that way on more than one occasion." I say, "Yes, I know exactly what you are talking about. It is rare but he can really get steamed. I think he solved that problem and went over their head." She asks, "How so?" I say, "He called the Director of the CIA and told him what was happening." She says, "Wow! That took a lot of nerve. Do you think his job will be in jeopardy?" I say, "I doubt that since he worked for the Director before in a different capacity. They both were in the Corps and they respect each other. The Director knows what he is up against here in Chicago. He gave him the green light to do what he feels is necessary to protect the Chief." She says, "I guess it's good to have him in your corner then." I say, "That is for sure. Our agency doesn't have any muscle and we don't scare people the way the CIA does. We have to be diplomatic at all times, they don't. They just make things happen." She says, "I never heard it explained that way before. You really think that is the way it is?" I say, "From where I stand right now, Yes." She says, "Enough shop talk. I made a meatloaf, I couldn't think of anything else to whip up for tonight." I say, "That sounds great to me. I love homemade meatloaf." After dinner I tell her I need to pick up McCray at ten-thirty and go make a phone call at eleven. She says, "Don't wake me when you get home if I'm asleep." I say, "I'll be really quiet." We talk until I have to pick up McCray and I kiss her goodnight. She says, "Be careful."

I pick up McCray and we go to my office to make the call. After about three tries, we get the right person and he does speak English. I tell him who I am and what I am trying to find out. He says, "I need to know dates and the person's name." I give him "Nikoli Filchev." After a few minutes, he comes back and says, "Nothing on him. Does he have an alias?" I say, "Not that I know of." He says, "Next name." I give him the doctor's name. He says, "We have an alert for him. It seems he left the country in some sort of trouble. We are to detain him at a point of entry, should he decide to come back to Dubai. His visa was pulled." I ask, "Has anybody been in contact with you about him or his whereabouts?" He says, "Last week some people from Saudi were looking for him and I said we have no information. Why do you ask?" I say, "He had some visitors with Saudi credentials." He says, "Interesting, I wonder what he did to warrant their interest." I say, "I was hoping you could help me with that." He says, "Sorry! I only handle Visas. You might try Intelligence. They might be able to help." I say, "Thank you. You have been a big help." McCray says, "You did well, I am glad I wasn't needed." I say, "You want to contact Intelligence?" He says, "I think we found out something from him that will help us. At least we know Nikoli is not involved in this. This is all Arab interest. So I think we will have McElroy take him in. Let him squawk diplomatic immunity and get his father involved. I think he doesn't want to face his father right now. My feeling is he will sing like a bird once we go through the house and find his real reason for being here. Mark my words. Tomorrow we will earn our money."

I drop him off at his place and go back to Vicki's. She is sitting on the couch, the TV is playing, but she is out like a light. I go to bed and let her sleep. About two, she comes to bed and says, "You didn't wake me." I say, "No, but you woke me." She snuggles up close to me and says, "You didn't tell me not to wake you." She kisses me and curls up next to me. The next thing I know it's six-thirty and I need to get up. She pulls my arm and says, "No, don't leave yet." So I stay there for another half hour. I kiss her and go get ready for my day. Seven-thirty she comes out wrapped in her sheet and says, "What do we have going on tonight?" I say, "I think Natalie has a game, but I don't know that I will be able to make it. Today will be very crazy. I'll call you later." She kisses me and says, "As long as it isn't too crazy to where we don't get to spend an evening together with no interruptions." I say, "I'll work on that after today. I promise."

Chapter 33

I drive to the office and go make coffee and go into my office to figure out the best plan for this mission. The doctor is at UIC from around eight a.m. until after two based on the reports from McElroy and his time log. He logs everybody in and out every day. His men are very thorough in their reports. They know pretty much the comings and goings of everybody in that area. In my mind, I am thinking two-thirty should be the ideal time. I read through the log sheet to see when others will be arriving home. We want to do this without a lot of distractions. The phone rings and I answer it. It is Buranski. He says, "I told Mariano there was a problem with the system. I can't pinpoint the problem right now. I know nobody has tampered with it, but there is a glitch. Give me a couple of days." He says "Our pigeon is supposed to be in town this weekend. We need to get it fixed." I told him, "Get me back in there tomorrow, I need three hours." He says, "I'll take care of it." I tell him, "After tomorrow, I don't think he will have to worry about the doctor." He says, "Why so?" I say, "I think he will be heading back home. His father will raise a big stink and he will be sent home. End of problem."

I call McCray and we talk for a while about my plan. He says, "If you think that is the best option, let's go with it. Have McElroy's people pick him up once he gets home from UIC, but let's be there for the search just to see what gets uncovered." I say, "I was thinking along those lines too since there is so much mystery behind this whole operation. I was wondering if perhaps the visitors were actually messengers bringing things to the doctor so he would not arouse suspicion trying to get all the things necessary to pull this off." He says, "That could very well be and the conversations taking place were merely staged in case somebody was listening." I say, "That's why when the other conversations took place they were completely different than the first one we heard." McCray says, "Well we will know one way or the other by the end of the day." I say, "I will call McElroy and go see him around eleven to get this operation set up." He says, "Pick me up around two if nothing changes." I say, "Will do." After I get off the phone with McCray, I call McElroy to meet him at eleven to go over the plans. I tell Denise I will be gone the rest of the day on business.

I go meet Lt. McElroy at his office at eleven, and we go over what needs to happen. He says, "I will have two of my men go to the house right after the doctor gets home and tell him he has to go with them to police headquarters to answer some questions about the recent visitors." I say, "He will probably play the diplomatic immunity card right off. Let him squawk. We want him to draw attention especially from his father." He says, "We have a person at the station who can translate if that becomes an issue." I say, "McCray and I will be here to conduct the search with your other team." He says, "I will be with my team also as the officer in charge." I say, "I expected that, you are as interested as I am in what this guy had planned." He says, "I guess I'll see you and your boss at two-thirty. Meet me at my office, then we can all go in my car." I say, "Works for me." I call McCray to tell him everything is set, and Vicki answers the phone. I ask, "Is he available?" She says, "He is on an important call with Washington. He will have to call you back." I say, "Tell him I will pick him up about ten to two." She asks, "Is your day still crazy?" I say, "Extremely so, I may be late today. I will try to call you later." I go grab lunch since if I don't eat right now I will not eat until dinnertime.

I pick up McCray outside his office at ten to two and we head to Lt. McElroy's office. We get there about twenty after two and we go inside. McElroy is on the phone to verify if the doctor is home yet. He says, "This might get pushed back a little. The doctor hasn't made it home yet." So I asked, "Does that seem strange to you?" He says, "Not really, I mean there have been days that he gets home a little later. Let me check my log sheet." He goes and gets the log sheet. Every Wednesday he gets home at two-fifteen. The only day he comes home later is Thursday and that is at three fifteen. I mean he has only logged the doctor for three and a half weeks I think. So it's hard to know for sure what his schedule really is. I ask, "Is there some way we can check with UIC to see if he attended his classes today?" McCray says, "I can call the Dean of the Medical School and ask him to check." I ask, "Do you know him?" He says, "I have talked to him before on a different matter, so I know who to call in the event I need some medical information verified." McElroy says, 'You can use this phone, I'll go get coffee." I say, "I'll join you." We head to the area where this coffee pot is going. He says, "McCray seems to have a lot of contacts outside the norm in your business." I say, "I know, he even has a friend on the Blackhawks staff that gives him free seats. They were in the Corps together." McElroy says, "You don't say, I would love to get tickets." I say, "I took my daughter to the Sunday late-afternoon game a few weeks ago since he was going to be in DC."

We get coffee and I bring one for McCray. He is just getting off the phone. He says, "The dean said the doctor was a no-show today. He checked with the professor to verify the information." I say, "I wonder if all the activity spooked him or what he was supposed to do was out of his league and he got scared." McCray says, "Maybe the net for him from Dubai got turned over to a freelancer to haul him in. You know the type bounty hunters that know no borders." McElroy says, "Do you want us to go into the house and check it out?" I say, "Let me make a phone call." I go outside and call Buranski on my cell to ask him about Mariano. He answers his cell phone. I ask, "Did you go to the house today?" He says, "No Mariano called this morning and said it would have to be tomorrow. He couldn't set it up for today." I ask, "Did he say why?" He says, "Giovani was busy today and couldn't get us access." I say, "Thanks, we have a potential problem. The doctor is missing. He didn't show up for classes today. If Mariano calls you let me know."

I go back inside. McElroy is on the phone with his guys and I raise a hand to ask a question. He says, "Yes, the doctor left this morning at his usual time carrying his backpack and boarded the same bus he usually takes. I just verified that with my men." I ask, "Can we get in there without breaking down the door?" He says, "We have a locksmith that can open any doors, but we might need a signed search warrant to get in there." McCray says, "I'll call the judge. He will issue it and we can have an officer pick it up to play it according to the book." He calls the judge and says, "Thirty minutes. Have a man at Judge Callahan's at the Criminal Courts building." So now we are looking at least four-thirty before we can do anything. We sit there and talk until almost four and then head over to the house. The officer will meet us there with the search warrant. McElroy calls the locksmith and tells him where to meet us. We get to the house and wait for the officer with the warrant. McElroy's team is there waiting for us. We park in the driveway and here comes the FBI guys from next door to see what is going on. One of them sees McCray and asks, "What brings you down here Director McCray?" McCray says, "We have a possible missing person. The doctor didn't show up for classes today." The agent asks, "How did you get involved?" He says, "We were going to nab him and check out the house based upon recent activities that took place here." He asks, "How come we weren't briefed?" McCray says, "Ask Washington, they might know. I informed them." The agent turns and walks away.

After the locksmith opens the door, McElroy says, "Leave me the master key. I will return it to you after we are finished and lock the place up." We walk inside, and the place stinks like ammonia and some stronger cleaning solutions. We search the first floor and find some heavy-duty military-type vests with pockets in them loaded with cartridges for an AK47 along with some bottles of liquid that get confiscated for evaluation. We find some caps like the ones used to set off dynamite but don't find any explosives. There is a manual written in Arabic and notes scribbled on the margins with numbers. We are amazed that all this stuff was here in this house, and there was no clue how it got here. I say, "I think those visitors must have hid the stuff in their long gowns, they didn't get subjected to searches since they had letters clearing them to be here." In the sink there are bowls of food that were partially rinsed and the place was mess. Papers and trash were lying all over the place. For a doctor he was a slob. There was no computer or laptop and no phone. There were several changes of clothes plus one traditional Arabic gown with sandals and turban hanging in a plastic garment bag. There was a large duffle bag, probably used for his everyday clothes. No identification or anything with his name on it. This guy really is a mystery. After we conduct a thorough search, we check the basement. We find nothing out of the ordinary in there.

We figure that whatever happened to the doctor happened while he was on the bus or after he got to UIC. We can check the security cameras at UIC to see if he got off the bus. McElroy sends his guys over there to look at the security tapes. We take the other stuff to his office to try and figure out what we have. McElroy has his translator look at the manual, and he says, "This is typical recruiting literature for some small terrorist groups. It gives instructions on how to make certain explosive devices using common household ingredients and ways to make a vest that will explode when you are within the area where you are to detonate the devise. It's really crude but at close range, effective for a suicide mission." We stand there shaking our heads. This doctor was recruited to blow himself up along with somebody else, either that or this was his punishment for whatever he did in Saudi Arabia. We need to talk to that contact in Dubai again. He said the Saudis were looking for him plus Dubai had a bulletin out on him. That means another eleven o'clock phone call to Dubai. We are finishing up our evaluation of all the stuff we took from this place and the phone rings. It is one of McElroy's men. On the tape from the riders on the bus that got off at UIC, the doctor did not get off the bus. So, either he got off the bus before it arrived at UIC or he was taken off somewhere between his stop and UIC. That means a lot of security cameras need to be looked at to find out where he got off the bus and whether it was by force. McElroy makes a couple of phone calls, so McCray and I go get some coffee. I say, "I need to call Vicki about tonight." He says, "Go call her. This is a real puzzle." I call Vicki to tell her and she says, "I understand. I will try to wait up for you." I say, "You can go to sleep. I'll wake you, but we might be here all night long."

We go back to McElroy's office and he says, "I called my wife and told her don't hold dinner. This will be a long night." He looks at the clock and says, "I'll order dinner since I guess we'll be here until we find something out. What would you two like to eat?" I ask, "What are our choices?" He says, "BBQ ribs and broasted chicken from the place across the street or Chinese." I say, "My choice would be ribs." McCray says, "Ditto." McElroy orders three slabs plus a bucket of broasted chicken and potatoes. He says, "You'll enjoy the combo with the ribs. It adds something to the dinner." After dinner arrives, we adjourn to the lunch area in his office and he turns on the TV. The Hawks are on tonight. Damn! I didn't even think of that before. He says to McCray, "I hear you have some pull with the Hawks?" McCray says, "I have a friend that gives me his coaching seats. I try not to overuse my welcome. I can get you tickets for the next home game if you like." McElroy says, "That would be fantastic. My son would be ecstatic." McCray says, "Consider it done. My thanks for all your help." Around ten, one of his guys calls and says "I think we found what we were looking for. He was escorted off the bus by three men in long Arabic gowns at 55th Street and put in a cab. We got the number on the cab and called the cab company. They have no record of a fare from 55th at that time. We told them we have a picture of four men getting into that cab. We repeated the cab number, and he told us that cab was reported stolen two weeks ago."

Somebody went to an awful lot of trouble to get their hands on this doctor. You have to give them credit. They planned it out very carefully and made sure they had authorization to be in the area and to go to his house. Somebody with a lot of connections had to be involved, and I think it has to be his father. He is high up in the Kuwait government and has all the contacts. He must have heard what happened. So he sent this team in to grab him before he did something stupid. It sounds like a classic case of protecting his son at all costs so that his name does not get drug through the mud because of an ugly scene brought about by his son's misdeed. McCray and McElroy listen to my analysis of this whole situation and ask, "How can you be so sure?" I say, "Look at all the facts." So I lay them out one by one based upon what I was told by the guy in Dubai and the fact that the visitors on Saturday talked about something completely different than the visitors from Thursday. We don't know what the other two visitors talked about since we didn't have a listening device in place. These three all came Saturday to case the joint and find out his routine. Then they watched him and grabbed him since they knew the timeline for his mission. He may have let something slip figuring they were part of the other organization. So they had to act fast and stop him since his father was furious that his son had gotten mixed up with that group. They both listened and say, "Since you put it like that, I hope you are right."

I ask, "May I use your phone, I will charge this to my office?" He says, "Where are you calling?" I say, "Dubai." I call the operator and tell her what I need and she connects me. I ask for Hakim, and he gets on the phone. He asks, "How may I be of assistance Director Huggins?" I say, "Can you tell me if the alert for the doctor I called you about has been rescinded?" He says, "Hold on for a moment please." He comes back on the line and says, "He is no longer a threat to Dubai or Saudi Arabia. It was a terrible misunderstanding according to the letter issued by our director of security." I say, "Thank you very much. You were a great help. Look me up if you get to Chicago." He says, "I will be in Chicago in June at a convention in Rosemont promoting Dubai." I say, "I rest my case gentlemen." At five to twelve, I drop McCray off at his apartment and head home to Vicki completely exhausted. I walk in at about twelve-thirty and she runs and jumps in my arms and says, "I decided to wait up." I say, "So I see." She kisses me and says, "Do you want to take a shower?" I say, "Why not." So we go get in the shower. Two o'clock we go to bed and I say, "I'll tell you all about the doctor tomorrow, I mean later today when we get up."

Chapter 34

Six-thirty I am awake. I feel groggy like I was out all night drinking and think, Today is Thursday. We are supposed to go take Natalie out for dinner so she can meet Vicki. I wonder how her game was last night. I should call her this morning before she heads to school. I call her on my cell phone. She answers the phone, and I say, "I am sorry about not making to your game last night. I was tied up on a case until almost midnight." She says, "You told me you didn't know if you could make to that game but you would be here Friday for our home opener." I say, "That is still the plan. I was calling about dinner tonight so you can meet Vicki. Can you make it?" She says, "I asked Mom about it and she said wait until today, your father might cancel." I say, "Not on your life. Vicki wants to meet you before everything gets crazy. I already marked it on my desk calendar at the office as a reminder." She says, "I'll tell Mom you called and that you will pick me up after work around six. OK?" I say, "That sounds fine. We will have a couple of hours so you and Vicki can talk." She says, "I love you Dad." I say, "I love you too sweetie." I get off the phone and Vicki comes out and asks, "Are you coming back to bed?" I say, "Can't. Too much to do. We are picking up Natalie at six so you two can meet over dinner and get to know each other a little bit." She says, "When do I get you all to myself?" I say, "It looks like Saturday night I'm yours." She says, "I guess I'll have to live with that." I kiss her and say, "Sorry, I have to run."

I get to the office a little after eight and make the coffee. I go into my office to work on my report that McCray needs to send to Washington. About eight-thirty the phone rings. I answer it and it is Buranski. He says, "Mariano just called and says I can get in there today. Giovani and his men will meet me at 55th at ten. What do you want me to do?" I say. "Hook it up and run the backup too and we will see what happens over the weekend. Then we will decide if we need to shut it down completely. McCray gave me the OK to do whatever we need to do. I am just curious why Mariano was so insistent upon the thing being fixed by this weekend. From what I found out this is just an overnight stay to meet with some personal friends and go out to dinner someplace downtown." Buranski says, "I'll call you later after I get back to the office." I am working away and I hear Denise when she gets there. A few minutes later the staff starts arriving, so I figure I should go talk to them and check the progress on the cases they are working on. I go to the break room and they are talking about last night's game. I saw some of it at McElroy's office but don't know what the final score was. From the mood, I would say they won.

I say, "Good morning. Tomorrow we need to have a round table discussion about a couple of the projects that we are working on to see what we can do to wrap them up. Plus there are still some reviews that need finishing. Today I will try to take care of two of them, so be available. I know this week has been crazy but trust me things will quiet down and you will be going crazy since you can't really do anything. Do any of you have questions or problems you want to discuss with the group?" No one says anything, so I take that to mean there are no questions. I go back to my office.

A few minutes later Erika comes to my office and asks, "Do you have a few minutes? I didn't want to say anything out there." I say, "Come in and close the door." She says, "Some of the staff are giving me the snub. They think you are favoring me by having me stay after or coming in your office to translate." I say, "I will clear all of that up tomorrow in the meeting. Don't worry about it. You have special skills that the others don't possess." She says, "Thank you, I mean I try to be friendly with them but it is really difficult. I don't get all excited about sports like they do either and I think that might also be part of the problem. They only watch them, I participate." I say, "I have an idea. Let's do a benefit for your neighborhood group, I'll call Lt. McElroy and have him put a team together from his office at CPD. That should shut them up. Ask a couple to volunteers to play on your team. It will be Co-Ed." She says, "That's a neat idea. With

Thanksgiving coming up and then Christmas, we could raise money for the needy. Do you think we can pull it off?" I say, "We can at least try. It will shut them up or get them excited about something worthwhile." She says, "Thank you." I jot down some notes for tomorrow, and I call McCray to tell him how my morning has been. He says, "That is nothing new. They did the same thing before after I paid more attention to Erika based upon her other talents. I do like your idea for the benefit. I think it would be good to get them involved to see how hard Erika pushes herself. She doesn't go hang in the bar and drink like they do. She will join them for a couple from time to time but then heads to the gym."

After lunch I complete a couple of more reviews. I am glad that I have an easy day today after last night's ordeal with the missing doctor. The phone has been quiet and I catch up on all my paperwork. Around three a courier brings a packet from McCray on Michigan Avenue. I open the packet and McCray scribbled a note on the outside of a large manila envelope. There was also a sticker FYO. That probably means read and destroy after I read it. There is a report about Nikoli Filchev. It seems he is branching out and doing some freelance work for some other clients. He recently made a couple of trips, one to Iran and one to Syria. McCray's note says, "Maybe he is not just selling info to the Russians. He is trying to peddle it to a few others. This weekend should tell the tale if we see increased activity next week in either of those countries. I already talked to the Director of the CIA to monitor all activity in those two countries. I don't know what benefit they could possibly gain by the Chiefs overnight stay here. We have run backgrounds on the people he is dining with, but there doesn't seem to be anything out of the ordinary. If he plans on talking on the phone to other close friends or political cronies, I don't know. He is always on the phone to someone, so we will wait and see. Feel Karl out about Nikoli and see if he had any recent contact from him. He seems like he smells an opportunity to make some big bucks from the information." Rodge

At four, Denise says "Phone call for you on line one." I pick it up and it is Buranski. He says, "I hooked everything back up, including the backup unit and tested everything. There was some activity next door and they were checking all three levels of the house again. When we were leaving, your friend from next door came up to us in the driveway and said, 'This house is off limits as of right now. I hope you finished what you needed to do since you can't get back here for a while'. By the way, what happened to the doctor that was living here?" The driver said, "I haven't heard anything, what are you talking about?" So the agent told him about the ordeal yesterday. The driver shook his head and said, "I hope he left for good. I didn't like the looks of him the first time I saw him." The agent says, "Fancy that you and I thinking alike." He asked me and I said, "Neyt, I heard nothing. I just fix things." I ask, "Are you busy Saturday early, we need to talk?" He says, "Sure I'll be in the office. I am meeting Radko for breakfast at seven-thirty. I'll be in my office around nine." I say, "I'll see you at nine."

I leave my office around five to pick up Vicki to go take Natalie out to dinner. On the way out to get her, I tell her about the doctor. She asks, "So where is the doctor now?" I say, "My guess is on his way back to Kuwait. His father spread some money around and he is not wanted anymore, but that doesn't mean the element he got involved with won't try to come after him." She asks, "Where are we going for dinner?" I say, "I haven't really decided. I wanted to wait and see what you two had a taste for rather than just picking a spot. There are several decent places to eat and one real nice place. Me, I'll eat just about anything. I skipped lunch today." She says, "I opt for the really nice place then, so we get a full dinner." I say, "We'll let Natalie decide." She says, "I can go along with that." We get to Natalie's at almost six. I go to the door and ring the bell. Rachael answers and then here comes Natalie. I invite Rachael over to meet Vicki and one thing leads to another and we wind up all going out to dinner. I feel like a fifth wheel so to speak with all the girl talk going on. We had a real nice dinner. They got along extremely well. It was almost like Rachael and Vicki were old friends from school. Rachael told Vicki, "It was a pleasure meeting you," when I dropped them off at home after dinner. Natalie couldn't believe how well they got along and said she wanted to see her more often. I was glad that this meeting was behind us. Now we could concentrate on other matters.

On the drive home, Vicki said, "Your Ex is a charming lady, I can't believe you two didn't stay together." I say, "That is now, you have to remember, I am not the same person now as I was when I was married to her. My job was very demanding and my schedule was not your normal seven to three-thirty job or a nine to five job. I was on like twelve—or fourteen-hour days most of the time back then." She says, "I understand. Even now your hours are not normal." I say, "In this business it never changes, whether you are in the field or in the front office, hours don't mean anything. Only the results." She says, "I can live with that if you at least come home when your day is done and don't go out carousing at the bars." I say, "Those days are long past for me. I'm not in my twenties anymore." We get back to her place and spend the next couple of hours just talking and then go to bed.

Chapter 35

Friday morning, I'm up at six-thirty and head for the shower. I feel better this morning. She met my daughter and my ex-wife, and it didn't put a strain on our relationship. In fact, I think Rachael and Natalie might join us for Thanksgiving dinner with Vicki's parents who are divorced but friends. I fix my coffee and am thinking about everything that has happened in the past seven weeks. I went from being a full-time loan wolf field agent to Director of Field Operations for the Midwest office. I went from not having a steady relationship to having a brief romance and then making plans to get married in December. What a crazy couple of months this has been. I mean I was single for more than ten years with no romantic interests and then out of the blue all of this happens. About seven-thirty, Vicki comes out and gives me a kiss and says, "I'm glad I met your ex and your daughter last night, I think we will be fine together. I am not a threat to your daughter. She understands and your ex is really understanding. I think we could become friends down the road." I say, "I hope so, but not too good please." She just kisses me again and says, "We'll see." I say, "I have to go to Natalie's game tonight. Are you going to tag along?" She says, "No I promised my Mom I would go out with her. I talked to her while you were wrapped up with the missing doctor, so I agreed to meet her after work today." I say, "That is fine. The game is at five-thirty or six, so I'll be back by nine or nine-thirty." She says, "Then we should get home about the same time, I'll see you then." I kiss her and tell her, "I love you," and then leave for the office.

At nine, I get everybody together in the break room and say, "I want to clear up a couple of things for all of you. First and foremost, this office operates as a team, we are all here for the same purpose and that is to gather highly sensitive information and pass it along to the proper agency for further action. Second, I try to show no favoritism, but sometimes, I need some specialized help. So I pick the person that has those skills. Right now, Erika has been a big help since she can translate foreign languages. Next week it might be Adam's turn to pitch in or Mark's turn. I don't know until the need arises. Third, on a different matter, Erika and her basketball team is going to play a game against CPD Lt. McElroy's team as a fundraiser in her neighborhood and she needs a couple of volunteers since this will be a co-ed game. It is just for fun, but the victors get to say they were on the winning team. I encourage you to help her out." They go, "When is the game and where. When do we practice?" Erika was smiling.

The rest of the day was a piece of cake. By the end of the day, they had a practice schedule set up and knew when and where they were going to play. Erika gave me the name of the gym where they play, so I called Lt. McElroy and gave him the details and said I'll even pay for the pizza and beer after the contest. He said, "I'll have no trouble putting together a team and we know the organization she is raising money for. So we'll get a good turnout for the game." I say, "Thanks I knew I could count on you. I saw some photos in your office and figured you were a softy for something like this." He says, "I don't play anymore but I can Ref." I say, "You're on and I will ask my old coach to help so you don't steal the game. He is eighty but sharp as a tack." He says, "Thanks for the warning." Around four-forty-five, I leave to go watch Natalie's first home game. They won in a squeaker by two points. I drive back downtown to Vicki's and get there at around nine. Vicki gets home a few minutes later and says, "My Mom is driving me crazy about invitations and all that stuff. So I told her next week we'll mail them out. I told her it's not going to be a big wedding. She said I already counted fifty people on my list." I say, "You knew that would happen. She has been waiting a long time for this day." She says, "Yes. I guess I did, but I did say I wanted a small wedding." I say, "I believe you. As for me, I only need about six invitations." She says, "I don't need a lot either, since my best friends are going to be in the wedding." I say, "We'll be alright. Now we have to find a hall or a restaurant." We talk until midnight and go to bed.

Chapter 36

Saturday morning I am up at seven. I take a shower and fix some coffee. I am on the computer and Vicki comes out and asks, "Where are you off to this morning?" I say, "I need to be in Orland Park at nine. Then I need to go by my place before I go for my instructions at the church and then I'll be back and I'm all yours until tomorrow morning when I go get Natalie for our day." She says, "OK, I'll call a couple of places about the wedding party and talk to my Mom. She said she had money put away but never thought she would get to use it." I say, "Offer for us to pay for it." She says, "I'll offer, but I know her answer." I say, "Tell her we'll split it then." She says, "I'll try." I ask, "What about the guy that owns this place. Have you heard from him yet?" She says, "No, but I will try calling him again, but really, I think once we get married we'll live at your place. I have been thinking a lot about it. I mean I love living downtown but your place has a lot more room and I don't think we can add a room for Natalie here unless we can take over the adjoining unit." I ask, "How much do they want for it?" She says, "They are asking almost three." I choke and say, "Are you kidding? In this market, if they can get one eighty, they should take it." She says, "They owe more than that." I ask, "How long have they been trying to sell?" She says, "Over a year." I say, "Good luck to them. Nobody will pay that much." She says, "Downtown is still hot, so if the right person comes along, they will buy it." I say, "I will see you later. I need to get a move on." She says, "I'll be waiting for you."

I drive to Orland Park to talk to Buranski and try to figure out what Nikoli is up. I get there at almost nine and he is not there yet. Five after nine, he parks in back and I pull around and park next to his car. He says, "Radko was in a talking mood today. Sorry I am late." I say, "No problem. I just got here a few minutes ago." We go into his office and he asks, "What is so important to drag you out here this morning?" I say, "I didn't want to talk to you about this on the phone. It seems your friend in Bulgaria made a couple of trips and we are thinking he is trying to peddle the same stuff he is passing on to the Russians. Have you had any recent contact with him?" He says, "Only when he said he got the information from Mariano." I say, "I figured that was going to be the case, so I wanted to see if you could sort of feel him out to find out if anything has changed. We think after this weekend we will know if there is any unusual activity next week. They are going to monitor both countries to see if any flags go up." He says, "I need to call him next week about Dragan and Sophia being there on their honeymoon. He is supposed to set up a meeting with Nadia to see about her coming here for six months or a year to train gymnasts in a new training facility we are trying to set up." I say, "Radko is your other partner in the training facility." He says, "Along with Grozdan, he thinks he can talk to one of the politicians and get a favorable deal on a building that has been sitting empty for almost two years. It is zoned industrial, but for a training facility, they might be able to change the requirements a little. The place is the right size and has enough parking. We only have to add showers and locker rooms a divide up the space between wrestling and gymnastics. I think if we can work it out, it will only take a month or two to get it in operation." I say, "Congratulations. I hope you can pull this off. It would be great seeing young athletes have a local spot to train." He says, "Nikoli seemed interested, but we are too far away, he likes to be right there watching them train and he can't do that being in Bulgaria." I say, "Thanks for the update and let me know what you find out." He says, "I will know if he received any information from Mariano by Wednesday." We shake hands and I leave to go by my house to look at the mail and talk to my neighbor and thank him for keeping an eye on my place.

 I get to my place around ten-thirty and I have a bunch of mail piled up in the basket I have on the floor below the mail slot. I weed through all of it and toss the ads and shred the credit card application forms. I finish and I have four bills and a note from my doctor about changing my appointment. He wants to see me today.

It was mailed Monday. I think why didn't they call me. I go listen to my answering machine. They did call. I wasn't here and the way my week was, I never checked for messages. I call his office, and they say twelve-thirty is fine. They held the appointment open just in case. I go next door and talk to my neighbor and tell him, "I really appreciate you keeping an eye on the place and I know I owe your son for mowing the grass and raking the leaves." I give him fifty and say, "If it's more, let me know." He says, "Ryan will be overjoyed. He was eyeing a new video game and this will cover it." I say, "By the way, I will be getting married in December, and we are going to live here after the first of the year as things stand right now." He says, "Congratulations, it will be nice having you around again."

 I go see my doctor for my checkup and then head to the church for my instructions. Father Duggan says, "One more week and you should be finished with this. Then we need to go over everything." It is four o'clock and I head downtown to Vicki's. I am beat. I swear today was worse than any day this week. I will be glad when all of this is over. I call Natalie on my cell about tomorrow to see what she wants to do. She says, "We don't have to do anything special tomorrow. I mean if you want, we can just go to your place. I know you have a lot going on and you will need to start making room for Vicki to put her stuff." I say, "I haven't even thought of that. I guess I should start moving some of the stuff to the basement, toss it in the trash, or donate it someplace." She says, "After breakfast I'll change to old jeans and help you." I say, "I'll see you after church sweetie." She says, "I love you Dad." I say, "I love you too sweetie." I get to Vicki's, and she has invitations lying on the table and an address book. She says, "You're just in time to help. We need to stuff these in the envelopes, so they go in the mail."

 After we stuff the envelopes, she says "I got busy on these and forgot about getting dinner ready." I say, "I can see that, I thought you were going to have help doing these?" She says, "I was supposed to, but I decided I could do them while you went and did your thing. I saved a few for you and one to put in our wedding album." I look at them and say, "You did good, these aren't too fancy, nice but not too fancy." She says, "You should have seen the ones Mom picked out.

I said, 'Mother Please!'" I ask, "What did she say when you offered to pay or split the bill?" She says, "Absolutely not, I have waited too long for this and your Father even said he would throw some money in the fund if I didn't have enough. You know him, he never spends any money if he doesn't have to." I ask, "Do you want to order in or go out?" She says, "I need a shower if we go out, just order Chinese I guess. Nothing else sounds good." I ask, "Where is the menu?" She points to a rack by the fridge. I go dig out the menu and ask her what she wants then call up and order. About thirty-five minutes later, the food shows up and we eat. She says, "I had big plans for tonight, but I'm beat." I say, "Me too." After dinner we lounge around in the living room, flip through the stuff on TV and find nothing that grabs our attention. We turn it off. Vicki goes over to her stereo and puts some music on and turns down the lights and hands me a glass of wine, and we sit there listening to the music and sipping our wine. Not a bad way to spend Saturday night. Soft music, a lovely lady, and some good wine, what more could a person want? So we had a nice peaceful evening all to ourselves for a change. We went to bed shortly after midnight.

Sunday morning I am up at seven, go take a shower and get ready for my day. Vicki is still buried in the covers in the bed. I try to be quiet getting my clothes, fixing my coffee so as not to wake her up. Around eight-thirty she comes out wrapped in her sheet and says, "I really enjoyed last night. It was so nice just sitting in there. No TV, no computer, soft music, some wine and gazing at the skyline with you." I say, "I enjoyed it too. I never really thought that much about how great the view is from here, but after watching it change so much last night, I find it amazing." She says, "That is one of the things I'll miss when we move. I can just watch all the time. There is always something to see even if it is just the buildings encased in the clouds or the fog." I ask, "How big is the other unit?" She says, "Three bedrooms, two baths. Why do you ask?" I say, "Just curious. This is just a one-bedroom unit. Is it that much bigger or did they cram two bedrooms and another bath in without all the open space?" She says, "It is twice the size of this unit. This floor only has three units. Some floors have six units or five, except the penthouse. They have the whole top floor." I say, "Thank you. I figured they were all the same." At nine, I leave and say "I'll see you about nine I guess. Enjoy your day." She wraps up in her sheet and says, "I think I'll sleep for a couple of hours." I kiss her and leave.

I pick up Natalie after church and talk to Rachael for a few minutes and then Natalie and I go for breakfast. She opted for the crepe place this morning, which was fine with me. Then we went to my place and we both changed to old jeans and got busy going through stuff. I found stuff I had forgotten about. There were boxes of old Christmas decorations. I haven't put up a tree for the past few years, just a small pre-lit tree and a few choice ornaments. I don't bother with the other holidays as far as decorating goes. I am always working or was. I have six boxes of old clothes that I don't wear. I swear I wear the same clothes year round. I get rid of everything I haven't worn in three years. We load the boxes of clothes and miscellaneous nick-knacks and appliances in my SUV and take them to a drop-off place and donate them. On the way back to my place, we stop by a KFC to pick up a bucket of chicken and the fixings for Sunday dinner. We get back to my place and get busy working and the doorbell rings. It is Ryan from next door. I go to the door and he says, "Thank you Mr. Higgins. I bought the video game yesterday afternoon. Will you want me to shovel when the snow starts falling?" I say, "That would be great. Right now you only have to worry about Saturdays and Sundays since I am staying downtown during the week." He sees Natalie and says, "Hi Nat. I haven't seen you for a while. Where are you hiding?" She says, "I live with my Mom and I only come here on Sundays usually." He asks, "Do you want to see my collection?" She says, "Maybe next week. We are cleaning today and I'm a mess." He says, "Cool. I'll come over next week and you look nice to me." She says, "He always says things like that to me. I mean I can be wearing cutoffs and a sloppy top or be dressed up real nice, it doesn't matter." I say, "I think he has liked you since you were ten and going trick or treating together." She says, "I like him too, but only as a friend. He is into video games and paintball and things like that. I don't think he watches sports or plays sports. His taste in music is all loud rock stuff." I say, "Boys do change. He seems like he is getting more into working, I would see him all the time working around the neighborhood doing odd jobs. Painting trim and fences, mowing other lawns. So I ask him to do mine, and he is really good."

We eat our dinner and I say, "I think we made a lot of progress today. Thank you for your help. I appreciate it." She says, "I liked going through all the stuff. There were pictures I don't remember seeing, and the ones of your family you really should write stuff down on the back of them. Twenty years from now, nobody will remember who's who." I say, "Hold on. I'm only forty-five. I won't be senile at sixty-five." She says, "I was only joking. But it would be nice to have them identified." I say, "OK we will do that one Sunday when we can't do anything else. I promise." She says, "Dad you're the best." About seven-thirty, we leave so I can drive her home. We walk out to the car and here comes Ryan. He gives a package to Natalie and says, "I missed your birthday, sorry." She says, "Thank you Ryan, you didn't have too." He says "I know, but I remembered you like the group. So I bought the CD for you." She opens it and says, "How did you remember. We talked like last year about them?" He says, "Things like that I remember. School stuff I don't." She kisses him on the check and says, "I will play it tonight." He walks away beet red from her kissing his check. She says, "Now, I need to find something for his birthday. His is right after Thanksgiving, early December. I think the third. I wrote it down once." I drive her home, and Rachael asked what we did today since we were both still wearing jeans. Natalie told her and she says, "You can help me anytime you want I need to get rid of stuff too." She says, "Mom, I know you. You say we'll do it then you find other things to do. But if you want to, I'll help you. We should do it before we decorate for Christmas right after Thanksgiving." She says, "That we'll do. That's what two weeks away?" I say, "A week from Thursday." I say goodnight and head downtown.

Vicki is sitting on the couch reading a Sunday paper when I walk in. She asks, "How was your day with your daughter?" I say, "We had a busy day after breakfast cleaning out things and taking a bunch of stuff I don't use any more to a store where they resell it. I donated a bunch and threw a lot of stuff in the trash. I almost have room for your clothes now. She says, "I need to go through my stuff I know so I will not have all that much." I ask, "So how long did you sleep?" She says, "Only until eleven, my Mom called and offered to come over to help with the invitations, and I told her they were done. So she said then let's have brunch I'll pick you up in thirty minutes. So I took a quick shower and slipped into a nice dress and fixed my hair. We went to a place in Lincoln Park that she heard raves about. She wasn't that impressed, but the food was very good." I say, "We had KFC while we were working since we didn't want to stop to change and go out." She says, "Mom asked me about Thanksgiving and wanted to know how many were going to be here and did she need to bring additional chairs." I told her, "I think we will be fine. The table seats eight with the other leaves and there are four chairs in the locker down stairs." She says, "Did Jim say if his daughter and ex will join us?" I said, "After meeting them Thursday, I think both of them will be here, we got along really well." She says, "That is nice to hear. A lot of times there is so much animosity and hostility toward a new love." We talked until after eleven and went to bed.

Chapter 37

Monday morning six-thirty I am up. I slip out of bed, go pour a cup of coffee, and then go take my shower. My mind is running in circles. I look at the calendar and try to fix everything in my mind. In a little over a month, we will be getting married and taking three days off for our honeymoon in Bermuda. We get back and only have a few days until Christmas and then we need to pack her stuff to move it out to my house. She talked to Stuart and told him she would not need the condo after January and that she would pay the next three month's rent. He told her it wasn't necessary. He said, "The job in Washington looks like it will be over in January and he will be coming back to Chicago until they need him to go set up another office someplace." She said, "I think he was relieved in a way since he didn't want to call me and say I have to move before he gets back. So our getting married saved him that decision." We need to go shopping for a new bed and linens and I have to move some of the furniture to make room for her dressing table that is at her Mom's place. I write all this stuff down in my daily planner so I don't forget anything. Around seven-thirty Vicki joins me and looks at my notes and says, "Don't worry lover boy. All the stuff will get finished and we will not have to move anything. Dad says he hired a mover to do it when we are ready. They will even get my dressing table from Mom's." I say, "That was generous of him." She says, "I think he felt he had to do something since Mom said she could handle the wedding cost." I kiss her and say, "I'll talk to you later. I have no clue what today will be like." Then I head to the office.

I go to the office, make a pot of coffee, and look at what is working this week. I make some notes to ask the staff about the various projects they are working on to see what we can clean up this week. Next week we have a long weekend for Thanksgiving. So we will only have two and a half days basically to try doing anything. I see some notes on the calendar that Vicki had given me concerning vacation days and requests for time off. Four members of the staff are looking to take the whole week off if they are not needed since they have family out of town and like to go home for Thanksgiving. I look at what each of them is working on this week and decide those projects should take priority to maybe finish up this week. I can juggle a couple of people to help if needed. McCray hasn't given me any other top priority projects that need doing in the next couple of weeks. Satisfied that we can handle all the projects we have, I look at the report that McCray gave me from Washington regarding a swap of an agent for six months. I really don't know which one I would like to give up. Adam is probably the one that would fit the best based upon what his long-term goal is, but Mark is also a good candidate for the job. I'll feel McCray out before I make the decision.

Around ten o'clock I go into the break room and Erika is talking to four other members of the staff about the basketball practice and when the game will be played. Glad to see that idea is going to help them work closer together and not treat her as an outsider. I fix my coffee and ask, "How was the first practice?" They say, "We had a good time. Erika and her girls play serious basketball. We were really surprised. They are very competitive on the court but seem like friends off the court." Erika says, "They played hard, and with a few more practices, they will be ready to play against the team from Lt. McElroy." I say, "I know he has some good players. Just remember this is for charity. It doesn't matter which team wins the game." After the break I ask them to hang around a few minutes to talk about the schedule for next week. They all seemed to understand the situation and didn't have a problem with the four requests for the week off. I say, "Next week, I plan on letting everybody leave at noon on Wednesday to enjoy the four days off. We'll just have to push a little harder this week to make that a reality."

Three o'clock Denise says, "Phone line one." I ask, "Did they say who was calling? I'm in the middle of something." Denise asks and says, "He says, you'll know when you pick up the phone." I am like "OK. Who is playing games." So I say, "Tell him I'll be with him in a couple of minutes." She says, "He said Fine." I finish what I am working on and pick up the phone. The guy says, "Hey Jimbo, where the heck you been hiding. Did you forget about your sorority brother when you decided to get hitched again?" I say, "Stan, I was thinking of calling you, but the last I heard you left for points unknown." He says, "That was only so my ex couldn't track me down. She was driving me crazy, calling all the time. I had to split town. We made up and now she wants to get back together. I guess I wasn't that bad of a husband after all." I ask, "How is your son, David?" He says, "He is fifteen and plays football and is getting looked at by the coach from Illinois." I ask, "So how did you find out about my plans?" He says, "I saw Rachael at the mall yesterday and she told me all about it and your promotion." I ask, "Where are you working now?" He says, "Right now, I'm between jobs. I was working on construction, but the jobs have dried up." I say, "I know the economy is tough for a lot of occupations. I thought you had a cushy office job." He says, "I did before 9-11. But that company went belly up and I took a job in the trades since I have always been doing handyman stuff." I say, "We should get together and catch up. Give me your number and I'll see what works and call you." He says, "Thanks Jimbo and if you need a best man I'm available." I say, "I asked my old boss McCray and he is doing it but I will invite you and Judy."

About four o'clock I call McCray to discuss Adam and Mark and which one I should tap for the switch. Vicki answers the phone and asks, "How is your day going?" I said, "Interesting. I got a phone call from my buddy from college about our getting married. So I told him I would invite him and his ex since she wants to get back together. I told him we need to get together to talk and catch up on things so I said I would let him know what works best." She says, "Thursday would be OK with me. I am meeting the girls again for our final fitting." I ask, "Is Rodge around?" She says, "He left a little while ago and said he would be back after five if anybody was looking for him." I say, "Leave him a note or ask him to call me when he gets back. I have a question for him." She says, "I'll probably be here. I have a ton of reports that are due, so I am working on them while he is out of the office. I figure I'll be here until after six." I say, "That sounds like my plan too. Why don't I pick you up when you are finished and we'll go over to Ed's for dinner." She says, "Gets me out of cooking. Fine by me."

McCray calls me at about five-thirty and asks, "What can I do for you?" I say, "I am trying to decide which one I should swap with Washington, Adam or Mark?" He says, "I see your dilemma, me I was leaning toward those same choices before, but now I am thinking more along the lines of Erika. She is far more qualified than she lets on and it would surprise the heck out of the brass in DC. She is much more than another pretty face to dress up the office." I say, "I had a hunch that you were going to pick her. But truthfully, I prefer to keep her in light of her translating ability." He says, "I gave you mine, but it is your call. It would be a good move for her, whether she wants to be in that circus is another matter. I talked to her a while back about DC and how they operate, and she did seem like she would be interested if the opportunity came up. She asked me about living in the DC area and I told her it is expensive and the extra security there is unbelievable. I think she wants to witness it first hand to understand the difference between here and there." I say, "Thanks for your input. Now you have given me something else to think about. I have to let them know after Thanksgiving. The swap would take place in January for six months."

Vicki calls me at six-fifteen and says, "I will be ready to go in twenty minutes." I finish up what I was working on and shut everything off and lock up to go pick her up. I get to her office around six-forty and she walks out the front door and gets in my SUV. Then I head over to Ed's on Wells Street so we can have dinner. She says, "This is a nice change. I didn't realize they offered more than burgers and shakes." I say, "I found that out the last time I was here. I brought Rodge here. He had heard of the place but never managed to make it here." We had burgers and shakes for dinner along with an order of Onion Rings and then we headed to her place. She says, "What a day. I have never seen so much paperwork or reports before. I thought we did a lot of paperwork at your office. That is nothing compared to all the stuff over here." I say, "I can imagine. That is why Rodge was happy to steal you away. He knows you are efficient and get things done." She says, "I know but that wasn't the primary reason." I say, "I know it was so we would not be together all the time and get on each other's nerves." She says, "So far it is working out fine this way. The lady that was Director Schaunessy's office manager decided to retire once I came over with him. The other ladies just do their job and figure I'm in charge since I am always in his office." I say, "Are they giving you any flack or make you feel like an outsider?" She says, "No, I think they didn't really like Erma. She was a tough cookie and what she said went." We watched the weather and half way listened to the sports and then we headed to bed.

Chapter 38

Tuesday morning I am up at six-thirty feeling rested. I don't think we have gone to bed that early since we have been living together. I get up, take a shower, and fix my coffee and decide I should have something for breakfast. I look and there is cereal in the pantry and the milk is fresh. I look in the freezer and there is a bag of mixed berries. I take some out and top off the cereal with them and add a little sugar and some milk. I am eating and here comes Vicki; she eyes the bowl and says, "For me?" I slide it over and say, "Sure." I go fix another bowl and she says, "Thanks, I mean to eat the cereal this way but never remember to add the berries." I say, "I didn't want to stop to get a cinnamon roll this morning or get donuts." She says, "This is better for you too." I say, "I know. I really need to stop the sweets and get on an exercise program, now that I'm in the office I am not running around like I was in the field." She says, "I don't give you enough exercise?" I say, "That doesn't count. Besides, that is pleasure."

I head to the office around eight o'clock. I am working away at my desk and the phone rings. I answer it and it is Buranski. He says, "I talked to Nikoli last night. Mariano sent him a plum from this weekend's meeting. He said the big man has strong feelings about what is going on in the middle east and he plans to make an announcement very soon about what action his administration will take in regard to Iran and Syria. That should send the oil prices higher for quite a while." I say, "Now we will see who does what and we'll know if he is selling the info to the Russians." He says, "I asked him what he has been up too and he said. I am working on a couple of prospects for the next Olympic games. I made a couple of trips to see them in competition." I say, "That is what two years away?" He says, "Yes in 2012. It takes time to train the athletes. That is why we are trying to get our facility ready." I say, "Thanks for the info. I will call McCray and tell him what you found out." I think to myself Nikoli can use that line with him, but I still wonder if he isn't trying to feather his nest by lining up some more clients for information. We will know by the end of the week. McCray has the other posts listening and watching to what is going on in the area. I look at the clock and figure McCray isn't in his office yet. He stayed late last night from what Vicki said to finish up his reports.

I call McCray at nine-thirty and he says, "Why don't you meet me for lunch and we will talk about this rather than kick it around on the phone." I say, "The usual spot at one." He says, "Yes, that works. It gets a little quieter in there since the regular lunch crowd is gone by then." I tell Denise, "I will be out of the office most of the afternoon. I have a meeting with the Director. If anybody calls looking for me, tell them I should be back around five." She asks, "Is it OK if I leave early today. My son has to go to the doctor today?" I say, "Sure just turn on the answering machine and I will check the messages when I get back. What is wrong with your son?" She says, "I think it's just a virus. He is listless and can't do anything. So I thought I should have the doctor look at him." I say, "That is probably all it is. I know my doctor told me Saturday they are seeing a lot of this new flu going around and they don't have enough medication to fight it. He is glad I am healthy. Otherwise he would want me to get a shot."

I leave the office around twenty to one to meet McCray at the restaurant. The weather is getting a little cooler and I debate about driving, then decide I can walk it. I really don't get enough exercise. It only takes about fifteen minutes to walk there, and I felt better doing it. McCray gets there at a couple of minutes after one and we go in. He says, "I see you walked today. It's not that bad of a walk. My new office is far enough that unless I have a lot of time, I just take a cab." I say, "This latest piece of news from Buranski about Nikoli to me doesn't wash. I mean it could be true, but I just have a feeling that he is looking for more clients to sell info to." He says, "I know what you mean. I called Washington to have them keep an eye on unusual developments in that region." I ask, "What are your plans next week?" He says, "I will be in Virginia from Tuesday through the weekend. My wife already laid down the law. We are having a big Thanksgiving with her family and then Friday she wants to get the house ready to decorate. Fortunately, my children will be there and they can help pacify her. They enjoy decorating. I hang the lights around the gutters since the boys are too young to do it. They hand me the strands so they get to help me and my daughter does the inside stuff with my wife." I say, "That is a good plan. Vicki is having Thanksgiving at her place and my daughter and my ex are coming too." He says, "I'm glad to hear that. It's nice to be on good terms."

I ask, "Any word from DC about Buranski's status?" He says, "They promised me a decision before Thanksgiving. I am still waiting, but my gut feeling is he is in." I say, "He has proven his worth in my mind." He says, "To my way of thinking too." I ask, "What should we do about this project in Hyde Park? I know you want it shut down. Buranski said he would do it. He knows he will get heat from Nikoli if the information dries up. But he said he would tell him it is only temporary. Mariano is who I'm worried about. If this gets shut down, he might not be real happy. He was going crazy when it was down for five days." McCray says, "I can get the boys at the Bureau to make an unannounced visit to his business and try to find out what else he is up too. That should get him wondering." I say, "I know what you mean there. Nobody likes them snooping around or knocking on their door." He says, "Let's let it ride until after Thanksgiving and then we'll talk more about shutting it down. I don't think the big guy will do anything in Chicago over the weekend. Last I heard, he has a big to do in DC." I looked at the clock and it was already three-thirty. McCray says, "I should head back to the office. I still have a bunch of stuff to take care of and more cases to look over before I send them your way." I say, "Remember, I will be shorthanded next week." He says, "There isn't anything extremely urgent that I have seen yet, but there are a bunch of files stacked up on my desk. I can't believe all of the activity right now for this office." We go outside and he spots a cab and the cab pulls over, he says, "Get in we'll drop you."

I get back to the office. Denise is gone. I check for messages and there are three. I write down the info and walk to the break room to see what is going on with the staff. They are sitting around talking about practice tonight after work. I say, "You guys are taking this serious. I'm glad to see you all involved. Tomorrow morning we have a meeting at nine-fifteen to discuss progress. Enjoy your evening and play hard." They say, "Do you want to watch?" I say, "I would love to, but I have a prior commitment. My daughter plays tonight. In fact if I don't leave pretty soon, I'll miss the game." They say, "You just got back." I say, "One of the messages was my daughter. I thought her game was Wednesday, the schedule was wrong." I go to my office and make two phone calls then tell everyone, "You can all leave. Don't forget tomorrow nine-thirty." They salute and say, "Aye, Aye Captain."

I call Vicki on my cell phone to tell her I will be home around seven-thirty and she says, "Bring dinner. I'm sticking around here again for a couple of hours." I get to Natalie's game right after tip off. She sees me in the stands and gives me a little wave. They lost by three points, but they played a really good school. After the game Natalie came over and said, "Thanks for coming. I wanted us to win this game." I said, "Your team played well. They are just faster on the breaks than your team. That is what beat you. Your team is making great strides from what the coach told me." She says, "Mom is supposed to pick me up, but I haven't seen her.'" I say, "I'll hang around a few minutes just in case. I can drive you home." She goes and changes and then we walk outside. Here comes Rachael and she says, "I was tied up at work and lost track of the time, then I had to race to get here. I'm sorry." Natalie says, "That's alright Mom. We just came out. The game was longer than I thought." I say, "You two are still coming Thanksgiving right? Vicki wanted me to make sure since she is ordering the turkey this week. She wants fresh not frozen." Rachael says, "Yes, but can you pick us up, I don't want to drive downtown." I say, "I think I can arrange that. I'll get the details and let you know the time."

I head back downtown and think I am supposed to bring dinner. Tuesday night what sounds good. In the old days, I would just stop at the Maple Street Café and go with what Val said was good. I really should go by there sometime before the big day and see them. I owe Tony a story even though this case isn't settled. It is still an ongoing case. Once DC decides the status on Buranski, I can probably close the book on this case. Val has a new suitor, at least from the last time I talked to Tony that was the case. Think Jim, what is Tuesday. Pork chops, with applesauce and au-gratin potatoes with fresh parsley. I call Vicki on my cell to ask her how that sounds. She says, "Whatever you decide will be fine. Right now the plastic fruit on the table looks good." I say, "I'll see you in about forty minutes." I call Tony and say, "Do you have the pork chops today?" He says, "Who is this?" I say, "Jim." He says, "So you are alive. I was beginning to wonder. I haven't seen or heard word one." I say, "I need two dinners to go. Please." He says, "Ten minutes they will be ready." I ask, "How's Val?" He says, "Fine. She is not here tonight. Her boyfriend wanted her to take tonight off to be with him." I say, "I'll see you in ten." I drive over there and notice things don't seem the same. He says, "Val's new boyfriend thinks she can just take off anytime he wants to be with her. I told her, 'Ask him if he is going to marry you?' She says, 'I'm not going to put it to him like that'. I said, 'Why not? That is the way he is acting. He wants you to cow-tow to his every need'. She got hot about that remark and stormed out." I said, "I could tell something wasn't right when I walked in. What about the other gal that comes in when she is off?" He says, "She was complaining about female problems." I say, "I hear you loud and clear." I tell Tony, "I'll see you Thursday. You remember Stan. He is back in town and wants to get together. I'll bring him here." Tony says, "I'll see you then. Do you want me to tell Val?" I say, "It doesn't matter. It's just guys' talk." After I leave, I'm sure Val will be there, so I best have something to say to her.

I get to Vicki's and we have our dinner. She says, "That was really good. Where did you get it?" I said, "The old place I used to go all the time. I was close by there when I called you and know their food is good. I remembered on Tuesday Tony always made the pork chops." She asks, "What other good things does he make?" I say, "Once a month he makes Yankee Pot Roast, except in the summer he says nobody wants to order it. It's too heavy. Friday's he makes fish at least two types." I say, "I asked Natalie and Rachael about Thanksgiving. They will be here, but I have to pick them up. Rachael doesn't like to drive in downtown Chicago." She says, "I don't blame her. The drivers down here are crazy and then you have the cabs everywhere and half of them can't drive, I swear." I say, "I know it is not my favorite thing to do either, but I need to drive." She says, "We could take the train from by your place and not fight the traffic." I say, "Don't think I haven't thought about that when we move out there." She says, "It's not like when you were a field agent. Now you are in the office almost all day every day except if you have to meet somebody or check on a particular case." We talk until eleven and then go to bed.

Chapter 39

Wednesday morning bright and early I am up. I smell the coffee brewing and think I might as well get up. I have a meeting with the staff at nine-fifteen. I go take a shower and fix my coffee and debate about fixing a bowl of cereal. This morning I am like maybe I'll cook up some eggs instead. So I make an omelet with eggs, cheese, peppers, and bacon bits. I am just about to dish it up and here comes Vicki and she says, "Whatever you are cooking smells really good. Do you have more?" I say, "In the skillet, I figured that you would smell that cooking and come out." She says, "It worked." So I cook the other omelet and we eat breakfast together. She says, "You are nice to have around. Here I should be getting up and cooking for you and you cook for me." I say, "I like to get up early and get ready for my day. Most mornings I don't feel like cooking, but this morning I did." She says, "All the same, I'm lucky to have you." I head to the office and say, "I should be home on time, but don't hold me to it." She says, "I know, you have no clue what today will have in store for you. I saw the pile of stuff Rodge was working on last night. You will get it this morning sometime." I kiss her and say, "I'll call you later." She says, "I love you." I say, "And I love you Vicki."

I get to the office, set up the coffee pot, and grab the reports for the cases we are working on this week. I am sitting at my desk and the phone rings. I answer it and it is Stan. I say, "Stan, Thursday I'll pick you up and we will go see Tony at Maple Street Café and talk." He says, "You remember where Judy lives?" I say, "How could I forget? If she hasn't moved, I can find the place in my sleep." He says, "She told me I could move in with her until I find a new job, and in the event we get back together, I will not have to worry about paying rent. I was staying at the Country Suites place and she said 'Save your money and move over here.' So I did. Right now I am staying in the guest bedroom. It feels really strange, but I think maybe we can work it out and get back together but I need a job." I say, "I'll talk to a couple of people in the neighborhood. I know a couple of the guys working in the trades. Maybe we'll get lucky." He says, "I'll be in your debt if you do." I say, "Not at all. That is what friends are for." He says, "You sure have changed. You didn't seem concerned before when I left town." I say, "I learned a lot in the past few months about friends and what they should do. It's a long story, but I learned a lot." He says, "Now you sound like the Jim I went to school with." I say, "I'll pick you up around six on Thursday."

Around nine the staff starts showing up. So I gather all my folders and head to the break room for our meeting. Some of the staff seemed tired so I ask, "How was practice?" They go, "Practice was fine." It was the shooting hoops for beer after that got them. I say, "You were playing make the same shot the other player made?" They go, "Yes, How did you know?" I say, "I did the same thing with my daughter a few weeks ago, but no beer and it's tougher than you think." They say, "That's for sure. Erika I think made every shot." I say, "Does that surprise you?" They say, "Not anymore. She is deadly with her shots." Erika takes a bow. I say, "OK, now down to business. Let's go over the reports. So I start with Adam. He says, "We should wrap this up by Thursday afternoon there is only one more piece of information to verify." Next I ask Mark. He says, "I thought this one would be finished by now, but there is a little detail nobody checked before. He was out of the country for six months and there is no data available about where he was or what he was doing." I say, "That definitely calls for more research. May I see the report?" Mark hands me his report. I look at his report and I look at the file from my office. I go, "Half of your report is missing. The file here has more information than you have there." He says, "Maybe it is just misplaced, I'll go look in my cubbyhole." I go to Erika and she says, "My report is finished. I just want to proof it before I turn it in." She hands me her report and I look at it and say, "It looks perfectly fine to me. Everything looks to be in order along with your recommendation. I will give it back to you after I read it completely." Next I call on Steve. He says, "This case should really belong to somebody else. I couldn't get any help at all. I called several organizations to get information and nothing."

He hands me his case file and I say, "I see what you mean. I see your notes, so it's not like you didn't try to find the information so it could be verified. I'll look at it." Next I ask Robert about his case. He says, "Cindi has been helping me on this case since she has a better understanding of the language than I do." I look at the name and I see a familiar name and wonder how did somebody I grew up with get into a position to be under the scrutiny of the IIA. I haven't seen him or heard from him since our high-school days. He went into the service after high school. I went to Illinois. I say, "I will look into the matter thank you." We still have Eugene and Willard's case to review, but it is already lunchtime. I say, "Everybody takes forty-five minutes. We'll meet back here at one." Denise says, "Boy you sure were thorough with the staff. I never saw anybody go over every case like that with all the rest of the staff there." I say, "I hope they will learn, we are a team. It is not each individual case. It is the team." She says, "I would think they have gotten the message and I have six messages for you along with the packet from Michigan Avenue." I say, "Do me a favor, Denise?" She says, "Sure. What?" I say, "Bring me a sandwich from the place where you and Vicki had lunch when you come back from lunch." She says, "What kind?" I say, "Ruben on dark rye with thousand island dressing on the side." I hand her fifty and say, "Lunch is on me."

After lunch, I gather the staff again and say, "Thank you all for being so cooperative. I received a new packet from Director McCray, and there are a couple of cases that we need to jump on right away. The other case at this point is not as pressing as these new ones. I know four of you will be off next week, so I am assigning these cases to new teams and we will see how the new teams do. Mark found a bunch of the missing information for his case, so I'm hopeful that case can be finished off. I will take over Robert and Cindi's case, since I know something about the subject. The case that Gene and Will are working on will be shelved until after we take care of these new cases." Then I announce the teams for next week, and I get some strange looks. I say, "This is only temporary since we have four teams that are one person short. I decided to do two teams of three and one team of two based upon what I feel each team can handle. Once our other members get back, we will see where we are at on these cases and what other cases come up that need attention. We need to finish up the old cases that are almost finished by three on Friday then I will give you the new cases. Any questions? If not, let's get cracking."

Around five o'clock the phone rings, and I answer it. It is McCray. He says, "I need you to call Buranski and have him come downtown tomorrow afternoon around two." I ask, "What is the occasion?" He says, "Washington is having a man from Central come in tomorrow to ask him some other questions. If he passes those, we will make him an offer." I ask, "What, they want to make sure he will not be a double agent?" McCray says, "That's pretty much it in a nutshell. They like everything he has done so far and the fact he hasn't told anybody that he is helping us. I really don't know what Central intends to talk to him about. They are pretty tight lipped over there. Usually they only get involved right before we take on a new agent from a foreign country. I have only been around long enough to see them bring in two from Eastern Europe. One didn't cut it and wound up back in Russia after six months." So I call Buranski at his office and ask if he can be down here at two. He says, "I'll rearrange my schedule, but we have a bachelor party for Dragan tomorrow night. So I need to be back here by seven." I say, "That will not be a problem. This should only take an hour or two at the most." I call McCray and say, "It is all set. He will be at my office at two." He says "I'll see you then. I'll bring the man from Central and he can do his interrogation. We'll hide out in the break room to give them privacy." After I get off the phone with him, I decide it's time to go home. What a crazy day. I call Vicki to see if she is ready to leave and she says, "I am." So I pick her up and we go home.

We get to her place and she says, "I hope you aren't looking to eat right away." I say, "I'm fine I ate lunch late why?" She says, "I was planning on making a roast tonight but forgot to take it out. How does baked chicken with vegetables sound?" I say, "That sounds fine to me." I look at the coffee pot and there is still a couple of cups in the pot, so I fill a mug and zap it in the microwave. Vicki says, "I'll make you a fresh pot once I start the dinner if you want." I say, "No this will hold me. I really should cut down on my coffee, but I have a taste for it right now." She says, "Do you want wine with the dinner?" I say, "That sounds good for a change." She gets dinner started. I drink my coffee and turn on the TV to see if there is anything worth watching. Nothing of interest to me. I flip to the weather channel and they are showing some snow to the west and north of Minnesota. I guess we might see snow before December this year. We have an enjoyable dinner and talk about our plans for tomorrow and figure the roast will be dinner on Friday night. Around ten-thirty we head to bed, we are both beat tonight for some reason.

Chapter 40

Thursday morning I am up before six. The coffee hasn't even started yet. I feel refreshed. The sleep felt good. I must have needed it. I go take a shower and then fix my coffee. I turn on the computer to do a little searching. The case that Robert and Cindi were working on got my attention. I need to clear this up and try to find out what happened to this guy. Paul Wisnowski class of '83. I look at the member page and sure enough his name is on the list. I plug in his address and it shows him still registered to the same address. I think maybe his folks had trouble and he took over the house. I remember he wasn't at our twentieth class reunion. He sent a reply back that he was out of the country. I figured he career was with the military. I look at the message board to see who was looking for whom from our class recently. Stan's name came up and Paul's name came up. I wish I knew who was looking for both of them. I look and somebody was looking for me too. I never updated my information after our twentieth. I didn't figure I would be going to anymore class reunions until maybe our fortieth, and that is not for a long time. I write down the address and search for a phone number. I'll be damned, I think that was the same number from high school. The area code is different but the number I bet is still the same. I'll call the number later just out of curiosity and see who answers. About eight o'clock here comes Vicki and she says, "You got up early." I say, "I couldn't sleep anymore. It felt good going to bed early." She asks, "What are you looking up?" I say, "I'm trying to track down a guy I went to school with and it shows he is living in the same house he did when we were in high school." She says, "A lot of times the son takes over the house if his father dies." I say, "I don't remember getting a notice his father died." She says, "There could be a lot of reasons. Especially, in light of the state of the economy these days." I say, "I'm sure you are right." We talk for a few minutes and I say, "Have fun with the girls tonight." She says, "Have fun with Stan tonight." I say, "I'll be home probably around ten, unless he gets carried away telling his tales."

I head to the office and get ready for the day and our visitor from Central. I tidy up my office to make it look presentable. I remind myself again I need to add some new photos to the walls and some pictures of Natalie on my desk. I wonder if she got her basketball pictures taken yet. I'll have to ask. That would be neat. I wanted one of her in her Blackhawks jersey just to show her off but haven't gotten around to taking the picture yet. Denise comes in and says, "My, you are ambitious this morning." I say, "We have a guest coming this afternoon." So I tell her the plan and then I bring two more chairs into my office from the break room. The phone is busy all morning with calls from different people wanting some answers. Finally, around noon it quiets down a little. Denise says, "I am going out for lunch. Do you want me to bring you back anything?" I say, "That would be a big help. Yes bring me a half-pound burger on dark rye with raw onion and mustard." I start to hand her money and she says, "I never gave you the change from yesterday. I still have thirty dollars of your money." I say, "I completely forgot about it too. Thanks." While she is at lunch, I try the number for Paul and get a recording. It is in Polish and I can't understand what it says. I am like that is probably why Robert couldn't get any answers. I wonder if Erika understands Polish. I'll ask her after lunch.

Around one I find Erika and ask her if she understands Polish and she says, "Yes. Do you need me to translate something?" I say, "Come to my office and listen to this message and tell me what it says." She follows me to my office and I call the number. She listens and then holds her hand up and then there is a beep. She says, "It says, 'We are not available to answer the phone. Please leave a message and we will call you back as soon as we can, thank you.'" She says, "I know a lot of ethnic people don't like to be bothered with sales calls, so they put a message in their native tongue and if the caller understands, they leave a message. Other times, they are home but don't want to talk to people they don't know, but if they know you and want to talk, they will pick up the phone once you start to leave a message." I say, "Thank you, Erika. Why didn't Robert or Cindi ask you for help?" She says, "I don't know. I guess they didn't figure I knew anything other than English like them." I say, "Good point. I think I'll give you a title linguistic expert." She says, "Are you serious?" I say, "No, I think I'll keep that information to myself."

At ten to two, I get a phone call from Ramon at the parking garage. He asks, "I have a gentleman here who said he has an appointment with you at two. Can he park here?" I say, "Yes, is he driving a silver gray BMW?" He says, "That is what he is driving." I say, "Yes, I was going to tell you this morning but had other things on my mind." He says, "OK." Buranski parks and walks up to the office. Denise shows him into my office. I ask, "How are you doing today?" He says, "A little nervous, I thought all the questions were answered." I say, "I did too, but with Central they have their own thoughts and we have to let them do their thing. I'm sure you have nothing to worry about." He asks, "Did you hear anything about the latest information?" I say, "We will find out when they get here I'm sure." Five minutes later here comes McCray and the agent from Central. Denise shows them in and McCray introduces the agent to Buranski and me. We exchange small talk for a few minutes then McCray and I leave my office so Agent David Smith, former Corps officer during the Gulf War. He has been at IIA since it began he is the Senior Interrogation Agent for the agency. He is a tough old bird if I ever saw one. Still has the mojo to go with it. Gruff, all-business no-nonsense approach. In a way, I feel sorry for Buranski, but he is a tough cookie too so he'll be alright.

Around three-thirty Denise comes to get McCray and myself from the break room and says, "Agent Smith buzzed me and asked me to get both of you to go back into the office." We follow her back and go into the office. Agent Smith says, "I have no problem with Mr. Buranski joining our operation. I will give Washington my full report. But as of right now, I would consider him one of ours." We both walk over and shake Agent Smith's hand and Buranski's hand and say, "Welcome aboard." McCray says to Agent Smith, "Jim and I both have been impressed with his contributions and help thus far. He is a man of his word and doesn't talk about what he does. He just does his job." Buranski says, "I am honored to be a part of your organization and I will do my best to live up to your expectations." McCray says, "We need to get you officially installed and get you a badge and go over all the fine print. I figure that will happen after Thanksgiving and Washington gives us the green light." Agent Smith says, "I am going back to Washington tonight and tomorrow I will present my report to Central. Normally, it takes about a week to process all the necessary paperwork. Good Luck Mr. Buranski and I hope to meet you again under different circumstances." McCray and Smith leave and I tell Buranski, "I told you, that you would be fine." He says, "Thanks Jim, I am really surprised I passed. He asked me all sorts of questions about Nikoli and Mr. Mariano and I told him what I knew. That was the extent of his questioning. I guess they have been monitoring both of them and it jived with what I said." I said, "Enjoy the bachelor party tonight." He says, "I will. Thank you again for your faith in me."

Finally, we have an answer on Buranski, now I need to figure out how we will use him and his talent. McCray didn't say anything about any unusual activity in regard to last weekend's conversation and what Nikoli told Buranski. I felt sure he would have heard something from our agents in the area. I'll call him later. I know Agent Smith was going back to DC tonight. I look at the clock and I need to leave pretty soon to pick up Stan. I try the number for Paul once more, when it beeps I start to leave a message and he picks up the phone. I say, "Paul, this is Jim Huggins from the Class of '83. Can you talk tonight?" He says, "Jimbo, why are you calling?" I say, "I have report on my desk that concerns you." He asks, "What sort of report?" I say, "Intelligence." He says, "I work the overnight shift tonight, what time are you talking?" I say, "I am picking up Stan and we are going to the Maple Street Café for dinner. How about after that? I need an hour of your time." He says, "You remember where I live?" I say, "Same place you lived in during high school." He says, "Yes, Dad is in a bad way and Mom couldn't handle him alone. So when I got of the Army, I moved back home. Twenty five years of that was enough." I say, "I'll see you around eight." He says, "My wife lives here too and she will be home by then. I met her overseas and we hit it off so we got married. Her name is Ursula." I say, "I am looking forward to it."

I leave and go pick up Stan and we head over to the Maple Street Café. We walk in and Tony sees us and comes out to meet Stan. I introduce them and look around and Val is waiting on a table at the other end of the place. Stan and I sit down, Tony sits down with us and we talk for a few minutes. Val comes over and says, "Hi stranger, how are things?" I say, "This is a friend of mine. We went to high school and college together and he moved back here recently." She says "Nice to meet you Stan. What do you do?" He says, "Right now, I'm looking for a job in construction and they are in short supply." She says, "My boyfriend works in construction and they are looking for help. What can you do?" He says, "Everything." She says, "Give me your information. I'll have Rory call you." Then she looks at me and asks, "So what's new with you?" Before I could say anything, Stan says, "He is getting married next month." She says, "Really?" I say, "Yes that is a fact. I didn't have any idea that it was going to happen. It just did." She asks, "So who is the lucky lady?" I say, "A lady from downtown. She is McCray's secretary and we just hit it off. One thing lead to another and all of a sudden we decided to get married." She asks, "You going to live downtown?" I say, "No we are moving out here after the first of the year." She says, "No hard feelings, Congratulations Jim." Stan looks at me and after Val takes our order I say, "I dated her, but it just wasn't going to work. She is a nice lady and she deserves a good man. Hopefully, this Rory is the guy." He says, "It would be great if I can get a job with him." I say, "Val is a good judge of character, so if she gives you high marks, he'll call you." We eat our dinner and catch up on things and I drive him home and ask him to call me after Rory calls him. He says, "Thanks Jim, I'm glad you asked me to go to dinner so we could catch up on things."

Then I head to Paul's house. I ring the doorbell and he comes to the door and invites me in. I see his mother and she looks at me and says, "Jim Huggins from high school, right." I say, "Glad you remember. She winks and says, "Paul told me you were coming. You were a good kid in school and you went to Illinois that I remember."

His wife comes out of the kitchen to the living room and he introduces her to me. I think he can pick them. She was about five nine, slender, with an athletic body and beautiful eyes. Paul says, "I met her while I was in Berlin and she was in the Russian Army as a liaison officer between the different sectors. We met for coffee and wound up together after that. I caught hell from the brass, but I didn't care. She is so beautiful. How could I stop seeing her. I had enough years in to retire. So I decided to retire and asked her to marry me and move to the States. The Red Tape was incredible, but we did it. It took almost eight months to get everything finalized. Mom called me about Dad and we caught a plane here. That was six months ago." I asked, "Where did you live for the months you were waiting to get cleared to get married?" He says, "I had a flat in Berlin, in the Western sector and I was getting my pension from the Army after three months." I ask, "Did you share any secret information with Ursula before or after you were married?" He says, "I never had access to any secret information. What is going on?" I say, "Probably a misunderstanding." I ask what he was doing now. He says, "I got hired at the Ford Plant. Dad's old boss got me the job but I have to work third shift for a year. Something to do with hiring Vets and I qualified." I say, "Good luck Paul, and it was a pleasure meeting you Ursula." Paul's Mom comes back into the living room and says, "Leaving already, Jim?" I say "Yes, I hate to run, but I know Paul has to go to work. I'll see you again soon I promise." She says, "You're always welcome." I say, "Give my regards to your husband." She just shakes her head like it won't do any good. I know Paul said he was in a bad way. Then I head downtown to Vicki's.

    I get there at almost ten and she says, "Was your friend talkative tonight?" I say, "No, we had a good dinner and I dropped him off at home and then had to see an old school chum about a report one of the staff was investigating. I recognized the name and figured I could handle it since I went to school with him. I knew you were going out with the girls and since I could see him tonight I took care of that. Sorry I didn't call you, but it worked out fine." She says, "I just got home myself. The girls were all talkative tonight and planning a party for me. I tried to talk them out of it, but they said, 'We are doing it and you will have fun.'" I say "Lucky you." She says, "Yes, just what I need. A party to celebrate finally getting married." I say, "Just go along. How bad can it be? It's only one night." She says, "When you have to help me upstairs, you'll know." I say, "Fat chance of that happening, I know you and how you are. You'll be fine." She kisses me and says, "That is what I love about you, nothing fazes you. Your motto, just do it!" I say "Mine and MJ's."

She says, "So tell me about Stan and your old school chum." So I told her all about both of them and she asks, "Are you always this helpful to old school buddies?" I say, "No. Before I figured it wasn't my place to get involved in their lives but I learned something over the past couple of months and I guess it changed me." Then I proceeded to tell her about Karl Buranski and the fact that he will be joining us as a freelance agent for special jobs. I would like to bring him in full-time but he prefers only part-time since he has other things going and told her about the training facility for wrestlers and gymnastics that they are trying to setup in Orland Park. She says, "He sure does have a full plate of activities going."

I say, "I feel relieved. One chapter can be closed now and a new chapter will begin after Buranski joins our organization officially." We talked until almost three a.m. and then Vicki asks, "So what are you thinking about now?" I say, "You, my love, and shopping tonight for a new bed for my house." She says, "Is that why you are smiling?" I say, "No, I'm smiling because I'm so damned happy I found you. You bring out the best in me." She says, "It was always there. You just kept it hidden. I'm the lucky one. Somebody else could have nabbed you." I said, "Nope, you're the one for me. I think after our first night together I knew it, but couldn't believe it. I can't wait until the eighteenth to make it official. We will be together for the rest of our lives." She says, "I love you so much Jim." I say, "And I love you just as much."